SAINT OF LOST SOULS

SAINT OF LOST SOULS

A NOVEL

TRISH MCGARRAHAN

ISBN 979-8-9917861-0-2 (paperback)
ISBN 979-8-9917861-1-9 (ebook)

Published by Angel's Share LLC.
Cover and book design by Christian Storm.

This is a work of fiction. Names, characters, places, and incidents are the product of the author's imagination or used fictitiously, and any resemblance to actual persons, living or dead, businesses, companies, events, or locales is entirely coincidental.

For Isabella Rose —

A bushel and a peck

SAINT OF LOST SOULS

PROLOGUE

I KNOW HE'S THERE.

Waiting.

Calculating.

Choosing the perfect moment to attack.

I stand, eyes closed, trying to slow my breathing, but my heart's racing, my pulse pounding. I inhale for a count of two, exhale for four, straining for a sound, any change that would indicate movement.

Two can play this game. But I'm fooling myself.

He's bigger, stronger, faster.

And he's waiting.

For me.

Then it happens.

Large hands seize my neck; my eyes fly open in surprise, even as I'm expecting this, and I gasp for air.

I reach up to break my attacker's grip on my throat but he sweeps my legs out from under me, catching me off guard. Suddenly I'm flat on my back and he's straddling me, his entire weight on my ribcage. Again, he tries to choke me, so

I tilt my hips upward to throw him off balance, forcing him to place his hands on either side of my head to keep himself from falling forward. Then I raise my right leg in toward my body and lever it across his torso, before shoving and rolling with all my strength.

The tables have turned. I'm on top, no victim but an aggressor, striking with my knees, palms and elbows, inflicting as much damage as I can before staggering to my feet.

My attacker lies on the ground, his face turned away.

There's a long moment of silence. Then he gets fluidly to his feet, six feet of muscle and menace, pulls off his mask and headgear, and grins.

"Well done, Wheels," Raj says, clapping a now-friendly hand on my shoulder. "You got in some really good shots there." Leaning down, he adds, "Thank God for the cup."

We're both smiling, slightly winded and pumped full of adrenaline, as we join our classmates in the center of the gym.

ONE

THE SHRILL RING of the office telephone cuts the silence of the room. I glance up from my computer at the sound, annoyed at the interruption, my concentration broken. It's ten o'clock in the morning on my first day back to work after a two-week vacation, and I'm in email hell. The number on the caller ID isn't one I recognize, so I let the call go to voicemail.

I'm drowning in military jargon and acronyms when I should be in the field, where the summer dig season is well underway. But here and now, my first priority is finding out if the government awarded the Dragonfly contract, which they've postponed once already.

Dragonfly is a next-generation armed drone that we hope will turn the tide in Ukraine's favor in the war against Russia. I desperately want us to win this contract, although any of our competitors could likely do the job just as well. As a senior contracts administrator for Tate Walker, I'll be the one signing it, if we win. To finally see that homicidal maniac in the Kremlin get what's coming to him and know that I'd played even a tiny role in it would be priceless.

I've just returned from two weeks in Europe, the first week in Seville and the second week in Avignon. I've been traveling internationally since I was old enough to hoist my own backpack, but France is where I'm happiest and where I feel most at home. My mother was French, and I've been speaking the language almost as long as I've been speaking English. When I'm in France, a lighter, happier version of me emerges.

I'd arrived in Europe in the midst of the Ukraine war and felt uneasy about it. Part of me couldn't shake the feeling that I shouldn't have been flitting around acting like the world wasn't on fire, when only a few thousand miles away, it really was. I also had my old friend Viktoriya, my former Durham roommate, on my mind. She'd returned home to Odesa after graduation. During the war, had she evacuated along with so many others? We'd lost touch, and I wish I had a way of contacting her now.

As the conflict rages on with no end in sight, merely donating to Ukrainian charities isn't nearly enough. I wish I'd done more, could do more still.

But maybe, just maybe, there will be Dragonfly.

There's still an unread message count of 357, though.

Lovely.

I've worked at Tate Walker, a defense giant based in McLean, Virginia, for longer than I care to admit, on our Army team. It was supposed to be temporary, something to get me back on my feet for six months or a year, tops. It's worlds away from medieval archaeology, my true love. But, after defending my PhD dissertation, I was forced to return home to Virginia from Durham, England, when my parents died suddenly, right before the congregation ceremony.

So many years ago, but some days it feels like yesterday.

A friend of my father's helped me to get a job here at Tate Walker several months after my parents' deaths, when I'd still been shell-shocked with grief. A contracts training course gave me the basics, I learned on the job, and I've been promoted several times since. But now I'm stuck – paid well, but dreaming of a different life. My only chance at a hint of heroism is Dragonfly.

What's more, I'd been beating myself up about my ex-boyfriend. Handsome, self-absorbed Noah, a brilliant foreign policy senior fellow at the Brookings Institution. We'd been together for a year, and it all came crashing down right before our planned European vacation this summer. He left me standing in my front hallway, dressed to the nines for a black-tie dinner at the French embassy. We'd argued over the dress I was wearing, which Noah said was too revealing. When he insisted that I change into something else and I refused, he drove off in a huff and went without me. That charming episode had been the beginning of the end.

Damned Noah.

The computer mouse in my hand is suddenly no longer a mouse but a soft-bristled brush. I'm in the ruins of a medieval abbey in the north east of England, kneeling in a shallow trench, one of a handful that we'd been excavating among the mossy remains of what had once been an impressive building.

I'm brushing hardened soil from a large shard of stained glass. My heart pounds as the ancient design begins to reveal itself.

My muscles are tight from crouching too long in the same position, the soil still slightly damp against the knees of my hiking trousers in the early-morning hours. Voices come to me from across the site, and some laughter. Second- and third-year students side by side with the post-grads, chatting, flirting, but mostly working steadily until the long summer daylight is lost. We're all looking forward to a shower and the upcoming night at the pub.

There will be breaks for sandwiches, tea and biscuits on the damp, dreary days when the low clouds hover, everyone's eyes on the piles of nearby tarps. On the hot days, there is bottled water instead of tea, not cold by any standards, but it will do the job in the heat. The next find might come at any moment or not for days. Or not at all.

The uneven edges of the glass shard blur and fade, and the computer monitor fills my vision once again. The tool in my hand is no longer a simple brush but a wireless mouse.

Reluctantly, my thoughts return to the present and Dragonfly. I enter 'Daniel Atkinson' into my email search bar and wait for the results. Atkinson is a government contracting officer whose very name makes me want to head for the nearest bar for a bit of day drinking. His default attitude toward contractors alternates between suspicion and contempt, and that's before he gets up a head of steam and starts yelling. Negotiations with him leave me dry-mouthed and sweating because there's no way to know what kind of mood he'll be in. We stupid contractors take his abuse because we have no choice, but he's also the contracting officer on Dragonfly; so, if we win, I'll have to deal with him whether I like it or not.

I scan the handful of messages that appear in the results window. None of them is the Dragonfly award notification I was expecting. No news is good news, maybe? At least we haven't been notified we lost. Foreign military sales need all sorts of congressional notifications and hoop-jumping. Since Dragonfly is my first, I'm no expert on whether or not delays are the norm for foreign arms sales. I'll have to ask my boss about it when I see him. There's been talk that no matter who wins, the award will be protested by a losing bidder. It wouldn't surprise me if all the bidders' legal teams have drafted protests in anticipation of the award announcement, just in case. Dragonfly's a pretty big deal.

I glance with distaste at the remnants of a dry blueberry scone and the cup of now-tepid tea sitting on the far corner of my desk. Hard to believe that only two days ago, I was eating a freshly-baked chocolate brioche at a café table opposite the Palace of the Popes in Avignon. I can still recall the sense of peace I'd felt in the quiet square in the cool stillness of the morning, before the arrival of the tourists with their selfie sticks and the long admission queues that snaked up the palace steps. Peace that had otherwise eluded me for most of the trip but had finally settled over me on that final day.

I now sweep the pastry crumbs, paper bag, and to-go cup into the wastepaper basket next to my desk. The gym awaits me later today. Some time on a punching bag is bound to help get my head back in the game. I hope so, anyway.

"You're back!"

Startled, I jump and look up. Standing in the doorway is a tall, slim, elegant woman with long blonde hair parted precisely in the center. There's not a single strand out of place, even in the mugginess of this early-July morning. I'd have hated her on sight if she weren't my best friend.

"Well, it's about damn time," she says. "I was beginning to think you'd decided to stay in France indefinitely."

Simone Ellis is an attorney on the company's legal team and, in my opinion, the best attorney we've got. Legal and contracts are separate entities in large companies such as ours, but we often work closely together.

She crosses the small office in a few long strides, then lowers herself gracefully into the visitor's chair next to my desk. "God, I missed you."

"Missed you, too, Simone. This place, not so much."

"No surprise there."

"I'm ready to jump off a Beltway overpass, and I've only been back for three hours."

"Yeah, you poor baby, strolling around Europe while the rest of us have been dealing with the usual bullshit here at the office."

"Okay, okay, message received." I hold up my hands in surrender. "I'll stop acting like a self-entitled ass now."

She laughs, leans over and gives me a one-armed hug. "So, did my self-entitled friend have a holiday tryst with any hot Spaniards or Frenchmen?"

My answer is written all over my face.

"Kate Barrow, have I taught you nothing?"

"One-night stands aren't my style," I remind my friend for about the hundredth time. "Besides, I don't need any more drama in my life."

"Who said anything about drama? I'm talking about having some fun for a change. You remember what fun is, right? It might've helped get Noah out of your head. The fucking psychopath."

Noah hadn't taken it well when I'd ended it, to put it mildly. The dress incident had been bad enough, but there had been others. How could I have been so stupid, so blind, not to see him for who he really was?

Simone is looking at me inquisitively.

"I'm over Noah, Simone. Let's not talk about him anymore, okay?"

"Yeah, well, I still wish you'd had some good revenge sex."

I laugh. "Better than sex, Simone. I explored ancient ruins, hiked during the day, and drank really good wine at night. What about you? Did you piss off anyone while I was away?"

She airily waves a dismissive hand. "Of course, I pissed off someone. You know that's part of my job description, right?" She taps her lower lip as if giving my question serious thought. "Let's see, Delgado over on the Air Force side has his tighty-whities in a twist over a conflict of interest. He's not happy because I reminded him that if we help define the government's requirements, we can't bid on the actual work when the time comes. I'm sure he'll try to submit a proposal behind our backs anyway, the fuckwit. How he ever got promoted to director is beyond me."

"You and me both."

"Oh, and then I had to break up what was sure to be a catfight between two of the admins in the eighth-floor admin pool. It's like *Mean Girls, the Office Version* up there some days. I told them to get their acts together and behave like the professionals they're being paid to be or they'd find themselves cleaning the fridges and microwaves every Friday for the next six months. I get death stares every time I go up there now. I never thought my job would require hazardous duty pay, for fuck's *sake*."

Simone. The face of an angel. The mouth of a sailor. And a heart of gold, although that last fact is known to only a select few. We became fast friends many years ago, bonding over the long hours and late nights it took to resolve a crisis caused by a defective part on a shoulder-fired missile. Her brilliant legal arguments saved the day, and we've been close ever since. On the worst days, it's Simone who keeps me from completely losing my mind in this place.

She'd worked for a DC defense attorney for a few years after passing the bar exam, then joined Tate Walker's legal department. It's a shame, really, because I've often thought her talents are completely wasted in corporate law. I can easily imagine her eviscerating a witness under cross-examination in a courtroom. Working eighty hours a week at the law firm had been too hard on her marriage with Luke, a gorgeous Aussie chef, so she ended up here. Bored to death, like me.

"I didn't forget your chocolate, Simone," I say, trying to make her smile. I open my desk drawer to pull out a beautifully-wrapped box. "It sounds like you earned it."

Her eyes light up as she recognizes the signature teal-colored box from a Parisian chocolatier. "Thanks, Kate. You're an angel."

"I really missed you," I say. "And all the while I *wasn't* having hot revenge sex, I couldn't get Dragonfly out of my head. Have you heard anything? It should've been announced by now, but I haven't seen any emails about it." I swivel slightly back and forth in the high-backed ergonomic desk chair as I face my friend.

She suddenly sits up straighter, if that's possible, as a thought occurs to her. She has the perfect posture of a classical dancer. I've learned through the course of our friendship that, as a child, she studied ballet for many years before abandoning dance for riding. I think I was probably studying French, Latin, or Greek in my spare time when I was a kid. Not quite the same thing, right?

"No, nothing on Dragonfly that I know of. But have you seen any of the emails from Charles?" she asks. She's referring to Charles Burton, CEO of Tate Walker.

"No, I haven't gotten that far. What's going on?"

"You're not going to believe it. Anne Marie was killed in a car accident."

"Anne Marie Clark? The Army contracts admin?" My voice has gone up at least an octave, I'm sure.

"Uh-huh. It happened right after you left. The theory is she fell asleep behind the wheel. She went off the road on the George Washington Parkway and hit a tree. They think she probably died instantly."

"The GW Parkway?" I inhale sharply, then seeing Simone's concerned expression, exhale slowly. Get a grip, Kate. It happens every day; you know that. Still, there's a tremor in my voice I can't quite disguise. "You're right. I can't believe it."

I hadn't worked closely with Anne Marie, but as fellow contracts admins on the Army account, we reported up to the same manager, sat in on the same weekly contracts staff meetings, and occasionally covered for each other in a pinch. From what I did know of her, she was a competent employee with two teenagers and a husband who also works in defense.

"Her poor family," I say, still trying to take in the news. "I spoke with her the day before I went on vacation. All she could talk about was her daughter getting into UVA and the plans they had for her dorm room. She was so proud. You just never know, do you?"

"I take it that means you haven't heard from Josh yet?" Simone asks, referring to my immediate manager.

As if on cue, there is a knock on the partially-closed office door.

"Is this a private party, or can anyone join?"

Josh Hudson appears in the doorway, a welcoming smile on his face. He is a large man, a few inches over six feet tall, with wavy sandy hair and warm brown eyes. For some reason he reminds me of a great big teddy bear. He can quote the Federal Acquisition Regulation's parts and subparts like a devout Christian can quote the bible's chapters and verses. He also has a wonderfully dry sense of humor, which goes a long way in this job. Most importantly, he is a complete gem of a boss.

"Great to have you back, Kate. How was your trip?"

Before I can reply, his gaze shifts between me and Simone, his expression changing. "Oh, so you've told her about Anne Marie, I take it?" he says to Simone. He picks up the spare visitor's chair and sets it across from me and Simone before sitting down heavily. "Not exactly the way I'd hoped to welcome you back. I spoke to Anne Marie's husband after the funeral. They're all still completely shell-shocked."

We sit in silence for a moment, thinking about our late colleague, then Simone looks at her watch and gets to her feet. "Gotta run," she says, her phone in one hand and the box of chocolates in the other. "Thanks again for this. Let me know if you need anything from me once you've made it through your inbox. Or if you want to talk about Anne Marie."

As she strolls out the door – Simone never appears to be in a hurry, even when she is – Josh and I turn back to one another.

"This is unbelievable," I say. "How is everyone doing? I mean, the team must be reeling. It's one thing for someone to leave the company for another job, it's totally different to have someone die so suddenly."

"Yeah, EAP has stepped up, made more counselors available for whoever feels they need it. We had a few rough days initially, but I think the team's coming to terms with it."

"She fell asleep behind the wheel?" I'm still unable to process what I just heard. "Does that sound like Anne Marie to you?"

"No, it doesn't. But you know how it is with proposals. This summer's been insane, as usual. Everyone's been working flat out trying to meet all our damned deadlines." He shrugs, looking miserable.

We sit in grim silence for a moment, then I say, "This job's going to be the death of us all."

He gives a short laugh, then stands. "So, with Anne Marie gone, this means the rest of us will have to divvy up her portfolio until we can hire her replacement. I've handed off her smaller contracts to the other CAs. But there is one important, $500 million contract I'd like you to take on. It's Ares, a five-year contract for virtual-reality headsets for the Army. I have to admit, it's had its problems from the start."

He flashes me an apologetic smile.

"You really love me, don't you, Josh?"

"If there were anyone else, you know I'd gladly spare you this headache right now. But the timing..." He holds up his hands in a gesture of defeat. "I don't know what else to do."

"It's fine, really," I say. "It's only until we hire Anne Marie's replacement, right? So, let's see exactly what you've gotten me into." I swivel around in my chair so that I'm facing my computer, open our contracts database and pull up Ares.

Josh pulls his chair next to mine so he can see the screen that's displayed. "The weird thing is, no one can find Anne Marie's laptop," he says. I look at him incredulously, and he nods. "I know, crazy, right? Security and HR checked her work locker, and her husband swears he hasn't seen her laptop bag since before the accident. He's asked the wrecking company who towed the car to track it down, but it's the least of his worries right now." While I ponder that little mystery, he continues, "Thank God for the cloud, at least. I've skimmed through her folders on the team's shared drive; maybe those will help. She might've saved files there that she didn't upload to the contracts database. IT has given me access to her emails for a few months, so we have those, too."

I scroll down to the points of contact section and read the names of the key players. Seeing a couple of familiar names cheers me up a little. I won't be starting completely from zero, at least not with the team. I continue down the page and pause when I get to the section on subcontractors.

"Eight subs? That seems like a lot."

"Yeah. Lots of moving parts on this one. I've already spoken with the VP and the program manager, so they're aware you're taking over. Let's set aside some time later this week so I can get you up to speed. I'd suggest you start with the proposal to get a read on all the subs and what their roles are. The PM should be able to fill in some blanks for you there, too."

"Okay, sounds good."

"Thanks. You'll be saving me a lot of grief." He stands and slides the chair back to where he found it.

"Thank *you* for covering for me while I was away." I swivel away from the desk and reach beneath it to pull out a soft-sided cooler bag. "A few goodies from France, as my way of saying thanks."

"Oh, wow."

I'm pleased at his reaction to the assortment of French cheeses and to-die-for – his words – butter amongst the ice packs. I'd thrown in some pricey chocolates for good measure, too. "It was only fair that I brought you back something."

"You didn't have to do that," he says, all the while eagerly checking out the contents of the bag.

"I know, but I wanted to. Hey, one more thing, Josh. Have you gotten wind of anything on Dragonfly? I thought maybe Atkinson emailed you since you were covering and left me off the message. That wouldn't surprise me. It's also my first foreign military sale, so I wasn't sure if they typically get held up."

"Nope, crickets." He scrolls through the emails on his phone to be sure. "If anything comes through and you're not copied, I'll forward it."

As Josh leaves the office, I suddenly see the face of Anne Marie, smiling, the last time I saw her. Even though it wasn't her proposal, she'd been asking questions about Dragonfly. I thought that was kind of strange, but she'd probably just been curious. If we get it, it will be a very big win for Tate Walker, regardless of who the contracts admin is. Now she'll never know the outcome of the award. Or anything else, for that matter. Shit.

I open another browser window on my computer and type, 'GW Parkway June traffic fatality' into the search bar and hit enter. Time to do some digging of my own.

TWO

"YOU'RE KILLING ME, WHEELS."

I laugh as the younger man lies spent and winded on the floor, grinning up at me. "You're killing me, *Kate*," I correct him, offering him an outstretched hand to help pull him up. He doesn't need my help but takes my hand anyway in a gesture of good sportsmanship.

"You're getting *really* good," Raj says, coming to his feet and brushing off his form-fitting T-shirt and loose-fitting sweatpants. Tall and muscular, he has dark, liquid eyes, lashes most women would kill for, and a ready smile. He's newer to the gym than I am but obviously not new to the self-defense tactics that are taught here. We've worked out together only a handful of times; but even I can see the quiet, unassuming young man knows his stuff in this space. "How'd you get the name Wheels, anyway?"

"Oh, that. My last name is Barrow, so one of the guys started calling me Wheelbarrow when I first joined. A retired Navy pilot with a thing for callsigns changed it to Wheels. His was Rebound – I can only imagine why. He's not around much these days, but the name kind of stuck."

"Oh, yeah, I know Rebound. He's been coming in most afternoons. Do you mind it, being called Wheels?"

"Nah, I was just giving you a hard time. I've been called worse, believe me. What about you? Did Rebound give you a nickname, too?"

He hesitates for a minute then breaks into a sheepish smile. "Choirboy."

"Do you —?"

"Nope. My last name is Singh."

"That is so bad," I say with a laugh.

"Yeah. But at least with Rebound, it's friendly. It means we're one of the guys. Well, you know." I nod to show that I'm not offended to be considered one of the guys. A shadow briefly crosses his face. "It's better than Bollywood, which is what some of the jokers in my old MP unit used to call me."

My laughter dies as I stare at my workout partner, feeling both sympathetic and outraged on his behalf. And there's something else I can't put my finger on. Uneasiness, maybe? Raj had once been a military policeman – I hadn't known that.

"Not a lot of soldiers looked like me, you know? That's the way it is." His tone is casual but I can tell the barbs had hit their target.

"I'm really sorry, Raj."

"Thanks." His expression turns playful. "You can make it up to me by taking it easier on me next time."

"Fat chance."

We laugh as we make our way around the cushioned workout mats toward the hallway. We're both sweaty, having gone through thirty minutes of self-defense moves and countermoves. It's physically and mentally exhausting; exactly what I need to clear my head. I'd spent the last two hours of my workday in a meeting with our risk team, debating the morality of using directed-energy weapons against human subjects. Just another fun afternoon in my contracts world.

Meditation and mindfulness do nothing for me; I'm too impatient and restless to sit still and focus on my breathing. When you're faced with an opponent who outweighs you by a hundred pounds and whose aim is to cause you grievous bodily harm, even in theory, it forces you to focus in the moment like nothing else. I'll take sessions like this any day when I need to quiet all the noise in my head.

When I'd first looked into taking self-defense classes last winter, one of my program managers, a retired Marine, had suggested Trident when he'd walked me to my car late one evening. Last fall, there had been an alarming series of assaults around the Silver Line metro station just steps from the office. It was only when a co-worker's attack had hit too close to home that I'd finally gotten serious about learning to defend myself. I'd initially worried I wouldn't fit in at Trident because most of the members here seemed to be in law enforcement or the military. The bottom line was, I didn't want anything pseudo-spiritual, just basic, no-nonsense self-defense training. Trident Tactics & Training, under the guidance of its owner, Hicks, turned out to be exactly what I was looking for.

A retired Navy SEAL, Hicks started up the small, no-frills gym ten years ago. The gym offers ongoing self-defense training, compressed self-defense seminars for women, and workout classes that anyone who'd served in the military would recognize from their trainee days.

I know Hicks' parents must have given him a first name, but I have absolutely no idea what it is. In typical military fashion, everyone refers to the former naval officer by his last name. As we leave the practice space, I see Hicks watching as Raj and I head for the locker rooms. He peels himself away from the wall where he's been leaning and walks next to me as I veer off in the direction of the water fountain to fill my water bottle.

Tall and lean, Hicks still has a military bearing. Even though this is a civilian gym and no one here is under his command, I can sense that everyone respects as well as likes him. He's here more often than not, although he has enough staff to cover most shifts. His is a calm, steadying presence even in the midst of all the shouting, punching, and bodies flying all over the place.

"Looking good, Kate," he tells me as I wait for the water to run cold.

"Thanks, Hicks," I reply with a smile, pleased that he's noticed my progress. My moves and responses are becoming second nature. My goal is to get to the point where I don't have to think but instead simply react the way I've been trained to.

"How're things?" I ask before taking a long swallow of water.

He smiles. "All good. Heading up to Deep Creek next weekend for a bit of R&R. Looking forward to getting away for a bit. Missed you the past couple of weeks. Been taking a little R&R yourself?"

"Yes, and it shows. I didn't work out at all while I was on vacation, so I'm really going to pay for it later."

In a moment we're joined by Declan O'Rourke, a gym member and part-time instructor. He and Hicks go back a long way, from what I understand. Declan fills in occasionally when a class needs to be covered; when he's not leading a class, he works out along with the rest of us.

Declan's nearly as tall as Hicks, around six feet, and he has a similar way of carrying himself. I don't think he's been in the military, though. Maybe it's just all the training. He's also more reserved and less approachable than his older friend. While Hicks is slim with a head of silver hair and is in his mid-sixties or thereabouts, Declan is broad-shouldered, with close-cropped dark hair going slightly grey at the temples and intense blue eyes. I'm not great at guessing ages, but I'd say he's closer to my age than to Hicks'.

Declan makes it clear that he's there to work out and nothing more; I've witnessed him subtly deflect a few women's attempts to get to know him better. Although I'm still recovering from the disaster that was Noah and another relationship's the last thing I need, there's nothing wrong with my eyesight: Declan's a very good-looking man. Plus, his accent is as warm and smooth as the finest single-malt Irish whiskey. Or so I imagine, since I'm not much of a whiskey drinker myself.

As I'd told Simone, though, I don't need drama in my life. For the past six months, Trident has been my refuge. I plan to keep it that way.

"Hello, Declan."

"Kate." A slight nod of his head. "Looks like you gave Raj a run for his money today."

"He gave as good as he got, I'd say." I take another sip before raising my water bottle to both men in salute. "Time to hit the shower."

They nod in acknowledgement. As I turn away, I see them walk back toward the main training room to square away the space for tomorrow. By the time they're done, everything will be as orderly and immaculate as a new Marine recruit's footlocker. Exactly the way Hicks likes it.

In the women's locker room, I strip off my sweaty clothes and enter one of the shower stalls, standing gratefully under the bracing, cool spray. After drying off, I gaze at my reflection in the wall of mirrors before getting dressed. Although my fortieth birthday looms on the horizon, I'm in the best shape of my life, thanks to my time here at the gym and a somewhat balanced diet.

Thinking of Hicks' earlier comment makes me smile; I know I've come a very long way since my first day here. At a few inches over five feet with a small frame, I'm still amazed to discover I can defend myself very effectively against opponents nearly twice my weight and often a head taller.

I'm no Puritan, and I enjoy my fair share of wine – okay, probably slightly more than my fair share of wine – which I blame entirely on Simone's influence. Good wine and Wegman's gourmet cheese and bakery departments are the extent of my vices. Apart from my gym workouts, about which I'll admit to being a tad obsessive, my life these days is pretty much about moderation and balance.

Pretty much.

AS I DRIVE THROUGH the congested streets of Herndon on my way home to North Arlington, I think again of Anne Marie and how she died. One of the major downsides to living in the Northern Virginia area is the endless traffic. There are well-paying jobs, excellent schools, and an overall good quality of living, but all the things that make the area so attractive and make people want to live here contribute to the daily grind of sitting in traffic. Gridlock is a fact of life on the Capital Beltway and the other major arteries that connect DC, Virginia and Maryland.

The GW Memorial Parkway, where Anne Marie died, is a scenic byway that is also one of the main routes to the Ronald Reagan Washington National Airport. It's heavily traveled by commuters during the week. On weekends, it's jammed with cyclists, walkers, and boaters of all kinds, drawn to the nearby Potomac. Tourists visiting the monuments, museums, galleries, and other attractions in DC rely on it, too.

The news articles I'd found online about Anne Marie's accident had said she'd gone off the road around midnight and hit a tree. There didn't appear to be any other vehicles involved, according to what I'd read. Alcohol hadn't been a contributing factor, but her speed definitely had.

If she'd fallen asleep, wouldn't the car have slowed down, though? I think about all the deer that cross the heavily-wooded parkway and wonder if she'd swerved to avoid hitting one. I've had a few close calls with deer myself. That makes more sense to me than falling asleep. There would have been signs of braking, though, and the police would have checked all that, I suppose. I know very little about her life outside of work aside from the few details she'd shared about her family. Even so, I can't help but wonder where she was going and what possibly could have happened.

Life happens, I tell myself as I signal and change lanes to exit onto the Dulles Toll Road. Sometimes life is random and tragic; that's the way it is. I lost both my parents in a crash with a drunk driver on the same stretch of roadway where Anne Marie died. This has me spooked, understandably. I'm sure traffic statistics would confirm that dozens of people have been killed on the same spot over the years, but the knowledge still unsettles me.

I follow the now-familiar route home, occasionally checking the navigation app on my phone for any traffic tie-ups or alternate routes. Fortunately, there are no major delays tonight, and I'm on autopilot as I drive through the neighborhood streets as the evening closes in. This time of year, it's not quite full dark at this hour. There are still sounds of families out in backyards and on front porches, as well as the occasional chirp of crickets and cicadas.

The house is blessedly quiet when I let myself in through the front door. As always, I take a moment when arriving home to savor the simple pleasure of being home, in this space, at the end of a long day. It's not a large house, just a three-bed, two-bath Craftsman-style bungalow, which I'd inherited from my parents. The original bedrooms and closets were on the small side, but a major renovation several years ago changed the footprint and layout considerably. Now the house where I'd grown up is nearly perfect for my needs.

After many years as a student in the UK, I'd developed a fondness for backyard conservatories from visiting friends' homes during term holidays at university. One of the major changes I'd had made to the house was the addition of a large sunroom to the length of the house, behind the kitchen and living rooms, facing the back garden. It's one of my favorite places in the house. Too bad there's no time to relax in there tonight.

Once I've changed into a comfortable sundress, I return to the kitchen and glance at the clock. Since it's nearly seven-thirty, it's too late for a heavy meal, so I settle for a light supper of store-bought pasta salad with a glass of Sancerre. Taking the plate and glass through to the front of the house, I enter what used to be my late parents' shared study and is now my office.

After setting down the plate and glass on the desk, I turn on the Anglepoise lamp in the corner, then switch on my laptop and close the plantation shutters that face the front of the house while I wait for the login prompt.

This is another space that brings me great pleasure, most of the time. The walls are lined with floor-to-ceiling built-in bookshelves that are filled with my parents' beloved book collections. Both professors, my mother taught French history and my father, English literature. Books were a kind of currency in our family, given as gifts for every occasion or no occasion at all. The large bookshelves flanking either side of the generous front windows contain my own books. There are neat stacks on the floor in front of the shelves, and I can put my hand on almost any title I'm searching for in a moment.

During the renovation, I'd had the dark wood trim and beams throughout the house painted a glossy white, and the walls in this room are a soothing robin's egg blue. It's a comfortable, cozy space, with a handful of framed pictures of me and my parents on the bookshelves and the low wall that divides the office from the rest of the downstairs.

On good days, when I enter this room, I feel as though I'm in the company of old friends and happy memories. On bad days, when I feel the loss of my parents so intensely, when I still can't believe they're gone, I have to resist the temptation to never set foot inside it again.

Today is one of the good days.

Once online, I use my authentication key to access my company's intranet and internal applications. A few more login and password entries grant me access to the contracts database. I likely won't have an uninterrupted block of time during the workday to read through all the Ares documents, so it's worth giving up a few hours of my time tonight to get a head start on the task. I take a sip of wine followed by a few bites of pasta salad, contemplating this new contract Josh dropped in my lap, wondering how much it's going to add to my workload. At least it's only temporary.

The first piece of bad news comes when I see the name of the contracting officer on the most-recent modification: Daniel Atkinson. That's the last thing I need right now. Bad enough that he'll be the contracting officer on Dragonfly, if we win it, but Ares is going to be a royal pain, I can tell. I've worked with some excellent contracting officers over the years and have learned the best ones are those who treat their contractors as partners, not adversaries. I've even become friendly with a few, within the strict guidelines that dictate such government-contractor relationships and interactions. Daniel Atkinson is definitely not among the best ones, and he and I will never be friendly.

The second piece of bad news comes when I do a quick scan of the award and modification amounts in the database. Contracts admins are required to enter all awards and modifications into our system within forty-eight hours, and sometimes mistakes are made in our rush to get the information entered. We're responsible for entering information such as the value of the award, the amount of funding received, the contract type, and all the pertinent terms and conditions, whether we have to notify the government when we expend a certain percentage of funding, and any negotiation notes or other information that the team might find helpful. All of our processes are tied to the contracts admin's timeliness, and work can't start until the contract is entered and set up, so there is a bit of pressure there.

Now I'm finding all sorts of errors and can't understand how they weren't caught earlier. A great deal of the information Anne Marie – or someone – had entered into our system doesn't match the contract. Granted, we admins cover for one other and are in and out of each other's contracts all the time. It might not have been only my late colleague who entered the data. But as the Ares contracts admin, she'd have been responsible for cleaning up any errors she'd found, regardless of who had made them.

We all make typos and transpose numbers – I get it – but a lot of the data we enter triggers automatic notifications to other departments, like security, finance, our small-business office, and subcontractor reporting. The dollar amounts have to be correct, and those notifications have to be made.

Just what had she been doing the past two years, for Pete's sake? There are too many checks and balances built into our processes for her to have done anything underhanded financially. It's never *seriously* crossed my mind – well, you know, except for those moments when I dream of living out my days in a secluded villa on the Amalfi Coast – but if I decided to suddenly go rogue and figure out how to skim funds, I'd make darn sure not to be sloppy about it. Criminals often get caught, though, right? The stereotype of the bumbling criminal exists for a reason.

Sipping my wine, I consider the idea for a moment.

What would be the magic number? One million? Five million, maybe? Yeah, it would have to be at least five million to make it worth the risk.

In your dreams, Kate Barrow.

The carelessness really annoys me, though. I'll admit I can be over the top with my color-coded folders, index tabs, and volumes of hand-written notes – slightly out of step in this digital world. All of that documentation is for my own use and isn't part of any official records, since we've supposedly gone paperless. That's never going to happen, by the way. But this is *government contracting,* not blending an overpriced, pretentious-sounding drink at some upscale coffeeshop. Details matter. Accuracy matters. If Anne Marie had been this cavalier with basic data entry, what else might she have let slip?

I save the spreadsheet I'd created to compare the funding amounts, turn off my laptop, and sit for a minute in the quiet office. I make a note to schedule a meeting with the business analyst to make sure our financials match the funding as shown on the contract, for starters. I'll also need to let Josh know the database entries are a mess. I curse silently at the realization that Daniel Atkinson's hostility might be the least of my worries with Ares.

While I finish my meal, I scroll idly through the unread emails on my phone, pausing briefly when I see an email from a familiar address. The third in as many days. My finger hovers over the latest message, ready to delete it. Instead, I close the email app and rise from the desk.

Fiona. I'll have to reply to her eventually, but not tonight.

THREE

"HEY, KATE. Got a minute?"

I look up to see a smiling Josh standing in my office doorway. "Hi," I reply, happy to see him.

"You had a few hours blocked out on your calendar this morning, but I wasn't sure if it was for meetings or real work."

I return his smile. "It was for real work, but I always have time for you. What's up?"

I've been back to work for nearly a week and haven't seen much of my boss, aside from the meeting where he got me up to speed on Ares and once or twice in the kitchen as we waited for the Keurig to do its thing. I've seen his calendar – it's insane – and I don't know how he manages it. Nothing seems to ruffle him, and his is not an easy job. He has ten administrators under his supervision who oversee contracts worth billions of dollars. I'm willing to bet no one calls Josh to say hello or when they're having a nice, uneventful day. If such a thing exists in this place.

While he'll occasionally make a purely social call to chat, I can tell from the expression on his face that today he doesn't want to talk about where he placed in Loudoun County's cycling event last weekend. He sits down in the visitor's chair next to my desk and gets right down to it.

"Bad news on Ares. The contracting officer's rep has told our program manager the government plans to speed up delivery of the augmented-reality training devices."

"Seriously? From what I can tell, we've just barely gotten back on track with the new schedule."

"I know. The VP's about to have a stroke, and word has already made its way up to Charles. We need to call the contracting officer ASAP to find out if it's true. If it is, we've got our work cut out for us in figuring out how we can make this work."

I was feeling as though I'd finally gotten back on top of things work-wise, and now this. Bad enough that sorting through Anne Marie's files and cleaning up her haphazard admin work had taken up most of my time since I'd returned; now the government's decided to drop this bombshell.

On the bright side, our business analyst and I had concluded the errors I'd found hadn't been anything more than carelessness on someone's part. The contract values and funding amounts all tally in our financial systems, and the data will be corrected once our analysts work their magic. If I quit my job tomorrow – I can dream, right? – my successor could pick up without missing a beat. Truth be told, most government contractors live in abject terror of a random government audit, myself included. I know for certain my official files would hold up to any government bean counter's scrutiny, though. Anne Marie's, on the other hand, were a complete shambles. I remind myself the poor woman is dead, give myself a good telling off for being so heartless, and focus once again on what Josh is saying.

"Let's go through the changes clause as a refresher. Then we need to review all the clauses in the contract that would apply in this situation. But first," he says, getting to his feet, "I need more damn caffeine for this. Coming?"

"Right behind you."

After Josh gets his coffee fix and I make myself a cup of tea, we spend nearly two hours wading through the contract and the defense and federal acquisition regulations to get ready for the call with Daniel Atkinson. We wouldn't be in such an untenable position if we hadn't made the decision to buy some of the scarce components in advance, even before we'd signed the final contract. It was a calculated risk on the company's part; now we have to live with it. The possibility of being saddled with parts we wouldn't be able to use and the financial penalties that could be imposed, in addition to having a contract termination in the public record, make us both understand how high the stakes are here.

Now Josh sits at my desk, his dress shirt sleeves rolled up, an empty coffee cup at his elbow. Empty foil wrappers from my not-so-secret chocolate stash litter the desktop. He's reviewing the notes he's written in a leather-bound notebook, making sure he hasn't missed anything. He worked as a government contracting officer for several years before joining Tate Walker. I suspect he loves using that knowledge to turn the tables on the government whenever he can, especially if they try to play dirty.

"Let's call Atkinson now and get this over with." He sets his notebook next to the phone so he can refer to his notes during the call. "Fasten your seatbelt. Things are about to get very interesting."

"I should've stayed on vacation," I grumble good-naturedly.

"What, and miss all the fun?"

"You really love this, don't you?"

"I really do." His wide grin makes him look years younger.

"I hear there's a support group for that."

"Wise guy. Keep that sense of humor, will you? We're going to need it."

I press the speaker button and dial the contracting officer's number. The phone rings several times; Josh and I exchange a resigned look. It was a long shot, thinking we'd catch him on the fly. My hand hovers over the phone, ready to end the call, when a harried-sounding male voice answers.

"Atkinson."

"Mr. Atkinson, this is Josh Hudson from Tate Walker calling about the Ares contract. We spoke briefly a few weeks ago when I called to tell you Anne Marie Clark had died."

"Why are you calling? Has someone else died?"

"No, Mr. Atkinson, no one else has died, I'm happy to say. During our previous call, I'd mentioned Kate Barrow would be temporarily taking over until we fill Ms. Clark's role. Kate's here with me now. Is this a good time to talk with us about Ares?"

"It's not a good time, actually. Wait, Barrow, you said? Are you the contracts admin who submitted the Dragonfly proposal? Those were *your* exceptions and assumptions?"

The team's lead engineer, program manager, Simone, and I had meticulously crafted watertight exceptions and assumptions. The contracting officer darn well knows it, too. That's probably why he now sounds as though he'd like to wring my neck.

"Yes, I was the contracts admin on our Dragonfly proposal."

"You do understand the government is under no obligation to consider exceptions and assumptions unless the proposal is incorporated into the contract?"

I can't tell if it's a question or a statement. I start to answer but Atkinson continues speaking as though he hasn't heard me.

"Why aren't you taking over Ares on a permanent basis? This is a high-visibility, defense priority contract. We need continuity, not a revolving door of contracts admins."

Josh and I are silent while we consider the contracting officer's comment. This *is* a high-visibility, don't-screw-it-up contract, which is one of the reasons he had given it to me.

My boss takes a deep breath, dives right in. "We understand your concerns. Tate Walker is doing everything we can to support the Ares project. Kate is—"

Daniel Atkinson cuts him off. "Why are you calling, Mr. Hudson?"

"We're calling because we've heard the government plans to modify our contract to expedite the delivery schedule. As you're aware, with the government's blessing, we're working through some supply chain issues that were beyond our control. Any change in schedule is a complete surprise to us."

"Tate Walker accepted this contract with the full knowledge it contained the changes clause and that it was a defense priority. Are you telling me that you're no longer able to fulfill the requirements of the contract? Because if you're not, I'm sure one of your competitors would be all too happy to."

"That's not what I'm saying at all," Josh replies diplomatically. "Of course, we intend to fulfil the terms of the contract. What I am saying is, we'd like to know when you expect to send us the modification so that we have time to review the changes and weigh our options."

"Weigh your options? Your *only* option is to accept the modification or find yourself in default."

Josh, bless him, is totally ready for this. "According to the Code of Federal Regulations, if a change to a rated order substantially alters the original production or delivery schedule, it's considered a new rated order. As such, Tate Walker can accept or reject the changed order. There's also the matter of consideration and equitable adjustment. We'd need time to determine the additional costs for expediting the delivery of components, the additional labor, as well as any other expenses associated with accelerating the delivery schedule."

"Also, as you're surely aware, Mr. Atkinson," I add, "we have several subcontractors on this contract who will also be impacted by any changes to the prime contract. It will take time to evaluate our contracts with them and flow down any changes."

"Tate Walker's subs are your responsibility, not the government's," he snaps. "Correct me if I'm wrong, Ms. Barrow, but you're not a *subcontracts* administrator, are you? The subs shouldn't be your concern. Unless you're also taking over for Ms. Cooper?"

Neither Josh nor I reply, since Atkinson has a point; neither of us knows who'll be taking over for Laura Cooper, the subcontracts admin who recently retired. What *I'd* give to be retired. I try not to dwell on the fact that I have decades of working still ahead of me.

Atkinson's voice snaps me out of my brief reverie. "If you have any questions once we've sent you the document for signature, email the contracts specialist. You'll have forty-eight hours to respond."

Even as I'm stinging slightly from the contracting officer's rebuke, I remember to ask the one question that's been on my mind since I returned from vacation. "Mr. Atkinson, one more thing before you go," I say quickly. "Has the government made an award decision on Dragonfly? The original decision was expected several weeks ago, isn't that right?"

There's a heavy silence before Atkinson replies. "Tate Walker will learn of the government's decision at the same time as the rest of the bidders. I wouldn't get my hopes up, if I were you."

When the line abruptly goes dead, Josh and I stare at each other, momentarily speechless at the man's rudeness.

"Nice to see that Atkinson is his usual charming self today." Josh's tone is dry but his expression is concerned as he rests his elbows on the desktop and rubs his hands over his face. He closes his notebook before getting to his feet.

I can't hide my disappointment. "Do you think he meant what he said about our losing Dragonfly? We put everything we had into that proposal, Josh. To make matters worse, we have to tell the VP and possibly Charles about Ares."

"Not just yet." He looks thoughtful. "We don't have the modification, so we don't know exactly what we're dealing with. I'd rather hold off on saying anything until we've seen it and have had a chance to run it by Simone."

"Oh, she's going to love this."

"My thoughts exactly." No longer looking worried, Josh is now grinning like the Cheshire Cat.

I'M STILL REALLY ticked off at government's high-handedness with Ares and the possibility we've lost Dragonfly. By the time I pack up my laptop bag at the end of the day, I feel like hitting something – or someone. So, I do what I usually do when I feel like this – I go to the gym. Some intense cardio and time on the boxing bag will do wonders for my stress levels right now.

I head straight for the weight room when I arrive. After a brief warm-up, I pull on a pair of boxing gloves and move to one of the free-standing bags. Concentrating solely on the bag in front of me, the rest of the world a million miles away, I vent the day's frustrations. When I take a breather for some water, I notice Raj watching me from across the room; we nod at one another in greeting.

He heads in my direction as I position myself back in front of the bag. "Hey, Wheels," he says with a sympathetic smile. "Bad day, huh?"

"Hey, Raj. How can you tell?" I exhale as my fist connects with the bag. With every strike, I'm picturing Atkinson's smug little face.

"Let's just say, if looks could kill, I'd be seriously worried about my life expectancy at the moment." One eyebrow is raised in amusement. "I know you're not in the seven o'clock class, but I have time for a few drills if you're interested. No big deal if you're not, but I thought I'd ask."

"That'd be great, thanks."

"Sure. Let me gear up, and I'll be right over."

I watch as he puts on basic protective gear: a mouth guard is followed by shin and chest protectors. A safety helmet with a cage for his head rounds out his ensemble. I decide to go slightly easier on him than usual because he might be missing one final but essential piece of equipment for our impromptu session: an athletic cup.

There aren't too many other folks using the weight room, so we're able to find a space off to the side where we'll have room to maneuver.

Raj asks, "Which one do you want to start with?"

"How about a rear chokehold? I still have some work to do on that one, if that's okay?"

"You're the boss."

I take a deep breath, already trying hard to control my breathing, knowing what's coming.

"You ready?" he asks.

"Yes."

I close my eyes and wait. Five seconds, ten seconds …

A strong arm is locked around my neck, and my head is pinned against the solid wall of a muscular chest. I open my eyes, gasping. I've found that no matter how many times I've practiced this, even though I know exactly what's coming, I still freeze at the moment of initial contact.

Once I recover from my usual panic, we work our way through the moves, eventually settling down on the mats to run through some options for releasing a front chokehold when an attacker is on top of you.

"Can we go back over the two-handed choke release one more time?"

"Yep."

We get back into position, run through the moves again, then one final time. When we're done, Raj gives me a hand up from the floor.

"Don't forget, Wheels, practice makes perfect. Remember to breathe and get through that initial reaction." He takes off his protective gear and stows it away. "You got this."

"Thanks, Raj. I appreciate it."

I take a long drink from my water bottle and pick up my boxing gloves from where I'd left them in the corner. Putting them back on, I once again square myself in front of the bag.

As he's leaving the room, Raj calls out, "I'm glad I'm not the one who ticked you off today."

"Yep. Consider yourself lucky, Choirboy." I manage to laugh even as I'm trying to concentrate on a series of jabs and cross punches.

"You know what they say about payback, right?" His tone is teasing as he points a finger at me.

A voice from behind me interrupts my quiet laughter.

"May I make a suggestion?"

Startled, I look over to see Declan standing behind me, slightly off to my left, arms folded across his chest. I hadn't known he was even in the room.

"May I?" he asks again.

I shrug. "Sure."

He moves directly behind me, taking me lightly by the shoulders. "Try a jab."

I do as he instructs.

"See where your shoulders are? You're too tense, relax your shoulders. Drop them slightly, like this." He demonstrates with his own body, corrects my form again. "Better." He watches as I throw a few more punches. "You're holding your breath on your combinations. Always remember to breathe."

With that, he turns and walks away to join the class that's starting in the other room.

"Thanks, Declan," I call to his retreating back. When he doesn't reply, I say under my breath, "You're welcome, Kate."

Then I smile and hit the bag again.

After more than an hour, I've had enough for the night. I lie down on the mat to stretch and cool down, looking forward to the leisurely soak in the tub that awaits when I get home. I think about how differently I'd have handled this afternoon's phone call with Daniel Atkinson if I hadn't discovered Hicks and Trident last winter.

I'd probably be on my second glass of wine by now trying to unwind after a stressful workday and an ugly commute home. That would be followed by a restless night's sleep because of the endless to-do list scrolling through my head. I'll always have those occasional nights when sleep is elusive, but since I joined the gym, they're not nearly as frequent as they used to be.

I think now of the other, more chilling reason I'm grateful for everything I'm learning here. When Noah left me high and dry and went to the French Embassy dinner by himself, I did what any self-respecting woman in my position would've done – I went out. I spent the evening at my favorite bar, drinking and enjoying the music. I'd posted pictures of myself with my friends, laughing and dancing, obviously having a great time. Noah was livid when he saw my posts. He'd apparently told everyone that I'd had to miss the dinner because I wasn't feeling well, so when my pictures showed up on social media, he'd texted that I'd made him look stupid. I'd replied that he hadn't needed my help for that. That had earned me four days of radio silence.

He and I had met last summer when he'd been the keynote speaker at a Brookings Institution presentation on the global impacts of the war in Ukraine. I found him fascinating, and we immediately hit it off when I approached him after the Q&A. In addition to being extremely good-looking, he came across as intelligent and well-spoken. His mother is a former senator, still a heavy hitter in DC; consequently, Noah's path in life has been paved smooth by connections and money. He had name-dropped shamelessly, expecting me to be impressed with all the people he knew. I wasn't. I was more impressed with him. Like me, he loved travel, art, history and wine. He'd checked all the boxes – at first.

I'd barely even registered his early attempts to control my behavior and his suggestions as to what I wore or his questioning how much time I spent at the gym or with my friends seemed harmless enough at first.

As our relationship progressed, I'd had the feeling that I was being followed, but Noah's late-model white BMW SUV was fairly common. Sightings of a similar vehicle when leaving the gym or after having dinner with a friend could have been a coincidence. Just fleeting glimpses, never close enough to see a license plate or catch sight of the driver, though. One more white SUV in a sea of them. It seemed not only melodramatic but also paranoid to think that it would even cross his mind to follow me.

I mean, it was, wasn't it? I'd thought so at the time.

But the clincher for me was what happened after the embassy dinner fiasco. When he finally deigned to speak to me again several days later, it was to show up at my house unannounced.

As soon as I answered the door, he pushed his way past me into the foyer, insisting that we needed to talk. I told him I was on my way out and it had already been four days, so what was his hurry? He didn't like my flippant tone and told me so. Then he grabbed my arm, hard, and twisted it painfully behind me, shouting at me to give him my keys, that I wasn't going anywhere.

At first, I had frozen in shock and nearly dropped my keyring. This was Noah, after all, not some creep in a dark alley or sketchy parking garage. But when he wouldn't let go, despite my protests, everything I'd been learning at the gym kicked in. I'd let my shoulder bag fall to the floor, then twisted and ducked away from him. Almost instinctively, I'd positioned myself in a fighting stance, raised my fists and tucked my elbows, ready to defend myself if he moved any closer.

We'd stared at each other in disbelief for what seemed like a very long time but was probably only a few seconds. In that moment, we became two complete strangers – no longer lovers but bitter enemies. I told him in a calm, quiet voice to get the hell out of my house. He tried to make light of his behavior, insisted I'd overreacted. The expression on my face and my body language said it all, though.

It was over.

He called me a useless bitch and slammed the door as he left, swearing that I was going to regret this. In hindsight, the only thing I'd regretted was not punching him in the mouth when I'd had the chance.

A few of the instructors have suggested that I test out on the self-defense training, try to advance my official standing. That's not why I do it, though. I don't need colored belts or certificates to know that I'm making progress. I simply want to stay in shape and know how to defend myself if I ever have to. For me, that's enough.

FOUR

THIS CAN'T BE RIGHT.

It has to be a mistake.

I clear the page's history and browsing data before trying again.

One of the things I loved about archaeology, aside from field work, was the research: coming up with a theory, then methodically finding the data to back it up, putting all the pieces of the puzzle together. My morning has been spent doing precisely that – not on some exciting new archaeological find, but on Ares. Reading the contract and identifying the clauses we're bound to and those that can trip us up is only the first step in learning a new contract as a contracts admin.

The government often restricts bids to small businesses, which means that if a large business wants a piece of the action on a particular project, it has to act as a subcontractor, or sub, to a small business rather than as a prime contractor. A contracts admin's due diligence in that situation includes running Dun & Bradstreet queries, confirming that a company is registered to do business with the government, and taking into account our own past experience with them.

Since Tate Walker is the prime on Ares, Laura, as subcontracts admin, would have confirmed the eligibility of our proposed subs before we included them in our proposal. Subs can range from small businesses with little knowledge of government contracting to large companies that have been in business for decades, such as ours. Federal contracting makes for strange bedfellows: one day you're competitors, the next you're teammates. It's all part of how the game is played.

Any entity wanting to do business with the federal government needs to register with SAM, the System for Award Management, an online database of companies and individuals authorized to contract with the government. Searching the site is a quick way to find pertinent information about potential competitors or business partners.

Users can also search SAM for companies or individuals who've been debarred. Debarments, also known as exceptions, are temporary and typically last from one to three years, depending upon the reason. Contractors or individuals can be debarred for fraud, falsification of records, embezzlement, non-performance, and non-payment of federal taxes, among other things.

Once I've confirmed that all the subs are registered with SAM, as expected, I scan through the entries, looking for anything that might raise a red flag. Finding nothing out of the ordinary, I close the web browser and open another window to display the Federal Procurement Data System.

The FPDS is a comprehensive database of government contract awards. It contains information regarding the awardee, the amount of the award, the period of the performance, and other details. There's nothing here that I really need to see, but I do a quick search of each of the subs, anyway, wanting some idea of how many contracts they've had or now have with the government.

I'd worked with Laura for years before she retired, and I always had the impression that she paid close attention to detail and was very good at her job. It looks like she'd done her usual due diligence on Ares, and I'm satisfied with the result of my morning's research.

Until I look at Tate Walker's monthly report of prohibited companies and debarred entities, that is.

Prohibited companies end up on our list primarily because of late or unpaid invoices or for poor performance. Once bitten, twice shy and all that. My first pass through the list doesn't turn up any of the Ares subs for the current month. When I remove the filter for this month to show all the entities for all the months in the spreadsheet, however, one name jumps out at me.

Puzzled, I check the name again, scroll across to the date field.

Huh.

Returning to the SAM site, I quickly type the sub's name into the exclusions search field, then watch with dread as the results appear on the screen.

There it is: Michelangelo Enterprises.

I double-check the name and the Unique Entity ID, just to be sure it's the same company. There are several with similar names, but there's no mistake: Michelangelo Enterprises, one of our subcontractors on Ares, is on the government's exclusions list. The exclusion started before the Ares award and ends six months from now.

What on earth?

I switch back to FPDS to look at their award information. Scrolling through the entries, I'm bewildered to find that ten prime contracts and a handful of subcontracts were awarded within the exclusion period. This goes against everything I knew – or thought I knew – about debarments.

What I wouldn't give for a heart-to-heart with Laura and Anne Marie right now.

My next-best option: Josh. When I hastily ring his mobile number, it goes straight to voicemail. I check his calendar and see he's in a meeting with our contracts vice president, David Kersey. There's no way I'm interrupting that little tête-à-tête.

I could wait. I could text. I could try Simone.

I open MS Teams, see that her status is set to red – she's busy, too. I pull up her calendar, but the meeting details are private. Crap.

There's only one way to resolve this. I pick up the phone and dial.

"Atkinson." The familiar irritable voice of the contracting officer comes on the line.

"Mr. Atkinson, it's Kate Barrow from Tate Walker."

"I told you and your boss that you'd hear about Dragonfly at the same time as the other bidders. Did I not make myself clear?"

"That's not the reason I'm calling. I'm calling about Ares, but not about the contract modification we're expecting. I wanted to talk to you about one of our subcontractors."

"Ms. Barrow, the government has no privity of contract with Tate Walker's subs. They're your concern."

"I understand that, Mr. Atkinson, but there is something I wanted to make you aware of."

My heart is pounding as I consider my next words. "According to the data in SAM, one of the Ares subs was awarded the contract during an active exclusion period." My words tumble out in a rush, and I have to force myself to slow down. "It's not just the Ares contract, either. If SAM and FPDS are correct, the government has awarded at least ten contracts directly to this contractor during the same active exclusion period."

For a long moment, the only sound I hear is my own nervous breathing.

"Which sub are you referring to?" His voice is quiet now, very deliberate.

"Michelangelo Enterprises."

Another long silence.

"Who else have you discussed this with, Ms. Barrow?" Again, a very quiet, measured tone. I think I prefer the ranting, snarling version of the contracting officer to his unfamiliar, unnervingly quiet alter ego.

"No one. I haven't had a chance to speak with my senior manager yet, but I plan to as soon as we end this call."

"You've made a very grave, unfounded allegation to a warranted contracting officer of the US government. For the sake of your career, I'm willing to forget we ever had this conversation. I suggest you do the same."

I can't possibly have heard him correctly.

"I'm not sure I understand, Mr. Atkinson. If the information in SAM is incorrect, shouldn't it be reported? Contractors rely on the accuracy of that data to make all kinds of decisions."

"I'll say it again, just so there's no misunderstanding. Forget this, Ms. Barrow. And I would tread very carefully in the future if I were you."

Am I dreaming? Did a government contracting officer just *threaten* me?

There is a long silence. I'm speechless, with no clue as to how to end this call. Daniel Atkinson's next words unsettle me more than what he's just said, if that's even possible. His voice is subdued, the iciness gone. He sounds weary or maybe resigned – like an actual human being, for once.

"Let it go, Kate. Please." Five simple words far more terrifying than his outright threat had been. Then the line goes dead, and he's gone.

I feel a chill run down my spine as I replace the receiver.

"YOU DID WHAT? Have you completely lost your mind?"

I'm in Josh's office, and he's as angry as I've ever seen him. Which is saying a lot, because I don't recall ever seeing him truly angry.

Until now.

"I admit I may have jumped the gun by calling him, but—"

"Jumped the gun? You think?" He's standing behind his desk with his back to me, looking out the window at the cluster of high-rise office buildings off in the distance. Maybe he's looking for inspiration. Or patience. Maybe he's thinking of jumping. There's no telling at the moment.

The knot in my stomach cinches tighter as the seconds tick by.

When he eventually turns around to face me, some of the anger is gone. I'm not out of the woods yet, though. I may consider Josh a friend, but above all, he's my boss.

"Show me," is the first thing he says.

I do.

"Call Simone," is the second.

"PRETTY GUTSY MOVE, KATE. I didn't think you had it in you." Simone can't hide her delight as she sits down beside me at the small conference table in Josh's office.

I give her a mock-outraged look but stay silent. Josh still isn't happy with me, and I'm not about to push my luck by doing anything stupid — like opening my mouth.

"Don't encourage her, Simone. This is your fault. I knew you were a bad influence."

"Sorry, Dad. Are we grounded this weekend? Or are you taking away our PlayStation?" Simone does a remarkably good imitation of a sulky teenager.

Josh and Simone have an interesting relationship. I know deep-down they really like and respect each other, but sometimes they act like a couple of squabbling siblings. Simone can get away with a lot more than I can with Josh because he isn't her manager. Her own manager probably gave up trying to rein her in years ago. She's very, very good at her job, and that tends to earn you a bit of leeway.

Her poor boss, though. I can't begin to imagine what my friend's annual performance review says in the interpersonal skills and relationship building category.

Josh doesn't reply as he joins us at the table.

"What's this?" he asks suspiciously when Simone slides a small napkin-covered paper plate and a steaming cup of coffee next to his notebook. One thing about Josh is that he can never resist anything chocolate, hence his raid on my stash yesterday and his habit of grabbing leftover brownies that've been put out in the kitchen after a working lunch. Luckily for him, his other obsession – cycling – cancels out his sweet tooth. He spends most of his spare time with his wife, Priti, on the W&OD Trail or competing in local races.

"I thought you could use it." She winks at me as my long-suffering boss uncovers a chunky, walnut-studded brownie the size of his fist. The scent of hazelnut fills the air as he removes the lid from the cup. Simone is obviously pulling out all the stops – hazelnut is Josh's favorite.

He looks down into the cup before taking a sip. "Did you spit in it?"

"I didn't, but I can."

Eww. These two.

"It'll take more than this to get Kate out of the doghouse. But thanks."

Okay, that's enough.

"Why am I in the doghouse for something the government did? Why is this my fault?" I ask defensively.

"You're not in the doghouse because of what you found out. It's what you did with it that's the problem here. Geez, Kate, could you not have waited to talk to me first? You know what a – you know how difficult Atkinson is. Would one hour have made a difference?"

"You're right. I should've waited and talked to you first." I'm the first to admit when I've made a mistake, which I obviously have here.

He looks slightly mollified as he breaks off a chunk of the brownie. When he pushes the plate in my direction, I know he's forgiven me. I can tell he's relieved when I decline his unspoken offer, though. Despite the slight thawing in his attitude, he's still ticked, which I suppose he has the right to be.

"Has either of you ever seen a contractor show up on the list by mistake?" I have to ask.

They both reply in the negative.

"Okay, then. Some intern probably entered the dates wrong, and this is an old debarment. Or it's the wrong company." I think of the other companies I'd found with similar names. Even as I say the words, they don't ring true. My gut is telling me that something is seriously wrong here.

"There's an exception in the FAR that permits an entity or individual to do business with the government even if they've been debarred or suspended, but I don't think that applies in this case. The contract value's way above the threshold amount, for starters, and Michelangelo's not providing commercial items. I'll have to call the SDO tomorrow to find out if the data was entered by mistake or if SAM is correct," Josh says. The SDO is the Suspending and Debarring Official, the individual who makes these decisions for each agency. "Are you both free at ten o'clock? I need to run this by David beforehand." This potential fiasco is not going to make our VP's day.

Simone and I check our phones – we're free at ten, or we'll make ourselves free. Either way, we'll be in Josh's office tomorrow for the call.

My boss polishes off the last of the brownie and smiles for the first time since I'd come to his office with my news. His expression is almost smug as he chases the last of the crumbs around the plate with a finger.

"What?" I ask.

"You've had the Ares contract for a week, Kate. One damn week."

"What's that supposed to mean?"

With the crumbs finally cleared from the plate, he looks up at me and Simone. "It means," he pauses for emphasis, "that I gave it to the right CA."

"Maybe not." I take a deep breath, bracing myself for their reactions. Then I tell them what Daniel Atkinson had said before abruptly hanging up on me. As I'd thought, they both stare at me in surprise for a moment before I continue. "Yeah. And we all know Atkinson can be an arrogant little shit, but this was something else entirely."

As I glance at my two colleagues around the table, I suppress a shiver. Why would he have said what he had if this had just been some administrative screw-up? I'm not sure I want to find out, but I have a feeling I'm about to anyway.

FIVE

"NO. EFFING. WAY."

Simone's voice is steely; but there's an undercurrent of humor there, too, a glint of challenge in her eyes. I can practically see the wheels turning in her brain, can see that she's girding herself for battle. No one loves a good legal skirmish more than Simone.

I smile to myself at my friend's toned-down language. She feels free to let fly with profanities when it's only the two of us but tends to ratchet it down if anyone else is around. Depending on the circumstances, of course. She's certainly not sparing Josh's feelings because he's witnessed Simone's colorful vocabulary as much as I have. Maybe she's feeling uncharacteristically mellow this morning.

Right.

More like the calm before the storm. A category five hurricane, to be precise.

"I know DC legalized weed and all, but the moron who wrote this mod must've been smoking crack."

It's the following Friday morning. Josh, Simone and I are sitting in her office, each of us looking at the Ares contract modification on our laptop screens, which the contracts specialist had emailed to me an hour earlier.

We're still waiting for the Suspending and Debarring Official to investigate the possible issues we'd found with Michelangelo Enterprises earlier in the week. Until we hear back, it's business as usual. Our most pressing issue with Ares is still this mod, which could potentially upend the entire project's schedule.

"Glad we all agree." Josh is smiling broadly. "The lead engineer and program manager will be ready for a Webex call in about twenty minutes. I've asked the subcontracts manager to join us, too, since they still haven't found a replacement for Laura. We'll need someone to weigh in on the impact to our subs. We have forty-eight hours to draft our reply and throw this steaming pile of crap back over the fence to Atkinson and company. I say we do it in twenty-four."

FREEDOM. FINALLY.

I enter Sam's and let my eyes adjust to the dimness of the restaurant, then make a beeline for an open seat on the opposite side of the crowded bar. It's nearly standing room only as office workers from the nearby defense and tech companies stream in for happy hour.

A tall, slim, sandy-haired bartender catches my eye and heads in my direction as I slide onto the soft high-backed leather barstool.

"You're the best, Paolo. Thanks a million for saving me a spot."

"You're welcome, Kate. Your text was a nice surprise. I didn't expect to see you tonight."

My favorite bartender places a Cosmo on a cocktail napkin on the gleaming wooden bar in front of me, stepping aside slightly to allow a hovering server to set a small plate at my place. Paolo grins when he sees my grateful expression.

"I figured you must've had a hell of a week to be in here on a Friday, so I put the crabcake order in when I got your text."

"Marry me," I say with a laugh.

"Name the date," he replies without missing a beat. "Enjoy, and I'll give you a minute to look over the entrees." He's already opening a new screen on his tablet, stepping away to attend to the latest arrivals.

Paolo's a single woman's dream when it comes to bartenders. He dotes on his regulars and often comps a drink or dessert. Even better, he warns about the married guys who pocket their wedding bands when they arrive, and takes my glass off the bar for safekeeping if I make a trip to the restroom. Best of all, he can discourage unwelcome attention without saying a word. One lift of an eyebrow is all it takes to get the message across to someone who otherwise won't take the hint.

I simply love the guy.

After taking a sip of my icy drink, I briefly close my eyes, savoring the moment. Friday night, and I'm out of the office – at last. We've sent our response to the government on the Ares mod, which is a massive weight off my shoulders. Now I can kick back and enjoy some great food and live jazz, maybe even an interesting conversation or two. Let all of the rest fall away, at least until Monday.

I swivel slightly to face the small stage where the jazz quartet is kicking off with 'Fly Me To The Moon.' My smile widens. I'm not familiar with this band, but they're pretty good. While it's still too early to get out on the tiny parquet dance floor, the temptation beckons.

Later, maybe.

I scan the now-crowded bar, searching for familiar faces. But since this isn't my usual night at Sam's, my initial sweep doesn't turn up anyone I know, aside from a few of the bartenders. Maybe it's just as well. I can relax, enjoy my meal and the music, no awkward conversations with strangers or shouting to be heard above the racket in the packed bar.

The hum of conversation fades away as I slide into the music, people-watch, and sip my drink. My martini glass is soon empty. Paolo raises a questioning eyebrow at me from down the length of the bar while holding up a bottle of Sancerre. I smile and nod.

When he appears a few minutes later with a glass of wine, I accept it with a smile of thanks and place my dinner order. Turning back toward the band, I feel the tension seep out of my body with every cool sip of wine and every brassy note of the trumpet.

For the next couple of hours, it's me and the music. Everything else can wait.

A HANDFUL OF tech companies have office space on the higher floors of the building where Sam's is located, so there's a reception area in the center of the lobby, not far from the restaurant's entrance. The desk is staffed by uniformed guards who direct wayward visitors and restaurant patrons while keeping an eye on the security camera feed.

On my way to the elevators that will take me down to the garage, I see that one of the guards on duty tonight is Poppy. She's a twenty-something computer science undergrad, which makes her a bit older than most students heading into their final year, but not by much.

She and I have become friendly over the course of my visits to Sam's, maybe because she reminds me of myself when I was her age. She's incredibly bright, and after our first few conversations, we discovered that we're kindred souls, both total nerds: Poppy with her software and data analytics, me with my medieval archaeology.

She's tiny and intense, with a nervous energy that practically radiates from her small frame. Even when she's sitting, she seems to be in motion: a knee bouncing, a Doc Martens-clad foot jiggling. Her jet-black hair is cropped into a messy pixie cut. I notice that, today, the ends are tipped electric blue. While she's not exactly Goth – she doesn't wear a lot of makeup or have any piercings other than one earring in each ear – I wouldn't describe her as a ray of sunshine, either. She does smile occasionally, but it can take some doing.

She's not smiling now.

"That is not a happy face," I say.

She glances up at me, her expression brightening somewhat when she recognizes me. "Hey, Kate."

"Is everything okay?"

"Nah. The stupid security cameras went down a while ago, and I can't figure out why. The techs were just here last week. But it's getting late, so the morning crew will have to deal with it tomorrow."

"Yep, tomorrow's another day. Any fun plans for the weekend?"

"Just a day shift at H&M and back here tomorrow night."

"All work and no play," I remind her gently.

That does raise a wry smile, at least.

"Tell that to our landlord and the bursar's office. Tuition's going up again this fall."

"Well, at least it's your final year, right?"

"Yeah." A shrug. "Have a good weekend."

"You, too."

I step off the elevator three floors below the mezzanine level where Sam's is located and am hit by an oppressive wave of heat and humidity, even though it's almost nine-thirty at night. The setting of the sun hasn't done much to dispel the day's warmth, especially in the close confines of the parking garage.

I have my keys in my hand and my shoulder bag slung over my arm. As I walk toward my car, I'm thinking about how good a nice long shower is going to feel before curling up in bed with the latest thriller. And tomorrow is Saturday – hallelujah. No need to set my alarm.

Humming 'The Very Thought of You,' which the band was playing as I left the restaurant, I realize I'm finally shaking off the black mood that had been following me around since I'd gotten home from vacation. About time.

Even though it's on the late side, this section of the parking garage is still nearly full, with only an occasional empty space scattered among the high-end SUVs and sedans. I walk purposefully toward the row of cars where I'd parked, my block-heeled sandals clicking loudly in the quiet space. My eyes scan the dank concrete floors and the rubber- and paint-streaked support columns as I walk, my focus now on getting to my car, getting home.

I'm mere steps away from my SUV when a large man emerges from behind a Lincoln Navigator. Startled, I walk in a wide arc to avoid bumping into him, a polite smile on my face, ready with the kind of comment we sometimes make to strangers in public places.

My smile dies instantly.

The man is not smiling. At all.

His blue eyes, set in a pale face, are like ice. He is big and silent and — dear God, he's wearing black leather gloves — in *July*.

And those gloved hands are reaching, grabbing for me.

I'm paralyzed with terror, unable to move. Every instinct is shouting, "Run!" yet I'm frozen to the spot.

The man catches me in a chokehold, one beefy arm cutting off my air supply as he tries to drag me down onto the grimy concrete between the vehicles.

You're not in the gym, my brain is screaming.

This isn't Raj. Or Declan.

This is real.

My panic escalates as I struggle to breathe.

A flash of memory breaks through my terror. Raj again.

"Remember to breathe. You got this."

In that instant, I find a strength I hadn't known I possessed.

In the next, all the training, all the drills, for this exact, terrifying scenario, come back to me.

I turn my chin toward my attacker's elbow, desperately trying to take some pressure off my throat. As I manage one heaving breath and shift my body weight, I brutally shove an elbow into my attacker's solar plexus. There is an exclamation of pain as my elbow connects. I have only an instant to break free and I take it, dropping my body and pivoting away, breathing hard.

I take another huge gulp of air, trying to fill my lungs.

My attacker and I face off against one another, my eyes going wider when I hear the wicked snick of a blade as he snaps open a knife.

Fuck, fuck, *fuck*.

How many times have I practiced how to react in this situation – how many times have I defended myself against a knife?

But this isn't a training scenario with a harmless rubber knife.

This is a waking nightmare. It's really happening.

Motor memory kicks in as the man once again lunges toward me, the knife blade glinting even in the garage's low light. With a silent prayer and a sudden surge of fury, I fight back as though my life depends on it.

Because I know it very likely does.

SIX

WHAT THE HELL just happened?

And what had I done?

I jam a fist against my mouth to stifle a sob, then quickly pull back my hand when I'm hit by a stabbing pain in my lower lip. I stumble from the car towards the familiar building in front of me: it's Trident. Hicks and the staff here have taught me everything I know about self-defense. He'll know what to do now, surely.

How had I gotten here? I have no memory of the drive.

I'm standing at the gym's entrance, rapping against the glass door. There is a light on in the back, maybe in Hicks' office.

Please be here.

It's late on a Friday night, and the last class will have ended at nine o'clock. Have I missed him? I wait, knock again. Still no sign of movement from inside.

Overhead, a determined moth flutters near the security light above the door. I'm about to turn away when I see a shadowy figure coming toward the entrance from the back of the gym. I sag with relief, thinking that it's Hicks. But as the person comes closer, I see that he's too broad, too wide across the shoulders. Tension once again tightens my own shoulders, my neck. I'm not prepared to deal with anyone else right now.

I hear the lock release, and the door swings open. I can't see the person's face from where I'm standing because of the glare from the overhead security light. I hold up a hand to block the brightness.

"Kate?" I recognize the voice before I see the face. Declan O'Rourke.

The lilting Irish accent is unmistakable, and so is the height and build. I should have realized. No mistaking him for anyone else I'd find here.

"It's kind of late, isn't it?" he asks.

"Declan. Is Hicks around?"

"No, he left this morning for a fishing trip. He'll be back on Monday."

My shoulders drop.

His blue eyes are sweeping over me now, and I hear his sharp intake of breath, see the alarmed expression on his face. "What's happened to you?" Swinging the door open wider, he says, "Come in, and let's have a look."

I step around him, enter the reception area. Everything here is familiar, even in the dim lighting – the space, the smells, the smoothness of the polished floor. I'm alert enough to register the snap of the deadbolt as Declan locks the door behind us but feel as though I'm moving through water. He starts to take my elbow then thinks better of it. Instead, he nods his head in the direction of the kitchen at the end of the passage. It's lit only by emergency lights, but I know the way well enough.

It's eerily quiet as we pass the darkened spaces – reception on the left and a training room opposite, followed by the locker rooms and a glass-enclosed lounge. Inside, the large wall-mounted television screen stares vacantly at us, reflecting only our images as we go by.

In the kitchen, where the first-aid supplies are kept, there's a round table with four chairs. Along one wall, there are knee-high padded benches with cubbies for storing running shoes and water bottles during classes. The larger of the two training spaces is straight ahead, flanked by a low retaining wall that separates it from the kitchen. To the left, Hicks has a small office.

"I was on my way out," Declan says by way of explanation for the darkened rooms. Switching on an overhead light, he looks more closely at my face. "Do you need the hospital?"

I shake my head.

"The police?"

Another shake.

His brow furrows as he gestures to one of the padded benches.

I tentatively run a hand over my throbbing face. Not the best idea in the circumstances, since even the lightest contact sends fresh waves of pain to every nerve ending. There is blood – a lot of blood – on my fingers when I pull them away.

"Sit here while I get the first-aid kit." He starts to walk away, then turns back. "Hicks keeps whisky in his office. Shall I get the bottle?"

I finally find my voice. "No whisky, thanks. I could use some water, though." I walk toward the water dispenser but the room starts to spin. I stop, slowly turn, and lower myself unsteadily onto the bench instead.

So much blood. But head wounds do that, don't they? Bleed a lot? Dazed, I wipe my bloodied hand on my shirttail, which has come loose from the waistband of my skirt.

"Stay put," Declan tells me. "I'll get you some water."

More lights come on overhead as he flips switches, crossing from where I'm sitting to the place where the chilled water dispenser and first-aid kit are located.

I feel strangely detached as I sip cold water from the paper cup he gives me. When I notice that my hands are shaking, I put the cup down and clench my hands into fists, trying to stop the trembling. Then I feel the trickle of warm blood running along my left forearm, adding to the red stain already soaking my sleeve. I slowly raise and turn my arm to look, remembering the slash of the knife, which I hadn't been able to step away from in time.

As Declan sifts through the contents of the large white box with its familiar red cross, he glances over at me and sees the same thing I'm seeing – the slashed sleeve, more blood. His mouth tightens into a straight line. I know his anger isn't directed at me, but in light of what's just happened, it's unnerving all the same. He must see something in my face because his expression softens almost imperceptibly.

"Who did this to you?"

"I don't know." I shut my eyes, see the stranger's face. Open my eyes again. "I was at Sam's, in Tysons. I was almost to my car. He came out of nowhere." My voice is shaking now. "Like he was just waiting." I can't wrap my head around it.

I stop myself even as the thought forms: "Why me?" Logically, I realize this happens every day, maybe even every hour, all over the world. It's a sad and tragic fact. But this was Sam's. I've been going there once a week for as long as I can remember. I've never, ever, felt unsafe, even as creepy as I find parking garages, in general.

I can sense he's looking at me closely, but I can't meet his eyes. If I see the slightest sign of sympathy, of kindness, I'll completely lose it. So I look at the first-aid kit instead, focus on the neatly-organized gauze pads, alcohol wipes, bandages, and tiny packs of antiseptic cream. The work of Hicks, no doubt.

"Let me wash my hands, then we'll get you cleaned up and sorted, all right?"

He moves to the sink, pumps liquid soap from the dispenser with a bit more force than is necessary, then scrubs his hands vigorously. I'm sitting with my back against the wall, looking at his broad back and shoulders. I can feel his tension, can practically see it radiating from him.

I mentally kick myself. How could I have forgotten that Hicks was away this weekend? Not surprising, given the circumstances. But I'm here now. And where else would I go?

So. About Declan.

He had taught the first introductory self-defense class I'd taken; and now, six months later, I don't know him much better than the first time we'd met. He helps out with teaching when someone cancels or is on vacation, and he's almost as much a permanent fixture here as Hicks. He's always polite but he never has much to say. Not to me, anyway.

While we're friendly enough during workouts and self-defense drills, the extent of our conversations to this point had been: "Hit like you mean it, Kate," and "It's no time to be nice. You're fighting for your life here." You know, the deep, meaningful exchanges that lead to lifelong friendship.

It was for that reason that I usually don't mind working out with him. Declan's a good sparring partner when I want to hit the bag, correcting my form without being chatty. Some days, I like being able to get in a solid workout without having to be social. The bootcamp workouts are basic exercises and drills, nothing trendy, and I can lose myself completely in the mindless repetition. Basically, show up and sweat.

The self-defense sessions are the exact opposite. I have to stay focused and alert to every movement, anticipating what my partner might do next. Some weeks, I skip self-defense classes altogether if my head isn't in the right place and take a fitness class or hit the bag instead.

We train for a reason, so if a situation like tonight ever arises, we'll be prepared. In the back of my mind, though, it had always been theoretical. Not when, but if.

Tonight, 'if' became 'when.'

I can't believe this happened to me.

Declan turns to me after drying his hands on some paper towels, tossing them in the trash bin at the end of the counter. After unspooling a few from the roll, he carries them over to the table and pulls out a chair, setting it opposite me. Sitting down, he opens the kit, takes out a gel icepack, snaps the tab inside to activate it. He wraps it in the paper towels before setting it aside.

"For your face, once we get you cleaned up."

He's watching me closely as he tugs on latex gloves and starts to clean the cuts on my face.

"This needs to be stitched."

"No stitches." My is tone adamant. There is no way, in this moment, that I'll admit to a lifelong, completely irrational, fear of needles.

"But it's your *face*."

"Listen, I'm no Helen of Troy, okay?"

His eyes widen briefly but he says nothing.

"Please." My voice is quiet, weary. "If you could just patch me up with whatever you've got in there." I gesture to the box on his lap. "That's all I need. A couple of butterflies should do it, right?"

Realizing that I'm not going to change my mind about getting stitches, he nods and tilts my chin up slightly toward the overhead light.

"Your call. This'll sting a bit," he warns.

I don't even flinch when the cold antiseptic makes contact with my skin. My eyes fill with tears, but that's about all the reaction my battered body can summon at the moment. Declan deftly closes the wounds on my cheek and eyebrow with a few butterfly bandages, then cleans the graze on my lip. I can feel that it's already starting to swell, and I have the same curious feeling as when I've had Novocaine at the dentist's. This time, there's no numbing effect, but my mouth still feels like it belongs on someone else's body.

"For your face." He puts the wrapped icepack in my right hand and gently lifts my left forearm, cautiously rolls back the sleeve of my slashed blouse, frowning again as he inspects the wound. "Now this definitely needs stitching, Kate."

"It's not my *face*, though. No one will notice it."

He looks about to argue, finally concedes the point. "It'll scar badly, then. Are you sure?"

I nod.

"Come over to the sink." He helps me to stand and carries the first-aid kit with him. He turns on the tap and tests the temperature with his hand, and when he's satisfied, he adjusts the flow of water to a gentle stream. "Ready, then?"

"Yes." I press my lips tightly together, and he guides my arm under the warm water.

He washes the blood from my arm and then begins to rinse the wound itself. I breathe in sharply when the water hits, and I feel light-headed when I see the two-inch slash on the outside of my forearm, now starkly visible under the LED lights of the kitchen. It's not very long, but it does look deep. It's still oozing blood.

Declan, who'd been standing to my left as he'd cleaned my arm, now shifts so that his right leg is slightly behind me in a protective gesture. "You all right there?" He glances down at what I'm sure is my very pale face, one gloved hand pausing from its task, ready to grab me if I fall.

I close my eyes and inhale deeply, then exhale. I move the icepack I'm still holding from my face to the back of my neck. "I'm fine," I say, which is the one of the most blatant lies I've ever told in my life.

After turning off the taps, he takes a sterile gauze pad out of its wrapper, placing it gently against the wound. "Let's get you off your feet."

He guides me back to the bench and proceeds to carefully apply antibacterial ointment and several butterfly closures to the wound. Nodding, satisfied for the moment, he covers the area with a fresh gauze pad and secures it with tape. "A fan of Seamus Heaney, are you?" He gestures at the faded ink on the inside of my left wrist.

"The tattoo has nothing to do with him." My tone is flat, unemotional, yet I cradle my injured arm protectively against my midsection, suddenly self-conscious of the tattoos I'd never been concerned with hiding before.

'*Noli timere*' – 'Don't be afraid' – in elegant cursive script graces my left arm. The delicate outline of a small hummingbird, my right. I'm left feeling strangely exposed but unwilling to explain or defend choices and mistakes I'd made a lifetime ago.

Declan doesn't comment, he simply gathers together the detritus of his late-evening stint as Florence Nightingale, still regarding me intently. As he sits back down across from me after throwing away the empty bandage packets, bloody gloves and gauze, he pulls the first-aid box onto his lap, attempting to leave the contents as organized as he'd found them.

"Is there someone waiting for you at home so you won't be alone tonight? Or someone who can give you a lift?"

I lean back against the wall, and as I stretch out my legs, I feel a twinge of pain in my knees. Realize they've taken some abuse, too, and are scraped raw.

"Can you keep that kit out for a sec, please? I need to clean my legs."

When he sees my bloodied knees, which he'd missed, his brows come together in a scowl. He's doing a lot of that tonight. "For the love, Kate," he mutters. Out comes the bottle of antiseptic again, with more gauze pads and first-aid tape.

"I'll survive," I tell him. "But no, there aren't any friends I want to call right now."

Diane, my long-time next-door neighbor, and I sometimes share a bottle of wine on a weekend evening or a pot of tea on a Sunday morning while we catch up and swap the latest neighborhood gossip. She and my mother had been friends ever since they became neighbors more than three decades ago. She has a sweet Southern accent that could be misinterpreted for fragility, until you get to know her. The woman does not take guff from anyone. She does tend to hover a bit, though.

Right now, I can't handle the thought of anyone hovering or fussing over me.

Simone, wonderful friend — and expert lawyer – that she is, would be full of righteous feminist indignation about how women can't even walk in a parking garage alone at night. Granted, she'd set me to soaking in one of her decadent tubs with a bottomless glass of wine and high-end French chocolates, if I wanted, but not before frog-marching me to the ER for x-rays and stitches, which would result in a police report being filed.

I can't stomach that at the moment, either.

Avoiding these possible scenarios might've been why I'd instinctively found my way to the gym tonight. I can barely handle my own emotions after what happened, never mind anyone else's. Hicks has always given off a vibe of calmness, which I desperately need tonight. He'd once been a Navy

SEAL, after all. I figured he'd patch me up and send me on my way, with maybe a question or two. No pressure. No emotion.

My face and arm are throbbing, my knees are stinging like the devil, and I'm aware of pain in my midsection now that some of the shock is wearing off. The stunning, staggering impact of the man's fists comes back to me. The human body is remarkable, but being punched and assaulted on a concrete floor by someone twice your size is going to leave its mark no matter what kind of shape you think you're in.

Physically or mentally.

This is not the way my evening was supposed to go. I'd missed my usual Wednesday night at Sam's this week because of some stupid work crisis – wasn't there always a crisis? – and I'd decided to go tonight instead. All I'd wanted was a good meal, a glass of wine, and a few hours of jazz.

Not *this*.

"Why no police?" There is an edge to his voice now. "You've let whoever it was get away with it. What if he attacks someone else?"

He meets my eyes, and when I look away, he rises from the chair, first-aid kit in his hand. I wait until his back is to me, watching as he returns the kit to its place on the counter.

"I don't think he will." My voice is quiet. An image of a large man, lying on the pavement, blood on his face, flashes through my mind, followed by the thought that he'd been waiting. Not for just a random target, but for me. My opinion of the police and my reasons for not immediately calling them aren't something I'm inclined to share with Declan, at least not now. Maybe especially not now. After what I did.

Maybe it's odd that I've chosen a gym that has so many cops and sheriffs as regulars. But I'm here for Hicks and what his team can teach me, not for the clientele. "There wasn't any point in calling the police. Nothing was stolen, and I don't need the hospital. The police would've taken a statement and told me to go to the ER. I could've done that on my own, if I'd wanted."

He looks unconvinced but doesn't argue. "Whatever you say. Feel like that whisky yet?"

I'm not a whisky drinker. I've had it once in my entire life, on a visit to Edinburgh back in my student days. A bunch of us had gone to the Fringe Festival, and I don't remember much about the week we spent there. I do remember taking a single sip of whisky in a pub on the Royal Mile, then handing the glass to one of my friends, who was all too happy to finish it.

I suppose it's offered at times like this for a reason, though.

"Sure, why not? Thank you."

Declan crosses the kitchen to Hicks' office and returns a minute later with a bottle and two glasses.

I look at the bottle's label. "Are you sure Hicks won't mind? That's not inexpensive whisky."

"Whisky's meant for drinking. And Hicks has it for a reason. All contingencies." He pours a generous finger's worth into both glasses and screws the cap back on the bottle before setting it on the table.

Handing me a glass, he says, "*Sláinte*" and raises his own.

"What're we drinking to?" For some reason his tone strikes me as cavalier, and I bristle. This isn't a happy hour toast with friends – far from it.

"You're alive, you're safe, and that's more than some people in your position can say."

I let that sink in for a minute. Repeat his toast. Take a tentative sip. The expected burn doesn't come. I work my jaw from side to side, run a careful tongue along my teeth. No damage there that I can tell. Small mercies.

The room is quiet as we sip our drinks. I feel the spreading warmth, and my sense of taste and smell start to return. The whisky's not as bad as I'd remembered. But if it's as expensive as I think it is, it should be palatable, at the very least. I look down with surprise at my empty glass, look over and see that Declan's is empty, too.

Time to leave, I suppose. I've kept him long enough as it is. I try not to wince as I reach for my shoulder bag where I'd left it on the bench.

His face darkens as he watches me lift the bag.

"What?"

Wordlessly, he turns it so I can see what had prompted his latest scowl.

There is a six-inch-long slice through the beautiful black Italian leather.

"Oh, no," I whisper, closing my eyes against a flood of warmth as they fill. It's astonishing that this, of all the things that had happened to me tonight, should reduce me to tears.

I take a shaky breath. "It has a lot of sentimental value." I pick up my empty glass and reach for Declan's, rising unsteadily to my feet.

"I can get those," he protests, but I brush past him and walk to the sink.

"Least I can do." Washing and drying the glasses gives me a minute away from those blue eyes that don't miss a thing. I blink rapidly several times to stop the tears before facing him again.

He thanks me as I hand him the clean glasses and returns a minute later from the darkened office, minus the glasses and the bottle. "Are you going to be okay? You shouldn't be alone tonight."

"I'll be fine. Really. Thank you for all the first-aid." I gesture vaguely at my bandaged, battered body.

My psyche is a completely different matter. But that's not Declan's problem. None of this is.

"You're welcome."

I pick up my bag again.

"Look, do me a favor, would you?" He runs a distracted hand through his cropped, dark hair. I realize it's the first time I've seen the man look awkward or uncertain. "Hicks would have my head if I let you go home alone tonight. You came here looking for him, and I know he'd feel the same way. I have two guest rooms, plenty of space for you if you don't want to be alone. You can leave in the morning. Humor me, all right?"

I hesitate. "I'll be fine."

He raises his hands in a defensive, frustrated gesture. "I have sisters. And a mam. I wouldn't want them to go home alone if they'd gone through what you have tonight." He catches my look of surprise. "Yes, I know you find it hard to believe, but I do have a mam out there in the world. I wasn't raised by wolves. Hicks trusts me, so you can trust me. The bedrooms have locks on the doors, if that makes you feel better. Just—don't go home if you're going to be alone tonight."

I look at him, then away, toward the darkened workout space, weighing his offer. I must be in shock because ordinarily there's no way I'd even consider going home with a relative stranger. It's only because of Hicks. Hicks trusts him, right? But he's a two-hour drive away.

Our eyes meet, and I can tell by his body language and expression that he's expecting me to turn him down, that he's already preparing more effective ways to plead his case.

"You're probably right. So, yes, thank you. I will go home with you." Surprising him, I think. Surprising myself, definitely.

He gives a brief smile. "Okay, then. Shall we go?"

He switches off the lights as we leave the kitchen. Darkness follows us as Declan extinguishes the rest of the lights as we make our way to the front door and out into the humid night.

SEVEN

LEANING BACK AGAINST the headrest as Declan drives my car, I close my eyes, feeling completely drained. Neither of us speaks during the fifteen-minute drive. When we turn off a paved road and the smooth surface beneath the tires changes to gravel, I look around with interest. We're on a long driveway that takes us through a large, heavily-wooded lot. As we approach a barn and a detached two-car garage, motion sensors trigger floodlights that illuminate the entry and the area in front of the garage.

Declan looks at me once he's shut off the ignition. "I should have asked you earlier. How are you with dogs?"

"Good. I like dogs."

"All right, then. I've an Australian Shepherd and a Golden Retriever. They're fairly well trained but can get over-excited with newcomers. I'll go in first and get them sorted because I don't want them jumping on you."

Declan unlatches his seat belt and exits the car before coming around to the passenger door, once again opening it for me. I release the hatch to the cargo area and pull out my gym bag, which I keep packed and ready with a towel and toiletries.

He takes the bag and closes the hatch as I step away. "This'll take only a minute," he says, leaving me standing on a wide, covered wooden porch. I hear excited barking as he enters, then a low murmur as he speaks to the dogs. The front door opens a short time later, and Declan is standing in a brightly-lit entryway.

"Come in. I've put the lads out in the back garden for a bit."

When I enter what appeared from its exterior to be a barn, I stop, staring in astonishment.

We're standing in an enormous open space with soaring, beamed ceilings and huge, high windows. There are several sets of French doors straight ahead, leading to the back garden. Taking up the left wall is a large kitchen area with a long granite-topped island and gleaming stainless-steel appliances. Adjacent to the island is a massive walnut dining table that could easily seat ten or twelve. Opposite is a living area with a generous, comfortable-looking couch and several overstuffed chairs and ottomans. A flight of stairs topped by a highly-polished oak railing leads to a second story to the right of the living area.

This is no barn, I realize, although it obviously had been in a previous life.

It is, in a word, spectacular.

"This is incredible," I manage to say, turning slowly around to take it all in.

"Thank you. Can I get you something to drink? Water, or maybe some tea?"

"I would kill for a cup of tea, if it's no trouble."

Declan genuinely smiles for what I think is the first time tonight. He sets my gym bag on a living room chair before crossing to the kitchen. I drop my shoulder bag beside it, deliberately setting it down so the ugly slash doesn't show. I know it's there, but I don't want to have to look at it right now.

I walk toward the wall of French doors and peer out into the sprawling back garden. I'm startled by the sudden appearance of two large dogs staring back at me from the other side of the glass. "May I let them in?"

Declan comes over to stand beside me. "You'd better let me do that, or they're likely to knock you over." I step aside to let him open the door. As soon as the dogs enter the house, Declan quietly commands, "On your beds."

The dogs look from me to their master, curious about their visitor but too well trained to disobey. They go to their beds and don't lie down but sit, tails thumping rhythmically against the deep bedding. Their eyes are bright with friendly curiosity.

"Finn is the shepherd, Jasper is the retriever," Declan explains. "Lads, this is Kate," he tells the dogs, gesturing for the dogs to come. They sit obediently in front of me while I pet them tentatively. Sore as I am, I'm not inclined to crouch down next to them, so I stroke their heads and sleek coats for a few minutes while Declan returns to the kitchen to finish making our tea. To my surprise and pleasure, he asks, "Earl Grey or Ceylon?"

"Earl Grey, please."

Maybe I should have known he wouldn't settle for your garden-variety Lipton. Not after seeing this house, anyway. It occurs to me now that Declan O'Rourke is not likely to settle for garden-variety anything.

I give the dogs a final pat and join Declan in the kitchen, awkwardly maneuvering onto one of the high-backed stools at the island. I know that tomorrow or the next day, I'm going to feel as though I'd been used as someone's personal punching bag. Which I guess I kind of was tonight.

"Milk or sugar?" he asks.

"Milk, please."

Another surprise comes when Declan places a delicate floral teacup and saucer on the counter in front of me with a matching small pitcher of milk. He fills our cups from a bone china teapot; no teabags casually dropped into mugs in this house. He doesn't sit but stands at the island opposite me.

"Do you need something for the pain?"

"I have some ibuprofen in my bag."

"This one?" he asks, walking over to the chair and lifting up my shoulder bag.

"Yes, thanks."

He goes to a built-in pantry, pulls out a decorated tin from a shelf, then carries it and my bag over to the island. He pops the lid on the tin, setting it on the counter next to my cup.

"You should have something to eat if you're going to take pain meds, especially after the whisky. I'm not sure if you're into sweets, but this should do the job for now."

There are two opened packages of biscuits in the tin: one of chocolate Hobnobs and one of Jaffa cakes. They're both brands that I recognize from my time in the UK.

"I haven't had these since I was at university," I say.

"Where was that?"

"Durham, up in the north east of England."

After indulging in one of each biscuit, I take a sip of tea and can't resist a smile. It's as strong as builder's tea – another reminder of my time in the UK. It had taken some getting used to, but I'd eventually grown accustomed to 'proper' English tea.

Declan catches my smile. "What?"

"You could stand a spoon up in this tea."

"Is there any other way?" he asks lightly, not offended in the least. "If you've spent time in the UK, I'd think you'd be used to it."

"I was used to it, once." I realize that the exhaustion I'd felt earlier was lifting, along with my mood, alleviated in part by the hot tea and the sweet biscuits.

Declan notices me eyeing the tin, pushes it closer. "Go on, then."

"Thank you." I help myself to another Hobnob.

Despite my comments about the tea, I drain my cup after taking two ibuprofen. I absentmindedly start to rest my elbows on the counter after setting aside the cup, then wince as they make contact with the cool granite. I carefully sit back instead, looking around the vast main level.

"I can't get over how beautiful your home is."

"It's a work in progress," he says modestly. I don't see a single thing that I'd change, though.

"I want to apologize if I was snippy or anything back at the gym tonight. I guess it was the shock."

Declan raises his hand slightly before I can go any further. "Absolutely no need."

"I'm not usually such a bitch."

He looks surprised, then recovers. "Cut yourself some slack, would you? You'd just been attacked. You weren't a bitch, but even if you had been, you'd have been entitled."

"It still would have been rude, especially after everything you've done." He makes no comment, so I continue, my tone more thoughtful now. "You know, up until tonight, except for training at the gym, I've never raised a hand towards another human being. Not in my whole life." I meet his eyes. "It's shattering, really."

"I can understand that."

"Even with all the training, as scary as that can be, even when you're expecting it, this was—" I lift my hands in a gesture of defeat. "I can't find the words to describe it. When we train, the instructors wear protective gear, and no one gets hurt." I close my eyes briefly, remembering, then open them again. "He was big and blond. Not tanned like someone who spends a lot of time in the sun. Just big and pale and—cold."

The word takes me by surprise. "He didn't want my wallet or my phone. He never said a word, he just kept coming at me. All he wanted to do was hurt me. Why would anyone want to hurt *me*?" We both know it's a question with no answer and sit in uneasy silence for a minute. I look at him consideringly and finally summon the courage to ask another question. "Have you ever had to defend yourself outside the gym? In real life, I mean?"

His eyebrows lift briefly in surprise, and he takes his time replying, his focus at first on his teacup. He pushes it away after realizing it's empty. Then he meets my gaze directly, understanding that I need to know, that his answer matters to me.

"Just once," he admits heavily. "I tried to walk away, but that turned out not to be an option. In an ideal world, we'd never have to use what we learn at the gym. But the sad fact is, that's not the world we live in. Sometimes we have no choice but to answer violence with violence."

I see the blond man lying on the concrete, his square-jawed face covered in blood. How had I been able to do that— to anyone? The words stick in my throat, and I can't bring myself to say them out loud.

In the end, I'd *wanted* to hurt him. And I had, badly. So what does that make *me*?

Declan's words bring me up short. "You've had a hell of a night, and it's late. Let's get you to bed, shall we?"

He places our cups and saucers in the sink and fixes the lid back onto the biscuit tin before returning it to the pantry. I get down gingerly from the high barstool and follow Declan to the stairs.

"Good night, lads," he says to the dogs, who are already half-dozing on their beds. A wag or two of their tails indicates that they've heard him, but then they're back in dreamland.

"After you." Declan gestures to the stairs. "Can you manage on your own?"

"Yes, thank you." I take a deep breath and make my way deliberately upward, holding onto the railing for support, my abused body protesting with every step.

When we reach the top of the stairs, he says, "This is you on the left," and leads me into a spacious, airy bedroom. It has several of the same large, reclaimed-looking windows as the main level. I walk over to them and glance down at the back garden, now in darkness.

As well as a queen-sized bed and night table, there is an upright dresser with a mirror above it and a compact writing desk and chair. Tucked into one corner by the window sits an oversized chair with a matching upholstered ottoman. A floor lamp for reading is nearby, and thick, colorful area rugs are scattered over the rustic wooden floorboards.

"My sisters use this room when they come to visit, so I think you'll be comfortable here." He opens one of the dresser drawers and takes out a pile of folded clothing. "They're forever leaving things behind." He sorts through the clothes and pulls out a pair of soft cotton work-out shorts and a T-shirt. "Will these do for sleeping?" he asks. "I've laundered the lot, so everything here is clean."

"They'll be fine."

"The bath is across the hall there. If you want to have a shower, there's an assortment of things in the bath, as well."

"You don't mind?" I ask, realizing that I want nothing more than to stand in a stinging hot shower and wash away every trace of what happened tonight.

"Help yourself. We can take another look at your bandages in the morning."

He starts to leave the room, pauses briefly when I say, "Thank you again, Declan. For everything."

"Sisters and a mam," is all he says as he closes the door.

Once Declan has left, I carry my gym bag and the clothes he's loaned me into the bathroom. The room is sparkling clean and bright, with a long clerestory window on the exterior wall and a stained-glass transom window above the door.

I strip off my clothes and step into the tiled Mediterranean-blue shower, closing the frameless sliding-glass doors soundlessly behind me. The water runs hot almost instantly, and I use the handheld shower rather than the main showerhead, mindful of my bandages. I shampoo my hair and try to keep the bandages on my left arm and my face mostly dry. It's not easy, but I manage. I gingerly wash the rest of my body with lavender-scented body gel, aware of my aching abs and the scrapes and cuts that are scattered over my legs and arms.

An inspection of the contents of the vanity beneath the sink turns up a hair dryer, which I use to quickly dry my hair. After awkwardly dressing, brushing my teeth and gathering up my belongings, I return to the bedroom.

I close the door quietly behind me and organize my clothes and repack my toiletries. The blouse I'd worn tonight is unsalvageable, and I'll throw it away once I get home. I don't think I'll ever want to wear the skirt again even if the dry cleaner can miraculously get the oil stains out of it; but I can decide what to do about it later. I bundle both items into my backpack for now.

Turning out the light and slipping beneath the coverlet onto crisp, smooth sheets, I sink into the softness of the bed. Closing my eyes, I pray for sleep.

I wait.

And wait some more.

It doesn't come.

Glancing at the clock on the small night table, I see that I've been lying awake for more than an hour. I wonder how it's possible because I'm beyond exhausted, completely drained.

My mind, however, has other ideas. Even though I've tried to quiet my thoughts and slow my breathing, my brain insists on replaying images in my head, like the old slides my parents used to take of our family birthdays and holidays.

Instead of being curled up on the couch with a bowl of popcorn watching happy images of our trips play out jerkily across the flocked wallpaper that once covered the living room wall, my mind replays images of horrors instead: A sinister-looking man appearing out of nowhere. The same man grabbing for me. Being punched and slammed to the ground. A knife slicing my arm.

My cuts are throbbing, the bandages on my knees are snagging the soft sheets, and I can't get comfortable. There is a water carafe and glass on the desk; I slip quietly out of bed and take the glass to the bathroom to fill it. I return to the bedroom, not bothering to close the door. I stand by the window and sip the water, looking out over the darkened grass and the trees beyond.

I hear the quiet patter of steps along the wooden floorboards in the hall and turn to see the Australian Shepherd, Finn, appear in the doorway.

"Hey, boy," I whisper, setting down my glass. He pads toward me silently, nudging my palm with his nose. I carefully lower myself onto the ottoman, and Finn takes this as the invitation that it is. He sits next to me, although with none of his earlier exuberance. He has a mission, and it's not to play. We sit there for a while, me petting his head and back, feeling myself relax as I rhythmically stroke his soft fur. Eventually, I simply lean gently into his warm body, one arm around him, taking comfort in the dog's calming presence.

"You're still awake."

Declan's voice is low in the moonlit room from where he's standing in the doorway. Even though Finn's ears perk up at the sound of his master's voice, he doesn't leave my side.

"I'm sorry. I was trying to be quiet."

"You were. But it's my house, and I know the sounds it makes at night." He's wearing a T-shirt and cotton shorts similar to mine, although I'm not sure if he typically wears them or if he's put them on for my benefit. A very random thought, that. "What can I do?"

It's a simple, thoughtful question. It doesn't have a simple answer.

"Nothing, thank you. You've already done too much. I didn't mean to wake the whole house. I'll go back to bed shortly."

Declan runs one hand over his face, rubbing the rough stubble of his cheeks, surveying his houseguest and his dog for a while. Walking over to us both, he scratches Finn's head, looking thoughtful. "Good lad, now back to your bed." Finn doesn't respond until Declan says, "Go on, then. I've got this." I give Finn one last hug, and he pads quietly away, back down the stairs to his bed.

Declan reaches out a hand to help me up from the ottoman. "Come with me."

He lets go of my hand once I'm upright, and I follow him down the hall to his bedroom, where closed wooden shutters block out most of the light from outside. He gestures to the bed.

"It's a king, plenty big enough for two." His eyes meet mine. "All I'm saying is, you don't have to be alone tonight if you don't want to be."

I'm too surprised to speak for a minute. Then the words spill out before I can stop them, so very quiet in the dark room. "I really don't want to be alone tonight."

He merely nods.

I move around to the side of the bed where the pillows haven't been disturbed and pull back the covers. After I lie down and settle back against the plump pillows, he asks, "All set?" before getting back into bed himself.

"Yes."

"You'd better not snore, because if you do, I'm tossing you down with the lads."

I find myself laughing, then clutching my sore midsection. "Don't," I protest but continue to quietly laugh helplessly.

Soon Declan joins in. A nice sound, that laughter, given the night we've had. "Good night, Kate," he says after a while, into the darkness.

"Good night, Declan."

For months, our interactions had been relegated to the worlds of self-defense and exercise. We'd sweated alongside one another; he'd partnered with me on the bag and corrected my form. He had also straddled my torso with his large body; pinned my arms to the floor above my head; attempted to choke me; pulled my hair from behind; grabbed me from behind in a bear-hug and lifted me off my feet; threatened me with knives and handguns and gripped my wrists like a vice. I had come away bruised and sometimes bloody, with scrapes and skin rubbed raw from repeated contact with the rubber flooring.

I, for my part, had kicked, punched, and pummeled him in return; twisted my body and thrown him to the floor, aiming with hands and knees and elbows for whichever vulnerable spots I could reach in my attempts to defend myself. I'd never thought that I could be a match against a man of his size, but I had learned to be, with the right training and guidance.

We had been nearly as physically intimate as lovers, wrestled and tangled in a heap of bodies as we practiced moves over and over again, a carefully-choreographed ballet of self-defense. And now here we are, those same two bodies, sharing a bed in an unfamiliar dance where neither of us knows the steps.

As I lie next to him, my brain feels like it's in overdrive. Who was the man in the garage? Why did he attack me? Why did it feel so personal, yet he never spoke a word? Why didn't I shout? Why didn't I—

Stop. I close my eyes and try to relax; but even after the hot shower, the tea, and the painkillers, I'm still tense and uncomfortable. I want nothing more than to close my eyes and sleep, and forget. The terror. The panic. Those chilling blue eyes. But I can't.

I feel a shift in the mattress as Declan changes position.

"Kate." His voice is very quiet.

I open my eyes and as my vision adjusts to the darkness, I see only one thing.

Declan, the man who for months has taught me to always be aware of my surroundings; to question a stranger's motives; to protect my personal space; that the words *Stop* and *No* are complete sentences; and to defend myself as though my life depended on it, is lying next to me now, one arm held open, offering me his embrace.

Without hesitating, heedless of the brief stab of pain it causes me, I slide toward him and let his arms enfold me, surrendering. To the need to be held, to be comforted, to be safe.

Finally, sleep comes. And with it, blessed oblivion.

EIGHT

I AWAKEN SLOWLY, vaguely aware of the steady patter of rain against a nearby window. As soon as I open my eyes, I know that something's off. The shutters on the large windows are still closed, although diffuse gray light seeps in around the edges of the wooden louvers. This isn't my bedroom – it's Declan's. I glance over and see with relief that I'm alone in the bed; the only sign he'd slept beside me is an indentation in the down pillows piled next to my own.

Rain is beating steadily on the back porch's metal roof. I listen for a few minutes, lying quietly, trying to enjoy this brief interlude of peace before facing the day ahead, whatever it might bring. The attack in the garage had been one of my worst nightmares come true, and every movement reminds me of the injuries my attacker had inflicted. *You're alive, you're safe.* Declan's words from last night. That's all that matters now. I let my mind drift back to the moment I'd fallen asleep in his arms. Even as a memory, it's surreal, like an inexplicable dream that you remember long after you've woken up and gotten on with the day. When you shake your head and wonder how on earth your subconscious ever came up with *that* in the middle of the night.

Sleeping with Declan was very different than sleeping with Noah. Even taking into account the very obvious. Of course, Noah and I had slept together – but apart. He hadn't been particularly affectionate, and we'd pretty much gone our separate ways in his bed whenever I'd stayed over. It had always felt odd to me, and more than once I'd considered getting up and going home to sleep in my own bed. I never had, though. Now I find myself wondering why. Why I'd put up with that, and so many other things, from Noah.

Water, bridge. Nothing to be done for it now but to remember and learn.

I put aside interesting thoughts of a warm and sleeping Declan when Jasper and Finn unexpectedly bound into the room and stand by the bed, tails wagging. I can't help but smile at their happy faces and their exuberant personalities; although I'm grateful that they don't make any attempt to jump on me or the bed. Their master has trained them well.

"Good morning, guys," I say cautiously, not wanting to show any signs of encouragement that might tempt them to join me. As suddenly as they appear, they bolt out of the room. Puzzled, I call after them. "Was it something I said?"

"Is she awake, then?" I hear Declan speaking to the dogs as he starts down the short hallway to the bedroom and have to smile at their excited, answering barks as they greet their owner.

He appears in the doorway, freshly showered and shaved, wearing jeans and a well-worn T-shirt. His feet are bare, and he's carrying a steaming teacup and saucer in one hand and something I don't immediately recognize in the other. The dogs are behind him, jockeying for position, trying to nose past him into the bedroom.

"Settle down, lads," he tells the dogs quietly. They follow him, tails wagging enthusiastically, as he enters.

"Good morning," he says to me, then winces slightly as he looks more closely at me before setting my tea on the bedside table. "You're a sight."

"That bad, huh?"

"I'll let you be the judge." At least he's smiling.

"Thank you for that," I say, glancing in the direction of the cup.

"I think it's the way you drink it." He sits gingerly on the edge of the bed, mindful not to move the mattress too much. "My nan would roll over in her grave if she knew I'd made something like that and passed it off as proper tea. For that face of yours," he says, handing me what I now realize is an icepack wrapped in a washcloth. "You should be doing twenty minutes on, twenty off, as often as you can for a few days."

I thank him, take the pack, and gently hold it to my cheek.

"Are you hungry?" he asks.

"Very," I tell him. "Do I smell bacon?" I reach slowly for the tea and lean slightly forward to take a cautious sip, then lie back against the mound of pillows behind me.

"Comfort food. Fancy a sandwich?"

"I'd love one, thanks. I don't think I've had a bacon bap since Durham. It was my favorite breakfast on rainy mornings when I didn't have an early lecture or tutorial." I smile at the memory.

"Aren't most mornings rainy in Durham?"

"Says the man from Ireland."

"Fair point." Declan stands. "Leave the bed as it is, I'll sort it later."

"Thank you for everything you did last night. I appreciate it."

"No need. Hicks would've done the same." He turns back to me as he reaches the doorway. "I've left one of Orlagh's shirts and a pair of jeans in the hall bath. She's about your size, a bit taller, but the clothes should get you home."

"Thank you."

"Come on, you two, out you go," he says to the hovering dogs as he walks toward the stairs. "You'll be tripping her up with your nonsense, and we can't have that. Besides, it's time for breakfast." The word 'breakfast' seems to do the trick because the next thing I hear is the dogs clambering down the stairs toward the kitchen, where I'm sure they're making a beeline for their bowls.

I smile at the easy affection between Declan and the dogs, remembering back to my childhood when I'd have given anything to have a dog. My parents wanted no part of pet ownership, had insisted it wouldn't be fair to any animal; given that we traveled every summer and during most school breaks and holidays. Now looking back on our lifestyle from an adult's perspective, I have to agree for purely practical reasons.

One day, I tell myself now, as I often have over the years.

Despite Declan's admonition, I can't resist straightening the bed covers and pillows a tiny bit on my way to the guest bath.

I groan when I see my reflection in the mirror above the vanity. There's a cut through one eyebrow and another one high on my cheekbone, and both areas are swollen and bruised. I resemble Rocky after a few too many rounds with Apollo Creed.

No wonder Declan had winced when he'd seen me. I'm tempted to remove the butterfly bandages and thoroughly wash my face and replace them afterward, but I decide to leave it for after breakfast. Peeling off the borrowed clothing, I cringe when I see the angry bruising on my midsection where I'd been punched. I know it will only get worse before it gets better, the way bruising often does.

Once I've very gently washed my face around the bandages, brushed my teeth, and gotten dressed, I feel slightly better. The clothes fit pretty well, but as Declan mentioned, the jeans are long. A few turns of the hem, though, and they're no longer hitting the floor. The last thing I need right now is to trip and fall on my face.

With my teacup and saucer in one hand and the ice pack in the other, I slowly descend the stairs to the main level. Despite the rain and lack of bright sunlight, the soaring space is still incredible. I linger on the way down, my gaze taking in the artwork and framed photos that cover the high walls.

The photos are mostly of landscapes, lush, green spaces and windswept seas; they appear to be predominantly of Ireland, both the Republic and the North. Some are dramatic black-and-white images that capture the steep seaside cliffs, the basalt columns of the causeway and ancient forts; while the colored images show the impossibly green spaces and the meandering dry-stone walls of the small island.

The dogs, having had their breakfast and some attention from Declan, are slightly less boisterous than they were earlier. They greet me with cold noses and wagging tails as I pet them and accept the plush toys they bring as offerings, which I set on a nearby barstool.

"You look better," Declan says as I join him in the kitchen where he's turned the heat back up under the bacon.

"Nice try, but I've seen my reflection. I look ready for Halloween."

"Let me take you to A&E after breakfast. Your arm needs stitching, and an x-ray might not be a bad idea."

"I'm fine." My tone is deliberately casual. I step around him, reaching for the teapot. "More tea?"

"Don't change the subject." He looks me briefly in the eye before turning the bacon in the skillet. "But it's your decision, and that's the last I'll say about it." Gesturing to his cup, he says, "I've just poured myself a fresh cup, thanks. The kettle's boiled if you want to add some water to what's in the pot, though." His mouth twitches with amusement but he manages to restrain himself from making another disparaging remark about my tea preferences.

He switches off the flame under the skillet and piles generous heaps of bacon onto soft rolls that are split open on waiting plates. We take our drinks and plates to the dining table where Declan has put out silverware and napkins.

"Perfect," I say, after taking my first bite. "American bacon doesn't hold a candle to this. It's even better than I remembered, if that's possible."

"I don't indulge very often myself, but today seemed as good a time as any." He takes a bite of his own sandwich before wiping brown sauce from his mouth with a napkin.

We eat mostly in silence, looking out to the back garden and the falling rain. It's not pouring but it's raining hard enough to deter the dogs from going outside. They sit, side by side in front of the French doors, looking glumly out at the offending rainfall.

Once we've eaten, I ask, "When did you want to get your truck from the gym parking lot? I'm ready to go as soon as we're finished here, if you want."

"I need to be there by noontime to open up. I'm covering until five, and Raj will lock up at nine." He's scanning the headlines of today's edition of *The Washington Post*, which had lain undisturbed on the table throughout our meal.

I rise from the table and start to clear my plate and cup but Declan stops me.

"I'll clear up. If you want to get your things together, we can head out in a few minutes. I'm fine with getting to the gym early. If nothing else, I can get in a workout before anyone shows up. You must want to get home."

I don't, actually, feeling oddly comfortable in this beautiful house with Declan and the dogs. The prospect of spending the rest of a rainy Saturday morning here, listening to the rain drumming on the skylight and metal porch roof, is very appealing. But I've imposed enough and should get out of Declan's way.

I say, "Yes, of course," and make my slow careful way up the stairs to get my things.

We're both quiet on the drive to the gym. The regular movement of the windshield wipers is almost hypnotic as I look unseeingly out the window, holding Declan's icepack to my cheek. He'd handed it to me once he'd seen me into the car, saying, "Take that home with you. I've plenty of others."

It's all a blur of grey – light fog, steadily falling rain, and rain-covered roadways. My mood now, too, it seems like. Declan pulls into the space next to his truck and puts the car into park. After switching off the engine, he turns to me. "Are you all right?"

Realizing that we've arrived at the gym and Declan's expecting me to get out and move into the driver's seat, I give a distracted shake of my head.

"Oh, right, sorry. Zoned out there for a minute. I'll get these clothes laundered and will get them back to you the next time I'm at the gym, if that's okay?"

"There's no hurry." Then Declan opens his door, an umbrella in one hand, and exits the vehicle. Coming around to my side, he opens the passenger door and holds out a hand while sheltering us both from the rain. He watches me slide behind the wheel and closes the door after me.

I lower my window. "Thanks again. For everything."

"You're welcome. Take care of yourself, will you?"

I start the engine and sit for a minute or two, watching through the rain-spattered windshield as he lets himself into the gym. I see him set down the wet umbrella next to the door and start turning on the lights. He turns and looks back, watching as I switch on the car's headlights and pull out of the parking lot.

I drive home on autopilot, wishing now that I'd thought to take some ibuprofen with breakfast, but it had slipped my mind. My entire body feels battered, and my head is throbbing. When I get home, I plan on collapsing into a hot bath and changing into the coziest clothes I can find.

Once in the house, I tell Alexa to start one of my music playlists. Soon the space is filled with a track from Sara Bareilles' *Amidst the Chaos* album, good company on this rainy Saturday. I turn on the taps to the clawfoot tub in the upstairs bath and toss in a couple of lavender bath bombs, inhaling deeply as the scented steam fills the air. While I wait for the tub to fill halfway, I go into my adjoining bedroom.

I pull out the clothing I'd worn to Sam's last night, staring at the blood-stained blouse, at the jagged tear in the fabric made by the knife's blade. Later I'll bury it at the bottom of the kitchen trash bin; simply looking at the dried bloodstains has me feeling slightly nauseated. The skirt isn't torn, just dirty, so I add that to the pile of clothes that I'll take to the dry cleaner on my next visit. If the oil stains are permanent, the skirt will join the blouse in the landfill: more collateral damage from last night's incident.

I force myself to examine my shoulder bag, trace a finger over the angry slash in the soft leather. The bag had been a graduation gift, which I'd found in my mother's suitcase after the car crash that had taken both my parents' lives; the gift they had never been able to give me themselves; the one that might very well have saved my life last night. The second swipe of the blade might have been fatal at worst, devastating at the least, but the large bag had prevented it from finding its intended target.

It's only a bag. You can buy another one.

I don't want another bag, though – I want this one. And I know exactly the person who can fix it, if anyone can. Feeling slightly less depressed, I empty the contents onto the bed with a plan now in mind.

After undressing, I lower myself gingerly into the steaming, scented bath, hissing in a breath as the silky water hits my various cuts and scrapes. I rest my head against the curve of the slipper tub's high back, another indulgence of the renovation. I close my eyes, drape my arms along the tub's cool porcelain rim, try not to think. And it works, for a while. As "Orpheus" plays in the background, I let the tears come, reaction finally hitting me. All the things that could have happened on the floor of the parking garage but didn't race through my mind. All the ways it could have been so much worse haunt me. The fact that I'm here now is nothing short of a miracle. I wipe my eyes, sink back into the water. Thank God for Hicks and Trident. And Declan.

The music plays, the steam swirls. I stay in the tub long after the water has gone cold.

THE RINGING OF the small bell above the door to the shop heralds my arrival. The air is heavy with the smells of leather and polish, and I breathe in deeply when I enter, letting the scents and the memories of past visits wash over me in a comforting wave. I pull back the wet hood of my rain jacket and run my fingers through my hair as I approach the counter, my eyes drawn to the dozens of cubbies that line the walls opposite, every one of them full, their contents bearing a beige paper tag attached by a short loop of similarly-colored beige string. The wall of cubbies is broken by a doorway, which is covered by a navy velvet curtain. A large glass jar of foil-wrapped Baci chocolates is in its usual spot on the counter. Some things never change – thank God.

When I was a child, I'd always felt that this shop was a bit enchanted. I had no idea what took place out of sight behind that curtain, but it seemed magical.

Since both my parents were educators, the leather satchels they favored were constantly stuffed beyond capacity with books and papers; broken buckles and worn straps were commonplace. And if I hadn't outgrown them, my leather Mary Jane school shoes – tennis shoes weren't allowed at my strict parochial school – were almost always in need of some TLC, as well.

We would surrender our broken and abused items in exchange for a simple beige ticket. A few weeks later, the items would be returned to us, wrapped in paper and tied with string, whole and new again, smelling of fresh wax; the shoes resoled or reheeled and shined to an impossibly-high gloss, and the well-worn satchels restored to their former glory.

The man primarily responsible for this sorcery sits behind the counter, now elderly with gray hair and slightly-stooped posture. His weathered face breaks into a welcoming smile at my greeting.

"*Buongiorno*, Marco," I say, returning his smile. My parents were both gifted linguistically; although I'm not as fluent as they had been, I've continued their custom of mostly speaking Italian with our long-time friend and owner of the shop. It had taken me a while to agree to call him by his given name rather than the more formal "Mr. Colletti" of my childhood, but he had insisted many years ago. When speaking Italian with him, I do still use the more formal "Lei."

"Caterina, *cara mia*," he exclaims warmly, and comes from around the waist-high counter to greet me with a hug, arthritic hands warm on my shoulders. I try not to stiffen and keep a slight distance to spare my bruised midsection.

"*Come stai?*" he asks, and I reply that I'm well and ask about his family. His wife, Leonora, died several years ago; and his son, daughter, and their families all live in the area. His daughter, Francesca, aka Frankie, and a grandson now do the majority of the work, but Marco Colletti still comes in five days a week and works as much as his ancient hands and eyes will permit.

Throughout my childhood, the Colletti family had been in and out of our home frequently, since we had all lived in the same neighborhood. My parents had been very social, helping to host annual block parties and Christmas Eve gatherings; and all the families in the neighborhood had looked out for one another's kids. While Frankie and I hadn't necessarily been close, we'd been on friendly terms and, being the same age, were often in the same classes throughout our elementary and middle-school years.

Marco's gaze slides to my bruised, bandaged cheek, one eyebrow rising almost imperceptibly, but he doesn't say anything. We exchange pleasantries for a few minutes, me in my rusty Italian, while Marco is indulgent and gracious as always, even when I mangle a verb ending or tense.

Walking back around the counter, he asks, "So, what can I do for you?" Taking pity on me and switching to English.

With a regretful sigh, I lay my shoulder bag on the counter between us. The slash marring the beautiful soft leather looks ugly and brutal in the unforgiving overhead light. We both look at the bag wordlessly for a few moments.

I finally bring myself to ask, "Can it be repaired?"

Instead of replying to my question, he asks one of his own. "Are you all right, *cara*?"

His kindness is my undoing. Not trusting my voice, I move my hand from side to side in the universal so-so gesture.

I've spent the past few hours trying to pretend that this is normal. That bringing in a leather bag with a slash caused by an attacker's knife for repair is a common, everyday occurrence. Just another Saturday errand in a laundry list of them. That the things I did to survive and walk away were of no importance. But this isn't normal. I'm not all right. But I will be. I force myself to get a grip on my emotions.

"I've been better." The understatement of the century. "But I've been worse." Somehow I manage to summon a smile for this kind man.

His sorrowful expression of a moment ago lightens then, and the familiar light returns to his eyes. "So will she," he says with a smile, holding up the bag for a closer inspection. "Maybe not quite as beautiful as before, but..." His voice trails off briefly as he shrugs in a typically Italian way. "Sometimes scars have a beauty all their own."

I look down at the bag again and nod, thinking of the scars that I'll end up with across my cheekbone and forearm, permanent reminders of last night's encounter. A small price to pay for having defended myself, for standing here today.

A sound from the back of the shop makes us both turn. The heavy curtain separating the shopfront and the workshop is pulled aside and Anthony, Marco's son, appears in the doorway.

Anthony is four years older than Frankie and I. Not much of an age gap now that we're adults, but as kids, it had been huge. It had kept him on the periphery of my life – he was in high school when his sister and I were in middle school, then down in Blacksburg at Virginia Tech when we were in high school. Always a flirt, his easy charm had made him popular in high school and college, from what I heard back then. I'd never seen the attraction, but I suppose it's because I'd always thought of him as a big brother of sorts. Now our paths cross only every few years or so, if we happen to be in the shop at the same time, like today.

"Hello, Anthony," I say with a smile, trying to regain my composure. "It's been a while. How've you been?"

"Hey, Kate, good to see you." He's wiry and of average height, and he reminds me a lot of his father. From what I understand, he pitches in with the books and the finances; while Frankie, her son, and Marco do the actual repair work. When he sees my face more closely, his expression changes. "What the hell happened to you? Are you all right?" Anthony is less tactful than his gracious, old-world father, obviously.

"I'm okay, thanks. Just a little accident," I say, trying to downplay my appearance. "Frankie's not working today?"

"She'll be in later. I came in to do the accounts. I heard the bell and wanted to make sure Papa was taking care of you."

As he turns back to the open doorway and begins to close the curtain, he says, "Be careful out there, Kate."

I nod in acknowledgement, then look back at Marco.

"It might take a while, maybe a few weeks?" he says now, running a hand over the soft leather. "We're a little busy right now."

"*Grazie mille.*" I swallow hard past the lump in my throat.

"*Riguardati, cara.*" Take care of yourself. I nod in agreement and turn to walk away when the old man's voice stops me. "*Il tuo biglietto.*"

I turn back with a smile and wait while he scribbles on a familiar ticket, then take the half he tears off from his outstretched hand. He holds up a finger in a gesture for me to wait a moment and retrieves two Baci from the jar, like I'm ten years old still. My smile widens as I accept them, and I reach up to kiss his weathered cheek. Marco never forgets the chocolates.

"*Grazie,* Marco. *ArrivederLa.*"

With a wave, he bids me goodbye.

I can feel his eyes on me as I pull up my hood, exit the shop and close the door behind me, the tinny bell now signaling my departure.

One more stop to make, and then I'm going home. To a pile of pillows and a blanket on the couch. And a book. The right book can heal almost anything.

NINE

BY SUNDAY MORNING, yesterday's rain has cleared out, and the day dawns bright and sunny, lifting my mood slightly.

I take my time with breakfast, making eggs and toast and lingering over the weekend newspaper with a second cup of tea. I remember Declan's advice and use an icepack on my face until I get tired of holding it after about twenty minutes, thinking I'll do it again later.

After washing the breakfast dishes and setting them in the rack to dry, I go into my office, where I log into my work laptop and take a look at my calendar for the coming week. I'm relieved to see that my schedule isn't completely packed with meetings, and I take a few minutes to block out time for my own work so that those periods of time won't show as free to anyone looking to schedule yet another meeting.

Since this is the height of the summer proposal season, I'm not surprised to find that three more request for proposals have dropped over the weekend. I confirm that they're assigned to me and set up folders for emails and documentation, glad to see that none are due within the next two weeks. So I have some breathing room on those, at least.

I'm in the kitchen debating if I want another cup of tea or a cold drink when the doorbell rings. Crossing the kitchen to the foyer, I look out the sidelight and am puzzled to see Declan standing on my front porch.

"Hello, Declan," I say once I've gotten over my surprise and have opened the door. He's wearing faded jeans and an equally-faded Boomtown Rats T-shirt, looking remarkably cool on this steamy summer day. I'm barefoot, wearing only a casual knit sundress, yet still feel like I want to turn the AC down a notch a two.

"Afternoon, Kate." He's holding his sunglasses in one hand and looking past me through the open front door. "I wanted to check in on you and see if you needed anything. Is this a bad time?"

"Uh, no, it's not. I was just about to take a break. Come on in." I lead him into the kitchen where it's cool and pleasant compared with the heat of the front porch. "How did you know where I live?"

"It's in your membership file at the gym." He tilts his head slightly, picks up on my discomfort. "Ah, I've overstepped, haven't I? I'll leave, if you'd rather." He's standing between the foyer and the kitchen, not yet committed to staying or leaving.

I have to admit, it is a little strange. I mean, he *could* have called or texted. Then I remember that he'd stepped up when I'd gone looking for Hicks, I've been to his house, and I've slept in his bed. A little late to wonder whether or not he's an ax murderer, Kate. Not to mention, he makes a killer bacon bap. Poor choice of words, maybe.

"It's fine. Although wouldn't it have been easier to call?"

"Easier, yes, although I expect you'd have told me not to come. I wanted to see for myself how you were doing."

He does have a point.

"Even more colorful today." He appraises my bruised face. "Have you been using any ice?"

"I did earlier." I feel oddly guilty that I hadn't really stuck with it for long. Oh, well, it is my face, after all. "Can I get you something to drink? Water, sparkling water, or iced tea? It's scorching out there."

"Whatever you're having is fine, thank you."

The kitchen wall clock reads nearly one o'clock. It's later than I realized. "Have you had lunch?" I ask. "If you like shrimp, you're welcome to join me. It won't be anything fancy, just shrimp and vegetable skewers on the grill. It's too hot to cook indoors."

"If you're sure it's no trouble, I'd like that. What can I do?"

"Since we're having lunch, add wine to that list of drinks I offered you, because I'm having a glass."

He smiles. "Wine it is."

"Good," I say, happy to now have something to do other than stand awkwardly in my kitchen. I point to the wine refrigerator in the corner. "There's white wine on the top shelf. Please grab whatever looks good to you. If you wouldn't mind opening it while I run out and turn on the grill, that'd be great."

He nods and crouches down in front of the fridge, pulling out bottles and examining labels while I take down two glasses and put them next to the corkscrew on the counter. By the time I come back inside he's poured two glasses. He hands one to me and picks up the other.

"*Sláinte.*"

I don't know about Declan, but I'm thinking about another toast we'd recently shared, but with whisky, not wine, under very different circumstances. Was it less than two days ago? It feels like forever.

"You have a nice home," Declan comments.

"Thank you. It's not nearly in the same league as yours, though."

"They're completely different spaces. This suits you."

I take it as a compliment, because Declan is right, it is a nice space. It suits me, too. I'd taken care with choosing the right colors, pale blue and muted green walls with crisp white beams and trim, touches of William Morris-inspired wallpaper and textiles scattered throughout the space. Nothing overwhelming or overdone, just understated accents of color and contrast that suit the craftsman design of the house.

"The house has good bones." He studies the beamed ceilings and built-in shelving, the nooks in the living room and the deeply-cushioned window seat in the kitchen. "Have you lived here long?"

"My whole life." I absently plump a throw pillow on the window seat as Declan wanders into my office. I stiffen slightly, then force myself to relax. It's not as strewn with emotional landmines as it used to be, but it's still a place I tend to tread lightly around visitors. "I grew up here and then inherited the house from my parents when they died."

"Were you working when I rang the bell?" His gaze sweeps over the open notebook and the folders I'd left on the desktop. "You should be resting today, streaming a rubbish film on Netflix, not working."

"I wish. I'm a contracts administrator for a defense contractor, and it's July. That means working on proposals, even on Sundays. Sometimes, especially on Sundays, because there's no time during the week with everything else that's going on."

I gather some scattered papers together, tap the edges on the desk to straighten them, and tuck them into a folder. "It's par for the course. I've also started filling in for a former colleague who died unexpectedly. A car accident. You really never know, do you?"

Declan is quiet for a long moment. "No, you never do."

I try to lighten the suddenly serious mood. "You mentioned having sisters. Do they visit you often?"

"Not as often as we'd like, perhaps once a year, whenever they can get away. Orlagh, whose clothes you've borrowed, is a GP in Dublin. Her husband's a doctor, too, a surgeon. I don't know how they have any time together, their schedules being what they are. Maeve is the youngest. She lives with her husband and two daughters just outside Galway. They have a small business making cheese and soaps on a bit of a farm with goats and chickens and all of that. Her husband runs a pub.

Different as chalk and cheese, the two of them." His voice is affectionate.

He's examining the bookshelves, pausing occasionally to read a few spines more closely. "May I?" he asks before reaching for one of the books.

"Yes, of course."

"Bit of a book lover, are you?" His tone is dry as he scans the walls of bookshelves, the stacks on the floor.

I have to force myself to smile, to keep my tone light. I'm not sure if it's because of all the strain since Friday night or hearing about his family in this room, but my emotions feel raw and close to the surface. I choose my words carefully. "Quite a few of them are mine, but the majority belonged to my parents."

"I'm sorry." He carefully places the book back where he'd found it.

My voice is quiet when I reply. "It's been a long time. They'd have been happy to know the books they loved are still being read." I stand next to Declan and remove the last book he'd been looking at, holding it out to him. He'd chosen a collected work of W.B. Yeats. One of my father's favorites. The smile I give him now is genuine, nothing forced about it. "Please take it." He accepts the book from me with some reluctance. "If there are any others that are of interest, help yourself."

"Thank you. Maybe another time."

His gaze falls on a display of diplomas and certificates. He skims them briefly, then stops and turns to me, looking puzzled. I haven't had the heart to get rid of my parents' diplomas, either, so theirs are hanging in one corner of the office along with my own. Claudette Angelique Lambert Barrow. Philip James Barrow. Catherine Isabelle Barrow. It makes for quite an impressive little collection, I must say. We were a family of high academic achievers.

"You have a PhD in archaeology?" He looks back at my diploma as if to confirm he's read it right.

"Yes, I do."

"Why are you a contracts administrator, then?"

"It's a long story. Maybe another time." Unconsciously mirroring the phrase he'd said to me. I look at my watch. "I should be getting the shrimp on the grill. Would you like some more wine?"

"Not right now. Perhaps with the meal, though."

TWENTY MINUTES LATER, we're sitting at the farmhouse table in the kitchen, enjoying our lunch in the cool dimness of the house. I've closed the sunroom blinds to keep out the worst of the afternoon heat, and it's comfortable and quiet. The only sound is the occasional excited bark from Diane's neighboring back yard. Luna, her rambunctious black Labrador, sounds as though she's having quite a time in the wading pool Diane fills for her when the weather is unbearable, like today. I smile at the sound, thinking of Declan's two dogs.

"Have you had Finn and Jasper since they were puppies?"

"Yes, well, nearly. They're both around three years old. I adopted them from a rescue when they were less than a year. A lot of pet owners aren't prepared to handle such high-energy dogs. I take them running and hiking quite a bit, so that helps."

"They're very well trained."

"That's a work in progress," he admits with an exasperated but fond expression, and I laugh sympathetically. "The books, have you read all of them?" He glances in the direction of the office.

"Not all, but quite a few."

"My formal education was in software engineering, and it was a bit lacking in most other areas. You know, the classics, art, literature, all of that. As I've gotten older, I've been trying to make up for it, fill in the gaps. It's not easy, but I'm enjoying trying."

"You're in software?"

"You sound surprised. Why is that?"

"Well, you're not like most software, uh—" I hesitate. Way to go, Kate, and English is your first language? Good for you.

"Nerds? Geeks?"

"Your words, not mine," I say, recovering. "I was going to say 'professionals.'" A tiny fib. "But yes, now that you mention it. You're not like most software geeks I've known."

"I'll take that as a compliment, then."

"It was meant as one." I'm desperately trying to climb out of this mortifying hole I've somehow dug myself into.

I take a large, fortifying sip of wine. "What always appealed to me about archaeology is that it touches on so much. Art, literature, history, architecture. My parents exposed me to all of that at an early age. Archaeology was the perfect fit for me." I idly twirl the stem of my wineglass on the table. "Guess I'm a bit of a nerd myself."

"It's good to have a passion." His voice is matter-of-fact. "We all need something that drives us, gives us a reason to get up in the morning."

I glance wistfully at the overflowing shelves and stacks of books. "Yes, we do. Would you like more wine, or coffee or tea?" I realize belatedly that our plates and glasses are all now empty. "There's likely something sweet for dessert, if you're interested?"

"No dessert, thanks, but I will have coffee if you're making it. I'm not big on sweets. Do you do much hiking?" he asks, nodding in the direction of my hiking boots that are sitting on a boot tray in the adjacent mudroom.

"Not nearly as much as I'd like."

"The next time you do, let me know if you want some company. The lads would love a day in the woods."

"I just might take you up on that. I'd been meaning to get out this spring, and now here it is, July already." There was a time I'd spent almost every Saturday on a day hike with a local outdoor meet-up but for a reason I can't remember now, I'd stopped going. Work, maybe. Noah, more likely. He wasn't the type to sweat or get mud on his boots, and he got all moody and silent when I wanted to do things that didn't involve him.

"Are you able to work from home until you've healed a bit?" Declan asks when we're sitting back down at the table with our cups.

"Yes. Our team only has to be in the office two days a week. Wednesday is the one day we're all in McLean. Sometimes I go in more often because my boss is always there. He lives within walking distance, so he doesn't have to commute like most of us."

We finish our drinks, and I walk Declan to the door. He's carrying his sunglasses and the Yeats volume.

"Thank you for the book and the lunch. I wasn't expecting either."

"Thank you for checking in on me." It's one of those awkward moments, like being tempted to send a thank-you note for a thank-you note; it could go on forever if you don't nip it in the bud. "Enjoy the rest of your Sunday."

I watch as he descends the porch steps and puts on his Ray-Bans.

"Put some ice on your face," he calls back to me.

Yep, definitely a software geek.

While I wait for the kettle to boil for another cup of tea, I take a couple of mint Milano cookies from a packet in the pantry and put them on the waiting saucer. Replacing the packet, I'm reminded of his comment about not being big on sweets. Yet he'd had that tin of English biscuits that he'd offered me on Friday night. Huh.

Only after I've deflected a barrage of anxious texts from Josh and Simone do I decide to take Declan's advice. I pass the late afternoon and evening curled up on the couch, streaming far-fetched doomsday movies involving earthquakes, tidal waves, and volcanoes. If you think your life's going to hell in a handbasket, five hours of watching people trying to avert Armageddon is surprisingly therapeutic. Also taking his advice, I alternate between pressing an ice pack to my face and eating half a pint of raspberry sorbet, figuring one or the other will likely do the trick.

TEN

I USUALLY FIND Monday mornings depressing and have to psyche myself up to get back into work mode after the weekend – no big surprise there. Today, though, I'm happy to get back to work and focus on something other than what happened Friday night. I work until one o'clock, then send Josh an IM to let him know I'm taking a late lunch. He knows to call or text if he needs me.

In the car, I start the engine and open the app on my mobile to select a favorite playlist before backing out of the drive. When the music doesn't start once I'm on the street, I notice the dashboard display is showing a Bluetooth sync error. Since my phone's in my bag in the passenger-side footwell, the music will have to wait until I get to the gym.

As I pull into the parking lot, I'm relieved to see Hicks' SUV parked several spaces down from the entrance. I take out my phone, check for any work texts, and reconnect my Bluetooth. Almost immediately, a notification pops up on my mobile's screen: *"Unknown AirTag."*

I stare blankly at the message, not understanding what I'm seeing at first. Then realization finally hits me – this is a notification from a tracker app I'd installed for keeping tabs on my luggage during my recent trip. And it's telling me that there's an AirTag in the vicinity of my phone.

My mouth momentarily goes dry. What does this mean? Is someone tracking me?

Following the on-screen instructions, I tap the notification and a map appears, showing the area of Reston near Trident. I tap on the 'Play Sound' prompt and listen but don't hear anything.

My heart pounds and my pulse races. Not with fear, but with anger. Blazing, red-hot anger.

After the absolute nightmare of Friday night, feeling for the past three days like someone's punching bag – aching, bruised, and stiff – I am done being anyone's victim.

I remember something Noah had said the night I'd told him it was over. "If I find out you've been seeing someone else, you'll be sorry."

Is he actually tracking my car? *No.* No way. I tip the contents of my backpack onto the passenger seat, combing through all the items one by one. I search through all the exterior pockets and the zippered lining, cursing under my breath.

Nothing.

Through the haze of anger, I remember that this bag is new; I'd only just put everything in it before going to Marco's shop. There's nothing in it that I hadn't put there myself.

Looking again at the message on the screen, I take a deep breath and exhale. I can't deal with this right now. I replace everything into the pack and grab the plastic shopping bag that's on the passenger seat, which is the main reason for my visit today. I'm practically radiating with anger as I approach the gym's entrance.

When I enter the building, it's quiet with only a handful of guys working out in the weight room. Hicks is sitting at the reception desk, talking on the phone. He wraps up the call and hangs up as I approach. I force myself to calm down before speaking. Hicks is not the target of my fury, and I won't take it out on him.

"Hello, Hicks. Do you have a minute?"

"Hi, Kate. Sure, c'mon back." He leads me into his small office, closing the door behind us. He gestures to one of the two chairs that faces his desk, and I shift uncomfortably as he silently assesses the cuts and bruises on my face, the worst of which are now more or less concealed with makeup.

"How are you?" His concern is obvious.

"I'm doing okay, I guess. Declan told you." My tone is flat but there's also a slightly accusatory note in my voice.

"Only because I asked," Hicks says mildly, defending his friend.

"What do you mean?"

"You were on the security footage." His hands are steepled in front of him, elbows resting on the desk, his green gaze steady. He doesn't look away from my battered face, and his quiet voice is reassuring. I guess as a former SEAL, he's seen way worse than this.

"So you saw me?"

He nodded. "I saw you'd come by late Friday night, that Declan let you in when he realized you needed help. I called him a while ago, and he filled me in. Do you want to talk about it?"

His tone is kind but not patronizing. I remember that Hicks, unlike Declan, has a wife and daughter, and it occurs to me that he's probably a lot more comfortable in this role than Declan had been.

"Thanks, but I'm all right. A bit banged up, a few bruises. Nothing major." I force a smile.

"It's all major, Kate. I'm glad you felt you could come here at a time like that. I wish I'd been here for you, but since I wasn't, it's good that it was Declan. Don't get me wrong," he says, taking a moment to weigh his next words, "anyone who covers for me while I'm gone would've stepped up to help you last week. I have no doubt of that. But he and I have been through the wars together, and I've learned that if you ever want someone covering your back, it's him. He's a good man."

"I'm sure he is," I say, feeling a little awkward. Not really knowing what else to say, I return to the real reason for my visit. Taking a large bottle from the shopping bag, I set it on the desk in front of Hicks. "Declan and I hit up your whisky stash the other night. I noticed that you were getting low, so I wanted to bring you this. Thank you."

"That's kind of you, Kate, but this is too much."

"It's not too much. If it weren't for what you and everyone else here has taught me, I'm not sure you and I would even be having this conversation. I'm pretty sure we wouldn't. So, please, it's the very least I can do."

"Well, I appreciate it. Declan gave me that bottle last year, I think, on the ten-year anniversary of my opening this place."

"Isn't that some kind of sacrilege, an Irishman buying The Macallan?"

"Probably, but he knows I enjoy it."

"I don't know how you can drink the stuff."

Now Hicks laughs. "Ah, well, like a lot of the finer things in life, it's an acquired taste, something you learn to appreciate over time." There's another silence, and then, looking thoughtful, he says, "You know that my wife and I have a daughter, Emma, who's now twelve."

I glance up at a family photo on the high bookshelf behind his desk and nod. "Yes, you've mentioned her."

"Emma was our miracle baby. Elizabeth and I had been trying ever since we'd gotten married to have children, and it had looked like it wasn't in the cards. We'd made our peace with it. When she was forty-two, Elizabeth found out she was pregnant. We were over the moon." His face lights up at the memory, then darkens as he continues. "When Emma was around two years old, she had to have emergency open-heart surgery."

I look at him in dismay, one hand going to my mouth. "What? Oh, the poor thing."

"I was away on a deployment and it took some time before I was able to get back home. It was Declan who stepped up and handled everything until I could be with Elizabeth and Emma. All of Elizabeth's friends, the other officer's wives, sure, they were wonderful. They're a special breed, military spouses," he muses. "The entire military would come to a screeching halt without them. But it was Declan who dropped everything as soon as he heard. His business was starting to take off then, and he turned it all over to his partners and took care of my family when I couldn't be there."

I continue to stare at him in surprise.

"He and Elizabeth took turns staying with Emma, and I'm told they practically threatened to throw Declan out some days. He talked with surgeons, consulted with specialists, and hunted down nurses because Elizabeth was already overwhelmed. If he wasn't with Emma, he was helping Elizabeth. If it weren't for him, I might not have a daughter – or a wife – today. I don't know if Elizabeth would've been able to forgive me if we'd lost Emma while I was deployed. She knew full well what it meant to be an officer's wife, but even she had her limits." He pauses as if to gather himself, then continues, "Declan's a man of few words, until you get to know him. Some people misinterpret that, don't give him a chance." He smiles. "Make sure you don't make that mistake yourself."

"Why are you telling me this?"

"Something to keep in your back pocket, that's all. And let me give you this." He writes something on a sticky note he peels off a pad on his desk. "They're my personal cell and home numbers. Call if you ever need anything."

Touched, I take the slip of paper he's holding out and stand to leave. With my hand on the doorknob, I hesitate.

"You wouldn't happen to know anything about AirTags, would you?"

"You mean those devices folks have been using to track their luggage, that sort of thing?"

"Yes, exactly. I have a couple I used for my suitcase and carry-on bag when I went on vacation, but they're back at home with my travel stuff. I could be wrong, but I think there's one on my car. I mean, there's a beacon showing that there's one near me, and I emptied my bag just now, but I didn't find anything. The only other option would be my car."

Hicks' expression turns serious. "May I see your phone, please?"

I reach into my bag, pull out my mobile, and hand it to him. "Here's what the app is showing," I say. He rises from his seat and I stand next to him. Together, we look at the small screen. "I've read that the app can pick up several tags at one time, so it might be not related to me at all. I have no idea."

"I don't know much about them beyond the basics," Hicks admits. "But we know someone who probably does. Do you have a few minutes?" When I nod, he says, "Good. Go on out to your car, and I'll meet you there in a few. It's the dark-blue Mazda, right?"

"Yes."

True to his word, he comes outside a couple of minutes later, and he's not alone. Raj is walking next to Hicks; both their expressions are serious.

"Hi, Wheels," Raj says by way of greeting, his smile faltering as the men get closer and he sees my face more clearly. He looks at Hicks, who shakes his head almost imperceptibly.

"Hello, Raj. I know this looks bad, but I'm all right. I'll tell you about it sometime, okay?"

Hicks gives me what I think is an approving look. Raj doesn't look entirely convinced, though.

"If you say so. Hicks says you think you've got a tracker on your vehicle, is that right?"

I see now that they're closer that both men are wearing disposable latex gloves, and Raj is carrying a small envelope. My pulse quickens when I realize how seriously they're taking this. I show him the screen that I'd shared with Hicks, and he nods thoughtfully.

"Raj, I'll start up front, if you'll search the back seat and the cargo area."

"On it." Raj opens the rear passenger door and starts by removing the floor mats. He expertly runs his hands along and between the seats, behind the seatbelt anchors and inside the pockets attached to the back of the front seats, anyplace something small could be hidden. Hicks starts to do the same with the front seat.

"I'll feel pretty stupid if you don't find anything." I'm only half-joking, a little nervous now. Afraid they won't find something and afraid they will.

"Would you mind popping the hood, please?" Hicks asks.

I open the driver's-side door and reach in, pulling the hood-release latch.

He takes his time searching the front seat and under the floor mats and has emptied the contents of the glovebox onto the passenger seat. Nothing too embarrassing in there, thank God. I watch him set aside the vehicle's owner's manual, registration and insurance cards. Then there's all the little, everyday items that end up in a glovebox: fast-food napkins, a bottle of hand sanitizer, a cheap plastic rain poncho, a couple of pens, and a tire gauge.

No AirTag, though.

As Hicks moves around the front of the car toward the driver's door, Raj calls out from behind the vehicle, "Found it, the little bugger. In the passenger-side wheel well."

Hicks looks concerned. "Know anybody who'd want to track you?"

A chill runs down my spine. "Yes," I admit. "I know someone who might want to. But I can't believe he'd actually *do* it."

The three of us are standing together near the still-open hood of my car, while Raj holds the tag in the palm of his gloved hand for us to see. It's a nondescript plastic disk slightly larger than a quarter. Such a small, harmless-looking piece of plastic. The feeling of dread that washes over me seems completely out of proportion to the size of the tiny device. Just a few weeks ago, I'd happily clipped a couple to my luggage, glad of the technology that allowed me to track my belongings across a few countries and through several airports. Now, I want to stomp on this little disk and smash it to pieces. Along with whoever hid it on my car.

"You should file a police report, Wheels," Raj says. "Tracking someone without their consent in Virginia is a class one misdemeanor. I'm not sure the police will get any prints from it, but you never know. It's possible to get the serial number of the AirTag and the last four digits of the owner's cell phone number, for starters. Then it can be disabled. I've seen some reports of car-theft rings tracking cars to steal them when their owners are away from their vehicles. Fairfax and Arlington counties are probably having the same issues as lots of other places."

"You think so?" I'm not sure which would be worse – being the possible target of a car-theft ring or having Noah tracking my movements. "My car is more than five years old and it's obviously not high-end. I can't imagine any car thief going to all this trouble for a Mazda."

"You'd be surprised," Raj says. "It's precisely the type of car that's being targeted. A few years old, not too flashy, a lot of them on the road. There's a big market for them out there."

I shake my head disbelievingly. "It's amazing the lengths some people will go to. Thank you both for doing this."

Raj goes back into the gym with a wave while Hicks hangs back. He unclips the hood support and snaps it back into its bracket before closing the hood.

"If Raj is wrong, why would someone want to track you?" His expression is troubled as he studies the envelope containing the AirTag.

"God only knows," I admit wearily. "If it's who I think it is, he knows where I live and work. He even knows about Trident. Doing this makes no sense."

"Is this person still in your life?"

"Not anymore."

"Glad to hear it," he says, looking slightly less concerned. "And I meant what I said – call me anytime, all right?"

I nod.

"Any objections to my keeping the AirTag? If the police ask for it when you file the report, let me know, and I'll drop it off."

"No objections at all, thanks."

He turns, starting to follow Raj back into the gym. "Oh, Kate?" he calls out to me when he's halfway to the gym's entrance.

"Yes?" I look up as I'm about to get into the car.

"I have it on good authority that your arm really needs to be stitched." He is smiling once again.

I return his smile. "So I've been told, Hicks. So I've been told."

My good humor fades once I get into my car and the reality of the situation starts to sink in. Reaching for my phone, I scroll through to the settings. When I reach the location function, I angrily toggle the setting to 'off,' swearing under my breath as I do so.

I can't help but feel slightly paranoid as I drive home, and when I realize I'm checking my rearview mirror more often than usual, I stop myself. The AirTag's most likely in Hicks' desk, and my phone's location is turned off. No one can track me now.

I consider going directly to the Arlington police station to file a report but catch a glimpse of myself in the rearview mirror and decide against it. There's no way I'm going anywhere near a police station looking like this.

I suppress a shiver as a sudden thought occurs to me: What if it wasn't Noah who'd been tracking me? What if my attacker knew I'd be at Sam's on Friday because he'd put the AirTag on my car?

By the time I get home, my head is throbbing and my thoughts are racing.

If it's Noah, I'm going to kill him. Figuratively speaking, anyway.

But if it's not – *who* is doing all this? And *why*?

ELEVEN

I'M IN MY HOME office the following morning, engrossed in a request for proposal that just landed in my inbox, when a new message from Josh appears in my MS Teams chat window.

"Are you free for a Teams call at 9:00? Simone should be able to join then."

Ten minutes from now. With no other meetings on my calendar, I reply back that I am. Making sure my laptop's camera is turned off before connecting to the call, I dial in a few minutes early and wait for the others to join.

When Josh and Simone's faces appear on the screen, they both ask what happened and how I'm doing. Avoiding any specifics, I say, "Just a little accident. A few bumps and bruises. I'm fine. Just not camera-ready at the moment."

Josh smiles, Simone scowls, and we get on with the call.

"I just got off the phone with Simone's boss and the Suspending and Debarring Official regarding Michelangelo. The SDO confirmed that they're on the exceptions list for non-performance and falsifying records, have been since the year before last. You were right, Kate. I don't know what made you check, but thank God you did. The SDO has no idea how any of these contracts were awarded since the exception was issued – ours included. Now we all have the fun job of cleaning up the mess."

Simone doesn't pull any punches, as usual. "Holy shit. How many contracts are we talking, Josh?"

"She said the government awarded at least ten contracts during the debarment period where Michelangelo is the prime. No idea at the moment how many where they're the sub. We have a dozen active subcontracts, from what I see in the contracts database. We'll have to issue stop-work orders on all of their contracts where we're the prime, and we'll be doing the same where we're a sub to them. The government's looking at shutting down all the contracts that were awarded during the exclusion period."

"As if that weren't bad enough, the Office of the Inspector General might pursue an investigation, and the Defense Contracting Auditing Agency has told us to expect an audit at any time. Simone, just a heads-up that you're about to get slammed, to put it mildly. Everyone in the company who's worked in any capacity on these contracts will have their emails and chat messages put under a litigation hold. Legal will be forbidding us from deleting any communications relating to all of the impacted contracts with Michelangelo. Brace yourself for emails and calls from some very unhappy people."

Until this moment, I hadn't considered all the implications of the situation because I'd convinced myself that it couldn't be true. Now that it's been confirmed and events are being put into motion, I'm stunned and more than a little overwhelmed by it all.

"Josh, I don't know what to say."

"All I know is it's going to take a very long time to sort out this mess. I've never seen anything like this in all my years of government contracting."

"Has anyone figured out the value of the contracts involved?"

"That's where it gets really complicated, Kate. Some are near completion, while others have just started. How they'll be recompeted, if they'll be recompeted, all of that has to be decided. The SDO said something like twenty-million dollars is at stake. That's just the contract values. That's not including government penalties or potential lawsuits from teaming partners who'll be impacted."

"What a complete clusterfuck."

"Agreed, Simone."

"We're in the clear for any contracts that were awarded before the debarment, though, right? It's not retroactive?" I ask.

"Right, those are all good. At least from a legal and contractual perspective, that is. I'm not sure if we'll attempt to close them down, too. That decision is way above my pay grade."

"When you spoke with the SDO, did you ask if there could there have been a delay in the government's reporting Michelangelo in SAM, and perhaps Laura honestly missed it?"

"It's possible, I suppose. Hard to say without talking with her directly, though. She should have documented all of her reviews and uploaded her checklists for auditing purposes. We haven't been able to find them yet. The subcontracts senior manager is working on that now."

Understandably, Josh looks more stressed than I've ever seen him.

"But it *could* have been an honest mistake?" I ask, trying to sound optimistic but knowing in my gut what Josh's next words will be.

"Once, yes, but we contracted with them as both prime and sub after the debarment. That means our contracts and subcontracts admins had to be aware there was an issue."

"This is unbelievable."

"Yep." Josh's tone is angry now. "We can only keep a lid on this for so long, and we expect it to be all over the local media eventually. Public relations is drafting a press release for our external website, and an all-employee email is going out before end of business today, telling everyone to refer any questions to public relations or legal."

"This is a dumb question, but has anyone tried to contact Laura directly?"

"Not a dumb question. Someone in legal tried to reach her but no luck. From what I understand, she's celebrating her retirement with a nice long European river cruise. Her calls have been going directly to voicemail."

"I wouldn't want to be her once she lands at Dulles," Simone says dryly.

"You and me both."

The understatement of the century.

THE DOORBELL RINGS just as I'm wrapping up my call with Simone and Josh. I open the door to find Raj standing on the front porch, wearing his usual workout clothes and a smile. He's cradling a simple but gorgeous bouquet of flowers.

"Hey, Raj. What's all this?"

"Hey, Wheels. You got a minute?"

"Sure. Come on in." I accept the paper-wrapped bundle and lead him into the kitchen so I can put the flowers in water.

"They're beautiful. Thank you."

"You're welcome. So, how're you doing? I already miss not seeing you at the gym."

"I'm doing okay. I've missed you, too. I'll be back once my arm heals. Maybe in a couple of weeks, I guess."

"I know it's none of my business, but what happened to you?" He flushes slightly. "Sorry. I understand if you don't want to talk about it. I just hate seeing you like this."

"Thanks, Raj. And I don't mind talking about it, but there's not much to tell, honestly." I describe my time at Sam's and the rest of what happened on Friday night. I include my visit to the gym and Declan's cleaning me up, but that's as far as I go.

"So you have no idea who this guy was?"

"Nope, not a clue." I try to lighten my tone. "I guess I was just in the wrong place at the wrong time." I don't believe my own words for even a second; from the expression on Raj's face, I can tell he doesn't, either.

"I call BS on that," he says.

I can't help but smile. "Yeah, me, too."

He tilts his head to the side, his expression turning somber. "So who was this guy and why you?"

I shrug, as lost as he is. "I wish I knew." We're both quiet for a few minutes, and I busy myself with trimming the flowers. I open a high cabinet above the microwave to find a vase, and Raj carefully pulls down the one I point out and hands it to me.

"Before I go, I wanted to ask, uh, did I do or say something wrong before?" He looks uncomfortable, as though searching for words. "The last couple of times we trained together, I don't know. You seemed ... different."

We're standing at the kitchen island. Raj watches as I put water and floral preservative in one of my mother's Lalique vases before adding the flowers. I look up at him from over a long stem of pale pink lisianthus and give him my full attention.

"You didn't do a thing, Raj." I feel like a complete ass. "It's me. I'm a total idiot, and I'm sorry if I made you uncomfortable."

A look of confusion crosses his face.

"I didn't know you'd been an MP, and it caught me off guard when you told me. Please don't take this personally, but I don't have a very high opinion of law enforcement, as a rule."

"I'd say you picked the wrong gym, then."

"I know, right? That has occurred to me." We exchange a smile. "I have a history with the police." At his look of astonishment, I jump in to reassure him. "That came out wrong." He looks at me expectantly, so I continue. "My parents died a while ago, when I was, I don't know, maybe your age. They were hit head-on by a drunk driver. They were killed instantly, but the other driver somehow walked away. What's the saying about God taking care of drunks and fools? Well, God – or someone – was obviously looking out for drunks that night. Someone on the department mishandled the evidence, so the case was eventually thrown out. The person who killed my parents never paid for what he did. To them, to our family."

Raj's eyes are wide with outrage.

"You're not those cops, and I'm sorry if I treated you like one of them, even for a minute. Forgive me?"

"Nothing to forgive, Wheels. I'm sorry about your parents, though. Thanks for telling me." His gaze follows me as I bundle up the discarded stems in the florist's paper and wipe down the counter. "So that was it? Whoever did it just walked free and went on with his life?"

"Yep. Pretty much. And I've spent all these years wondering how the police could possibly have been so inept and despising them for it."

We exchange glances, and I can't tell what he's thinking. Does he think I'm completely unhinged? Still vindictive and bitter, even so long after the fact?

He finally gives me the slightest of nods.

"You said you used to be an MP," I say. "Do you plan on joining one of the local police departments now that you're out of the Army?"

"I'm still deciding."

"You could always go back to school."

He's giving me the same uncomfortable look he'd given me earlier. "I already have a degree in computer science. I'm not sure it's the right field for me, though. That's one of the reasons I joined the military."

"You have options, then. If there's anything I can do, let me know. I work at Tate Walker, and we have a good program for newly-discharged service members. If you want to go that route."

"I'll think about it, thanks. I need to be going. I'm glad you're doing okay."

"Thanks again for the flowers. They're gorgeous. Your mother raised you right."

A shadow crosses his face, then clears. "Have you filed a police report for the tracker yet?"

"Not yet, but I will."

"Do it, Wheels. You know, not all cops are bad guys."

"I know, Raj. Thanks for the reminder. See you later."

TWELVE

IT'S EARLY AFTERNOON on Wednesday, and I wish it were already time to call it a day. I'm scattered and finding it hard to focus, preoccupied with thoughts of Friday's attack and the mysterious AirTag, which have my imagination going to some very dark, scary places.

I'm back in the office, even though Josh would've been fine with my working from home for as long as I wanted. I can only stand so much silence, though, and my house was beginning to feel too quiet. I'm at my desk, redlining a teaming agreement, when my mobile rings. Looking at the caller ID, I'm surprised to see Trident displayed on the screen. Usually if classes are cancelled or if there's any other kind of information that needs to go out to the gym members, we receive an automated text or email message.

"Hello, Hicks, this is a pleasant surprise." But the voice that I hear in reply to my greeting isn't Hicks'.

"Kate, it's Declan."

"Oh, hello, Declan. What's up?"

"I need you to listen very carefully to what I'm about to tell you." His voice is urgent, clipped, his Irish accent more pronounced than usual.

"What's going on?"

"Are you in the office today?"

"Yes, I'm in McLean."

"You need to pack up your things and leave as soon as you can. The office probably isn't a good place for you right now. Do you remember how to get to my house?"

"Well, yes, but, I don't understand."

"We'll explain it all when you get here."

"We?" I ask.

"Hicks will be here, too. Kate, I need you to trust me, please. Don't tell anyone where you're going and stay on the line until you get to your car."

I connect my earbuds so I can stay on the line and do as he says, shutting down my laptop, hands trembling, shoving files, power cord, and mouse into my laptop bag, waiting for the red power light to go out. Once I've crammed the laptop into its bag, I yank my shoulder bag from the lower desk drawer, and I'm half-walking, half-running down the hall, past the kitchen, in the direction of the elevators.

"I may lose you in the elevator," I tell Declan breathlessly, jamming the call button with more force than is necessary, as if pressing it harder will make the car arrive faster.

"That's okay. If we get disconnected, call me back as soon as you can."

But somehow, miraculously, I don't lose him as the elevator descends the six floors to the lobby. "I'm on the ground level now." I force a smile and wave to the friendly security guards manning the lobby desk, trying to look normal, when my palms are so sweaty I can barely keep my grip on the computer bag's handle.

"All right. Do you know how to remove your mobile's battery and SIM card?" His voice is calm, measured, the complete opposite of mine.

"Yes, I think so." *Do* I know how to take out the battery and the SIM card? It's been ages since I bought the phone, and I haven't given them a moment's thought since I first took the phone out of its box.

"Good. When you get to your car, I want you to switch off your mobile and take both of them out."

As I reach my car, breathing as though I'd sprinted a mile, I unlock the door, look around the general vicinity and check the back seat, as always, before throwing my bags onto the passenger seat and sliding behind the wheel. "I'm in the car."

"I'm not trying to frighten you, but I am trying to convey a sense of urgency here, all right?" he says.

I nod, and then I realize he can't see me. "Okay."

"Get to my place as soon as you can. No speeding, no drawing attention to yourself. You should be able to make it in about twenty minutes, yes?"

"That sounds about right."

"Take a few deep breaths, and we'll explain it all when you get here. Be careful."

"I will." I end the call, press the power button, and wait for the phone to shut down.

What the hell is going on? Why on earth are Declan and Hicks contacting me?

I wrench off the phone cover, then slide back the battery case and pull out the battery and SIM card. To my relief, they both pop out fairly easily, and I let out the breath I hadn't known I was holding.

One hurdle overcome.

I start the engine and back out very carefully after checking and double-checking that I'm in the clear. I try to control my speed as I descend from the third to the ground level, simmering with impatience as a driver slowly backs out of a space and takes his dear sweet time before he finally pulls forward and begins to exit. I wait irritably for the barrier to lift after swiping my employee ID on the card reader at the exit and drive through, glad there are no vehicles lining up behind me.

My mind is in overdrive, and despite Declan's suggestion that I take a few deep breaths, I find that focusing on my breathing only makes my anxiety worse, so I give up on that and turn on the radio. News, traffic, and weather reports fade into the background as my thoughts spin.

Finally, I turn into Declan's long gravel driveway and let out a pent-up sigh of relief. I pull my car in front of the garage alongside Declan's Ford F-150 and Hicks' Nissan Pathfinder. My hand is on the handbrake when Declan appears and opens the driver's-side door.

"No issues?" He steps aside to give me room to exit the car.

"No, none."

"Glad to hear it." He leads the way into the house where Hicks is waiting for us, sitting at the long granite kitchen island, a steaming cup of coffee in front of him.

"Kate," he says, standing when we enter the large room. "Sorry for the all the cloak and dagger, but we have ourselves a situation."

I look at first Hicks and then at Declan. "A situation? Would one of you please tell me what's going on?"

"Come and sit down," Declan says, so I pull out a bar stool from the island and sit next to Hicks. Declan doesn't sit but goes to the kitchen side of the island and fills the electric kettle. Tea: the universal remedy for every crisis – at least in my world. Apparently in Declan's, too.

"Do you want to start, or shall I?" he asks the older man.

Hicks begins. "When I first found out you'd been attacked, I put out a few feelers to some friends of mine in the county, asking them to let me know if there was any chatter about what happened that night."

I look at him in surprise.

"I didn't expect much, figuring the guy high-tailed it out of there, just another punk. On Monday, a body was found by a couple who own a condo in the high-rise and use the garage. Seems they'd stayed close to home over the weekend, and it was only when they went to leave for work on Monday that they discovered a man's body on the ground near their SUV."

"A *body*? What? It has to be someone else. The man who attacked me – he was alive when I left." I look from Hicks to Declan and back to Hicks. "I'm sure I broke his nose, and I hit him a few times, I think. It all happened so fast. But I didn't *kill* him."

I hadn't, had I? I know I'd injured him. But that's a far cry from what Hicks is saying. I cover my face with my hands, shocked and suddenly terrified.

Hicks, looking thoughtful, continues. "At that point the police had a body with no ID and nothing else. No witnesses and no hits on recently-reported missing persons. So not much to go on." He pauses and looks from Declan back to me. "Until today."

My head shoots up, and I stare at him. "Today? What happened today?"

"Fairfax County police received an anonymous tip." He scrolls through his mobile phone. Finding what he's looking for, he adjusts the volume and hands the phone to me. "It's not easy to watch, but you need to see it."

As a video begins to play, I watch at first with curiosity and then with horror, and my hands start to tremble. By the end of the short clip, I'm shaking so badly I'm afraid I'm going to drop the phone, and I hand it back to Hicks. Rising from the bar stool and turning to both men, I manage to find my voice enough to ask, "Where did *that* come from?"

"No one knows, but we're going to find out."

"That video only shows the end—it doesn't show *him* attacking me, it shows *me* attacking him—" I trail off, and

Declan takes the opportunity to put a cup of tea at my place at the island. I nod my thanks and drink too quickly. The hot liquid scalds my throat, but it brings me back to my senses. I realize, with growing terror, what this video represents. "So, am I going to be arrested? Is that why you wanted me to leave the office, so I wouldn't be arrested at work?"

"We wanted to buy you some time in case you needed it," Declan clarifies. "Right now, only the police have the video. But if it's released publicly or leaked, it could go viral, and things could get very ugly, very quickly."

I put my cup down on the counter and pace the long room, pausing at a set of French doors to look outside. Finn and Jasper are out in the back garden, and when they spot me, they approach the house joyfully, tails wagging.

"May I let them in?" I ask Declan.

"Sure."

Once I've opened one set of doors, I kneel down for stability and brace myself, since I know the dogs could easily knock me over in their exuberance. I pet both the dogs and bury my face briefly in the thick fur of Finn's neck, wishing I could hide, wishing this sudden nightmare would go away.

After a few minutes, the dogs retreat to the kitchen for water and then settle on their beds in the living room. I turn back to Declan and Hicks.

"The video isn't from the garage's security cameras; the angle's all wrong. And besides, the cameras were down Friday night," I say, remembering my conversation with Poppy. "The security guard on duty told me. This video was taken by someone who was *there* that night. How is that possible? I didn't see another soul." The two men watch as I resume my pacing. After a few minutes of silence, I ask, "What do I do now?"

Declan asks, "Do you have an attorney you can call?"

"Well, yes, but only a family attorney for wills and that sort of thing. Not a *criminal* attorney. Who does?" I am totally out of my depth here. Then I think for a moment. "My friend Simone's an attorney, she might be able to suggest someone."

"Do you trust her?" Declan asks.

I look at him in surprise, wondering if this is what my life has suddenly become – a question of those I can trust and those I can't. "Yes, absolutely."

"You should call her and get a name," Hicks says. "I don't know how long the police will sit on this video and you need to be ready for when this hits the fan. You'll need an attorney so you can post bond immediately. You don't want to stay in custody any longer than is absolutely necessary, if it comes to that."

I swallow hard, fighting a wave of panic. The words 'bond' and 'custody' are two words I never in my entire life thought I would hear in reference to myself. But then, I never thought that I'd have to one day possibly fight for my life, either. I reach for my bag to retrieve my mobile, and then remember I no longer have a working phone.

"May I use your phone, please?" I ask Declan.

"There's a landline on the desk in my office."

I find it strangely comforting to know that, in a world overrun with mobile phones, I'm not the last dinosaur to have a home landline. My contracts admin background has me cringing at the thought of how many supposedly private or confidential conversations are conducted over mobile phones every day, ripe for the picking. By hackers, by the NSA, by whomever has the means and the desire to eavesdrop.

"Thank you."

In the office, I sit down at Declan's desk and briefly lower my head onto my crossed arms on the desktop. I take the deepest breath I can, then let it slowly out. Raising my head, I reach for the phone. I know only a few phone numbers by heart and rely on the contacts list in my mobile phone for the rest; fortunately, I've memorized both Simone's office and mobile numbers. I try her office number first.

Please pick up.

To my unspeakable relief, she answers on the third ring. "Tate Walker, Simone Ellis speaking."

"Simone, it's Kate." I feel ridiculous tears of relief sting my eyes at hearing her voice, normal, wonderful Simone.

"Kate? My caller ID shows a private caller, so I almost didn't pick up. Where are you calling from?"

"I'll explain it all as soon as I can. But right now, I have an urgent favor to ask."

"Okay. What's up?" I'm sure she's thinking that it's something work related, that I'm about to ask for her help with a proposal or a conflict screening. The kinds of things that are dropped in our laps at the last minute all the time.

If only.

"Simone, can you recommend a criminal attorney? A very good criminal attorney?"

The silence, as they say, is deafening. When she speaks, her tone has completely changed, her casual, offhand manner replaced by concern. "For you or for someone else?"

"For me." My voice is quiet, subdued, as if saying the words will make it more real somehow.

"What the hell? Kate, are you okay?"

"Uh, yes, for the moment. I swear, I'll explain all of this, but right now, I really, really need the name of the best criminal attorney you know."

"You're on a landline?"

"Yes."

"Okay," she says. "You're now my client, and this conversation is covered under attorney-client privilege."

"What? Simone, you're not a criminal attorney," I protest, but she cuts me off.

"You are now my client," she repeats, with an odd note in her voice and an emphasis on the word 'client,' and I slowly understand.

"All right, whatever you say."

"How can I reach you when I have more information?"

It takes me a minute to reply. Since my phone is out of commission, and I'm assuming Declan and Hicks will suggest that I don't return home anytime soon, I guess this is the only way Simone can reach me, for now. "Hang on, I need to check." Before I can put down the phone, Declan appears silently at my side, holding a notepad with a phone number written on it. I nod my thanks to him before reading the digits out to Simone.

"Okay, I'll call you back as soon as I have a name for you." Less business-like, she asks, "Are you sure you're okay?"

"Yes. I'm with friends." Only as I say the words do I realize they might be true.

"Good. Call you back shortly."

I replace the receiver and sit for a moment, feeling completely overwhelmed. I've been through worse, though, and I know I can get through this. I don't really have any choice. But what exactly is *this*? I'm not sure I even know.

Declan and Hicks look up expectantly as I come to join them. They've moved from the kitchen island to the more comfortable couch and overstuffed chairs in the living area.

"What did your friend say?" Declan asks.

I sit in one of the large chairs opposite them, though I'm too tense to relax and I move forward, close to the edge of the seat. "She's going to call me back as soon as she has a name." Looking at Declan, I say, "I told her she could call back here, since my phone's not working. I called her on the office landline since she's in the office today."

"Good." Declan relaxes slightly.

"About your phone." Hicks gestures to Declan.

"Here's a new mobile phone." Declan hands me a generic-looking mobile phone. "It's programmed with numbers for me and Hicks with only our initials, not our names." My head swims at the implications.

I notice then that there is a mobile phone on the coffee table in front of each of the men, and Declan is gesturing to them now. "Even when you disable your phone's location feature in some apps, your mobile phone provider can still track your phone. For now, it's better to be completely safe and use these phones with no locations enabled for any of us."

I stare at them both uncomprehendingly. I know about the location features on phones and usually keep mine disabled unless I'm using a navigation app, figuring my location is my own business, not Microsoft's, or Google's, or whomever they want to sell my data to. Now the idea of being tracked through my phone has taken on a more sinister connotation, and I feel a chill run down my spine. The thought that law enforcement, and not some hacker or car thief, might want to track my whereabouts, might be attempting to right now, has me clenching and unclenching my fists nervously.

"It's okay, Kate," Hicks says reassuringly. "We'll get you through this."

I look at him and, for a moment, my brain struggles to find the words for what I'm feeling. Eventually I ask, "Why?" Both men look at me, uncomprehending. "Why are you doing this? Why are you helping me?"

Before either of them can answer, the phone in the office rings. I start at the unexpected noise, and my gaze shifts to Declan.

"That'll be for you, I imagine," he says.

I hurry into the office and pick up the receiver somewhat breathlessly. Relief washes over me. Simone. "That was fast."

"Yeah, well, I called an old friend, you might say." I close my eyes briefly, saying a silent prayer of thanks, and Simone goes on. "You'll be getting a call in the morning from Penfield Wainwright's paralegal."

I gasp when I recognize the attorney's name. He has an international reputation as a brilliant, calculating and extremely successful criminal defense attorney. And if memory serves, he was also a sitting judge at one point in his career.

"Penfield Wainwright? There's no way I can afford for him to represent me."

There is silence on the line for a long moment. "If this is as serious as I think it is, you can't *not* afford him. And we can talk about all that later." Her voice is casual now, as offhand when discussing money as only those who have lived with it their whole lives can be.

"Thank you, Simone."

"He wants me to get the basic details of your case and pass them on. When can I see you?"

I hesitate for a moment. "Let me check with, uh, my friends, and I'll call you back. Is that okay?"

"Sure. I'll give you my number at the house. Have you got a pen handy?"

Once I've written it down, we say our goodbyes and hang up. God bless Simone. I'm thankful that as an attorney, she also knows the legal significance of using a landline versus a mobile phone and has maintained one at her home all these years, too.

This time when I return to the living room, I'm feeling slightly better than when I first spoke with her. Hicks and Declan look at me expectantly. "Penfield Wainwright."

Hicks gives a long, low whistle. "Must be some friend you've got there."

Declan says, "Impressive."

"I know, right?" Then I bite my lip nervously. "I might be eating PB&J into my retirement years, but that certainly beats the alternative. Simone wants to see me. Do you think that's okay? When we talked earlier, she insisted that I retain her as an attorney so that anything we said would be covered by attorney-client privilege."

The two men exchange a look.

"I don't think that'll be a problem," Hicks says.

I pick up the prepaid phone that I'd left on the table and pull up the contacts list. As Declan had said, there are two listings: CEH and DO.

"So, you do have a first name," I say to Hicks, teasing. "What does *C* stand for, anyway?"

"That is a very closely-guarded secret," Declan says.

"Oh, come on. How bad can it be?"

"I'll tell you one day," Hicks offers.

"Will you tell me, then?" I ask Declan.

Declan gives an emphatic shake of his head. "Not even under threat of grievous bodily harm."

"Oh, well, it was worth a shot."

We all laugh.

THIRTEEN

AFTER CALLING SIMONE back and giving her Declan's address, I belatedly remember to call Josh to let him know I've left the office for the day. I tell him I've had a personal emergency come up and will be back online as soon as I can. As I hang up, I offer up a fervent prayer that I will be working from home tomorrow and won't be in police custody.

Declan has cleared, washed, and put away our cups and saucers, and we're still in the living room, trying to figure out who took the video and their possible motives for anonymously turning it over to the police. After spending a while in the back garden tossing tennis balls to the dogs to burn off some nervous energy, I've resumed my pacing inside the house. Hicks is busy with his prepaid phone, alternating between firing off texts and making calls.

Finn and Jasper both rise from where they'd been dozing on their beds, barking loudly. Declan quiets them with a look. They stop barking but their eyes are on Declan as he and I step outside to greet Simone.

Without hesitating, she wraps me in a hug when she reaches me, and I hold on as tight as my aching midsection will let me. She looks critically at my face, surveying the ugly bruises, the healing cuts.

"You have some serious explaining to do," she warns, then turns to Declan and Hicks, who have joined us on the front porch.

By way of introduction, I say, "Simone Ellis, I'd like you to meet Declan O'Rourke and," I hesitate for a moment, and Declan and I exchange a smile, "and Hicks. Declan and Hicks – Simone Ellis, my friend and colleague."

They all shake hands and exchange pleasantries, and Declan gestures to the front door. "Shall we?"

"I have a few things in the car, if I could please get a hand with them?"

We all walk toward her car, a vintage navy Mercedes E-Class sedan. Opening the trunk, Simone retrieves a paper Whole Foods shopping bag and her laptop bag, then gestures to the rest. "I figured you hadn't had anything to eat yet, so I picked up a few things on the way."

I see Hicks and Declan exchange an amused glance. 'A few things' amounts to two more overflowing bags and three bottles of wine in a canvas wine tote. Declan and Hicks get the remaining groceries while I carry the wine, and we all return to the house.

Simone hesitates briefly as she looks appreciatively around the large, light-filled space, the expansive windows and

French doors, reclaimed wooden floorboards and restored brickwork. "What a beautiful place you have."

"Thank you," Declan acknowledges.

"Good Lord, Simone. How many people were you intending to feed tonight?" I ask as Hicks and I unpack the food trays and set them on the island.

"Whatever we don't eat tonight will be here tomorrow."

"Or next week," Hicks adds, to everyone's amusement.

Simone notices Jasper and Finn sitting obediently on their beds. "Now look at you two beauties." She turns to Declan. "May I?"

"Of course. They tend to jump on newcomers, so brace yourself."

The dogs, realizing they're about to get some attention, wriggle excitedly on their beds, their large tails wagging in anticipation. As Simone approaches, they make a move to leave their beds, but before the dogs rise fully and before Declan can say a word, Simone quietly commands, "Stay." To everyone's amazement, the dogs sit obediently and wait for her to pet them. She strokes their heads and rubs under their necks, talking to them in a low voice while they bask in her attention.

"Huh," I say to Declan.

"Guess you need to work on your obedience training."

"Apparently."

Unpacking the wine tote, I see that Simone has bought a bottle of Sancerre, my favorite, one of cabernet sauvignon, and one of pinot noir. I ask Declan if it's okay to put the

Sancerre in the refrigerator to chill, and he does one better, gesturing to the glass-fronted wine refrigerator tucked beneath the island.

"This was here the whole time we've been drinking tea and coffee?" I joke, opening the tinted glass door and making room for the Sancerre.

"You never asked for wine."

I have to admit, he has a point.

After surveying all the food that Simone brought, we opt for chicken salad, an assortment of sushi and California rolls, and an artichoke and mushroom flatbread, which Hicks deftly slices and leaves on a wooden bread board for anyone who wants it. Declan asks about drinks and retrieves four wine glasses while, by mutual agreement, Hicks opens the pinot noir. Declan takes pity on me and opens a chilled bottle of chardonnay, filling my glass halfway and sliding it across the granite countertop in my direction. I smile at him gratefully.

Once we've all filled our plates and taken them and our glasses to the dining table adjacent to the island, we take our initial sips of wine and begin to eat.

"Thank you for this, Simone. I was slammed with meetings and didn't have time for lunch."

Declan and Hicks add their thanks, while Simone merely smiles and takes another sip of the pinot. Knowing Simone as well as I do, I brace myself.

"My pleasure." Her smile is genial as she looks around the table. "Now will someone please tell me just what the fuck is going on?"

There is silence for a full minute while Simone's words settle in the room. While I give Declan and Hicks time to recover — I think they've both accidentally inhaled wine mid-sip because they're coughing slightly – I turn to face Simone and explain.

I point to my face. "This is where it all begins, I guess. Last Friday, I went to Sam's for my usual supper and jazz. I was attacked in the parking garage as I was leaving."

Simone looks stunned, her wine glass halfway to her mouth. Slowly and deliberately, she places the glass back down on the table; I can tell she'd rather throw it across the room.

"Why didn't you *tell* me? My God, Kate. On Sunday when you texted that you'd had a little accident, I thought you meant a fender-bender."

"I didn't tell anyone except for Declan and Hicks." The men judiciously remain silent. "They're from the gym," I explain. Realization dawns in Simone's eyes, and she gives Declan a long, appraising look. "I went to the gym after it happened. Declan was there and patched me up."

"So, all those self-defense classes you've been taking, I mean, you're okay, right?" Simone, never at a loss for words, seems to be struggling.

I place my hand gently on her arm. "Yes, I'm okay. A few cuts and bruises, but I'm fine," I say, trying to reassure her.

She exhales sharply and takes a long sip of wine. "So, who attacked you? What did the police say? Do they have someone in custody? When is the arraignment?" It's Simone at her lawyerly best, her rapid-fire questions coming one after the other.

"Well, I guess that's part of the problem." I know she's not going to be happy when she hears what I have to say next, so I figuratively brace myself for her reaction. "I fought back and managed to get away, but I didn't call the police."

"Why the hell not? And why didn't you call *me*?"

"Honestly, I don't even remember leaving the garage and driving to the gym. Declan took one look at me and asked if I wanted the police or the hospital. At the time, I didn't see the point."

Declan rises from the table and returns a few minutes later with the bottle of chardonnay and the now-uncorked bottle of cabernet and places them on the table. Simone raises her glass in response to his unspoken question and nods her thanks when he tops it off. My glass is still mostly untouched.

Hicks picks up the thread. "I have some friends with the feds and the Fairfax police," he tells Simone without getting into specifics, "who told me today that the body of a deceased male was found in the area where Kate was attacked."

She looks at me, her eyes now wide with realization. "The *body*?" It takes a lot to shock Simone, but even she looks more than thrown by this news. "You mean, whoever attacked you is dead? And you didn't call the *police*?"

"He was not dead when I left, I swear." I raise my right hand for emphasis. If I say it often enough, will I somehow believe it?

"So how has this been tied to you? Were there witnesses or security footage from the garage?"

Again, Hicks speaks. "A video clip of the attack, well, part of the attack, was sent to the police earlier today. It wasn't security camera footage from the garage; it was taken by someone who was there that night. Someone who watched the whole thing and didn't help Kate. Someone who now seems to be trying to implicate her in this guy's death."

Simone, to her credit, takes it all in, nodding. "Why don't we all finish with our meal, then I'll take a look at the video." Addressing Hicks, she asks, "You do have a copy of it?" When he nods in confirmation, she seems satisfied.

"Okay. I suggest we wrap up here, I'll review what the police have so far, and then I'll tell you what I think needs to happen next."

Once we've finished eating and putting the dining table to rights, we load the dishwasher and settle in the living room, where Simone takes out her laptop and starts taking notes.

Declan excuses himself to feed Finn and Jasper and then he takes them out into the back garden where he tosses tennis balls for the dogs to chase over and over again until they tire of the game. Panting heavily, they patter into the kitchen for water and then into the living room for the comfort of their beds. I notice vaguely that Declan doesn't return with the dogs but remains outside on the covered patio.

Simone recites back to me what I told her over dinner, and when I've confirmed that it's correct, she turns to Hicks. "May I see it, please?" It doesn't sound like a request at all.

Hicks queues up the video and hands Simone the phone, and I watch her expression as the short clip plays. It is one thing to be on the receiving end of physical violence and to experience it as it happens. It is entirely different to see the incident take place from the perspective of an outside observer. I recall the horror I'd felt when watching the video for the first time. The horror for me had been not because of the attack itself, but because of what the video had shown and what it had not shown, which were the circumstances that precipitated my fighting back.

Simone looks at me, her eyes wide with disbelief, and I can't speak because of the enormous lump in my throat. Even now, I can recall my initial disbelief, the paralyzing fear. Then the anger, the outrage, and finally, the indescribable relief at managing to get away and to safety.

But at what cost? And what is safety without freedom? Because this video will surely cost me mine.

"Whoever's responsible is going to pay. Penfield will make sure of that," Simone snaps, and we all seem to exhale at once, the drama of the video sapping our energy suddenly. "But I still don't understand why you didn't call the police," she says, turning her attention back to me. "You might've been in shock when it first happened, but it's been five days." Her tone isn't quite as sharp as it was a minute ago, but I know that look.

I try not to sound defensive but can't quite pull it off. "The police didn't stop that guy from trying to kill me in the garage, did they? So, when they finally showed up, they'd have taken a statement, and they'd have suggested I go to the ER and sent me on my merry way."

"No," she says in the annoying tone you use when speaking to small children, "you'd have called the police, they'd have taken your statement and a description of the guy. They'd have been on the lookout for him, and when they found him, they would've pressed charges, and he'd go to jail. That's how the system works, if you let it."

"That's how the system is *supposed* to work, but it doesn't always," I say hotly. "And it doesn't matter now, does it? Because the guy is dead."

Hicks and Simone both stare wordlessly at me, surprised at my sudden outburst.

"I'm sorry," I say eventually. "That was inexcusable."

Declan, who has quietly made his way back into the living room, speaks first. "The police have the video, but we don't know what they've done with it so far. We had Kate come here today because we don't know if she's been identified, if there's an outstanding warrant, or any of that. We were trying to buy her some time."

Simone looks at them with renewed respect. "Thank you for taking care of my friend. As Kate's probably told you, Penfield Wainwright has agreed to act as Kate's defense attorney." She smiles suddenly, a complete departure from her earlier demeanor. "Penfield is my godfather, by the way, and he owes me a favor or two."

"Your godfather?" I ask in surprise.

Simone nods. "Well, one of my godfathers, anyway. I also

clerked for him when he was magistrate judge in Alexandria when I first passed the bar exam. So, I do have some knowledge of criminal law and Virginia statutes. In a best-case scenario, if Kate is charged, we'd argue that it was self-defense. That would result in the charges being dropped."

I relax slightly and take another sip of wine, which I hadn't finished during our meal and had brought with me into the living room.

My friend taps her lip thoughtfully for a moment. "That damned video, it bothers me. It all seems so calculated — first the ambush, then the attack. But the one thing the guy obviously didn't count on was Kate fighting back the way she did." She turns to Hicks. "Too early for a cause of death, I assume?"

He nods. "I'll see if I can get some information tomorrow, but it might take some doing."

"We'll get access to the autopsy as part of discovery, but I'd sure like to know as soon as possible what exactly we're dealing with. The prosecution could make a case for excessive or unreasonable force. Involuntary manslaughter is a class five felony in Virginia, with a prison sentence of one to ten years and a fine."

Suddenly I feel light-headed. "Ten years?"

"That's only if we can't get any charges dropped on the grounds of self-defense. Without a warrant or an arraignment, I don't have any idea what the prosecution's intentions would be, so I think it's best to be aware of the worst-case scenario. I'm sorry," she says, putting her hand on my arm. "But, listen.

Penfield's the best criminal defense attorney in DC, and he doesn't like to lose. He's not going to let you go to prison. *We* won't."

I wish I had her confidence. Right now, I just don't.

FOURTEEN

"TELL ME AGAIN how you all know each other?" Simone asks, saving her notes and shutting down her laptop.

"Hicks owns Trident, the gym, and Declan's a member and also runs some of the training classes," I explain. "Declan was closing up the night I was attacked because Hicks was away for a few days."

"So, you work for Hicks?" Simone asks Declan.

Both men seem amused by this.

"No, Declan doesn't work for me," Hicks corrects her. "He helps out when I need a class covered, or as Kate mentioned, when I need someone to close up so I can get away when none of the other instructors is available."

"And Declan, what do you do?" Her tone is seemingly offhand, casual, but I've never known her to ask a casual question.

An expression crosses his face that I can't quite read, and then it clears. "I do this, among other things." He looks around the large expanse of the converted barn's interior.

"This was a wreck and ready for demolition when I bought the land and buildings several years ago."

"It really is beautiful," she says, repeating her compliment from earlier in the evening. "How long have you lived in the States?"

I resist the urge to give her a sharp look.

"I don't see that it has any bearing on Kate's current situation," he replies, emphasizing my name, "but I've nothing to hide. I'm a naturalized citizen and have lived in the States for more than twenty years. I came over on a visa working for a software company, got my green card, and I've been here ever since."

"Declan's being modest," Hicks says smoothly, and a look passes between the two men. Declan doesn't appear to object when Hicks continues, "He and some colleagues started their own company once they'd worked here for a few years, went out on their own. They developed a proprietary algorithm that became highly sought after in the cybersecurity world, particularly by the US government. That's how he and I met."

I listen with interest, since this is the first I've heard any of this. I knew that the two men were friends but knew almost nothing about either one of their lives other than in the context of the running of the gym.

"I was a Navy lieutenant commander in charge of a SEAL platoon, and Declan was working as a contractor overseas. He trained my teams on a few occasions and acted as an advisor. We stayed in touch over the years, and when I retired from active duty and moved back to Virginia, we reconnected. He had sold his company by then, and he was looking for something to keep himself busy, so he started helping out at the gym. I'd originally offered to sell him a share in the business but, at the time, he wasn't interested in owning another business."

Again, both men exchange a look that I can't decipher.

Declan turns to Simone. "Anything else you'd like to know?" His tone is still a bit chilly.

"I have a question for Kate," Hicks interjects before she can answer. "Kate, what do you do for a living?"

I look at Hicks in surprise, realizing that just as I know almost nothing about Hicks and Declan outside the gym, they also know very little about me. "I'm a contracts administrator." I figure that with Hicks' government background, he'll have a general idea of what that entails.

"For the government?"

"No, I work for a defense contractor. Tate Walker."

"Oh, they're a decent outfit. I've worked with them a few times over the years."

"Being a contracts admin isn't the most exciting job, but the government couldn't run without us."

"No doubt."

"Whatever the reason, someone appears to have it in for you." Declan's tone is factual, unemotional. "We need to find out who it is and why."

Everyone is pensive for a moment, and the room is briefly silent.

"Well, I think that about covers it for today." Simone turns to me. "Have you given any thought to what you're going to do tomorrow?"

"I have absolutely no idea."

"Kate," Hicks says, his voice kind, "don't worry yourself thinking that you're going to be dragged out of your bed in some kind of pre-dawn raid and hauled off to the police station in your robe and slippers." I glance up at him in surprise because that is exactly what I'd been terrified was going to happen. I think about Raj and Hicks searching my car for the AirTag. They'd gone through only my car, and they were friends doing me a favor. What would it be like to have my entire home taken apart and searched? My finances examined? My whole life put under a microscope?

"It's simply a matter of how we'd handle your surrender if a warrant is issued or if officers do come to your home to place you under arrest." Simone's voice is reassuring.

"So, what do I do in the meantime?"

"What did you tell Josh when it first happened?" She looks at the two men. "He's Kate's simply adorable boss." The woman is hopeless, I swear.

"That I'd had an accident and had gotten banged up a bit and needed some time at home to recover."

My friend raises an eyebrow. "Yeah, that's what you told me, too." I give her a contrite glance. "Did he see you in the office today?"

"No."

"Good. Why don't you tell him that you overdid it today and you'd be more comfortable working from home for a while. He doesn't really care if you're in the office or not, does he?"

"No, as long as I'm online and everyone who needs to can reach me."

"All right, that's one hurdle overcome. I'll speak with Penfield first thing tomorrow, and once I've laid out all the facts, we'll be ready if and when a warrant is issued. His paralegal will email you an engagement letter in the morning." I must look worried, because she adds, "It's going to be okay. You're not a flight risk, you've lived here almost your whole life, plus you own property and have the means to post bond. Being arrested or turning yourself in will be scary as hell, I'm not going to sugarcoat it. But with a little preparation, we'll get you through it, okay? Are we good?" Her eyes search mine.

"Yes," I reply with more confidence than I'm feeling.

"Gentlemen, anything to add?"

When neither Declan nor Hicks say anything, Simone slides her laptop into her bag and stands, ready to leave.

Declan says, "Kate, hang on for a bit, will you? I'll see you home, but I need to let the beauties out for quick run before we leave." This is said with an ironic glance in Simone's direction.

Hicks adds, "I'll let Declan know if I hear anything about an arrest warrant, and we'll pass it on to you both ASAP. Declan, will you work on that video clip in the morning?"

"I will."

At the door, Simone hugs me and whispers in my ear. "I'm very glad these men have your back, but if they're just a gym owner and a former software developer, then I'm the bloody Pope." In a louder voice, she says, "Good night, everyone. Talk soon."

To my surprise, Hicks also envelops me in a gentle hug as he leaves. "Try to get some sleep tonight, okay? I know it won't be easy, but it's the best thing you can do to prepare yourself for what's coming."

"Why are you doing this?"

He looks briefly taken aback at my question. "Because I have a wife and a daughter." He glances at Declan. "And Declan has sisters and nieces."

Declan says nothing, his expression unreadable.

"No one should have to go through what you have," continues Hicks. "And you certainly shouldn't have to go through it alone. You're a member of my gym, so you're family. We take care of our own." He turns to his friend. "I'll call you in the morning." Then he follows Simone out the door.

Declan closes and locks the front door, and the house seems very quiet as we go back into the living room where the dogs have stirred and are vying for attention. I pet them absentmindedly as Declan opens a set of French doors to let them out into the back garden, where they run off into the darkness, triggering motion lights as they go.

"She's quite something, your friend."

I'm not sure if it's a compliment or not. I smile at him, a little apologetically. "Simone can be a bit much. Until you get to know her."

"Just a bit. I pity anyone who takes her on."

I move to stand at the windows, looking out into the darkened back garden. "Just a few days ago, my life was perfectly normal. Totally boring and uneventful," I say, almost to myself, pressing my forehead against the cool glass.

Declan comes to stand beside me. "It's going to be okay." His voice is calm and assured.

What I would give to feel the same way.

"That video." His tone is thoughtful. "Who would take such a thing, watch the whole incident, and not step in to help?"

"Oh, you see it every day," I remind him. "Videos that are posted online show people doing horrible things to one another, and yet so many people are more concerned with posting content that it never occurs to them to step in and help. That these are people's real lives, with real consequences, not simply another way to get likes on their Twitter feeds or some stupid TikTok challenge." I make no attempt to disguise my contempt of the trend.

"Have you ever had any issues at Sam's before?"

"Never. Since you and the other instructors have stressed the importance of situational awareness, I'm mindful of what's going on around me from the minute I leave the restaurant until I'm in my locked car. But I swear that guy came out of nowhere."

"Do you go there often?"

"Yes, most Wednesdays if I don't have to work late. There's a core group of us who show up every week. We vent about work, life inside the Beltway, the usual. We mostly work for defense contractors and consulting firms, so we have similar war stories."

"But the night you were attacked, it was a Friday. I was covering for Hicks, and he'd left for Deep Creek Lake that same morning."

"That's right," I agree, remembering now. "I had to work late, so I couldn't make it to Sam's that night. I went on Friday instead."

He's looking at me intently. "How many people know of your routine?"

I consider his question for a minute. "Simone and Josh, for sure, but they know it's not carved in granite or anything. Work always takes precedence."

"Who else?"

"The regular bar staff and servers, a few of the full-time security guards." I pause, thinking. "The staff at the host stand and the jazz quartet, although sometimes that changes at the last minute. And then the Wednesday regulars."

"How many would that be?"

"Let me think. Maybe eight or ten?" I make a mental list of the people I'm likely to see every week.

"That many?" Declan sounds surprised.

"It's a popular place. It's close to all the offices in Tysons. Plus the metro and the Beltway are right there, too."

"How well do you know these people?"

"It depends. The restaurant staff knows only my first name, but I've probably exchanged business cards with most of the regulars. You know how it is in this area – the first question people ask is, 'What do you do?' The second one is, 'Where do you work?' It's all about networking and connections, especially at a place like Sam's. Then they want to connect on LinkedIn. It's who you know and what you can do for someone."

Declan's expression is thoughtful for what seems like a long time. "When you found the AirTag on your car, Raj thought perhaps it was being used to target your vehicle, since there had been reports of gangs using the trackers to find suitable cars. But you told Hicks you know someone who might have put it there. Is it an ex?"

"What makes you say that?"

"Not much of a leap. Is it?"

"Yes. I have no proof, though. Just a gut feeling. He always wanted to know exactly where I was when we weren't together."

"Does this ex have a name?"

"I'd really rather not say, Declan, not until I know for sure."

"You do know I could find it in less than five minutes online."

When I don't reply right away, he picks up his phone.

"Oh, for heaven's sake. His name is Noah Blackstone."

His fingers fly across the screen, then stop. He quickly scrolls and reads for about a minute. Then he looks up at me.

"I'd say he deserves to be an ex."

"I'd say you're right." I think back to that day when he'd shown up at the house, when he'd grabbed me, gotten nasty. If I hadn't been going to the gym, hadn't learned how to handle myself, how far might he have gone?

I push the thought away.

"When was this?"

"I ended it about a month ago."

"Good to know."

He gives Jasper a final pat, then gets to his feet.

"What are you thinking?" I ask, looking up at him, a knot slowly forming in my stomach.

"I think your car might have been tracked for a completely different reason than Raj suggested. Not to learn your car's whereabouts, but to find out yours."

WHEN WE ARRIVE at my house, I sit in the car for a minute after shutting off the engine, looking at the dark windows and unlit porch, thinking about everything I've learned tonight and everything I still don't know.

I hear Declan's truck door closing behind me, and I look up to see him approaching my car. He opens the driver's door. "If you don't mind, I'd like to come in with you, have a look around."

I'm about to object but look again at the dark house with all its first-story windows that give onto the wide front porch and the manicured shrubs and flowering bushes of which I've taken such care. Easy access through those windows, and lots of places for someone to hide if they were so inclined. "I don't mind at all."

Motion-activated outdoor lights illuminate the house and side gardens as we approach the front door. Once we're inside, after locking the door behind me, I hang my bag and keys on hooks in the entryway. I glance at Declan curiously as he pulls the keys down and hands them back to me.

"Is there somewhere else you can keep these that aren't within sight or reach of your front door?" he asks, gesturing at the sidelights that grace both sides of the heavy wooden door. The sidelights have a subtle geometric pattern but aren't opaque when the lights are on inside the house. "Good to see that you have keyed deadbolts, though."

After setting the keys on the kitchen table, I move through the rooms, turning on a few lamps and overhead lights, closing shutters and blinds. Part of my evening ritual is closing the shutters and fabric Roman blinds at dusk, and I usually enjoy the sensation of being cocooned in my cozy space, symbolically closing out the world and all its cares for the night.

Now I have the sensation of locking myself inside a stronghold, fortifying my home against invaders who would do me harm. I think briefly of my long-ago medieval studies, learning how the upper classes petitioned to turn their manor houses and palaces into castles through licenses to crenellate, to literally turn a home into a fortification.

I understand their motivation more now than I ever did as a student, blithely tucking away the information to retrieve later for an exam or as a factoid when watching *Jeopardy* or attending a pub trivia night.

We climb the stairs, Declan taking the lead. It doesn't take long for him to check all the windows and for me to confirm that no one's been in the house while I've been gone today. We soon head back downstairs.

"Thank you for doing this," I tell him gratefully. "I'm going to be a bit spooked for a while, but I'll get over it."

"You'll be okay here on your own?"

"I'm safe here. I'll be fine."

Declan nods and smiles slightly. "Get some sleep and let me know how it goes with Wainwright tomorrow, will you?"

"Yes, I will."

I pick up my keys from the kitchen table and, as we walk to the front door, I see Declan glance briefly at the bookshelves in the darkened office.

"Go ahead," I say.

He looks at me, not following.

"If there are other books you'd like to borrow, feel free."

"It's late."

"Not that late. And I have a feeling you know which ones you want."

"Only if you don't mind."

"Come on." I walk into the office and switch on a lamp.

He follows me and goes immediately to the shelves he'd been perusing the other day, pulling out three books in quick succession. I glance at the authors and smile. Rumi, Khalil Gibran, and Seamus Heaney. "A bit of light reading?"

"A bit of enlightenment is more like it. As I said, I have some catching up to do."

I switch off the light in the office, and we walk back to the front door, where I unlock the deadbolt so that he can leave.

"Good night, Kate."

"Good night."

I stand in the doorway and watch as he gets in his truck and starts the engine, not turning away until the vehicle disappears from view.

It takes only a few minutes to undress and get ready for bed. After sliding beneath the covers, I lower my hand to the hardwood floor, stretching slightly to reach what I'm searching for. I'm relieved when my hand comes into contact with the cool metal of the 20-gauge Winchester pump shotgun, fully loaded.

Satisfied, I turn off the bedside lamp and roll onto my side to sleep.

FIFTEEN

IT TAKES A MINUTE for it to register that the unfamiliar sound I'm hearing is not part of the podcast I have playing in the background; rather, it's the ringtone of the prepaid mobile that Declan and Hicks had given me yesterday.

I snatch up the phone, hoping to answer the call before it drops.

"Hey, Kate. It took you a while. Is everything okay?" Simone asks when I finally answer.

"Morning, Simone. Sorry, I'm not used to this ringtone. Everything's as good as can be expected, I guess. I feel like I'm waiting for a bomb to drop."

"Well, I've spoken to Pen, and he'd like us to meet with him today. Can you be in DC early this afternoon?"

I look at my watch. It's ten forty-five. Mentally I run through my calendar, thinking of any meetings that I might need to reschedule. At the moment, there's nothing more important than this.

"Yes, I can. Are you driving in or taking the metro?"

"Driving. I'd like to come to your place and go over a few things with you first."

"Sure, what time were you thinking of?" I ask right as the doorbell rings. I walk to the front door and peer out the sidelight to see Simone standing on my front porch. She's smiling and holding up a paper bag from the Corner Bakery.

"How about now?" she says as I open the door.

"Wise guy."

She hands me the bag as I hold the door wider to let her pass; then I close and lock the door while she ends the call.

"This had better be a cream cheese brownie," I say, peering down into the paper bag.

"What else would it be? The lemon square is mine, though."

We walk through to the kitchen where Simone places her computer bag and purse on the floor next to the long farmhouse-style table.

"What time is our appointment?"

"Two o'clock. That should be enough time to go over my notes from the other night, make sure I have all the facts straight, and prepare you for the kinds of questions Pen might ask."

"Okay. I need to know how much his retainer will be, too. Did you discuss that?"

"Yes, I've negotiated that with him. We can talk about it later." She's deliberately not looking at me as she opens a cupboard and takes down two dessert plates.

"Simone," I say, a warning in my voice, "you are not paying my retainer."

"You're right, I'm not." I give her a pointed look until she finally caves. "If you must know, we agreed on a retainer of one dollar."

I look at her incredulously. "Do I look like a complete idiot?"

She's leaning against the edge of the table, arms crossed. I know that pose well – it's Simone at her lawyerly best. I'm fortunate enough to usually not be on the receiving end of the look she's giving me right now.

"I told you, Pen's my godfather. If he can't do me a favor, then who can?"

"He's *your* godfather, Simone, not mine."

"Then please accept this favor from me, okay? You're my good friend, and you're in trouble. I want to help any way I can, and I can do this. What's the point in having connections in this bloody town if I can't use them when I really need them? Please."

I hand her a dessert fork and take my plate and fork over to the table. Sitting down heavily on the long bench seat, I take a bite of brownie and chew, considering. "Okay." My tone is grudging. "But how can I possibly repay you?"

"You can't, and you don't need to. That's what this friendship thing is all about." She's smiling as she joins me at the table.

"So, I have to ask, though. What would his retainer be if he weren't doing you this favor?"

Exhaling, she grumbles, "And I thought I was stubborn." I can see her heart's not really in it, though. She arches one perfectly-shaped eyebrow. "Fifty thousand. To start."

I stare at her in disbelief. "I love you, Simone."

"I know you do."

She powers up her laptop and starts to read back to me her notes from last night's conversation with Declan and Hicks. When we've gone through them all and confirmed that everything is correct, she takes off her reading glasses. The look she gives me is long and considering. "So how are you *really* doing?"

"Physically, I'm healing. Mentally? I've been better. Even that ... thing with Noah was nothing compared to this." Simone's jaw tightens at the mention of my ex. I force myself not to react and continue, "With all the classes I've taken, all the hours of training, I thought I'd be prepared for something like this. God, what an idiot I was."

"Hey," she says gently. "I saw that video, remember? You were incredible. And I didn't even see the whole thing, only the tail end of it. I can't begin to imagine what the first part was like. I couldn't have done what you did and walk away." I give her a dubious look, and she reaches across the table to put a hand on my arm. "I mean it. You defended yourself, and you're sitting here today because you did what you had to do. You and I have both heard of too many women who weren't as fortunate. And," she adds with an expression that I know and love so well, "no one is going to set my friend up like this and get away with it. That I can promise you." Her fierce expression clears and she's smiling again, but with a hint of mischief now.

"What?" I ask warily.

"So, tell me again. Why on earth are you not sleeping with Dublin?"

I give my friend an exasperated but affectionate look. "It's Declan, as you very well know, Simone. Anyway, did you not meet the man?"

"Yeah, I did. That's why I'm asking. Seriously, Kate. I don't know why it took me so long to connect the dots the other night, but Oh. My. God. The man's gorgeous, and that accent. Throw in that house and the dogs – what more could you want?"

"Are you done?"

"Well, I had to try. Besides, the man's obviously got a soft spot for you."

"Don't be ridiculous."

"I have eyes."

"Well, you'd better get them checked. It was just his bad luck he was filling in for Hicks when I showed up at the gym on Friday. He's just doing what he thinks Hicks would've done."

"Nope, I call bullshit on that. Hicks is back from his trip now, and Declan is still around, isn't he? He feels something, and I'll bet Pen's retainer that responsibility's got nothing to do with it." She glances at her watch. "You need to get ready. What're you planning on wearing?"

I look over to examine my friend's outfit, which today is a navy pin-striped trouser suit with a dusty rose silk blouse, diamond stud earrings and a steel watch – a classic Cartier Tank. I sigh. "Well, it won't be my favorite navy pin-stripe."

Simone follows me up to my bedroom and sits on the edge of the bed, watching as I remove a plastic dry-cleaning bag from a charcoal grey suit. I select two blouses and hold them up for her inspection. "Royal blue," she says decisively. "Have you spoken with Josh today?"

"No, and I need to call him, especially since I'll be offline the rest of the day." I take a pair of black pumps from the closet and set them on the floor by the bed. "I don't know how much to tell him. What do you think? This could all blow over or blow up any minute, and I'm just waiting for one or the other to happen. But I really do think it's going to seriously hit the fan."

"I'd have to agree with you. Let's ask Pen this afternoon. There's no warrant and no charges have been filed. Simply tell Josh that you need to take some personal time this afternoon. For all he knows, you could be going to the doctor for a follow-up appointment after your 'accident,'" she says, putting verbal quotes around the word.

I know she hasn't completely forgiven me for not telling her right away about what happened, but she's getting there. I did get a cream cheese brownie, after all.

And a fifty-thousand-dollar retainer.

"DO YOU THINK your two gym pals are what they seem? I mean, really?"

We're in Simone's car, heading east on I-66 toward DC. I've cleared the decks of any meetings and texted Josh, who replied that he hopes I'm on the mend and to let him know if I need anything.

"What?" Her question totally catches me by surprise. "Of course they are. Hicks is a retired Navy officer, and Declan used to own a software company. What's wrong with that?"

"Nothing. Have you ever googled either of them?"

"It's never even occurred to me. Why?" I glance over at her. "You have, haven't you?"

"Uh-huh. Last night."

"And?"

"Hicks spent most of his career in Naval intelligence and retired as a vice admiral. I bet he still has a ton of connections in the service and in all those three-letter agencies, too. And your quiet Irish friend is a multimillionaire. Did you know that?"

"No, I didn't. I assumed he wasn't hurting financially since Hicks said he'd sold a software company. That was years ago, though. A lot could've happened since then."

"True. Although he doesn't strike me as the type to blow through that kind of money just for the heck of it."

"What kind of money?" I can't resist asking.

She names a figure that raises even her eyebrows, which is saying something.

Great. Just what the world needs – another obscenely wealthy software geek on the loose. Okay, so maybe Declan's not all bad. He had come through for me when I needed his help. That says something, right? He's just a little on the uptight side. That's not a crime, even if it is annoying. It sure beats the God complex too many wealthy tech bros seem to have these days.

I force myself to focus on my current situation and the reason for our trip into DC today and say a silent prayer that Penfield Wainwright will live up to his reputation.

Simone maneuvers the Mercedes into the parking garage beneath the imposing building where Wainwright and Associates' offices are located. Placing a hand on my knotted stomach, I take a deep breath and try to relax. She gives me a reassuring look as she shifts the car into park and shuts off the engine. "Don't be nervous. Pen's not nearly as intimidating as you might imagine."

I look at my friend dubiously, then pull myself together. "Right, let's do this."

～

SIMONE NAVIGATES US expertly through the lobby and up to the tenth floor, where Wainwright's practice occupies the entire level. In Washington, DC, office buildings are subject to a height restriction, and the office's prime location provides a spectacular view of the capital city's skyline without the risk of taller buildings obstructing the sightline.

Stepping off the elevator, we enter a hushed, subdued space with thick carpeting and tasteful décor. A handsome, impeccably-dressed young male receptionist sits behind a large mahogany desk and greets us as we approach.

"Ms. Ellis, how lovely to see you again." He stands and comes around the desk to shake Simone's outstretched hand.

"Hello, Thomas," Simone says. "I hope you're doing well." They exchange a few more pleasantries before Simone turns to me. "Thomas, this is Catherine Barrow. We have a two o'clock appointment with Pen."

My eyebrows lift in surprise at Simone's referring to the powerful Penfield Wainwright by his nickname to an employee, but the receptionist doesn't appear to be fazed in the least.

"Of course," he says smoothly. "If you'd please take a seat, I'll show you in shortly. May I get you some refreshments while you wait?"

"Water will be fine, please, Thomas." She looks to me for concurrence. I nod, and the young man slips silently away down the plushly-carpeted hallway. Simone winks playfully. "All part of the experience that is Penfield Wainwright."

My friend looks relaxed and totally in her element as she settles into one of the comfortable armchairs to wait. I couldn't be more uptight if I tried, completely intimidated by my situation and the surroundings. It's not just the fact that she's an attorney feeling at home in a law office; it's the kind of confidence that a lifetime of privilege and money brings.

Sometimes I'm surprised that we've become such good friends, so different are our personalities and backgrounds. I'm a card-carrying introvert who needs to recover after spending more than an hour or two with other people, while Simone owns every room she enters. Conflict and drama are her drugs of choice.

I'm the only child of two career academics and grew up in the suburbs of North Arlington. It was the kind of place where neighborhood kids ran in packs; our after-school explorations only ended when we were called home to dinner or when the street lights came on. Summer breaks were spent traveling wherever my parents' fancy and careful budgeting happened to take us, from national parks in the US to more international destinations than I can count. While this sounds extravagant, we were always watching our pennies, often staying in hostels or university residence halls that were rented out to visitors during term breaks. Every trip was seen as a great adventure, which was my parents' general philosophy toward life.

Simone, on the other hand, comes from serious generational wealth and attended an expensive New England prep school. I'm sure my family's vacations may have seemed exotic or excessive to some of our neighbors, but Simone's casual mention of summering at her godfather's beach house on the Vineyard, learning to sail in Cannes and ski in St. Moritz, left my travel stories in the dust. Nowadays you'd never know that she was a trust fund baby, aside from the understated elegance of her wardrobe and comments about catching up with a former president or tech billionaire at her parents' home in Georgetown.

At the moment, I'd give anything for her quiet confidence, for the security of knowing that any situation can and will be handled, discreetly and with no one the wiser. A word in the right ear at the right charity event or big-ticket political fundraiser, and – problem solved.

I'm too nervous to sit and have to fight the urge to pace, so I stand next to Simone and look across the waiting area to the sight of the city beyond. I don't often have access to a panoramic view of DC, and on this clear afternoon, it really is impressive. I pass the time trying to identify landmarks and monuments while we wait.

Thomas returns with a silver tray laden with crystal glasses filled with ice and a large bottle of Badoit sparkling mineral water, announcing, "Mr. Wainwright is ready for you now." While I'm sure Simone more than knows the way, Thomas escorts us down the long hallway past numerous offices and large conference rooms until we reach Wainwright's office.

The receptionist knocks discreetly, then smoothly opens the large door and gestures for us to enter ahead of him, expertly balancing the tray and its contents without missing a beat. He sets the tray on a credenza before silently departing.

A distinguished-looking, grey-haired man looks up from behind an imposing desk as we enter and smiles broadly when he sees Simone. Rising, he crosses the room and envelops her in a long hug which, for some reason, takes me by surprise.

When they separate, Simone says, "It's great to see you, Pen." I can tell that the sentiment is genuine.

"Where've you been hiding, Simone? I can't remember the last time we saw each other. I'm so glad you called." As though the reason for our visit were a social call and not a serious legal problem that needed solving.

They both turn to me, and Simone makes the introductions. "Catherine Barrow, I'd like you to meet Penfield Wainwright. Pen, this is my friend, Kate."

Penfield Wainwright is as handsome in person as he is in the images I've seen of him over the years. He is tall, a few inches over six feet, and is expensively but casually dressed in charcoal grey trousers and a softer grey cashmere turtleneck. His light blue eyes meet mine, and he takes one of my hands in both of his with a warm smile.

"Catherine – you don't mind if I call you 'Catherine,' do you? It suits you so much better than 'Kate,' I think."

I catch Simone's gaze, and she's rolling her eyes, but there's a softness there, too, that I don't often see in her, an obvious affection toward this powerful man.

"It's a pleasure to meet you. Simone's given me some background as to your current situation, and I have every confidence we'll be able to represent you successfully."

"Thank you for making the time to see us today, Mr. Wainwright."

"Call me Pen," he insists, waving away my formality. There is no way on God's green earth that I can imagine myself ever calling Penfield Wainwright by his nickname, but I let that one go for the moment. "Why don't we sit down and have a chat?" He gestures with an outstretched arm toward a sofa and three chairs placed around a coffee table, rather than the more business-like conference table that runs parallel to the floor-to-ceiling windows.

I sit down on one end of the sofa, while Wainwright takes one of the chairs opposite.

"Water, anyone?" Simone asks, moving to the credenza and the bottled water.

"Sit, Simone, I'll get that," Wainwright scolds, getting up and moving the entire tray from the credenza to the coffee table. He opens the bottle of sparkling water with a crack of its seal and fills the three glasses.

Simone sits next to me and after taking a glass for herself, opens her laptop in preparation for our chat. I accept a glass but am too nervous to drink just yet.

I'd spent hours last night reading online articles about Wainwright's cases and his personal life to get ready for this meeting. The man is even more compelling and charismatic in person than I'd expected, which is saying a lot. His reputation as a barracuda in the courtroom might be justified, but right now, he simply seems kind.

He takes a long drink before placing his glass back on the table. His eyes are warm but sharp as they meet mine. Then he turns his gaze to his goddaughter. "Tell me everything you know."

For the next several minutes, Simone succinctly lays out my situation: the circumstances of the attack, the discovery of my attacker's body several days later, and the existence of a video that shows the final seconds of the encounter but not the crucial piece making my case for self-defense.

Wainwright doesn't take a single note, he merely listens intently and interrupts only to ask clarifying questions. "I'm so sorry, Catherine," he says when Simone wraps up her summary. "You're recovering well, I trust?"

"Yes, I'm fine now, thank you."

"Who currently is in possession of this video?" His expression is pensive.

"Fairfax County Police, to the best of my knowledge," Simone replies, "as well as, um, Hicks, the owner of Trident." She looks slightly uncomfortable at not knowing Hicks' first name, at not being as flawlessly prepared as she usually is in professional situations.

"Do we have any of the metadata on the video, the date and time it was recorded, any location information?"

Declan had made good on his promise to Hicks to look at the video and had shared what he'd found with me and Hicks. "From what I've been told, the video was taken the night of the attack," I say, "but there's no location information in the video's metadata."

The attorney considers this for a moment. "Perhaps our initial position would be to question the legitimacy of the video, to suggest the possibility that it's been AI-generated or is a deep fake. If, as you suspect, it's been edited to show Catherine as being the aggressor, we could likely make the case that the entire video is a fiction. That she's being set up for the death of the unidentified victim in the garage." He picks up on my dubious expression. "Yes, we do need to refer to the individual as a victim in this instance, Catherine, difficult as that may be to swallow. Until such time as we can put our hands on an unedited video of the entire attack or otherwise cast doubt on its legitimacy. Or until we find the person responsible for the video and its leak to the police."

"Do you think we have a case for the video being a deep fake or being AI-generated?" I try not to sound as skeptical as I feel. This is the great Pen Wainwright, sure, but I have my reservations on this score.

"Have you seen some of the deep fake videos that have gone viral recently?" I say that I have, and Wainwright continues, "It's becoming increasingly difficult to tell the difference between fiction and reality. A picture has long ceased to be worth a thousand words. Pictures, and now videos, aren't worth a damn, given the latest technology. Now we have to discover who it is that would benefit from your being set up for manslaughter when you were, in fact, lawfully defending your own life."

He pauses to let us absorb that stark fact for a moment, and the room is quiet for a beat or two. Turning to me, he says, "Now let's talk about the administrative side of things, shall we? What you can expect from a legal perspective, and what our next steps are."

Just as we're wrapping up, Simone's phone buzzes in her handbag. Giving us both an apologetic look, she quietly excuses herself and steps into the hallway to take the call.

"Mr. Wainwright," I say, taking advantage of Simone's timely absence from the room, "there's something you need to know that I didn't mention earlier." At the attorney's mildly surprised look, I continue. "Simone's concerned enough about me as it is, and I didn't want to add to her worries." I tell him about the AirTag we'd found on my car, the discovery of which I hadn't shared with my friend; then I explain about Noah and our less-than-amicable breakup. Wainwright simply nods, then asks a few questions about the tracker. When he seems satisfied, I breathe a sigh of relief. By the time Simone slips back into the room, we're both smiling and chatting about this season's Kennedy Center lineup.

"All good?" she asks.

"All good," Wainwright and I both reply.

"CHAUNCEY."

"Cornelius."

"Clarence."

"Carmichael."

"Chesterfield. No wait, isn't that the name of a cigarette?" I ask.

"Uh-huh, and a style of sofa, too." We're kicked back on lounge chairs in the sunroom, having been driven indoors by mosquitos despite the citronella candles I'd lit. Since her husband, Luke, was working late dealing with café business, I'd invited Simone over for an early supper after our meeting with Pen.

While we'd sliced tomatoes from my garden and fresh mozzarella for Caprese salad, she'd made the mistake of asking what Hicks' first name was. I told her I had no idea and that Declan had been sworn to secrecy under threat of bodily harm. That started us down this slightly-twisted, rather ridiculous path of unusual men's names that begin with the letter *C*.

"I'll pry it out of him eventually, don't you worry," she says, leaning her head back against the headrest.

"I wasn't, really. But how bad could it be? It's only a name. And on the subject of names, has Luke decided what the new restaurant will be called yet?"

For the past few years, Simone's husband has run a small café not far from their home in Great Falls. It's a popular spot, with lines stretching out the door most days. I've had the pleasure of tasting his cooking, and it is pretty amazing. He's dying to expand his offerings from breakfast and lunch to a full dinner service, but it hasn't been easy.

As with Simone, there's a complete disconnect between the beautiful face and the words that come out of it. Tall, blonde, and muscular, Luke looks like he should be emerging from the surf off Bondi Beach rather than wearing chef's whites and directing kitchen staff. In the looks department, he could give the Hemsworth clan a serious run for their money. He drops the F-bomb like it's nothing and calls nearly everyone he doesn't like a wanker. But, similar to his wife, he's one of the best people I know. Potty mouth notwithstanding.

Simone turns back to me, her face animated. "He's got this idea of calling it 'The Twelve Apostles,' after the rock formation in Australia. Not after, you know, the original ones. It'll be primarily a seafood restaurant. He's thinking of maybe focusing on twelve ingredients at a time or something like that, playing off the number in the name."

"That sounds great, Simone. You must be really excited."

Her face clouds over. "Well, we would be, but getting financial backing is almost impossible. New restaurants have such a high failure rate, most investors won't touch one with a ten-foot pole. Since Luke refuses to accept any money from me, we're in a holding pattern for now."

"I'm sure you'll find the perfect investor," I say, trying to cheer her up. "He's a fabulous chef; there's got to be someone out there willing to take a chance on him. It'll happen one of these days."

ONCE I SEE HER out, I lock up and go back into the kitchen to clear up and load the dishwasher. Wandering into the office, I glance idly at the rows and rows of books, thinking not of my parents as I usually do, but of Declan. Sunday's lunchtime conversation comes back to me. Checking my watch, I see that it's nearly nine o'clock. Too late to call? Maybe, but I decide to give it a shot, anyway.

The phone rings three times, then four, and I'm about to end the call when Declan's voice comes on the line.

"Hello, Declan. It's Kate."

"Is everything all right?"

"Yes, everything's fine. I hope I'm not disturbing you. I was wondering, I mean, I know it's very last-minute, but would you be interested in joining me on a hike tomorrow?"

There is a long silence on the other end of the line. This was a bad idea.

"Yes, I'd like that," he says finally. So maybe this isn't the stupidest phone call I've ever made, after all. "Aren't you working tomorrow?"

"No, I'm not." Even though I haven't cleared this with Josh yet. "I really need a break, to go somewhere quiet and clear my head. Have you ever taken the dogs to Rose River Falls?"

"Yes. The trail has some stream crossings they enjoy, as well as the waterfall."

"Okay. How does nine o'clock sound? I can pick you up on the way."

"That'd be fine. We'll need to take the truck because of the lads, if you don't mind my driving."

"Of course I don't mind. See you in the morning, Declan. Thanks."

"No need. We'll enjoy it as much as you will."

We end the call and I'm feeling better already as I walk out to the garage and carefully carry one of the large plastic storage bins that holds my hiking and camping gear into the house. I sit cross-legged on the living room floor next to the bin and start pulling out the contents, setting aside the items I'll need. I know from long experience the essentials every day hiker should carry, so it doesn't take long to load up my day pack.

Once I've returned the bin with the rest of its contents to the garage, I send Josh a short text to let him know I'm taking a personal day and will touch base with him later tomorrow.

Tate Walker, like so many other companies, prides itself on promoting work-life balance and encouraging employees to take care of their mental health. That looks great on the company's recruiting page but tends to work better in theory than in actual practice. If there were ever a time I needed a mental health day, this would be it.

SIXTEEN

AFTER YESTERDAY'S preparations, it doesn't take long to get ready. I find myself smiling as I fill my water bottle and tuck it with a spray can of sunscreen into the outside pockets of my daypack. I add a small cooler bag with food that's more appetizing than trail mix with some ice to keep everything chilled for a few hours. I enjoy hiking but there's no need to be uncivilized about it.

Making sure I have my mobile phone and the one that Declan and Hicks had given me, I take my handbag and keyring from the mudroom, sling my daypack over one shoulder, and I'm out the door in no time.

The traffic gods are feeling benevolent this morning. I make the turnoff and drive slowly down Declan's long gravel driveway at 8:45. The front door opens before I've turned off the engine, and Declan steps out onto the porch to greet me.

"Good morning. I know I'm a little early. If you need more time to get ready, there's no hurry."

"No, we're ready. The lads saw me pull out the backpacks last night and know that means we're going out on the trails. They haven't given me a minute's peace since I got out of bed."

He closes the shutters against the heat of the day and locks up, and Jasper and Finn bound excitedly next to us as we walk to the truck. They jump into the back seat and after Declan connects their safety harnesses, they sit up straight, gazing out the side windows, happily anticipating the upcoming day in the mountains. I completely understand how they feel.

We spend the first thirty minutes of the trip in relative silence, Declan easily navigating through the neighborhoods and side streets until we exit onto Route 66 heading west. Even though we're heading in the opposite direction of the commuters who are streaming into Northern Virginia and DC from Bristow and Haymarket, there is still a lot of truck traffic to contend with. The dogs settle down and are dozing in the back seat, and traffic finally starts to thin out once we pass Gainesville.

"So how does someone with a PhD in archaeology end up in defense contracting?"

Declan's unexpected question cuts into the silence of the truck.

I think about it for a minute, choose my words carefully. Even now, my throat tightens a little. "My plan had always been to stay in the UK once I'd gotten my degree. I had my friends, a flat, and a job waiting for me. Then I got the news. The news that my parents had died." I swallow hard, remembering that awful call. "I didn't know what to do about the house and everything else that needed to be done back here. All the things that come with having both your parents die at once. I left everything in the UK behind and came home. Friends were telling me to sell the house and go back to Durham, but I wasn't ready to do that. To leave the house I'd grown up in and all the ties to my parents, like they'd meant nothing." The idea of never having the house to go back to still makes me sad. "A while after my parents died, I ran into a friend of theirs, quite by accident. We got to talking, and he offered me a job with Tate Walker. I think he might possibly have saved my life."

I look down at my hands, which are now clenched in my lap, glance at the fading ink of the tattoos on the insides of both wrists. I shut my eyes briefly, forcing a memory away.

Declan glances over at me, but I'm once again looking straight ahead at the road, unable to meet his gaze. I can tell the story, but I can't make eye contact and hold it together, too.

"The company had a leadership development program for recent college grads. We completed six-month rotations, with promotions and pay bumps after each phase. I knew I didn't want to work in finance, estimating, or supply chain, so I chose contracts. And here I am still."

"Not exactly a five-star review on Glassdoor." Declan's tone is wry. I look over at him, but he's not smiling, he just looks thoughtful.

"No, I guess not. But we all have bills to pay, and with my parents gone and no other family, I had to support myself."

Wanting to change the subject, I ask, "What about you? How did you come to live and work in the States? I know it's not easy to work in a foreign country these days, unless you're an academic. Digital nomads didn't exist back then, did they?"

At first I think he's not going to answer, but then I realize he's focusing on the navigation screen and isn't ignoring my question. Turning his attention back to me, he replies, "Not then, no. But starting in the mid-1990's, the Republic of Ireland experienced historic economic growth. The Celtic Tiger, as it was known. You've heard of it, I'm sure."

I agree that I had, and he continues.

"I was working for a company not unlike your Tate Walker, a global consulting company with headquarters in Dublin. I'd been there for several years and was given the opportunity to transfer to our Seattle office. It was a promotion and a chance to try something different, so I jumped at it. It was a great time to be in software. I burned out after a few years. Working for a big corporation, often on government contracts, started to be less fun and more work. More administration, more reporting, more numbers. I wanted only to write code and help build systems."

"A few of us had been knocking around the idea of starting our own business for a while, and one day, we did it. We qualified for a few small-business loans and signed our lives away, or at least it felt that way at the time. The first few years were brutal," he admits, "but we found our stride, grew our reputation, started getting some good contracts. I was traveling all over the world, to some real hot spots, training the military or whomever was buying our products, living out of a suitcase for months at a time. That's how Hicks and I met."

I try to imagine a younger Declan, working with Hicks and a platoon of combat-hardened Navy SEALs; despite my teasing him about being a software nerd, I can totally picture it.

"It was all grand until it wasn't." He doesn't say anything for a few minutes, checking the navigation screen as we get closer to the Fisher's Gap trailhead parking lot. "We eventually were approached with an offer to sell, which my partners and I agreed to accept. It was more money than we'd ever dreamed of making, and it was time to ... to move on."

"Now what do you do?"

"Now?" His expression brightens. "Now I do whatever I want."

Must be nice. The thought comes with not a small amount of envy.

Declan parks the truck and looks at me, and then at Finn and Jasper. "Shall we?" he asks. Our happy response is unanimous.

Once Declan and I have swapped our running shoes for hiking books, liberally sprayed ourselves with insect repellent and sunscreen and shouldered our respective daypacks, he guides the dogs from the back of the truck and hands me Finn's lead.

"You're okay with taking Finn?"

"Happy to," I reply, meaning it.

Declan takes Jasper, and after locking up the truck, we set off in the direction of Skyline Drive and the fire road that leads to the trail. Once we're on the yellow-blazed equestrian trail, by unspoken agreement, Finn and I take the lead. We turn right onto the blue-blazed trail that we'll follow for the next few miles, and a short distance down the trail, I hear a sound that is music to my ears – the rushing water of the nearby stream. My spirits lift even higher as we continue deeper into the forest.

"This is perfect." I look back at Declan and Jasper. Jasper, like Finn, is sniffing madly in every direction. "Am I going too slowly for you? We can follow you and Jasper, if you'd rather."

"Absolutely not. This is a hike, not a forced march. Let's take our time and enjoy this day while we have it, yes?"

"Yes." I focus my attention again on the trail in front of me as we approach a rocky section. There's a good bit of mud, and no matter how much I try, I can't keep myself on solid footing and keep Finn out of the mud. He doesn't appear to mind in the least.

It's a spectacular day for a hike. Beneath the dense tree canopy, the forest is cool and still. Eventually we pass the highest of the waterfalls, and I can tell the dogs are dying to get in the water. Declan judiciously leads us past the falls, and after we've hiked another fifteen minutes or so, he suggests we stop for a water and snack break.

"Then if you're inclined, there's a crossing a bit farther down where we can let the lads cool off in the stream. If you'd rather not, I can take them both."

"I'm fine with it if you think Finn will be."

"He seems to have taken to you, so I don't think there'll be any issues."

Settling down on a large boulder that is set back some distance from the trail, we fill the dogs' water bowls and give them some dry food and a few baby carrots, which they happily devour. As Declan and I share our packed lunches with the sound of the burbling stream in the background, I feel like the weight of the world has dropped from my shoulders. The first thing I'm going to do when I get home is look up my old hiking club.

We're all feeling slightly lazy from the break and not quite inclined to continue yet. I say, "You've told me a bit about your sisters. What about your parents? Are they still in Ireland?"

Declan nods, chewing a baby carrot that he's pilfered from the dogs' supply. In exchange, he's given them some cheese, which has them sitting close to his side, hoping for more of the same. He merely rubs their heads and refills their water bowls, which they empty within seconds.

"Yes, they're still in Galway. They own a couple of pubs, have done my whole life. My mother's happy to spend her days with Maeve and her kids and doing other things, now that my parents are getting on in years. My father can't stay away from work, even though they've hired perfectly capable managers so they could retire. My parents are talented musicians, so most evenings, they're back in one of the pubs for the music, pulling the odd pint or two if the place is overrun. They often are, especially in summer with the tourists."

"I've been there – it's lovely."

"Well, it wasn't always. When I was growing up, it was a bit rough around the edges. It's come up in the world, though. Now it's got some great restaurants and festivals, all sorts of things going on."

"When was the last time you went back?"

Declan's expression changes, clouds over. "It's been a while." His tone changes, and I realize too late that I've somehow put my foot in it. "Let's get moving, shall we? We don't want to be out too long in the heat of the day." I curse silently and then remind myself that I'm not psychic. It's impossible to avoid landmines when you don't know where they are or how they're triggered.

We pack up the remains of our light lunch, and I give the dogs a few more treats before we set off again. As we approach the stream where Declan plans to cross so the dogs can cool off, he says, "Follow my lead?"

I nod my agreement and try to take generally the same steps as Declan, but his stride is much longer than mine, so I'm not able to follow exactly. Thankfully, Finn behaves himself and doesn't try to pull too hard in his eagerness, which makes it easier for me to keep my balance on the slippery rocks. Jasper is barking delightedly ahead of us with Declan, who looks back now and then to check on us. "We're fine," I call to him, and he continues on without speaking.

Finn happily romps through the cold water, trying to paddle in the rare deep pools and splashing joyfully through the shallows, and we make it across without my boots getting completely submerged or, worse, my slipping and falling completely into the water.

As we exit the stream and regain the trail, Declan's warning comes a second too late. The dogs shake madly, and I can't react in time to back away. Looking down at my mud and water-spattered clothes and then up at Declan, whose expression is unreadable, I can only laugh.

"This close," I say, holding my index finger and thumb an inch or so apart. "I was this close to making it out of there with dry clothes. Thanks, guys."

Now Declan does smile, his earlier subdued expression gone for the moment, at least. Soon we're crossing a pretty footbridge with views of the gorge, and he warns, "A heads-up that the next mile or so is a bit of a climb."

"I'm fine." We walk in silence for a while, treading carefully on the wet, rocky trail as it slopes upward. For some reason this stretch of trail reminds me of hikes I'd taken with my parents. I find myself saying, "My parents used to love to hike. We did a lot of walking and hiking in France when we visited my grandparents when I was growing up."

"Your mother was French?"

"Yes. She and my father met while he was studying abroad in Paris. Love at first sight and all that." I turn my face up to a shaft of sunlight that's making its way through the dense tree canopy. "Maybe that's why I've never been married. They set an impossibly high bar. I know, looking back, their marriage wasn't perfect, but it seemed pretty close."

"You've never been married?" He isn't able to keep the surprise out of his voice. "Never even been tempted?"

"Yeah, I've had a couple of serious relationships, but they never stuck for whatever reason. Bad timing, different goals. The usual reasons why relationships end. What about you?"

"I was married once."

While the words are tossed out casually, his tone is not. I'm so caught off guard that I stumble briefly on a loose rock before regaining my balance and continuing along the trail.

"You all right up there?"

"Fine," I reply, but I'm not sure that I am. For some reason, the knowledge that Declan's been married throws me. I realize I'd asked the question with the expectation that the answer would be 'no.' No idea why. Statistically speaking, it would be more unusual if, like me, he'd never been married at all. I can't help but wonder what his wife was like and what caused them to split up. From his tone I get the feeling that follow-up questions are probably off the table, so I simply concentrate on putting one front in foot of the other on the rocky trail until he asks if I'm ready for a break.

We find another large boulder and set our packs down, then give the dogs some carrots and a few biscuits. Declan fills their water bowls and our bottles with the last of the water he'd packed in. "Do they get one last swim before we leave?" I ask, tilting my head in the direction of the dogs.

"Yes, they can have a quick dip, I suppose, when we're done here."

"Can we please stop for a break at Big Meadows before going home? It's a few miles from the parking lot."

"Sure. I could use a break, too."

"Thank you for today," I say. "I really needed this, and it was nice to have company for a change."

"We needed it, too, so I'm glad you thought to ask."

We lead the dogs to the nearby stream, letting them cool off one last time before getting back on the fire road toward the parking lot and Declan's truck. Neither one of us has much to say on the final leg of the hike back, each deep in our own thoughts.

SEVENTEEN

WHEN WE REACH the truck in the trailhead parking lot, we give Jasper and Finn more water and one final bathroom break. I wait outside the truck with them while Declan starts the engine and turns on the air conditioning. He powers down all the windows and waits for the built-up heat to dissipate before settling the dogs into the backseat for the drive home.

While we wait for the car to cool down, it's almost as if someone's flipped a switch — both our phones chime with missed call and text notifications. We look at one another questioningly. I can hear him listening to a voicemail message from Hicks, his expression darkening. He hits the call button on his mobile to return the call. I see that I've missed several calls and texts from Simone and Josh.

Hicks answers on the second ring. His voice sounds urgent over the Bluetooth connection in the truck's cab. I lean inside the open passenger window so I can hear.

"Declan, where have you been? I've been trying to reach you for hours."

"We've been hiking in Shenandoah," Declan replies. "Mobile coverage isn't great up here. We just got back to the parking lot, and our phones went crazy."

"We? Is Kate with you?"

"Yes, she's right here."

"Hey, Hicks," I chime in. "What's going on?"

"It's not good. Your video has gone viral. It's on social media and most of the local news sites." He pauses to let that sink in for a minute, and then he continues. "You've been identified as the woman in the video."

"What?" I look at Declan in disbelief as Hicks goes on.

"That's not all. The cause of death for the John Doe has been determined as massive blunt force trauma to the head."

I stumble away from the truck just in time, gasping and vomiting into the grass at the edge of the lot. Bending over, bracing my hands on my knees, I retch until my stomach is empty. Over the buzzing in my ears, I vaguely hear Declan saying, "I'll call you right back, Hicks." I breathe shallowly, fighting another wave of nausea.

A minute later he's standing next to me, holding out my water bottle. I take it from him and rinse my mouth and spit into the grass a couple of times. As I straighten up, I see Declan snapping a disposable icepack, rubbing it between his palms to activate the gel. He places it inside a bandana square and presses it to the back of my neck, holding it there. I close my eyes, feeling instantly better as the coolness hits my neck.

"Your video." That's what Hicks had called it.

It's not my video, I want to shout – it's someone else's. But whose? *Who* is doing this? And more importantly – had I possibly *killed* a man?

"You're not going to pass out on me, are you?"

I take the ice pack from him. "No, I'm okay."

Finn and Jasper begin to whine and bark in the back seat, and Declan leans his head into the truck and speaks quietly to them for a minute. They settle down, and he's back at my side, his concerned gaze sweeping over me.

Leaning back against the truck's front fender, I take a small sip of water. "I can't believe this is happening."

"It's going to be all right."

I look at Declan solemnly. "No, I don't think it is."

"Let's call Hicks back and head home."

Wordlessly, I get into the truck, and Declan closes the door behind me. I lean back against the headrest and close my eyes, the icepack clamped to my forehead with a shaking hand. Declan calls Hicks again, and we wait for the call to connect.

"Everything okay?" Hicks asks as he comes on the line.

"Kate needed a minute." An understatement if ever there was one.

"Hold on, I'm going to get Simone on the line. She's been trying to reach Kate all day, too."

There's a slight pause, and then we hear Simone's voice. "Kate, where have you been? All Josh could tell me was that you'd taken a personal day. Are you all right?"

Declan answers for me. "Simone, it's Declan. Kate's here with me, and yes, she's fine. We've been hiking in Shenandoah since early this morning and only now got your messages. Hicks gave us the basics. What else can you tell us?"

"You know about the video and the rest?"

"Yes," Declan confirms.

"Kate's been identified as a person of interest, but there's no warrant as of now. That could change, though. Kate, I've spoken with Pen, and he's arranged with Fairfax police to bring you in for an interview on Monday." When I don't reply immediately, she asks, "Are you there?"

"Yes, I'm here."

"It's going to be okay," Simone says gently. "I know it doesn't seem like it right now, but this is what Pen does, and he's managing it. We'll get you through it." Her tone changes, becomes more business-like. "What time do you expect to be back in Arlington?"

Declan replies for me. "We're going to mine since Kate's car is there. Depending on traffic, maybe five o'clock or so, I would guess."

"Kate, are you up to calling Josh to let him know what's going on? I can do it for you, but I think it might be better if he hears it directly from you."

"I'll call him," I tell her wearily.

"Let me know once you've spoken to him, okay? Call me if you need *anything*."

"Will do, Simone," Declan says. "Talk to you both later."

He ends the call and swears quietly but quite fluently, tossing his phone into the center console. I echo the sentiment, even if it's only in my head.

After a quick bathroom break at Big Meadows, we're silent for nearly the entire drive home, both of us occupied with our own thoughts. As we approach the exit off I-66, I gaze unseeingly at the stream of traffic ahead of us.

"Well, it's happened. The thing I've been dreading. At least the waiting is over."

Declan doesn't reply. Soon he's driving slowly down the long gravel driveway toward his house. He parks the truck next to my SUV and turns to me. "You'll want some privacy for the call with Josh. You can use my office, if you'd like. Best to call before it gets too late."

"Yes, I'll do it now."

The dogs bound out of the truck when Declan opens the rear doors and unlatches their harnesses, and we all walk up to the house together. He and I remove our mud-caked hiking boots and leave them on the outside door mat. He unlocks the front door and then, taking each of the muddy, wet dogs by the collar, he guides them straight through the house to the back garden and deposits them outside.

I feel grubby and disheveled, so I pick up my bag from the chair where I'd left it that morning and take it with me into the half-bath that's tucked under the stairs. After splashing some water on my face, I brush my teeth and run a comb through my hair, having mostly recovered from that lovely episode in the trailhead parking lot. Even though this won't be a FaceTime call, I need the mental boost of knowing I look presentable. The face reflected in the mirror is slightly pink from a day outdoors, but otherwise remarkably composed. I want to shout and throw things, but this isn't the time or the place. Besides, I don't think I've ever thrown anything in anger in my entire life. I bet it would feel amazing, though, if only for a second.

I take my bag and mobile and head to Declan's office in the far corner at the front of the house. After pulling up Josh's details from my contacts list, I enter his phone number into the landline on the desk and wait for the call to connect.

"Hello?"

"Josh, it's Kate. Kate Barrow."

"Kate, I've been so worried. Are you okay?" I've known Josh long enough to realize that he is genuinely concerned as my friend and as my boss, in that order.

"I'm all right. Is this a good time to talk? If you're in the car, I can call you later."

"Yes, I'm in the car, and no, you don't need to call me back. Route 7 is a parking lot, as usual, so I have all the time in the world." There is silence for a minute. "Can you please tell me what is going on?"

"Yes, but you might want to pull over for this one."

"It's that bad?"

"Yeah, Josh, it's that bad." I start talking, explaining about the attack, my injuries, the video, and finish with what I know from today's call with Hicks and Simone.

There's a silence, then I hear him take a deep breath. "I wish you'd told me all this sooner."

"I'm sorry. I wanted to put it all behind me and forget about it. I never dreamed it would turn into the nightmare that it has."

"Do you have an attorney?"

"Yes," I reassure him.

"A good one?"

"A very good one."

"I'm glad to hear it." There's silence on the line and, as it grows, I shut my eyes, knowing what he's about to say. "I had a call with David and HR this afternoon."

"They're firing me," I say flatly.

"No, no, they're not firing you. David and I went to bat for you, tried everything we could. But once your name was released, social media and the news sites got the company's name from your LinkedIn profile. Senior leadership is very worried. The optics aren't good, Kate."

"Are you kidding me? Josh, I never thought I'd hear you use the word 'optics.' After all these years, I'm nothing more than an optics problem?"

"Sorry. Poor word choice. I don't like this either. If it were up to me and David, there'd be no question. But HR's a different story. They answer to too many masters. They're putting you on a thirty-day leave of absence."

I take a deep breath, then exhale loudly. "And at the end of thirty days – then what? They *are* firing me, they're just too gutless to come right out and say it."

"When they send you the letter, please sign it. It's thirty days of paid leave. We can reassess later when all this blows over. And it will, I know."

"It's the height of proposal season, and we're already down one person. Doesn't HR understand that?" I can feel my temper flare into life. "There's no way our team can absorb two people's workloads on top of their own. Everyone's going to go ballistic when they hear this."

"I know, and we tried, I swear. But that's not HR's priority right now."

"Well, it should be, because you're going to have a mass exodus of CAs when this is all over." We're both quiet for a minute, and then I ask, slightly calmer now, "Do you want me to turn in my laptop and smart card?"

"No, there's no need for that right now. Hang onto them until this is all straightened out. Kate, I'm really sorry. For what's happened to you. For what's still happening. And for not being able to make HR see common sense."

"It's not your fault, Josh. Thank you for letting me know. I'll be in touch."

"Take care of yourself. Please let me know if there is anything – I mean *anything* – I can do to help."

"I will."

I leave my mobile on the dining table and remember that I still have the burner mobile that Hicks and Declan had loaned me in my bag, which Pen says I no longer need to use. I set it on the kitchen island, making a mental note to tell Declan I've left it there before letting myself out of the house through the French doors. Despite everything that's happened today, I can't help but smile when I step onto the patio and take in the scene before me.

Declan has taken off his socks, and he's barefoot on the now-wet lawn. Finn is leaping into the air trying to attack the jet of water coming from the hose that Declan's holding, while Jasper, whom Declan had to practically drag out of the river earlier today, is doing his utmost to avoid the water at all costs. Go figure.

"And?" He briefly turns off the nozzle as I sit down on the raised wooden patio to take off my own socks.

"Thirty-day leave of absence," I say coolly.

Declan, having worked for a similar company himself, knows the shorthand. "So, they sacked you."

"As good as. Fricking HR."

"Feel like helping out here? I could use a hand."

"Sure, if you'll show me what I need to do." I get to my feet. Maybe a distraction is exactly what I need.

He retrieves some beach towels, dog brushes, and a bottle of dog shampoo from a large resin storage bin in the corner of the patio, which the dogs immediately recognize. They start to run around the garden, barking nervously. He calls them with a low whistle, and they slink unhappily toward him, knowing what's coming next. It's all I can do not to laugh at their expressions, usually so exuberant and playful. They look like they're being led to the gallows.

For the next fifteen minutes, Finn and Jasper submit to being bathed, looking at us with sad, reproachful eyes. It's pathetic and hilarious. As soon as they're dried and we've let go of their collars, both dogs immediately chase each other around the lawn, eventually lying on their backs and rolling crazily on the grass. I look at Declan questioningly.

"One of the great mysteries of the universe. They can spend the entire day in the water, and when I get them back here to bathe them, this is what they do." He collects the wet towels and lays them out on the patio to dry, glancing out at the dogs. "Every dog I've ever owned has done the very same thing. Daft buggers," he says affectionately.

I lean back on my elbows with my legs stretched out in front of me. The warmth of the sun feels good against my damp clothes. The wet grass tickles my bare feet. My eyes close, and I'm vaguely aware of the dogs playing, Declan moving around on the patio.

"So, this Noah of yours." His voice is quiet as he sits on the wooden steps next to me.

"Not my Noah." Not anymore. But he never really had been, had he? And I'd known that from the very start. So why, then?

"Do you think he's responsible for any of this?"

I open my eyes and sit up, no longer lulled by the heat of the sun. "I'd say he's capable of being spiteful and petty. So maybe the tracker, yeah. But the other? Even for someone like Noah, I can't see it."

"Someone like Noah?"

"A jealous, controlling, egotistical asshole."

Declan's expression is impassive. "Well, that answers my next question."

"Which is?"

"Whether or not you're over him."

"There wasn't anything to get over." I hadn't been in love with Noah. If anything, I'd been in love with the idea of him. As far as I could tell, he hadn't ever been in love with anyone except himself.

"Maybe Mr. Blackstone doesn't entirely agree with you."

Well, that's just too bad for Mr. Blackstone. Even as the thought comes, Declan's observation unsettles me.

"What about you?" I ask, trying to lighten what has become a very heavy mood. "I bet you've left a trail of broken hearts behind, if the women at the gym are anything to go by."

"I think you've been out in the sun too long."

"Oh, come on. I can't even count how many women I've seen throw themselves at you during the self-defense seminars."

"They're supposed to throw themselves at me, remember?" He's trying not to laugh and failing utterly. "It's all part of the training."

I smack his shoulder harmlessly, but I'm sure he gets the message. "That's not what I'm talking about, and you know it."

"That would never happen, anyway." His expression is serious once more. When he can see that I'm not following, he explains. "Becoming involved with anyone at the gym. Any of the students. Think about it. The type of training we're doing, half the time we're rolling around on the floor on top of each other. The other half, the trainers are grabbing the students, using chokeholds, all of that. It's not pretty, and it's not elegant. Emotions can run high, especially with new students. They're reacting in real time, often for the first time, to those types of situations. We do our best to take the emotion out of it, to make it practical and rational. That doesn't always work, especially with students who might come to us after a previous assault. Literally one wrong move, one misunderstanding, and Hicks could find himself facing a 'me too' kind of lawsuit, even with all the releases and disclaimers we ask students to sign. He's drilled it into the instructors that we can't be too careful. None of us is willing to take a chance. The gym's got a great reputation, and we're not going to do anything to jeopardize what Hicks has built."

"Makes sense. But still – all those poor women," I can't resist adding. Then I have another, less humorous, thought: *No chance for you, then, Kate. You're a student, too.* Where did *that* come from? Maybe Declan's right – maybe I have been out in the sun too long.

He pointedly ignores my last comment and starts to clean up the dog-washing supplies. Once he's finished, he steps back out into the yard, away from the patio, and pulls his sodden shirt off over his head, shaking as much of the dog hair off it as he can. For the first time I notice he's wearing a silver chain around his neck, something I've never seen him wear before.

There's a small medal attached to it, resting slightly below the hollow of his throat.

"Is that a religious medal?" I ask, curious.

"It is," he says, sounding even more Irish than usual.

"Is there a Saint Declan?"

"Yes, actually, but this isn't of my namesake." He idly pulls on the medallion and runs it along the chain. "This is Saint Jude, the patron saint of lost souls ..."

"... and things almost despaired of." We both finish the phrase together.

"You're Catholic?"

"Recovering," I say dryly. "Not from my faith. Just the institution."

"Aren't we all? I went through a rough patch a while back, and Orlagh gave this to me. We Irish are a superstitious lot."

I think of the medal that's been on my keyring since my student days, more than a decade ago now. "You're not the only ones. I'd never noticed you wearing it before today, though."

"I don't wear it at the gym." He pulls his damp shirt back over his head, the medal hidden once again. "I say we hit the showers and have a proper meal. You did bring a change of clothes?"

"Yes, and I could definitely eat something."

"Make yourself at home, then. You know where the guest bath is. Shall we go out to eat?"

I raise a self-conscious hand to my still-bruised face. I'd noticed this morning that the bruises have morphed into a lovely shade of purple. "Maybe not today, thanks. The hike was one thing. I didn't care about how I looked out there. But now that we're closer to home, I don't want people to see us together and think you're somehow responsible for—this."

"For the love, Kate. The places your mind goes." He's smiling as he says it.

"Terrifying, isn't it?"

"You have no idea." I'm sure he also has no idea where my mind had gone a few minutes ago, when he'd taken off his shirt to shake it out. For the love, indeed.

EIGHTEEN

IT'S MONDAY MORNING and I'm at home. I'd barely slept last night because my mind had been on an endless loop of how today's interview might go and all the possible outcomes. I pace downstairs, straightening a magazine here, plumping a pillow there, unable to settle, before going into the kitchen.

I'd spent the weekend being as active as possible, trying to tire myself out so that I wouldn't lie awake each night, thinking. Saturday, I'd ridden my bike for a couple of hours on the W&OD trail, wondering how on earth Josh and his wife can happily cover a hundred miles some weekends. Great exercise, but not much fun when you're on your own. Sunday, I stayed closer to home and weeded all the gardens, then lugged around huge bags of topsoil and pine bark from a local garden center to perk up the flowerbeds.

It was physical, satisfying work. Still, I couldn't get images of myself being arrested and put into a cell out of my head. I don't even know what a police cell looks like, for heaven's sake. That only makes it worse, though. My imagination goes to some very strange places, none of them good.

I'm wearing my favorite trouser suit, a midnight blue double-breasted pinstripe, because it makes me feel very competent and confident. It's my power suit of choice when I'm facing off with a difficult contracting officer or internal client. I'd scrapped the idea of a skirt suit because I felt oddly vulnerable with my legs exposed. The heat be damned – government buildings have air conditioning, don't they?

My hair is straightened to within an inch of its life on this humid morning, and I've pulled it back in a navy hairband. My make-up is understated, though I have slicked on a red Chanel lipstick to lift my spirits. I love it but it might be slightly over the top for daytime. It reminds me of the shade my mother always used to wear, so I decide to wear it anyway, for good luck. What on earth would my parents think if they could see me now? It's something I can't bear thinking about.

From outside comes the sound of a heavy car door closing. Luna barks from the yard next door, and the doorbell rings. I freeze.

"Breathe." I hear Raj and Declan's voices again in my head. On unsteady legs, I move to open the door.

Simone is standing on the front porch and, behind her, I can see a late-model black Escalade idling at the curb in front of the house.

"Good morning," she says cheerily, following me into the living room. She's immaculately dressed and coiffed, as usual, wearing a perfectly-cut summer grey suit with an ice-blue blouse and square-cut diamond drop earrings. I don't recognize the designers offhand, but with Simone, labels aren't really necessary – you know by looking at her that whatever she's wearing probably cost a month of your salary and then some.

"Is there anything special I need to bring with me?"

"Just your driver's license. Are you ready?"

I nod and go back to the kitchen to get my handbag. As I slowly walk back to where Simone is waiting, I look around my comfortable, cozy home, wondering if I'll be coming back here tonight, and then I stop myself. That way madness lies, and right now, more than ever, I need to keep a clear head. I take another long look around, feel Simone's hand on my arm.

"We need to leave."

We cross the dew-damp lawn toward the waiting vehicle. As the black-clad driver holds open the door, I take one final look back at my house. My home. Then I'm in the back seat of the Escalade, fastening my seat belt, sitting stiffly next to Simone.

"Good morning, Catherine." Pen greets me heartily from the front passenger seat.

The driver meets my gaze in the rearview mirror and says, "Good morning, Miss Barrow. I'm Gabe. There's juice and water in the console. If you need anything, please ask."

I direct an overly-bright smile to the two men in the front seat. "Good morning, Pen. Nice to meet you, Gabe. I think I'm good for now."

Gabe expertly guides the enormous SUV through the back streets of Arlington on the way to I-66 west and the McLean District police station.

THE CLOSER WE GET to our destination, the faster my heart beats. I take a steadying breath. Simone reaches for my hand and grips it tightly as Gabe parks the vehicle.

"Pen is the best, and he's got your back."

"I know."

When I rummage in my bag for lipstick, my hand closes over an unfamiliar item, something I hadn't put there. Eventually the tumblers all click into place in my brain, and I realize what I'm holding. I open my hand to reveal a silver medal on a matching heavy silver chain.

Declan. How did he manage that?

"What's that?"

I open my palm more fully to show her.

"I didn't know you were religious."

"I'm not." Not really. Until I am. I say a silent fervent prayer that whatever miracles Pen can't work, that St. Jude can. Briefly closing my hand tightly around the medal for a few beats, I drop it back into my bag and snap the clasp firmly closed.

I force myself to smile at Simone now. "Thanks for not wearing your navy pinstripe today."

"Yeah, I figured you'd go with your favorite power suit," she says, now grinning at me. "Knock 'em dead."

As we both realize the incredibly bad taste of what she's said, she claps her hand over her mouth, and we stare at one in another in horror. Then we collapse into nervous giggles. "Not funny, Simone."

"I know, right? I'm a terrible friend."

We're both so exhausted and stressed, we can't help ourselves. It's like laughing in church and not being able to stop. She pulls some tissues out of her bag, hands one to me, and we both dab at our eyes, sniffling.

Pen smiles indulgently at us, like we're two misbehaving children. "If you ladies are done, I think we need to get in there, Catherine, and kick some proverbial ass, don't you?"

NINETEEN

"THIS IS ALL merely a formality, Catherine." Pen's tone is reassuring as we make our way from the SUV to the police station's entrance. "We'll have you back home in no time." I give him a grateful look, knowing that he's likely done this hundreds of times in his career and that for him, it's a walk in the park. Not so much for me, though, and my stomach flutters nervously as he holds open the door.

Picking up a beige wall-mounted phone in the lobby, he gives the duty sergeant our names and the name of the lead detective on the case. He's politely asked to take a seat while Detective Nguyen is notified of our arrival. In most places, Pen's name would turn heads and have folks bowing and scraping but not necessarily here in Fairfax County, which has its fair share of millionaires and people of influence.

It's a full thirty minutes before we're approached by a tall Asian woman in a nondescript navy trouser suit. She's about my age, with straight black hair shot through with grey, cut in a chin-length bob. I notice she's wearing minimal jewelry, only a leather-banded wristwatch and a wedding ring. She surprises me by holding out her hand and directing her greeting to me rather than to Pen, who stands protectively at my side, looking slightly amused at playing second fiddle.

"Ms. Barrow, I'm Detective Christine Nguyen. Thank you for coming in today." She turns to Pen, and the two of them greet each other and shake hands. From their demeanor, it appears they know each other, but I don't sense any overt hostility between them, which is something of a relief.

"My colleague, Detective Henson, has been delayed this morning, and he'll be joining us shortly. If you'll please follow me." She leads us from the bustling waiting area down a quieter corridor, stopping at a door with a large pane of reinforced glass.

The interview room that Detective Nguyen leads us into isn't quite as grim as I'd imagined, given that my only previous knowledge has been from television police dramas and movies. I was expecting dingy cinderblock walls painted a sickly, faded yellow, and a scarred utilitarian table bolted to the floor, surrounded by four hard plastic molded chairs with metal legs. Overhead, there would be six-foot fluorescent tubes providing harsh, unflattering illumination. And of course, one of the lights, always, would be flickering and buzzing, on the verge of burning out. The kind of space that gives off an 'Abandon hope, all ye who enter here' kind of vibe.

The room we enter is a step up from that, but only slightly. The space reminds me of the bland training rooms every person in corporate America or every community college student is familiar with: thin industrial-grade grey carpet tiles cover the floor, a four-person laminate-topped table in the same shade sits in the center of the room, and yes, there are four hard plastic molded chairs, two on each long side of the table. The lighting is also an improvement from what I expected; the same bright LED recessed lights that were in the lobby illuminate the ten-foot by ten-foot room.

The walls are grey – surprise, surprise – and the one personal touch is a colorful box of tissues on the corner of the table alongside a cup of pens and pencils. Perhaps it's not quite as depressing as what I was expecting, but it's still not exactly an inspiring space. I shudder to think what an actual interrogation room would look like compared with this delightful little setting.

Pen graciously pulls out a chair for me, ever the solicitous old-school gentleman, and I sit down stiffly, murmuring my thanks. He seats himself next to me and opens his Montblanc notebook, while I put my bag in my lap and try to relax my death grip somewhat. I notice there isn't a recorder in this room, although the large windows on an interior wall do look like they're two-way glass.

My attorney seems quite content to sit quietly while we wait for Detective Henson and makes no attempt at pleasantries or casual conversation to fill the silence. My strained nerves have just about had it by the time Henson appears fifteen minutes later, flinging open the door and entering the room.

"Detective Bill Henson," he says by way of introduction. He sits down heavily in the chair beside Detective Nguyen, making no apologies for his delayed arrival. He's kept us waiting and his attitude borders on rude – not the best of first impressions. But then, he's not the one being questioned here – I am. He obviously doesn't give a rat's ass what we think of him.

Henson is perhaps in his early forties, of average height and build, with dark brown hair and a neat mustache. His suit is sharply pressed and creased, and his gaze is equally sharp.

Pen kicks things off. "I realize this interview isn't being recorded, but I would like the record to show that my client is here voluntarily. She has made herself available in response to social media and news accounts suggesting that she's a person of interest. This relates to an incident that allegedly took place within the county's jurisdiction earlier this month. My client is not under suspicion, nor is there a warrant pending for her arrest."

It's a statement, not a question. Henson looks annoyed but says nothing to Pen in reply.

"Ms. Barrow," Henson begins.

I interrupt him. "It's 'Miss,' actually." I never use 'Miss' when given the option of a title, but this guy's attitude has already put my back up. I'm bristling at *any* assumptions he might have made, might be making, about me.

"*Miss* Barrow, then. Will you tell us where you were on the evening of July 14th?"

I don't reply but defer to Pen as he and I had discussed when I'd met with him and Simone last week.

"Detective Henson, it's our understanding that Fairfax County Police are in possession of a video purporting to show

Miss Barrow being attacked in a local parking facility. We're requesting to view the unedited footage at this time. Since the video has been released to the public, I assume the county has no objections to our request."

The younger detective tries unsuccessfully to hide his annoyance.

"We are also requesting the details of the video's metadata," Pen continues. "As you're well aware, detectives, pictures and videos are no longer worth a thousand words. In many cases, with the advent of artificial intelligence and deep fakes, they're completely worthless. The metadata will help to shed some light on the origins of this purported video." When neither of the detectives responds or makes a move, Pen prompts, "If you have no objection?" We can both tell that they object very much, but they grudgingly comply with Pen's request.

Detective Henson looks impatient while Detective Nguyen passes Pen an iPhone. Pen turns up the volume and taps the forward arrow to play the video. We watch in silence as the same footage we've already seen plays out, and I sense the two detectives watching me closely.

When the video ends, Pen hands the phone back to Detective Nguyen. "How did the county come to be in possession of this video?"

"It was sent to us through the Fairfax County Crime Solvers website," she admits reluctantly.

"An anonymous tip?" Pen asks.

"Yes."

"How convenient for you. And the video's metadata? What information do you have as to the date, time, location, and type of device used?"

Detective Nguyen sighs and consults her notepad. "There was no location data associated with the video, which was recorded using an iPhone 13. It appears to have been created on July 14th of this year."

"So this video could have been taken anywhere?" Pen contends.

She hesitates before replying. "Yes, that's correct."

"Given that my client does have a social media presence, albeit limited, it is possible that a public image of her has been manipulated and used to create this footage?" Pen's tone suggests that he's asking a question, but we all know that he's stating a fact.

"That is possible," Detective Nguyen grudgingly admits. "But not likely," she adds in an attempt to discredit Pen's suggestion.

"What motive would someone have in creating this video?" Detective Henson asks.

Pen looks frankly insulted. "Please, Detective. For the express purpose of implicating my client in a crime. Or simply because he or she could. In this brave new world of social media, as it were, it's all about likes and clicks, is it not? Videos are the new online currency, and who knows to what lengths someone will go in order to attract viewers or subscribers?"

For a few minutes, it appears we've reached an impasse, and we're all silent, looking at each other across the table.

"Would either of you like something to drink?" Detective Nguyen eventually asks.

Pen waves a hand in the negative. "Nothing for me, thank you, Detective."

"I'd like some water, please," I say.

The detective leaves the room briefly before returning with a store-brand bottle of water. I accept it with thanks, the flimsy plastic crinkling as I grip the bottle and remove the cap.

"Miss Barrow," Detective Henson asks, "will you please explain why on the night of the incident, possibly having been viciously attacked, you didn't report it to the police?" His gaze lingers meaningfully on the healing cuts on my cheek and eyebrow, the fading bruises that aren't quite concealed by my makeup.

I look at Pen, who nods, and I address both the detectives. "Detectives, I was brought up to respect members of law enforcement and first responders. It must be a difficult and sometimes dangerous job." I take a sip of water and continue. "Police cruisers no longer display the motto, 'To protect and serve,' and for good reason. I read recently that the Fairfax County police department alone has nearly two hundred vacancies they're unable to fill, and it's a huge county. It's almost impossible for such a short-handed force to adequately do their jobs when violent crimes are on the rise. I, for one, have never been under the impression that the police would be able to *protect* me, should the need ever arise." I direct that last comment directly to Detective Henson, since he and I are hitting it off so well. Or not. "Detective, are you familiar with the Fairfax County police department's closure rate for aggravated assaults last year?"

He looks briefly uncomfortable at my question. "No, not offhand, but I could get that information fairly quickly."

"Then let me enlighten you, Detective. The effective closure rate last year for this type of alleged crime was eighteen percent. Eighteen percent." I let the number sink in for a moment. "Do you really think it's worth a taxpayer's time and aggravation to report a crime when there's only an eighteen percent chance the perpetrator will be identified and prosecuted?"

The detective shoots me a look of pure venom, then recovers himself. "But you weren't aware of these statistics the night of the alleged attack, were you? Maybe you have a more personal reason for your obvious animosity toward law enforcement?"

I feel the blood drain from my face. Pen looks at me questioningly, and I shake my head, just once. We both wait for the detective to continue.

"We're aware of the unfortunate situation regarding your parents' deaths many years ago."

The color that had drained from my face a moment ago now rushes back; I can feel the heat rise up my neck and into my cheeks. With some effort, I fight to control my temper. "Leave my parents out of this, Detective. They have nothing to do with what we're here to discuss today."

Pen quietly clears his throat next to me, and I force myself to calm down.

"When a drunk driver responsible for the deaths of two people walks free due to the mishandling of evidence, that's more than an unfortunate situation," I say. "It's an inexcusable miscarriage of justice, and you know it." I glare at both detectives, no longer even attempting to hide my contempt. "May I remind you that I'm not suspected of committing any criminal offense. If this is how potential crime *victims* are treated by your department, I can understand the public's current disillusion with law enforcement."

Pen chooses that moment to speak, diplomatically attempting to defuse the situation. "On the subject of law enforcement and the reporting of a suspected crime, Ms. Barrow has reported a recent incident to the Arlington County police department." He slides a piece of paper across the desk to the detectives. "This is a copy of the report Ms. Barrow filed in connection with an AirTag that was discovered on her vehicle three days after the alleged incident. Someone had willfully and knowingly tracked Ms. Barrow's vehicle without her knowledge or consent."

The two detectives stare at me and Pen for a few minutes. I take a long swallow of water in the quiet room, waiting for someone to speak.

Detective Nguyen finally breaks the silence. "Are you trained in martial arts, Miss Barrow? Your actions in the video would suggest so."

"I'm five foot three in my bare feet, Detective Nguyen," I acknowledge, addressing the female detective directly. "That means I'm a lot smaller than the average male. So yes, I have taken some self-defense classes, but I don't hold any certifications or belts. My goal is to be as prepared as possible in case I ever need to defend myself. Is that now a crime in this country, Detective?"

She flushes slightly and shakes her head. "No, Miss Barrow, it is not a crime to use reasonable force in self-defense. It is, however, a crime to use excessive or unreasonable force." She pauses for effect, and her next words would have had more of an impact if I hadn't already known, hadn't already been expecting them.

"The man in the video is dead, Miss Barrow."

Pen interrupts. "If I may ask, what was the alleged victim's cause of death?" Which he already knows.

"The victim died as a result of blunt force trauma to the head," Detective Henson answers grimly.

"While any man's death is a tragedy, Detective, we find it interesting that this anonymous video, which appears to implicate my client in the alleged victim's death, doesn't show the precise action that led to his death. So perhaps, detectives, you have a great deal more work to do. Work that, I would suggest, does not involve my client." His tone turns cold. "In the future, you might consider not publicly identifying a private citizen as a person of interest before you have all the facts. In doing so, you have exposed my client to adverse public scrutiny and malicious speculation. You have also caused her to be placed on a leave of absence from her longtime employer. There may be legal grounds to pursue a case of defamation of character."

There is silence as the two detectives consider Pen's words.

"I trust you have no further questions for my client, detectives?" His voice is smooth.

The detectives exchange a look before Detective Henson replies. "No, Mr. Wainwright, we don't have any further questions at this time. Ms. – *Miss* – Barrow, if you can think of anything you'd like to share, here's my card." He places a business card on the table and slides it across to me. I don't take it, though; I merely look at Pen, who picks up the card and places it in his notebook.

When I finish the last of the water and place the cap back on the bottle, Detective Nguyen holds out her hand, reaching for the bottle. "I can take that for you."

I flatten the flimsy plastic bottle with a satisfying crunch. "No, thanks, Detective. I'm perfectly capable of disposing of my own trash."

My satisfaction is short-lived when Detective Nguyen replies. "Yes, Miss Barrow. That's exactly what we're afraid of."

Pen looks over at me and back at the two detectives. "I think we're through here." He stands and pulls back my chair so that I can get up from the table, and he picks ups his notebook. Taking my arm, he escorts me out of the interview room.

Neither of us speaks as we make our way through the building. I notice some heads turning as a few county employees and patrons recognize Pen as we pass by. He keeps us moving until we're back out in the bright sunshine. I shield my eyes from the light as they adjust to the brightness and take in a deep, shaky, breath.

Pen glances down at me as we approach the waiting SUV. "I'm sorry about your parents, Catherine."

"Thank you. You already knew, didn't you?"

"I did. I make it my business to know everything about all my clients."

"I would've mentioned it if I'd thought it was relevant."

"If anything, it helps our case. Gives more credence to why you didn't call the police or file a report." His eyes brighten with mischief. "Where did you get those statistics on closed aggravated assault cases?"

"From the FBI's Crime Data Explorer website. Although they may have actually been for Fairfax, Minnesota. Or was it Fairfax, Oklahoma? I can't recall."

He shakes his head in amazement, his eyes meeting mine. "Now I understand."

"Understand what?"

"Why you and my goddaughter get along so well. Your talents are completely wasted in contracts."

"You have no idea."

Despite my nonchalant words to Pen, my stomach is clenching at Detective Nguyen's parting comment.

That's exactly what we're afraid of.

I'm afraid of a lot more than that.

TWENTY

GABE PULLS THE Escalade up in front of my house, and I profusely thank both men for their help today. Pen promises to be in touch with any news. Gabe opens my door and assists me down from the SUV's high step, and I make my way wearily up the walk, Simone at my side.

"Kate."

I turn at the sound of my name.

Declan is standing at the curb across the street from the house. He has Finn and Jasper with him, and they're both pulling on their leads in our direction, having recognized me and Simone.

My friend gives me a sideways glance, one eyebrow raised. "Anything you'd like to share with the class?"

"If I did, you'd be the first to know."

Declan nods a greeting to Simone as he crosses the street and joins us on the path to the front door. "It must've gone well. You're home, at least."

"Maybe not 'well,' but they're done with me for now. Come on in, and I'll tell you about it."

As we all step inside the cool, shuttered house, I feel nearly weak with relief at being home. I had spent only a few hours at the police station, but it felt like an eternity. Simone and I both shed our suit jackets and step out of our shoes; I sigh with pleasure at the coolness of the wide floorboards on my bare feet. Whoever invented high heels must never have had to wear the wretched things.

"You made quite an impression on Pen today," Simone says when we've settled ourselves at the kitchen table with glasses of iced tea. "He couldn't get over your throwing the closed case statistics at the detectives."

I smile back at her. "Pen and I were civil initially, but that went out the window pretty quickly. I'd gone in voluntarily and they made me feel like a criminal. I could tell Detective Henson wasn't happy at all to see the great Penfield Wainwright in the interview room with me, so at least there's that."

She looks very pleased with herself. "I bet he wasn't."

"Simone, thank you for referring me to Pen. I could be sitting in a jail cell right now if it weren't for you."

"He's something, isn't he?"

"He certainly is."

I vaguely register Simone and Declan talking in the background. My mind has gone somewhere else, and I hear Declan's voice asking, "Are you with us, Kate?"

I'm not. All I can think of is Detective Nguyen's comment as we left. They obviously think that I'm capable of having killed a man. I'm beginning to think so, too, if the cause of death is correct.

But the video. I'm missing something crucial here, aside from the very obvious fact that someone has it in for me.

Two questions: Who? And why?

What possible motive would someone have for trying to set me up? It doesn't make sense. Until a few weeks ago, I'd have sworn on my life that I didn't have an enemy in the world. Because quite frankly, I don't think anyone would feel that strongly about me, one way or the other. But to attack and then frame me for killing a man?

Out of nowhere, a phrase comes to me: Beyond the pale. Thinking back to my student days, I recall how fascinated my small post-grad cohort and I had been with the etymology of words and expressions. We were a motley group of UK and international students, and it fascinated us no end to learn and share the origin of archaic and modern words.

Beyond the pale. There are multiple historical references to pales, including an area of Ireland that was under the control of the English between the late twelfth and sixteenth centuries. It can also refer to a stake that may have been used as part of a fence or barrier. In the example of the Irish and English, anything not within the pale was considered lawless and to be outside the protection of the crown.

The modern meaning signifies an act beyond the boundaries of acceptable behavior. And this truly is. Who could witness my being attacked without stepping in and, then possibly, *likely*, kill my attacker in order to frame me? Who could hate me so much? Or was I making it all about me when it really wasn't? I can't see it. For someone who's accustomed to solving problems – solving everyone else's problems – it's absolutely maddening not to be able to solve my own.

"Yes, sorry," I reply belatedly when I realize that he and Simone are both looking at me.

Another phrase springs to mind and I say it now to Simone. "*Cui bono?*"

"Who benefits?" she asks, familiar with the phrase from law school.

"Yes. Who benefits if I'm charged with manslaughter or negligent homicide or whatever, and why?" I get up from the table, too full of nervous energy to sit still. I stand instead, leaning slightly against the kitchen island. "Let's think about this. Why did it happen when it did? Did something trigger it, trigger this person? I'd been on vacation, having a great time. Then I came back, and suddenly everything hits the fan. I don't get it."

"Fucking Noah, probably, still ticked off about your dumping him," Simone says. "I wouldn't put it past him to hire some goon to do his dirty work for him."

"Tracking Kate's car is one thing. Hiring some low-life to attack her is on an entirely different level." Declan's tone is suddenly icy.

"Tracking Kate's car?" Simone looks astonished. "Someone tracked your car? When was this? And why does he know about this and I don't? No offense, Dublin," she says offhandedly to Declan.

"None taken." He seems to take her nickname for him in his stride.

"It was a few days after I was attacked. Declan knows because we found the tracker while I was at the gym. And I didn't tell you because you'd be giving me the look you're giving me right now."

Simone seems to recover quickly, but knowing her, she won't let it drop that easily. She'll wait to bring it up when it's only the two of us. "Maybe it's work. Maybe it's connected to Ares and Anne Marie," she suggests. "The timing works." She thinks about it for a minute, then waves her hand dismissively. "I'm just throwing pasta at the wall. Don't listen to me."

"What's Ares, and who's Anne Marie?" asks Declan.

"I think I mentioned Anne Marie to you," I tell him. "The contracts colleague who died?" I give him a quick rundown of everything that had happened on Ares in the short time I'd been responsible for the contract.

"It's a complete shitshow." As usual, Simone is brutally honest.

"Uh-huh. But it's not *my* shitshow anymore."

Declan looks at me. "I do remember your mentioning Anne Marie. Car wreck, wasn't it?"

"Yes." I feel like I'm working on a jigsaw puzzle — of which I am not a fan, by the way — trying to force a piece into a place where it obviously doesn't fit. "But you might be right, Simone. I mean, do we know for sure than Anne Marie's accident was an accident?"

"Sorry, my friend, but I think you've read one too many thrillers," Simone replies. Declan looks amused. He must have come across dozens of thrillers and crime novels in his exploration of my bookshelves. You can't be expected to read great literature and the classics all the time, can you?

"What if the two things are somehow related? Do you have a better explanation?"

"No, I don't. But don't mistake coincidence for causation." I recognize Simone's lawyer's voice.

"Declan, do you know if Hicks has any contacts in the National Park Police? They have jurisdiction over the GW Parkway, right?"

"They do. I've no idea if Hicks has any contacts there, but it'd be easy enough to ask him."

I glance at my watch and am surprised at how late it is. "Is that the time already? Simone, don't you have a meeting this afternoon? You can use my office if you want to take it from here."

She agrees that she does but declines my offer to stay. Once she's arranged for an Uber ride, she retrieves her shoulder bag and suit jacket and steps gracefully into her heels, power-suited once again.

"Do you mind if I stay for a minute?" Declan asks. "There are a couple of things I want to ask you."

"No, I don't mind. I want to change out of these clothes, though."

Simone, catching our exchange, tilts her head thoughtfully as she glances at me and Declan. With a straight face she says, "Fifty thousand, my friend. Fifty thousand dollars says you're wrong." She gives me a quick hug, saying, "Later," and sails out the door to her waiting Uber, leaving us speechless in her wake. As always.

"What was that all about?" Declan asks.

"Oh, just Simone being Simone. You get used to it."

"How does her husband cope?" He looks suitably bewildered.

"He's absolutely head-over-heels in love with her," I tell him by way of explanation. "Well, that, and alcohol helps, too, I imagine."

～

TEN MINUTES LATER, after changing into a sundress and flat sandals, I join Declan and the dogs on the sun porch. With the shades drawn, the porch is a comfortable spot despite the afternoon's heat.

"I don't know how you managed it, but thank you for giving me this." I hand him the St. Jude medal and chain.

"I didn't think it could hurt, in any event. And you can do something for me in return."

I look at him expectantly.

"You can tell me everything you know about Ares."

"Ares? Why?"

"Humor me."

"All right. It would be better if I showed you, though. Let's go to my office."

"They haven't cut off your access, even though you're on a leave of absence?" Declan looks skeptical once we're sitting at my desk and I enter my user details into Tate Walker's intranet.

"Only one way to find out. Nearly everything we need is on government websites anyone can access, though. Okay, I'm in. Here we go." I scroll through the contracts database to find what I'm looking for. "Here's a brief description from the statement of work as to what the project is." I give Declan a few minutes to read through the page, then continue. "We've got a bunch of subcontractors, and I checked them all out using a couple of government websites and our financial reporting system."

"Show me your data sources."

I start with the financials, walking him through what I've found, and he nods, satisfied. "Next?"

I pull up the federal procurement website, explain its purpose and the information I've compiled from it. "You're probably familiar with this from your days as a government contractor, right?"

"Somewhat. We left that to our contracts team, for the most part. We were focused on doing the work and didn't get too involved in these details."

I switch screens and display the government's award management website. As I scroll down the page, Declan asks, "What's this?" pointing to a heading titled 'Entity Information.'

"That's all the pertinent information regarding a company or an individual. Name, business size, location, reps and certs, that sort of thing."

"What's an exclusion in this context?"

"That's when a company or individual is prohibited from doing business with the government for a specified period of time. You might know it as a debarment. This is where the shitshow began, as Simone called it." I pull up Michelangelo Enterprises and show him the details of the debarment.

"Where's the owner information?"

"Here." Instead of a person's name, the owner is listed as 'Medici Holdings.'

"They're using a holding company, which isn't unusual." Declan types on his phone. "If Medici isn't registered with the secretary of state, I'll have some homework to do."

"You don't honestly think this is related to what happened to me, do you?"

"No, I don't. It's best to eliminate all the obvious things first, though. And if the police consider you a suspect and not a victim, chances are they're not going to be doing much investigating on your behalf. I'd say we're on our own here."

WE TAKE THE DOGS out back for a run around the yard, still thinking about what we've just discovered. Animated barking erupts from the opposite side of the adjoining fence, which sets off Jasper and Finn. They race over to the gate, sniffing and whining with excitement. I hear Diane talking to Luna.

"Kate, are you there?" she calls out.

"Hey, Diane. Yes, I'm here. Come on through, but brace yourself."

There's a slight delay, then the gate between our properties swings open. Comically, Jasper and Finn race into Diane's yard, and Luna runs into mine, which she thinks is an extension of her own. All three dogs eventually end up on my side of the fence, sniffing and greeting one another, tails wagging happily. No doggy drama or territorial issues to sort out, thankfully, just three, big, exuberant dogs excited to make new friends.

Diane is carrying a cake plate and wearing a broad smile as she attempts to keep out of the fray. "You did try to warn me, didn't you?"

"I did. Sorry about that." I haven't seen much of Diane since I'd returned from my trip, and I'm pleased she's come by, even though her timing might not be the best.

Diane is in her late sixties, I'd say, and is nearly a head taller than I am, with a trim, athletic build and the tanned complexion of someone who spends a lot of time outdoors. She runs religiously and is a keen gardener – a love she and my mother had shared. She is the best kind of neighbor to have – someone who keeps a general eye on things but who knows when to keep her distance. She also bakes for her church —

and the entire neighborhood — and is legendary for the killer margaritas she brings to our summer block parties.

She eyes Declan, who's stepped back toward the house, away from the frolicking dogs. "Diane Bradford. I live next door."

I remember my manners, rush forward with introductions. "Diane, this is Declan. Declan, my neighbor, Diane."

They shake hands, and she offers me the plate. "It's your mother's cherry almond cake, but it's just an excuse, really. I watched that video that's been going around online, and I wanted to check on you. I can see there was no need for me to worry. There isn't, is there? You're all right?"

I try not to visibly wince at the mention of the video, but at least her bringing it up does answer the question of just how viral it's gone. "Yes, Diane. I'm all right."

"Word is you didn't call the police when it happened. You and I know why you didn't, but that doesn't look good for you." We exchange a long look. She glances past me as if remembering that Declan is here. "We'll talk later."

I release a breath I hadn't known I was holding. "Thanks for the cake, Diane. And for checking in." The polite thing to do would be to invite her to join us for cake and a cold drink. Then I remember that Declan doesn't like sweets, and I hesitate. But he's a grown man and can make his own excuses. "Join us?" I finally manage.

"No, thanks. I have plenty of my own in the kitchen. You two enjoy, and we can catch up another time. Nice meeting you, Declan."

"And you, Diane. Watch those two on your way out. They might try to make a run for it over to your side."

"It's fine. Leave the gate open as long as you'd like. Maybe it'll tire them all out if we let them play for a while." She disappears through the gate with a cheery wave.

We do as Diane suggests and leave the dogs to it while we return to the relative quiet of the house.

"Your mother's recipe, she said. You've been neighbors all this time?"

"Yeah. She and my mother were pretty close. They had a lot in common, I guess. Successful, educated women. Neither of them afraid to speak her mind. It made for some very lively dinner-table conversations when I was growing up."

"Is Diane a professor, too?"

I laugh. "Um, no. Diane is CIA. She doesn't talk about it, naturally. She wasn't the only one in my parents' circle of friends who was, so no one made a big deal out of it. I think she's been bored since her husband, Vince, died last year. We visit and catch up every now and then, but it's not the same kind of friendship she and my mother had."

"How was it really, this morning?" he asks.

I glance at the clock. Not five o'clock yet – not by a long shot. Screw it. I open the wine fridge and pull out a bottle of Sancerre, gesturing for Declan to follow me into the sunroom.

Then I give him the highlights of our friendly chat with the two charming detectives.

HE ACCEPTS MY invitation to stay for an early supper since we both missed lunch. We take the path of least resistance in the heat and place an Uber Eats order from my favorite neighborhood Thai place. Jasper and Finn have been fed and are passed out on the tile floor of the sunroom after their impromptu play date with Luna, which went on for much longer than I'd expected. Diane had sneakily filled Luna's wading pool, and it kind of escalated from there. I'm exhausted from just having watched them.

Now Declan calls to the dogs for one final trip outside before the drive home.

I've loaded the dishwasher and am wiping down the kitchen table and counter top, moving Declan's keyring in the process. As I set it back down on the counter, I notice a man's wedding band, silver or platinum, threaded among the keys. It glints up at me in the bright overhead LED lights of the kitchen. Why would Declan have a wedding band on his keyring?

At that moment, the dogs come bounding in through the sunroom, happily heading for their water bowls and their beds, which Declan had brought with them for today's visit.

I gesture to the keyring. "Is that your wedding band?"

"Yes." He looks at me with an expression that I can't quite read. Not exactly sadness, or guilt, or regret. Perhaps a small measure of all of them.

"Have you been divorced for long?" I immediately wish I could take back the words but it's too late. "Sorry, I shouldn't have asked. It's none of my business."

"It's all right; it's not a secret. But I'm not divorced."

TWENTY-ONE

NOT DIVORCED.

It feels as though the bottom has dropped out of everything. Like that horrible carnival ride where you spin and spin before the floor drops out, with only centripetal force keeping you pinned to the wall. The one that always leaves me wanting to throw up.

"I'm not divorced," he says again. "I'm widowed."

I slowly turn around to face him, hardly able to believe what I've heard. "Widowed? Declan, I'm so sorry. I had no idea."

He shakes his head ruefully. "There's no way you could have, is there? And it's been more than ten years now." There is an awkward silence as he picks up his keys and looks at them for a long moment, then puts them in his jeans pocket. "I don't suppose you have any whiskey? This could take a while, and I might need more than coffee for this." One eyebrow lifts in that expression I'm starting to recognize.

"Actually, I do." It takes less than a minute to fetch a bottle of Irish whiskey from the bar cart in the living room and bring it back to the kitchen.

Declan gives an ironic smile when he sees the familiar label. "Expanding your horizons?"

"Something like that. Let's sit on the sun porch." Declan takes the bottle, and I follow him with two tumblers.

"You haven't opened it yet."

"Waiting for the right moment, I guess."

He doesn't say anything as he pours two fingers in his glass and one in mine. I watch as he takes a generous sip. Then he begins. "Her name was Cara, and we met at university back home in Galway."

It's very quiet at this hour, with only the night sounds of crickets and distant traffic to disturb the stillness.

"We met in the lunch queue at a campus coffee shop. She was in her first year, and I was in my last. She was studying art, and I was finishing my software degree. It was completely by chance that our paths even crossed. I mostly spent my days studying and nights and weekends working in my parents' pub. She was into the whole arts scene and was very outgoing, was always with a crowd of friends. She lit up every place she entered. I hadn't had many girlfriends before we met, and I couldn't understand why she'd even looked at me."

I think absurdly that the female population of Galway in the 90's needed to have their heads examined, because, really? He hadn't had many girlfriends? What the hell had been wrong with those young women? Software geek or not, the man looks like, well, *this*.

"We started to date and became inseparable, except for when we had to be in lectures and tutorials. We were both from Galway, living at home, and by the time she'd gotten her degree, we'd saved enough money for our first flat. We moved in together and got married not long afterwards. I had a decent job, and Cara was making a name for herself as an up-and-coming young artist. She'd already had a few exhibitions with a local gallery."

"At first, everything was grand. When I received a job offer to move to the States, Cara was thrilled. She'd heard about the arts scene there and loved the idea of living in America. All her friends were mad with envy and couldn't wait to come and visit."

The dogs are sleeping quietly on their beds. The night beyond the sunroom is still; the only sound I'm aware of is Declan's voice.

"Cara was in her element in Seattle. She found a job in a small gallery and continued to paint and did quite well. Those first several years in America were brilliant. We made a lot of friends, and family and friends from back home came to visit. But what I didn't realize at the time, and what I might have noticed if I hadn't been working so much myself, was that Cara had started using drugs. Probably weed at first, although it wasn't yet legal in Washington state back then. It didn't matter. The crowd she ran with seemed to always have a supply of something. I didn't learn that until later."

He runs a hand distractedly through his dark hair. "If I'd been paying more attention and hadn't been so caught up with my own work, I might've seen the changes. Seen that it was more than the occasional joint at a party or a gallery event. She never used at home or in front of me. It had never been part of my life, and for a time, I never suspected. I'd call her out on it when she came home reeking of it. She'd say that someone else had been smoking, and it was easier to let it go. I've never been one for confrontation, and I took her word for it."

"Declan, you don't have to tell me all this."

"I want to." But his eyes remain fixed on a point in the distance, past even the gardens and the tree line beyond. Thousands of miles and many years away from now.

I think back to our drive to Shenandoah, when I'd stoically told him the story of my parents' deaths. Staring out the truck window, unable to make eye contact. So I understand. As we continue to gaze unseeingly into the night, he continues his story.

"It was Orlagh who noticed and commented on it first. She'd studied medicine and had started her residency at one of the big teaching hospitals in Dublin, where there was more of a drug problem. She'd been exposed to a lot of users and addicts, knew the signs. She'd come for a visit and asked me if I'd suspected Cara was using. Cara had always had a lot of nervous energy, but she'd gotten almost manic by that point.

Of course, I denied it. Orlagh didn't want to start a row, so she let it drop."

"I told you a few colleagues and I decided to leave our jobs and start our own software company, yes? Once we got a couple of small-business loans and other backing, things moved more quickly than we'd ever expected. With all the new government contracts we were getting, my partners and I decided to move the business to DC."

"Was Cara happy about the move?"

He shook his head. "We started to argue. We'd never rowed before – ever. Cara didn't want to move, didn't want to leave her job and her friends and the life she had in Seattle. I couldn't make her see that it was an investment in us, that we'd be much better off working for ourselves, creating our own future. She hated DC," he says flatly. "Hated the endless political chatter, the traffic, and life inside the Beltway. Everything that she loved about Seattle, she said couldn't find in DC or Northern Virginia. I accused her of not trying, of not even giving it a chance. We both said hateful things, things I'd take back in a heartbeat if I could."

I watch him take another sip of whiskey, hear him exhale on a long sigh.

"I was training some clients in a classified location and had been away for a lot longer than we'd originally planned. Nearly a month rather than two weeks. I had to stay until we were done, though; there was nothing for it. Cara got fed up with being by herself and flew to Seattle one weekend. She planned to attend a few parties, some after-hours exhibits, the sorts of things she'd loved doing when we'd lived there. We texted on the Saturday evening while she was getting ready to go out. She was excited to be back there, couldn't wait to see her old friends."

I'm waiting for him to continue but praying that he'll change his mind and stop right this minute so we can go back – back to the time before I knew any of this. But his words can't be taken back; he can't stop after having come this far.

It's the rare book I don't read through to the end, bitter or otherwise. This is one book I want to close, though, to put back on the shelf, unfinished. Because anyone can see how this story is going to end. It's inevitable, isn't it? What happens to the beautiful young heroine. And she would have been beautiful, I know.

He continues the narrative, stoically shouldering some self-imposed penance for sins that were never his to atone for. "Cara's body was found the following morning in an alleyway not far from the gallery. The police didn't think robbery was a motive since her bag was found with her body and nothing had been taken. They suspected it was probably a drug deal that had gone bad."

I shut my eyes against his words, feeling again the shock and horror of learning that my parents had been killed. In an instant, lives and worlds changed forever. It happens every day. But not to you.

"Since I was out of the country and nearly impossible to reach, the Seattle police contacted Cara's parents, asked them to fly over and identify her body. In their eyes, I'm the reason she died alone and in a strange country. They've barely spoken to me or my family since."

"Dear God." It's all I can manage to say.

"It's a long time ago now." He takes a sip, swirls the amber liquid around in the heavy-bottomed glass. "Do you know about Emma's heart condition?"

"Um, yes." I'm slightly thrown by the unexpected change of subject. "Hicks told me something about it."

He nods. "It was Hicks and his team that I was working with when Cara died. When I got the news, I could barely function, let alone work. And much like your parents' friend saved you by offering you a job, Hicks saved me by offering me his home – and the gym. I couldn't face going back to the condo Cara and I had shared in DC, so I moved in with Hicks, Elizabeth, and Emma for a while. Emma was still recuperating, and Elizabeth needed a hand with that. Hicks was thinking about retiring. In the middle of all of that, my partners and I were getting offers to sell the company."

"So much for you all to deal with."

"All of our lives were at a turning point. Hicks came up with the idea of the gym. He brought in some self-defense practitioners to train me and the original team. He was relentless, let me tell you. There were days I'm sure he wanted to drop-kick me into next week. But he didn't. He stuck with me, wouldn't let me give up. First he got me into shape. Then he taught me self-defense, the focus and the discipline of it."

I nodded. I knew what Hicks' training had done for me.

"If it weren't for Hicks, his family, and the gym, I may have gone the way of Cara. On the wrong end of a whiskey bottle, not a crack pipe or a needle. It makes no difference in the end. The house gave me a new focus after the gym was up and running. I was helping out at Trident only part of the time, and I found the land with the buildings when I was looking for a house to buy. I'd never done anything like it before, and I learned as I went. I subbed out the electrical and the plumbing, but I put in months and months of hard graft, I'll tell you. I'd drop into bed each night more exhausted than I'd ever been in my life. It became another refuge, after the gym."

We're both silent for a minute or two. I'm still taking it all in, and Declan is – well, heaven only knows what's going on in his head. When he speaks again, his tone is less subdued, more pragmatic. "I lived to tell the tale, so they say. Here I am. Here we both are. On the other side of tragedy. Life goes on."

"It does. Sometimes whether you want it to or not." I think of the agonizing, early days after my parents' deaths, then glance at our empty glasses. "Stay tonight," I say impulsively.

Declan looks at his own glass before replying. "I'm hardly over the limit."

He's not, but I must be, if my last maudlin observation is anything to go by. I should never have mixed whiskey and wine tonight. "As a wise man once said to me, 'Humor me, will you?' It's late, we've had a long day, and I have a perfectly good guest room. You can leave as early as you want in the morning. I'd rather not have a DUI – or worse – on my conscience. There's enough to deal with at the moment, I'd say."

He glances back at the dogs, who are still sleeping soundly, now splayed out on the cool tile floor of the sunroom.

A momentary stand-off.

"All right, I'll stay. In that case—" He reaches for the whiskey bottle.

I SLIP BENEATH the cool sheets with a sigh of exhaustion, knowing that even as weary as I am, sleep won't come easily. When I'd gotten up this morning, my only concern had been my interview with the detectives. Declan's story had unsettled me far more than my own situation. What an incredible waste of a young woman's life. I can feel the beginnings of a headache tightening the back of my skull. I silently will the pain away.

My hand is on the lamp switch, ready to turn it off, when I see Finn standing in the doorway. A minute later, Declan appears, holding Finn's bed.

"I should've known he'd end up in here. Do you mind?"

"Of course not."

He sets the dog bed beneath the window on the far side of the bedroom and watches, arms crossed, as Finn takes his time getting comfortable.

"Good night, Declan."

"Good night."

Declan can't have made it halfway down the hall when Finn jumps up and lands on my bed with an audible thud. I stifle a giggle when Declan says, "I heard that, Finnegan." But he doesn't tell the dog to get back on his bed, so I let him stay with an encouraging pat. He curls up happily at my feet.

Two minutes later, Declan's back in the doorway, holding Jasper's bed, the retriever now at his side. "Who knew dogs had fear of missing out?" His tone is exasperated, but there's humor in it, too. He sets the retriever's bed next to Finn's. Jasper ignores it and joins his buddy at my feet.

"I really don't mind. It's only for one night."

"Just so you know, you won't get any sleep." He pauses. "It's not only you I'm worried about. The daft buggers will think they're allowed on my bed from now on. This could make my life rather difficult. You do know that?"

I've since turned off the light and can't completely see his face. Just how serious is he?

He considers the scene for about thirty more seconds. "For the love, the lot of you." He walks over to the bed. "Budge up, then. Seems like the party's in here tonight."

"Maybe it's not only Jasper who has fear of missing out," I tease, moving over to give him room. When the dogs see Declan on the bed, complete chaos ensues. They climb over and between us, barking excitedly, tails wagging, delighted that their master has joined in this new game.

When the laughter and the barking die down and the room is quiet, Declan says, "You didn't have to move over quite that far." I can definitely hear the humor in his voice now. I slide closer, and he pulls me against him, holding me the way he had that awful night not so long ago.

The night I'd been attacked and Declan had offered me his embrace, I'd been looking for comfort, nothing more. Strong arms and a warm body to maybe keep the nightmares away. Tonight, he'd come to my bed, Finn and Jasper's antics notwithstanding. I can't help but wonder if he's looking for the same thing – a warm body to maybe keep the ghosts at bay.

God, what a world we live in.

The room is quiet once again, the only sounds the settling of the house, the hum of the air conditioning, and the occasional snoring of two large, very contented dogs. I'm drifting off when I hear Declan's voice, almost inaudible in the darkness.

"You'd better not get used to this."

I wonder vaguely if he's talking to the dogs. Or to me. Or to himself.

That's a worry for tomorrow, though.

We sleep. We sleep like survivors of a great shipwreck, tossed and battered and eventually spat out onto a faraway, unfamiliar shore, not quite knowing what the coming dawn will bring. But hopeful of rescue all the same.

TWENTY-TWO

I HADN'T DREAMT IT.

That's my first thought. Before I've even opened my eyes, when I hear Declan talking in low tones to Finn and Jasper, when I hear the dogs scrambling down the wooden stairs toward the kitchen at the mention of breakfast. I turn my head on the pillow, catch Declan's lingering scent where his head had been. Sandalwood. Leather. Vanilla. Unexpected here in my bedroom but strangely familiar all the same. The scent triggers a memory, then another. Last night.

Yes, there had been whiskey. On top of the wine. What had I been thinking? I know better than that, know how I'm bound to feel the next morning. But even so, I hadn't been drunk, not even close, when I'd tossed aside the covers and let Declan into my bed. Have there ever been two more screwed-up people? I mean, who does this, just sleeps together? This isn't Kent Haruf's *Our Souls at Night*, for Pete's sake. That's twice now. *Damn.* I should go down and make coffee, should offer to make breakfast, say something. I need to clear my head, though. Shower first. Conversation later.

The hot water works its magic, pounding the back of my neck and shoulders, loosening the knots there. About a quart of water and some Advil will do the rest. It'll only be weird if I make it weird. And there's enough weird in my life these days. I dress and go downstairs.

DECLAN'S ALREADY BEEN busy, has filled the kettle and laid out cups and saucers for tea.

"Stay for breakfast?" As I say the words, I'm shocked to realize it's the first time I've ever uttered them in this house. I've never let a man spend the night here before. I've always made an excuse, always been the one to stay over and leave in the morning – if I'd even stayed the whole night. A thought to examine sometime, maybe. But not right now.

Declan slides a glass of water and a bottle of Advil in my direction on the kitchen island. He doesn't say anything, but I guess it's his way of apologizing for my current state. He'd been the reason I'd brought out the whiskey, after all. His eyes are clear and their usual bright blue, no sign of the excesses of the night before. Figures.

I down two tablets, drain the glass and go to the refrigerator for more water from the pitcher in the door. While I'm at it, I check to see what I can make us for breakfast. Maybe I should've looked before I'd offered. But no, we're good. There's enough here for a decent meal.

"Sure, if you're offering," he says. "I need to get my gym bag from the truck. Be right back."

A minute later he's back, his expression grim.

"What's wrong?"

"You need to see this."

I follow him onto the porch and glance around, puzzled. Our vehicles are parked in the driveway where we'd left them last night. There's nothing I can see that would've prompted Declan's unmistakable anger. I turn toward him to ask for an explanation; then I see it.

WHORE and *BITCH* are spray-painted in huge red letters across the front of the house and windows. I hadn't opened the downstairs shutters yet this morning, so I hadn't seen *this*.

I feel the color drain from my face. Looks like the universe has decided my life's not quite weird enough.

"YOU SHOULD CALL the police."

We've finished breakfast, and Declan is packing up the dogs' assorted paraphernalia.

"I just checked the county's website. Non-emergency police reports can be filed online. Vandalism's not an emergency."

"It should be, combined with your assault and the tracker." Declan's jaw is set.

"I agree. But Arlington County doesn't seem to."

"I've got a few things to take care of this morning. I can come back later and help you clean up the paint, if you want."

"Thanks, but I'll just YouTube it and figure out the best way to get rid of it. Fricking Noah. He must have driven past and seen your car was here."

Declan's eyebrows rise slightly. "You really think it was him?"

"Who else?"

"I'll know soon enough." He crouches down to zip up the dogs' duffle bag.

"You'll know what soon enough?"

"Ah, hell." He runs a hand along his jaw, the stubble rasping as he considers his next words. "Let's just say I've been keeping an eye on Mr. Blackstone."

"You've been following him?" I can't keep the astonishment out of my voice.

"Not exactly. Look, the less you know, the better. And you can't say anything about this to Simone, all right?"

"Say anything about what? You haven't told me anything."

"It's probably better to keep it that way. I'll know shortly if Noah's car or phone was anywhere near here last night or this morning. That's not to say he couldn't have had someone else do his dirty work for him, but we'll know where he was when it happened."

It takes me a minute to process everything Declan's just said. "You put an AirTag on Noah's car?"

He looks insulted. "I'd like to think we're a little more sophisticated than that."

"We?" I start to say, then hold up a hand. "Never mind. You're right. It's better that I don't know. I'm already a suspect in one crime. I don't want to be an accessory to – whatever you're doing. At this rate, Pen will be representing both of us."

"I know what I'm doing, Kate. I'll give you a call later, once I have more information."

I wave Declan and the dogs off at the front door and go back inside, thinking about what Declan had said. Noah's car or his phone. How on earth had he been tracking Noah's phone?

Simone's words come back to me now: "If they're just a gym owner and a former software developer, then I'm the bloody Pope."

"I REALLY APPRECIATE this, Hicks."

I watch him pull a pressure washer from the back of his SUV, see his expression of disgust as he takes in the ugly, dripping red words emblazoned across the house.

"Not exactly a Banksy, is it?" he asks dryly.

"Don't I wish. But unless his style's changed dramatically, I don't think my house value's about to skyrocket."

"I'd have to agree with you there. This won't take long."

We clear the plants away from the house and the cushions from the porch swing. Then I leave him to it, wondering what Declan had told Hicks about being here last night – or rather, this morning. Wondering what he's thinking. Wondering when my life will go back to normal.

"CAN I OFFER you lunch, at least, since you came all the way over?" I ask when Hicks has finally finished removing the paint.

"Thanks, but there's no need. Not that anyone's keeping score, but you still have a nice fat credit on your account from that Macallan you dropped off."

I try not to shudder at the mention of the gym owner's favorite whisky, watch as he expertly loops the power cord into a tight bundle. He's crouched down next to the machine, focused on the task at hand, not looking in my direction.

"Um, Hicks, does Trident have a policy against instructors dating students?"

I can feel the heat rising up my cheeks and can't bring myself to look at him. I focus instead on putting the potted plants in the exact same positions they'd been before, deadheading a few that need attention in the process. Looking anywhere but at the gym's owner.

"A policy? Nah, I've had my fill of policies and regulations from a lifetime in the Navy. We kind of self-police ourselves and each other, if that makes sense. The guys are all pros, though, and we've never had any issues with them crossing a line." He pauses. "Have a soft spot for young Raj, do you?"

I can't stop an outraged yelp of laughter. He chuckles and shakes his head.

"You worry me, Hicks. You're starting to sound like Simone."

"God forbid. I don't think the world could handle more than one Simone." His words are playful, and there's still a spark of humor in his eyes. "For the record, you haven't been a student for a while. You're a member of the gym now. And we're all consenting adults, last I looked."

Well, that answers that question, then.

"Everything okay? Aside from this, I mean?" He gestures at the damp façade of the house.

"Yeah, Hicks. Everything's fine."

The person who'd spray-painted the house had known that the truck parked overnight in the driveway wasn't mine. Had assumed that a man had spent the night. Who else could it have been besides Noah? Who else would have cared?

As Declan had said, we'll know soon enough.

"HAVE A LITTLE excitement this morning?"

I plump the last of the pillows on the porch swing and turn at the sound of my neighbor's voice. Luna bolts toward me, and I give the dog a hearty rub. Satisfied for the moment, she runs off to sniff and investigate the rest of the porch and the nearby shrubs.

Diane is giving me a concerned look.

"Not my idea of excitement."

"Noah, you think?"

"Why would you say that?" I ask in surprise.

She lowers herself onto the swing and pats the cushion next to her. "We need to talk."

I sit, nervously setting the swing into a gentle rocking motion. "What is it?"

"It's about Noah. If things had gotten serious between you, I'd have said something before now, but you've split up, haven't you?"

I nod, waiting for her to continue.

"There were rumors about him. You know how DC is – there's always gossip. You learn which whispers to ignore and which ones to pay attention to. Supposedly three women had filed charges against him – two for assault and battery and one for harassment. Physical abuse and stalking, basically. Marcia Blackstone was still a senator at the time, and she was up for reelection. Word was she paid off the women. Convinced them to drop the charges and keep quiet."

The news should come as a shock, but it doesn't. The incident in my front hall had only been the tipping point. There had been signs along the way that I'd chosen to ignore. A year with Noah had taught me a lot. If I'd learned anything, it's that psychopaths look just as normal as anyone else. That's what makes them dangerous. Having a powerful, influential mother covering your tracks only ups the ante.

My neighbor is watching me closely, gauging my reaction to her news. "You're not surprised?"

"No, not really. Thank you for telling me all this, Diane. Noah Blackstone's a bastard. I'm lucky I found out in time."

Diane nods, seems satisfied.

"Yesterday you said it didn't look good that I hadn't called the police," I say. "You think it makes me look guilty, don't you?"

"Ignore me, please. I had no right to bring any of that up. You did what you thought best. End of story." She looks back at the house, where there's almost no sign of the earlier vandalism. "Where did you find the handyman who was here earlier? I'm always looking for a good one."

I smile. "That wasn't a handyman. That was a friend of mine."

"You have a lot of new friends, Kate."

"I do." As I say the words, I realize it's true. Send up a silent prayer of gratitude for each of them: Hicks, Raj, Declan.

"Come over for a drink later?" she asks.

God, please, no.

I manage a smile. "Can I take a raincheck, Diane? Maybe this weekend?"

"Of course. You know where to find me." She rises from the swing and calls to Luna.

I watch as they cross the lawn to their front yard. Long after they've left, I sit and swing gently, wondering where my peaceful life has gone.

"IT WASN'T NOAH. At least, his phone and his car haven't been near your house in the past twenty-four hours."

Declan's called me on my office landline, which makes me nervous. But then again, he's admitting to having access to information about a private citizen that he legally shouldn't have. Being a private citizen himself.

"Well, that leaves me exactly nowhere." I can't keep the frustration out of my voice. "Sorry, Declan. That's not directed at you. Thank you – I think – for looking into it."

"Did you file a police report?"

"Yes, for all the good it'll do."

"Call me or Hicks if anything else comes up, okay?"

"Okay, thanks."

After I've hung up the phone, I sit for a minute in my peaceful office, just enjoying the quiet. Then a thought occurs to me, and I'm in motion once again. Turning to my laptop, I open a search window in my browser. Time to follow Simone's lead and learn a bit more about a certain retired Navy admiral and a wealthy software developer.

LIKE A LOT OF PEOPLE, I love a good mystery.

And usually, if I'm paying attention, by the time I get to the end of the thriller or crime novel, I'll have figured out who the culprit is. Most of the time.

At the moment, I'm struggling to find more than the bare bones about Hicks or Declan; there's surprisingly little information about either man online. Hicks has a small bio as the owner of Trident Tactics & Training, and there are some old articles where he's been quoted or featured as a high-ranking naval officer. Like Simone, I hadn't been able to find out his first name – on most sites, he's listed as C. E. Hicks or C. Edward Hicks. Strange. He's been awarded all sorts of medals and commendations for his military service – definitely the kind of man you'd want leading you into harm's way. No surprise there, knowing what I do know of Hicks.

A search for Declan O'Rourke returns dozens of links and pages for a well-known Irish singer and a few references to an advisor to the government of Ireland. But the Declan O'Rourke I'm interested in is a complete puzzle. There are some old posts from *Forbes* and *The Economist* about the sale of his former company, but almost nothing since. I know he's been dabbling in software again, but if he has a company, I can't find it.

I check Delaware's business registrations, knowing a lot of companies are incorporated in the business-friendly state; and then Virginia's, looking for anything I can tie back to Declan. I try all the words I think he might use for a company name: Finn, Finnegan, Jasper. I even try Cara – which is a long shot, I know. Nothing comes up related to Knappogue Castle 21, his favorite whiskey. Then I search using Galway and Ireland and some of the country's more famous landmarks – I'm grasping at straws at this point.

Intrigued and determined, I keep digging. There has to be something. I mean, the man has to exist somewhere online, doesn't he? Then it occurs to me that he's exactly the type of person who would know how *not* to have an online presence. Oh, well. It was worth a shot.

I'm just about to give up when an online post about whiskey catches my eye. The Devil's Cut. The Angel's Share. I quickly skim the paragraph, read it again: The devil's cut is the percentage of whiskey lost due to absorption into the casks used for aging. The angel's share is the percentage lost to evaporation.

I go back to the state registrations websites, try my luck there. In five minutes, I find what I'm looking for: a Delaware corporation named Angel's Share LLC. Owner: Declan Michael O'Rourke.

Bingo. It's all I can do not to raise a fist in triumph. I search a bit more and find a charitable trust under a similar name. Very interesting.

I remember my first reaction when Simone had told me that Declan had made an eye-watering amount of money on the sale of his business. I'd thought the last thing the world needed was another tech bro with more money than sense – or any kind of moral compass, for that matter.

Now, though, knowing the man slightly better, I have to smile.

Devil's cut. Angel's share.

At least he'd chosen the side of the angels.

TWENTY-THREE

THE FIRST FEW days of my leave of absence have taken on a familiar routine. I read the paper over breakfast and take a power walk around the neighborhood. When I get back home, I enjoy a second leisurely cup of tea in the sunroom, looking out at the garden and dreaming up landscaping projects and improvements that I know I'll get to – well, probably never, let's face it. I'm simply not that kind of person. Checkbooks and credit cards exist for a reason; I know it's better and probably safer for everyone concerned if I pay someone else to complete any home-improvement or major gardening projects at my house.

When you're working five days a week, you dream about having unlimited time off and not having to work. When you're forced to stop working, leisure time takes on a different quality because it's not your decision. I'll be the first to admit it, my job was not even close to ideal, and I know I griped about it as much as the average person, probably more.

Right now, though, I'd give my right arm to be working. I'm going out of my mind with boredom. It's great to be compulsive and organized and tidy, but the downside to living that way is you don't have any projects that need to be done at times like this. The house is clean, bills have been paid, junk mail has been shredded, medical bills and charitable receipts are in the folder titled 'taxes,' and the car has been serviced and detailed.

I wasn't one of those people who baked sourdough bread or learned a foreign language during the COVID lockdown. I love sourdough, but I have no desire to bake it. That's what Wegmans is for. I already have all the foreign languages I'll ever need on account of my parents' love of overseas travel and exploration when I was growing up, thank you very much.

It's only day three and I've resorted to reading every back issue of this year's *Archaeology* and *British Archaeology* magazines and most of last year's, too. I can spend just so much time at Trident before even that gets tiresome or Hicks throws me out. Not that he would, but he might want to. Anyway, while my arm is still healing, any strenuous upper-body work is off the table. Not much use when all you really want to do is punch something. And I'll never admit it to Declan or Hicks, but yeah, I really should've had my arm stitched.

I'm thinking of taking a bike ride on the W&OD Trail to get out of the house when my mobile rings. Seeing 'Dublin' on the display, I smile and swipe to connect the call.

"Good afternoon, Declan," I say cheerfully, happy for the distraction.

"Good afternoon, yourself." Declan's tone isn't nearly as light as mine.

"What's up?"

"Are you home this afternoon? Hicks and I need to see you."

"Yes, I'm home. I'll be here all day, since I'm not working," I say with bitter emphasis on the last word. "Sorry, not your fault, I know. Care to give me a heads up?"

"It's probably better if we explain when we see you. Maybe thirty minutes?"

"See you then."

I look down at my decades-old Levi's and faded T-shirt, smudged with traces of dirt I'd picked up from weeding in the back garden, then catch sight of my reflection in the hall mirror.

Darn it. I launch myself up the stairs, heading for the bathroom and a shower. Twenty minutes later, I'm dressed and nervously watching the street for a familiar vehicle, wondering what's so important that Declan and Hicks feel the need to tell me in person.

Declan's as good as his word. Twenty-five minutes after hanging up with Declan, the doorbell rings. I unlock and open the door, expecting to see Declan and Hicks. They're there all right, and standing off to one side behind them, is a very nervous-looking Poppy.

At first, I almost don't recognize her, since it's completely out of the usual context in which I see her; knowing she looks familiar but not exactly sure where I know her from. Kind of like running into your dentist in the wine section at Whole Foods on a Saturday. It takes a minute.

"Poppy?" I ask in confusion, looking from Declan to Hicks and then at Poppy again.

"Hello, Kate. I think we'd better come in. This could take a while," Hicks says.

I step aside to allow them all to enter and show them into the living room. Poppy sits nervously on the edge of an overstuffed chair, and I sit in the middle of the couch. Declan and Hicks opt to stand, at least for the moment.

"We need to show you something, and then I think we'll let Poppy tell you what she's already told me and Declan," Hicks says. Poppy nods.

The two men come to sit next to me on the couch, one on either side. Poppy pulls her mobile out of a large maroon purse embossed with 'Deathly Hallows' and has what appears to be a wand just below the leather handle. Harry Potter, I guess. In jeans, a T-shirt and red Chuck Taylors, Poppy looks far younger than she appears in her security officer uniform. Far younger and more vulnerable somehow.

She hands her mobile to me after scrolling through to find what she wants me to see. There is a video queued up on the screen, and I press the play arrow with some trepidation. Another video. Heaven help me if it's anything like the last one.

Hicks puts a reassuring hand on my shoulder as he looks on.

The video is clear but something about it is off, and then I realize what it is: I'm watching a video of a video. I stiffen slightly when I recognize the location as being the parking garage at Sam's. There is no activity for the first few seconds and then the elevator doors open, and a petite, dark-haired woman dressed in a slim skirt, crisply tailored blouse, and high-heeled sandals steps out of the elevator into the garage. The woman is me. I look questioningly across at Poppy, but she looks down and nervously picks at her cuticles, not meeting my gaze.

I see myself step out of the elevator, striding confidently, my keys in one hand, aware of my surroundings. My pace quickens as I head toward the row where my vehicle is parked. My heels click loudly on the cement floor. I've only made it a few yards when a large man suddenly appears from behind a Lincoln Navigator. I react quickly and swerve out of the man's way, a slight smile on my face. Our eyes meet, my smile disappears, and then he lunges toward me. He grabs me roughly, his arms locked around my neck, trying to drag me down onto the garage floor.

Initially, I appear to be frozen with fear. Then, as if someone has flipped a switch, I come to my senses. I break free from my attacker with a violent elbow jab to his solar plexus, dropping and backing away, putting as much distance between us as possible.

The man, angry now, pulls something out of his pocket and snarls at me before flicking open a lethal-looking knife. He lunges toward me with the blade. I try to sidestep it but don't move quickly enough; a slash of red appears on the sleeve of my white blouse. My stomach drops, remembering the white-hot pain that sliced through my forearm. In the video, I step back with a cry of pain, then raise my bag protectively against my torso as the blade comes up again. This time, the blade connects with my dense leather shoulder bag, filled as it is with all of my life's daily essentials and then some. The blade slices the leather, and I wrench the bag to the side, the jerking motion causing the man to drop the knife. I also lose my grip on the bag, which falls heavily to the ground.

He charges with a roar of fury and, with a vicious punch, slams his fist into my upper body, the force of which nearly knocks me to my knees. Doubled over, unable to breathe, I don't have time to recover before he brutally swings the same fist back up and into my face. He tackles me to the ground, and winded and injured, I struggle, kicking, scrabbling backward before he finally straddles my body and locks his hands around my neck.

Using one hand, I wrench one of his hands away, maintaining my grip, and with the other, I strike him hard in the throat, which causes him to reel back in pain. To give myself space to maneuver, I raise one knee diagonally between our bodies. Letting go of his hand, I kick out fiercely with the other leg, slamming one foot into his face, shattering his nose with a sickening sound. The man cries out in agony and totters backward, clutching his hands to his face, blood spurting from between his gloved fingers.

Staggering to my feet, I sway unsteadily for a moment, moving away from the man's body, where he now lies on his side, moaning and holding his injured face. I clumsily pick up my purse, my scattered keys and the other items that had spilled from my bag when it was knocked to the ground. I half-run, half-stagger away, no longer in sight.

Watching this, I'm nearly weak with relief, hardly able to believe what I've seen. This is what I've needed – the second half of the video, which shows my attacker was alive when I left, that I hadn't killed him.

I move to hand the phone back to Poppy, but Hicks says, "There's more. Give it a minute."

More? How could there be more? I glance back down at the phone, waiting.

A second man moves into the frame, of average height and wiry but otherwise nondescript. I feel a prickle across my scalp as I watch him move, thinking that there's something familiar about him but dismiss the thought as I continue to watch.

The stranger approaches the injured man, who is still lying on the ground. Leaning down, he shouts something into the man's face, and the man, injured as he is, recoils. I gasp out loud when the stranger delivers one vicious, knock-out blow to the side of the injured man's head. And then he hits him again. I want to turn my own head away, but I can't. I have to see this. With some difficulty, the second man on the scene drags the larger man so that he's hidden from view behind a parked car.

The man steps out from behind the vehicle, looks around, and finding what he's looking for, picks up an item from the concrete floor. It's the knife, I realize. He puts the weapon into his pocket and strides away. As he turns to leave the scene, his face is in full view of the camera.

I gasp, my hand going to my mouth in shock. "What …?" I can barely get the word out. I look at them all in disbelief. "I know him. That's Anthony Colletti."

Hicks and Declan react instantly, their bodies tensing next to mine. Declan, in particular, goes very still.

"This man is Anthony Colletti? And you *know* him?" Something in his voice, in the way he says the name, sets off alarm bells in my head.

"Yes. Do *you*?"

"No, I don't, I only know of him. I told you I'd do some digging on the holding company, remember? I hadn't had the chance yet to tell you what I'd found." His expression is grim. "Anthony Colletti is the owner of Michelangelo Enterprises through a shell company called Medici Holdings. He's your debarred subcontractor. It's not only his company. I did more digging: he's on the exclusions list, too."

Hicks, Declan, and I stare at one another in astonishment, reeling from yet another bombshell.

Hicks recovers first. "How do you know him?" He rises and moves to sit in a chair next to Poppy, handing her back the phone.

"Our parents were friends. We kids – Anthony, Frankie and I – practically grew up together. We lived in the same neighborhood; they came to our house. Marco Colletti, their father, runs a leather repair shop not far from here."

I stop and a chill of fear runs down my spine. "I just saw Anthony. The day after the attack. He was in the shop when I brought my bag in to ask Marco if it could be repaired. I talked to him, the very next day—" I'm breathless and bewildered with everything I've seen and learned. I can't take it all in.

"I'm so sorry." Poppy finally speaks, looking tinier and even more waiflike than usual as she shakes one leg nervously, seeming to shrink into herself. "I'm so sorry I didn't help you that night."

"From the beginning, Poppy, I think?" Hicks' voice is gentle, encouraging.

"I was working the night this all happened, Kate, you remember, right? I'd heard some of the girls at Sam's, you know, the hostesses and some of the wait staff, talking about Anthony Colletti a few times. He comes in pretty often, so most everyone there knows him."

"I've never seen him in all the time I've been going there."

"He usually shows up on Saturday nights," Poppy offers. "I don't work very many Saturdays, only if I really need the money. But I know who he is, and like I said, there are rumors about him. Like not accepting a drink from him if he offers it to you. Some of the girls have said he'd been physical with them, touchy, you know? I kind of knew he was bad news, but I never dreamt…" She puts her hand to her mouth, then gets her emotions back under control.

"I had no idea," I say, astonished. "None. How could I not have heard this about him?"

"Poppy, would you tell Kate what you told me?" asks Hicks.

She nodded. "I was checking the monitor that Friday night, and things were quiet, normal, on that garage level. Then I saw Anthony get out of his car and walk around for a few minutes, and then get back in. He didn't go to the elevator, he just sat in his car. I figured maybe he was waiting for someone who was up in the restaurant or in the mall, since he didn't usually come to Sam's on Friday nights. He'd have had to go upstairs to pay for his parking at the kiosk on our level at some point, so it all seemed a little weird to me. I thought it might be a good idea to keep an eye on him."

She takes a deep breath and says, "I don't know what made me do it, but I started to record the feed from that camera in the garage on my phone. It all happened so fast, and when I realized what I'd seen, I really freaked out. I was working alone that night because the usual guys had called out sick. I knew that when Anthony came up to pay for his parking, he'd see me alone at the desk. I freaked out, basically," she admits, playing with the handle of her bag. "I ran into the lobby restroom and stayed in there for, like, twenty minutes. I knew Anthony had to come up to the payment kiosk, but I had no idea what he was doing or how long it might take."

"You must have been terrified," I say gently.

She nods. "When I finally went back to the guard station and checked the monitors, I saw that his car wasn't in the parking lot, so I assumed he'd left. Remember I told you that the cameras had gone down that night, Kate? Well, the cameras themselves were working, they just weren't recording. I recorded the video from the monitor in real time." She looks imploringly at us. "I know I should have called the police, but I was so freaked out. I know that if I gave that video to the police, Anthony would know exactly where it had come from and could have found out from anyone at the restaurant that I was the only one on security duty that night."

"Oh, Poppy," I say, rising from the couch and moving to crouch next to her chair. "How on earth were you so brave?" I put an arm around her thin shoulders.

She turns her head into my shoulder and sobs. "I'm not brave. If I were brave, I'd have gone down to the garage to help you. I'd have gone to the police," she chokes between her tears.

Declan, Hicks, and I look at each other while Poppy cries quietly. Declan steps away and returns a minute later with a box of tissues from the half-bath under the stairs.

"It's okay, Poppy," Hicks says. "Take your time." He gets up from where he's sitting next to her so that I can sit in the chair and hold her hand, and he settles himself next to Declan on the couch.

She is so young, I think, as she blows her nose and wipes her eyes, trying to pull herself together. She's on her own, living far from home and family. What a terrible, traumatic thing to have witnessed.

"I didn't know how to get in touch with you, we'd only exchanged first names when we'd chatted, you know, when you're arriving for dinner or leaving. You're one of the few people who doesn't ignore us," she says, sniffling. "Most people treat the security staff like we're furniture, like a potted plant or something. But you always talk to me, you're always so nice."

"You're not a potted plant," I say with a smile, trying to lighten the moment.

She returns a weak smile. "I was a total wreck all weekend, you're all I could think about. I didn't know how badly you'd been hurt. God, the way he hit you and threw you. I don't know how you walked away." She presses a tissue to her eyes and goes on. "I wasn't scheduled to work until the following Tuesday night, so I stayed in my apartment all weekend. My roommates are gone for the summer, and I have the place to myself. I already had two summer jobs lined up at the end of the spring semester, and it made sense for me to keep the apartment during the break. I liked having the place to myself for a change. I went and saw Paolo to ask if he knew your last name, and he did, from your credit card. He knew you worked nearby but not the name of your company. He remembered the name of your gym because you guys had talked about working out a lot. He thought it was a really small place, so I decided to go over there and see if anyone knew how to get in touch with you."

"Did Paolo ask why?" I prompt.

Poppy shakes her head. "I told him I'd found an expensive earring that I thought was yours and wanted to return it to you. He offered to hold onto it until the next time you came in, but I told him I wanted to see if I could get it to you personally first."

"Then everything hit the fan when the other video of you went viral. I'd read that a man's body had been found, and I was even more scared than before. I knew there was only one person who could have taken that video, and it was Anthony. He must have been standing just out of range of another camera because that's the only way he'd have had the view he did.

"You don't remember seeing anyone else that night?" Declan asks. I shake my head no. I had been so intent on fighting back and getting the hell out of there. Then I must've gone into shock, remembering again that I couldn't even recall how I'd gotten from the garage to the gym. It might not have registered even if I had gotten a glimpse of anyone else.

"I read online that no one had been charged with the guy's death but that you were a person of interest. That totally freaked me out. There was no way I could keep quiet anymore, knowing what I did." She clears her throat.

"You're doing great, kiddo." Hicks gives her a reassuring smile. She smiles gratefully back at him.

"I'm working at H&M four days a week this summer, so I wasn't able to get to the gym until today. When I asked about you at the reception desk, the guy gave me a funny look and went in the back for a few minutes. When he came out a little while later, Mr. Hicks was with him, and he brought me back to his office. I explained everything."

"And that's pretty much where we are now," Hicks says. "I've sent a copy of the video to my contact at the department. The ball's in their court at the moment." Looking at Declan, he continues, "We called Simone before coming over, and she and Wainwright are aware of the video. They've asked us to meet them at four o'clock."

"We should just be able to make it if we leave now." Thankful that I'd showered and made myself presentable, I grab my keys and bag from the mudroom.

I'm proud of myself as I buckle myself into the back seat of Hicks' SUV next to Poppy, thinking I'm holding it together, all things considered. Then reaction sets in. My hands shake as I pull a compact mirror from my bag to check my makeup. My knees and legs tremble as if from the chill of the SUV's powerful air conditioning in my light summer dress. It's not the A/C that has me shaking.

Poppy's video. Anthony Colletti's involvement in my attack. Anthony *Colletti*, whom I've known since I was a child, witnessed my being attacked and did nothing to help. And then he likely murdered the man who attacked me.

TWENTY-FOUR

WHEN WE ARRIVE at Pen's office a few minutes before four o'clock, the ever-unflappable Thomas greets us with his usual aplomb, although there is no offer of refreshments this time. He merely escorts us directly into a conference room adjacent to the reception area and tells us that Pen will be with us shortly. If he's the one who had to rearrange Pen's schedule, he must surely be aware of the crisis that's brought us here.

Looking around the large meeting room, I see why Thomas didn't offer us anything to drink. A vast credenza on one side of the room is set up with two large carafes, a silver tray of cups and saucers, assorted teas, bottled water and juice, and two silver bowls filled with small bags of various snacks. There's also a platter of cookies and a bowl of fresh fruit.

"Ms. Ellis called to say that she expects to arrive in less than ten minutes," he informs us before he silently closes the door. Hicks and Declan exchange a glance, one with which I'm becoming very familiar. We all move to stand in front of the wall of windows to take in the view.

"Look at that, Poppy," Hicks says to her, pointing out the panorama of the city below. "You won't get a much better view of DC anywhere in the city." Such a kind man, I think, knowing that he's trying to distract her, given that she has a very tough task ahead, having to recount her story yet again to more strangers. They do as I had done on my previous visit to the office and look for recognizable landmarks and monuments while we wait.

The door quietly opens, and Pen enters the room. He smiles in welcome and greets me warmly, taking my hands in his and saying, "Catherine, I trust you're well. So very good to see you again."

I make introductions all around since I'm the only person in the room who knows everyone else. I see Poppy's eyes go wide when Pen turns to her with his usual charismatic smile. I'd thought there might be a chance she wouldn't recognize him, but I realize that's not the case.

"A pleasure to meet you, Poppy," he says to her. Turning to the rest of us, he says, "Let's sit and get started, shall we? Simone shouldn't be too much longer. We don't stand on ceremony here, so please help yourselves to refreshments."

"Poppy, I'm going to have some tea," I say, rising from my chair. "Would you like a cup?" She flashes me a grateful look and joins me at the credenza. We make tea while Pen, Hicks, and Declan talk about the view and the history of the building to pass the time.

There's a discreet knock at the door, and Simone slips quietly into the room. As if on cue, all three men stand when she enters, and she breathlessly greets Declan and Hicks before crossing over to Pen to give him a kiss on the cheek. Her gaze turns to Poppy, who looks suitably intimidated by the tall, imposing blonde woman. Despite Simone's unobtrusive entrance into Penfield Wainwright's office, she somehow gives the impression that she owns the place. "You must be Poppy." She takes in the raven-haired, gamine young woman who's staring back at her. "I'm Simone." Her smile is warm, genuine. "We're so glad you could come in today."

Poppy turns a little pink, and my friend directs her attention to me. "How're you holding up?" Her tone is casual while her gaze is anything but.

"Hanging in there. By my fingernails."

"Who has this video?" Pen asks once Simone has powered up her laptop.

Poppy's phone is passed down the large table to Pen and Simone, who are sitting next to each other, with me on Simone's right. Hicks, Declan, and Poppy are opposite us.

The room is nearly silent as the attorneys watch the video, the only sound being the scratchy audio from the tape. When it ends, no one speaks for a long beat. I would have thought that nothing would faze either one of them, especially Pen. Nonetheless, they both appear shaken by what they've seen.

Simone is the first one to break the silence. "Dear God in heaven."

"God has nothing at all to do with this," Pen corrects her. He looks at Poppy. "Now, young lady, if you would please be so kind as to tell us everything you know about what we just saw, I'd be most grateful."

For the next fifteen minutes or so, Simone gently but expertly guides the discussion, asking pertinent questions and taking notes.

Once Poppy finishes telling her story, I turn to the two attorneys. "I know the man – the second man – in the video."

"You *know* him?" Simone asks. Even Pen looks surprised at this revelation.

I explain our family's longtime connections, both personal and professional, and provide a few details about Marco's business. When I mention that I'd seen Anthony the day after I'd been attacked, Simone looks shaken.

"You saw him the next day?"

"Yes. I'd gone into the shop to ask Marco if my bag could be repaired."

"And what was his demeanor?" Pen asks. "He must have been shocked to see you turn up there."

"If he was, he didn't show it." Remembering now, I'm furious. "As I was getting ready to leave, he told me to be careful. What a complete psychopath." Another one, apparently.

"There's more," Declan says to Pen and Simone. He briefly explains what I'd found about Michelangelo Enterprises and what he'd later learned about the nature of Medici Holdings and Anthony's own debarment.

"This is incredible." Simone picks up the phone again, and I watch as she replays the video, fast-forwarding, then stopping. Turning up the volume as far as it will go, she hits the play arrow. The words that fill the room make my mouth go dry.

"You were supposed to kill her, you stupid fuck!" Those were Anthony Colletti's final words to my attacker before he fatally struck him.

Declan and I look at each other across the long table.

"He knows where you live." His voice is quiet, calm.

"I know." My voice is quiet, terrified.

"You can't be alone there," Declan says unequivocally. "Either I stay with you, or you come to mine."

"Declan," I start to reply, but he silences me with a look.

Hicks intervenes, his tone placating. "We'll sort all that out after we're done here, okay?"

Declan's face is hard. "You saw that video. The man wants her dead."

Hicks gives him a pointed look. Declan holds up both hands, palms out, in an 'Okay, fine, we'll do it your way' gesture.

The room is quiet as everyone takes in the significance of what we heard on the video. For the first time since I've known her, Simone's at a loss for words.

"Pen?" She looks to her godfather for guidance.

"Who else has a copy of this video?" Pen asks Hicks.

"The police and this young lady possess the only two copies of the video."

"Once the police identify Mr. Colletti and bring him in for questioning, he'll be shown the video and will make the connection as to where it came from," Pen says thoughtfully. He is quiet for a moment. "Poppy, my dear, where do you live?" His voice is kind. "Do you live with family or roommates, perhaps?"

"I'm living alone until my roommates come back in the fall."

"We need to rectify that situation immediately." His comment is directed to everyone in the room, his tone uncharacteristically severe.

"I have an idea," Hicks says. "Let me make a call, and I'll be right back. Please excuse me."

The mood is somber, and Simone breaks the tension by glancing over at Poppy. "Let's get a little snack, why don't we? I don't know about you, but I'm starving."

Poppy smiles faintly at Simone before joining her at the credenza. The poor young woman must be absolutely terrified. I am, and I've got decades on her.

Hicks returns to the room, a satisfied expression on his face. "I have a plan," he says. After helping himself to a cup of coffee and a chocolate chip cookie, he sits down at the table and fills us in. "A young man who recently separated from the military joined the gym a few months ago. He's been staying with me and my family while he decides what to do next."

"Raj," Declan says.

Hicks nods. "Yes, Raj. He's a former MP and he's been working a few odd jobs until he decides on his next career move. Poppy, since your roommates have left for the summer, how would you feel if this young man moved into one of their rooms so that you wouldn't be alone? I understand that he's a stranger to you, but as I said, he's been living with me and my family for a while. If I trust him to live under my roof, that's saying something. We'll understand if you're not comfortable with this idea. If not, we'll come up with something else, all right?"

We all look at Hicks in surprise at first. Once we've had a chance to think it over, there a few thoughtful head nods. Gradually we turn to Poppy who, poor kid, looks like the proverbial deer in the headlights.

"Well," she says, taking a deep breath, "my freshman and sophomore roommates were assigned by the college, so they were strangers to start with, too. I guess it wouldn't be much different than that. It would be nice to have company again. I can't afford to pay him or anything, though." She gives an embarrassed shrug. "I can barely cover my bills as it is."

Simone and Hicks both begin to speak, and Simone graciously defers to Hicks. "That's not something you need to worry about, Poppy. I know Raj, and he's not going to take a dime from any of us. He just wants to help. Right now, the only thing you need to focus on is staying safe. You did an amazing thing, taking that video and coming forward with it. The least we can do is make sure you're not put in harm's way because of it. You let us take care of the details."

Poppy genuinely smiles then, and it completely transforms her gamine features. For the first time since she appeared on my doorstep earlier today with Declan and Hicks, I recognize the Poppy I know from the guard desk outside Sam's.

After a few minutes, I say to no one in particular, "But what about when Poppy's at work?" I turn to her. "How many hours a week do you typically work?"

"Um, usually around thirty-five, between the two jobs, I guess."

"Thirty-five hours." I look at Hicks. "Raj can't be with her for thirty-five hours a week and work his own jobs, too. It's not possible."

"Do you have any vacation time coming?"

Poppy gives me an 'Are you kidding?' look. "Kate, I make minimum wage at two different jobs. I don't get paid vacation time."

"Sorry, I wasn't thinking. Okay, so what if I paid you to not work for a few weeks, until the worst of this blows over?" I look at Pen. "What do you think? If the police have the video, how long will it take for charges to be filed and all of that, until he's taken into custody?"

"Catherine, Poppy is a witness. If you were found to be paying her before the trial, you'd be in a great deal more trouble. Besides, you're working on the assumption that, even if this Anthony Colletti is charged, that he'd be held over until trial. Depending upon the circumstances, he might be allowed to post bond and be released. While that's unlikely given that the charges would likely be first-degree murder, there's no guarantee as to how this will play out. Even though we have Poppy as a witness, his counsel could use the same defense I'd proposed for you regarding the first video."

We all consider Pen's words for a while, searching for a solution.

Declan speaks first. "Poppy, what are you studying at university?"

"Software engineering. I'm not taking any summer classes, though, because I'm trying to finish a data analytics certificate. That's taking up most of my free time when I'm not working," she explains. "The cert is really inexpensive, compared with tuition."

"How would you feel about working for me?" More surprised looks from everyone, this time directed at my quiet Irish friend, as Simone once called him. Ignoring everyone but Poppy, he asks, "Have you ever heard of The Morrigan?"

"The video game? Well, sure, it's like, epic." Her obvious pleasure is like a ray of sunlight breaking through the room's oppressive atmosphere.

"It was my company that developed it. Among other things."

Defense technology and video games? *This* is how the man made his millions? And I thought my head hurt before I knew that.

"Seriously?" she practically squeaks. "Wait, the guy who developed that video game is Declan … oh my God, *you're* Declan *O'Rourke*?"

Simone and I exchange an indulgent, amused glance. Oh, to be that young.

"I am." His expression is completely deadpan. "What're you being paid per hour?"

"Twelve dollars." Poppy appears completely starstruck, looking at him as if she'd met Harry Styles or Timothée Chalamet.

"In Northern Virginia? That's not a living wage." He looks suitably outraged on Poppy's behalf. "A software professional should be paid accordingly. We'll start at twenty-five an hour and see how it goes. That way you can spend more time on completing that certification. Surely this will look better on your CV than what you're doing now. Do we have a deal?"

"Yes, yes, absolutely." The college student looks as though she's about to burst with excitement.

Declan glances around the table. "Well, that's sorted, then. Whenever Raj isn't available, Poppy will be working with me."

Poppy's face clouds over for a moment, and then she asks, "But why? Why are you all helping me?"

My eyes meet Hicks' and we exchange a smile, both of us remembering when I'd asked him that same question only a few weeks ago.

"It's simple, Poppy." I pause as my gaze goes around the table to Declan, Hicks, Simone, and Pen before returning to the young woman. "Like Simone said, you put yourself in harm's way to help me. That means something. To me, to all of us. Now it's our turn to help you and keep you safe."

I think suddenly of another group of people – a family – shattered, possibly sitting around another table not far from here. Struggling in the aftermath of inexplicable, violent death.

"Anne Marie," I say slowly, looking around the table at everyone. "It wasn't an accident, then, was it?"

Simone pales. "She must have found out about the debarment. But what about Laura? She was the subcontracts admin. It was her job to check the exclusions list. It doesn't make sense."

"What I also don't understand is how Anthony connected me to Ares, if that's what this is all about. That's the only thing that makes sense, right? How could he have known that I'd taken over for Anne Marie?"

"Who else knows?" Hicks asks.

"Only my boss, Simone, the vice president overseeing the account, and a few folks on the project team."

"And the ever-delightful Daniel Atkinson," Simone adds.

"How could I forget? And Daniel Atkinson, the government contracting officer." I remember his warning to me, and I suddenly feel cold. "Could he have something to do with this?"

"Only one way to find out," Simone says. "We need to tell Josh all of this ASAP. Once he contacts the contracting officer, if he's involved in any way, everything is going to hit the fan in ways he's never dreamed of."

I turn to Hicks. "Have we heard if the police have identified the man who attacked me?"

"Not that I've been told so far." Pen also shakes his head.

"Do you think you'll be able to find out anything from your contact with the Park Police about Anne Marie's accident? If it's not too late, that is. Aren't cars that are totaled by insurance companies usually sent to salvage yards?"

Before Hicks or anyone else can reply, Simone quietly says what we're all thinking. "If the car is gone, so is all the evidence that someone else was involved."

TWENTY-FIVE

AS MUCH AS I enjoy spending time in Declan's gorgeous house, I can't help feeling slightly resentful that my own place is out of bounds for the time being. After we'd wrapped up our meeting at Pen's office yesterday, Declan had hovered while I'd packed an overnight bag with some essentials, then I'd driven us to his house while Hicks drove Poppy back to her apartment. Anthony Colletti is the bad guy here, yet I'm the one under house arrest, or it feels that way, anyway. I know it's for my own safety, but I'm aggravated all the same.

Declan and I are lounging on his large couch, feet on the coffee table, books in our laps, when the sound of the telephone ringing in his office makes us look up. He slips a bookmark onto the page he's been reading, sets the book on the coffee table, and reluctantly rises from the couch. I hear his deep voice as he answers the call and speaks for a minute but can't make out the words.

"Kate? It's your boss." He's standing in the office doorway, holding the receiver.

A sudden knot of tension twists in my stomach. I accept the phone, taking a deep, steadying breath before speaking.

"Hey, Josh. What's going on?"

"Everything's completely hit the fan. It turns out Daniel Atkinson is the contracting officer on almost all the contracts where Michelangelo is the prime and most where they're a sub. We've tried to contact him to get more information but he's not answering his calls. The Ares contracts specialist said he didn't show up for work today. We issued stop work orders once Legal gave us the okay. It's been radio silence ever since."

"You mean that arrogant little bastard is behind all of this?"

"Not necessarily. He's involved somehow, but he's the government's problem, not ours. It's Michelangelo we're going after." His next words are jaw-dropping. "As if all of that weren't bad enough, it gets worse. We're looking at the possibility that Laura and Anne Marie were both caught up in it, too. We don't know for sure, but we can't see any other way this could have happened without some inside help. Laura should've vetted all the subcontractors as part of her due diligence. One time, maybe, something could have slipped through the cracks. But more than once? That's not the way we operate. The subcontracts senior manager is beside himself, and I can't say I blame him. We all are."

It takes me a minute to find my voice. "No one suspected that there were issues with Laura's documentation, that she might have hidden the fact that Michelangelo was on the list?"

"That's still being looked into. It's going to take a while." He pauses. "I'm so sorry."

"Why are you apologizing?" I ask him. "None of this is your fault. You trust your people to do their jobs. We have procedures and guidelines to follow for the everyday stuff. You're there for the big stuff, the problems. Everyone assumed that Laura was doing what she was supposed to do, too."

"Yeah, but Anne Marie? I have to answer for that."

"You don't know for sure, do you? I mean, she was only the contracts admin. It was Laura's responsibility to vet the subs on Ares, not Anne Marie's. I assume my subcontracts counterparts are doing their jobs like I'm doing mine. I don't go behind their backs to check. No one has time for that, and no one should have to. I did it on Ares only because there was no one left to ask."

"Still, as Anne Marie's manager, I am responsible if she had any part in all of this. It's going to take a while to figure it out, though."

"Have you and the subcontracts team talked about Michelangelo Enterprises at all? I mean, the people we've worked with on proposals, that kind of thing?"

"How do you mean?"

"Has the name Anthony Colletti come up in any of your discussions?"

"Not that I recall. Who is he?"

"He's registered as the owner, or one of the owners, of Michelangelo Enterprises. I was curious if there was any record of him in Laura's files."

"It's possible. Some small-business owners are more hands-on than others. He might've left the proposal work and actual execution to his employees."

"Could you keep an eye out for any mention of him, please?"

"If you tell me why it's important. What are you not telling me?"

I take a deep breath, and then I drop the bombshell I know he'll never have seen coming. "Well, I hate to be the one to tell you this, but it gets worse. It's not only a government contracting issue but it's also now a criminal issue."

"What?"

"It's looking more likely that I wasn't randomly attacked. There's evidence to suggest that Anthony Colletti, the owner of Michelangelo Enterprises, arranged for someone to attack me."

"Oh my God."

"My attorney has asked the police to re-open the investigation into Anne Marie's car accident."

"What?" I can hear the shock in his voice. "Why?"

"To make sure it really was an accident. Because there might be evidence to indicate that it was deliberate."

"I can't believe this. Are you somewhere safe?" Josh asks, his tone suddenly urgent. "I mean, this man, Colletti. He hasn't been arrested, has he?"

"No, he hasn't been, and yes, I am. I'm somewhere safe," I assure him with a grateful glance in Declan's direction. Maybe I'm slightly less resentful in this moment, given the concern in Josh's voice, to be at Declan's house with him and not by myself at home in Arlington. Where Anthony Colletti knows where to find me.

314

TWENTY-SIX

IT'S FRIDAY, slightly more than a week since Hicks shared Poppy's video with the police and our meeting with Pen. As the defense attorney had suspected, Anthony was released on bail despite what was shown in the video. His lawyers made similar arguments regarding the video that Pen had made on my behalf, so we don't have a lot of options. Anthony was described as a respected business owner with strong professional and family ties to the local community and all that jazz. And so, life goes on.

Simone and I are sitting at my kitchen table, looking at the blueprints for Luke's dream restaurant on her laptop screen. We've come back to the house so I can water the flowerbeds and pick up more clothes for my stay at Declan's. It's mid-afternoon, and Simone has been working from the kitchen while I run the sprinklers and do a bit of weeding. She, Declan, and Hicks have been watching me like a hawk, making sure I'm not on my own until everything with Anthony is resolved. Raj is keeping an eye on Poppy as agreed during our meeting at Pen's office. I love them all for it, but I'm starting to go slightly stir crazy.

I could've planned this better and not chosen to do this in the worst heat of the day, but oh, well. I'm sweaty and a bit muddy, trying not to get too close as Simone scrolls through the drawings. "It's gorgeous, Simone. I can just imagine what it's going to look like when it's finished. Thanks for letting me take a peek. Want something to drink?" I take the Brita pitcher from the refrigerator and pour myself some water while she decides.

"What time is it?" she asks pointedly.

"Not wine time," I tease.

"Killjoy. Water's fine, then."

I'm putting the pitcher back in the refrigerator when a movement in my peripheral vision makes me glance toward the front door sidelights.

Simone sees it, too. "Were you expecting someone?" She rises to go to the door, with me following only a step or two behind.

She's barely cleared the end of the bench when one of the sidelights explodes in a shower of shattering glass. We both scream. Simone ducks, and we watch with horror as an arm reaches inside the broken window frame, trying to unlock the door from the inside. But it's a keyed deadbolt, not a thumb lock. The key, thanks to Declan, is no longer on any of the hooks near the door.

"I know you're in there, you bitch!" Anthony Colletti calls out, and Simone and I clutch each other's arms in panic.

"Your mobile! Where's your mobile?" I whisper to Simone frantically as I realize that mine is charging on the counter on the other side of the room which, in this moment, seems impossibly far away. She pulls hers from her back jeans pocket.

"Upstairs, my bedroom, now!" I hiss. We stumble and scramble up the hardwood stairs. I'm urging, "Go, go, go!" as I trail Simone while Anthony continues to rage outside.

It's only a short flight of stairs, but it seems to take us forever to make it up the stairs and onto the landing. We sprint to my bedroom, and I slam and lock the door.

"Call 911," I urge her, "then get in my closet and close the door. He can't get in through the back without climbing the fence," I say breathlessly. "The gate's locked with a key, so he won't be able to open it." I think of all the glass in the sunroom, such an easy way in, praying he won't go over the fence.

"What's that?" she gasps as we hear more shattering glass from what sounds like the rear of the house. *Shit, shit, shit.* I'm not exactly sure where it's coming from because I can barely hear for the panicked pounding of my heart, the humming in my ears. I strain, trying to listen.

We stare at each other in horror as we hear rapid footsteps on the stairs.

"Kate!" Simone whispers urgently.

"Please," I beg her. "Get in the closet and call 911 – now!"

Kneeling, I reach under the bed and pull out the shotgun. Simone's eyes widen as I rise to my feet and raise the weapon to my shoulder.

"I don't want you to see this."

"You ruined everything, you fucking bitch!" Anthony roars from the upstairs hallway.

Simone turns deathly pale, but she nods and races for the closet just as the first kick hits the bedroom door.

Remember to breathe.

I push the safety button to the "off" position.

I take a deep breath, exhale. Nestling the shotgun into the pocket of my shoulder, I take another breath, begin to exhale.

Line up the sight on what I think will be slightly higher than center mass.

Another kick, and the doorframe splinters. The door swings inward, crashing against the wall with a loud bang.

Anthony is standing in the doorway, his chest heaving, his eyes lit with fury. Almost unrecognizable. A madman. With a gun in his hand.

I barely register his raising an arm in my direction—

I complete the exhale and squeeze the trigger. He staggers backward at the impact, his eyes now wide with shocked disbelief. He stares down at the wound in his shoulder, then he looks up at me. As our eyes meet, he very deliberately raises his weapon again.

"Anthony, don't!" I plead, but I don't wait, can't wait for him to do what he so obviously came here to do. Tears stream down my face as I rack the slide and squeeze the trigger again. I fight back a sob as he drops to the floor in a heap. *Anthony.*

Without the hearing protection that I'm accustomed to, the blasts from the shotgun are deafening, and the recoil has my shoulder throbbing from the impact. I bend over at the waist, gasping.

I close my eyes, swallow hard, then open them again, straightening to stand upright. Then I force my gaze downward, toward the floor and farther, to the doorway. I swallow again, harder this time, compelling myself through sheer force of will not to projectile vomit all over what is now the buckshot-laden, bloodied corpse of Anthony Colletti.

There is no doubt in the logical part of my brain that he is dead, but I'm so terrified and have seen too many horror movies where the supposed corpse rises just as the heroine turns her back. Believe me when I tell you, I'm not taking any chances.

After a few minutes that feel like a lifetime, I lower the shotgun, flip on the safety, and eject the remaining shells onto the bed. Then I lay the weapon next to the shells and walk over to the closet door.

Knocking gently, I say, "It's me."

The door slowly swings open. I sit down next to Simone in the shadows of the walk-in closet.

"Did you call them? Are they coming?" I ask, starting to tremble, reaction now setting in.

"Yes." I hear her sob. "Is he—?"

"Yeah. He's dead."

We sit there among neatly-ordered lines of shoes and purses, dresses and skirts, trousers and suits, the air sweetly scented with the French lavender sachets that are scattered throughout the closet. Waiting.

"Where did you get the shotgun?" she asks after a minute. She's trembling as badly as I am, I realize.

"You remember the guy I dated before Noah? Chuck, the ATF agent?"

"Oh, God, yeah, Upchuck." Her laughter is tinged with hysteria; I hear her fight to swallow it down.

"I forgot you used to call him that." I want to laugh with her, but I can't remember how at the moment. "He said I should have a handgun for protection, but I didn't want one. We settled on the shotgun, and he taught me how to use it. I've been going to a range in Springfield every few months since then." A pause. "You never liked him, did you?" I'm feeling slightly hysterical myself, the trembling in my legs nearly uncontrollable now. I wrap my arms around my bent knees, trying to make it stop.

"No. I really hated that cocky little swagger of his. But fuck me, I really love him right now," she confesses.

"Yeah, I know. Me, too."

Then we hear the sound we've been waiting for. Sirens.

Simone starts to get up, but I stop her with a firm hand on her arm. "Wait. Let them come to us." I don't want to explain in graphic detail what we'd have to step over to get out of the bedroom; I also don't want to contaminate the scene. Although I can't imagine much analysis will be needed in this case.

But anyway.

The sirens are louder now, there is hammering at the front door, the sound of wood cracking as the battering ram shreds the front door jamb. There are shouts of "Armed police!" and "Clear!" as they make their way through the small house's first floor. Still we sit, shivering and leaning against each other in the closet, waiting.

The pounding of booted feet on the stairs, the squawking of radio comms. Then a sudden, fraught silence. The discovery in the doorway.

"In here," I call out, my voice at first weak with relief, then stronger, more powerful. "We're in here."

HOURS LATER, after the police, forensics team and detectives have left, Hicks and Raj arrive with blue tarps that they use to cover the bedroom floor, walls, and hallway. Simone and I painstakingly look down at our feet as we walk out of the bedroom and down the stairs, like some twisted version of the 'step on a crack' game that we played as kids, neither of us wanting to take a chance of seeing any traces of what took place here hours earlier. I don't think Simone would ever be able to forget it if she did.

It's too late for me, though.

When we're safely in the kitchen, far away from the bedroom, I feel like I can breathe normally again. The broken glass has been cleared away, and Hicks and Raj are in the process of hammering plywood over the sidelight and sunroom window that Anthony had used to gain access to the house. The front door has been temporarily repaired, and it's good enough for the moment.

The police had taken into evidence a large black Maglite flashlight, which Anthony had apparently used to break the sidelight and the sunroom window. They also took possession of a nine-millimeter handgun, which they'd recovered next to the dead man's body.

We'd handed our blankets back to the EMTs when they'd left, and Simone and I are both wrapped in a couple of the fleece throws that I keep in the living room, rolled and stored neatly in a pretty basket. I usually reach for one to keep warm on chilly evenings when I'm curled up on the couch. Never in my wildest dreams did I imagine they'd be used at a time like this.

Declan and Luke have been summoned by Hicks, and they're both hovering anxiously, wanting to do something but not sure of their roles in this drama. In the end, Declan makes a pot of tea. Luke pours Simone a stiff whiskey.

We sit in shattered silence while Hicks and Raj finish whatever repairs they want to get done tonight before we all head out. When they're done, we thank them, and they depart with promises to check in on us tomorrow.

"Let's get you home," Luke says to Simone. We all get up from the table and make our way wearily to the battered front door.

Simone turns to me and hugs me fiercely, whispering, "Love you."

"Love you, too," I tell her as she steps back. Luke takes her by the arm and leads her out to the car. Declan and I stand in the doorway and watch as Luke carefully backs his Porsche out of the drive.

We're both subdued as we return to the kitchen. All I can think about is a shower and bed. Preferably not here, though. Not tonight. God knows how long it'll be before I'm able to face my bedroom and what happened up there.

"Did I hear Diane's voice earlier?" I ask.

"Yes, you did. She called 911 when she heard the gunshots. She said she'll give you a couple of days before checking on you. And bringing cake, probably."

He smiles, but his heart isn't in it. He runs a hand through his hair, seems about to speak, reconsiders. He's not looking directly at me, which isn't like him at all.

"What?" I ask.

"How long have you owned a shotgun? What *is* it with you Americans and your bloody weapons, anyway?"

I stare dumbly at him, unable to believe what I'm hearing. "Seriously? You think *this* is the time for a philosophical discussion about America's gun culture?"

He's gathering glasses and cups from the table, setting my teeth on edge as he puts them in the sink with a clatter. Every movement is jerky, exaggerated, punctuated by anger. To spare my mother's precious Waterford glasses and Wedgwood teacups, I gesture for him to move away from where he's started to run the water.

"Leave them. Then you can tell me what your problem is. I didn't see anyone coming after *you* with a gun tonight."

"*My* problem? *I* don't have a problem. You're the one sleeping with a shotgun under your pillow. For f—." He stops himself just in time, his jaw practically grinding with the effort. I know exactly what he was going to say. If it had come from Simone, I'd be smiling. But Declan isn't Simone, and this isn't funny.

"Don't be ridiculous. I don't sleep with it under my pillow, and you know it. I've been a responsible gun owner for years, and tonight is the first time I've fired that weapon outside of the range. Where I go regularly, by the way."

We're standing between the counter and the island, and the narrow space feels way too small, too crowded to contain all the anger and emotion that's suddenly swirling between us. Declan's jaw is clenched, his face is flushed; I can tell he's struggling to control his temper. I've never seen him truly angry before, certainly never like this.

"Why would you buy a gun in the first place?"

"Because the police aren't there to protect anyone, Declan. They show up after the fact, to investigate, when it's too late. And even when you hand them a killer on a silver platter, they still screw it up. I wasn't going to be another victim of their incompetence."

"What are you talking about? If this is about your parents, I don't see the connection. Your parents weren't killed by a gunman. They were killed by a drunk driver. What happened to them doesn't justify—"

I cut him off. "Justify? Are you kidding me? Simone and I would probably be dead right now if I hadn't had that weapon. Why do I have to justify defending myself against an armed madman in my own home? What is wrong with you?"

We're squared off, facing each other, nearly toe to toe in the narrow space. But unlike my confrontation with Noah a few months ago, I'm not concerned for my safety or feeling threatened in any way. Not with Declan.

Instead, I'm bewildered. That he doesn't or won't understand.

He looks at me for a long moment, his arms outstretched with his hands braced on both the counter and the island. He pushes off and walks around to the far side of the island, putting some distance between us. "You're right. Now's not the time. We can't talk about this tonight."

"*You* started this. Tell me."

"The bastard who killed Cara. He shot her. Did I not tell you that?"

I close my eyes tightly, drop my head at his words. "Declan, I—"

"Don't, Kate. Please. Just – *don't*."

We stare at each other across the granite slab, the anger gone now, exhausted as quickly as it had come, like a flame extinguished by a sudden gust of wind. There's only a heaviness, along with a strange emptiness.

His expression is weary and haunted now from dredging up memories he'd much rather have forgotten, I'm sure. Tonight's shooting had brought them all back. My heart breaks for him but I can't undo what happened. What's more, I won't apologize for doing what I had to do to save me and Simone.

Now, as we stand in my kitchen, both of us wearing the same pained expression, I know it's not only a few square feet of granite that separates us.

"Maybe you'd better leave," I say.

He exhales loudly, shakes his head for a moment, then looks at me. "I'm not leaving you here. The place is practically still a crime scene. Come back to mine. Until you can get things sorted, get the place cleaned up."

I sit down heavily at the kitchen table and massage my temples, trying to think straight. I know only one thing, in this moment: I cannot deal with this tonight. "Declan, we're friends, right? I'd like to think we are, anyway. You've been there for me through this entire nightmare, and that means a lot to me. And yet, we barely know each other."

He's leaning against the granite island, his arms folded across his chest, waiting for me to continue.

God, I'm tired. So unbelievably exhausted. I just want to curl up somewhere, anywhere, and sleep for a month. But I have to say this. "As much as I appreciate everything you've done, you aren't responsible for me. And you and I shouldn't be together tonight, because if we are, we'll say things we can never take back. I don't want to lose you as a friend. And I would, if I went home with you now."

I get up and look out through the sunroom windows to the house next door. A faint light is still on in the kitchen. "So, my friend, you need to go home. I'm going to go over to Diane's and spend the night there. All right?" My back is to him, and I don't turn around to face him.

When I hear the front door close, I grab my phone and keys and race out the sunroom door, across the yard, and through the gate. Diane opens the kitchen door almost immediately to my pounding, sees my expression, holds open her arms.

"You poor child."

I stumble across the threshold, sobbing, "I killed him, Diane. I killed Anthony. Marco's never going to forgive me."

She doesn't say a word. She simply holds me and lets me cry.

GOD FORGIVE ME, but when I shot Anthony and saw his lifeless body on my bedroom floor, all I could think was, "It's over." No more living in fear of what might happen next: no more hiding, no more of the pain and uncertainty that had plagued me in the weeks leading up to tonight. Nothing had prepared me for the way I'm feeling now, though, knowing that someone is no longer alive, no longer walking on this earth, as a direct result of something I've done.

Under the stinging spray of the shower, I try in vain to wash away all traces of what happened just a few hours ago. Soap and water can help with gunshot residue and any physical evidence, but there's no mental equivalent of soap and water for my shell-shocked mind.

Impressions from tonight flood my brain, everything coming back in a rush: the shattering glass, Simone's scream, the pounding feet on the stairs, Anthony's ranting.

Then the shots. The acrid smell in the air. The metallic tang of blood. So much blood.

I look down at my hands in horror. There's no blood on them, but there may as well be.

I killed a man tonight. I killed Anthony Colletti. Marco and Leonora's son. Frankie's brother. The shooting had been one of the most traumatic moments of my life. Something I'll carry with me forever.

So why is it the disagreement with Declan that keeps coming back to haunt me?

TWENTY-SEVEN

THE MORNING AFTER.

It's all I can do to drag myself out of bed, dress, and go downstairs to Diane's kitchen, but I manage.

When I see her on the screen porch through the kitchen window, I go out to join her there.

"Breakfast?" she asks.

"I couldn't. But is it all right if I make some tea?"

"Of course. You know where everything is."

I make the tea and take it outside to drink it. We sit quietly for a few minutes, looking out at her lush, thriving gardens.

"It was you or him, Kate. You had no choice. Whenever you go down that rabbit hole, remember that. The man was armed, and he came to your home to kill you."

I give her a considering look, wonder what she'd be like to work for. Tough and no-nonsense, for certain. Which is exactly what I need right now. Tea, but no sympathy. I finish my drink. After leaving my cup in the sink, I pick up my phone and keys and walk through the house and onto the porch. I look across Diane's wide lawn to my front yard. At least there's no yellow crime scene tape stretched across the front door, as I'd expected. And no reporters or news vans for now, thank God.

I lie down on the porch swing, one leg dangling to set the swing in motion and keep it swaying gently. I scroll through the new texts, ignore the voicemails. I see who they're from, know what they'll say, anyway. Time passes. Diane leaves a pitcher of lemon water with mint and a glass on the small table that's within arm's reach, then slips away quietly.

The phone rings. I ignore it, close my eyes, shut out the world.

ON DAY TWO, Hicks calls. I answer, hear him say, "I'm coming over." Then he ends the call.

Twenty minutes later, I see his SUV pull into the driveway from where I'm lying on Diane's swing. Same as yesterday. Same as tomorrow, probably. I stride over to his truck to greet him. He envelops me in a massive hug, then leads me back to my neighbor's porch. We both sit.

"Please don't say anything kind," I say. "I can't take it right now."

He doesn't speak, he simply takes my hands in his, gives them a gentle squeeze. I rest my head on his shoulder with a sigh of relief.

"I can help with that, if you want," he says, gesturing across the yard to my damaged front door. "I know some guys who do good work. They can replace the broken windows, too."

"That would be great, Hicks. Thanks."

"Want a quote first?"

"No, it's got to be done. If you trust them, that's good enough for me."

He hesitates. "I also know of a company that'll take care of the, uh, cleanup. Want me to make a call?"

I feel a huge weight lift from my shoulders. "Please."

"You're not returning his calls or his texts." His tone is factual, not accusatory.

"It's not just his. I will. Not yet."

"We're here for you, Kate. You know that. Whatever you need, whenever you're ready."

"I know. Would you mind running interference with the contractors? I'm not sure I can face going in the house anytime soon."

"Of course."

I dig in my pocket, hand over my keys. "Thank you."

"Simone's going to call you. Luke and Declan are having some folks over on Saturday. Thought it'd be good for us all to get together. For you and Simone."

"Luke and Declan?" I ask, wondering at the odd pairing. Setting that question aside for the moment, I speak with more conviction. "It's too soon, Hicks."

"Think about it." We sit quietly, lulled by the gentle swaying of the swing. "He's leaving for Ireland on Sunday. So you might want to be there on Saturday."

I turn to look at him, unable to hide my surprise. "Ireland?" I think that over for a minute. Maybe it's not so much of a surprise, after all. Maybe it's long overdue.

He lets go of my hands and stands up. "I'll let you know when I get the work scheduled, okay?"

"Thanks again. For everything."

"Take care of yourself."

I watch him leave, then lie back down on the swing. Same as yesterday, same as tomorrow.

ON DAY THREE, Josh sends a text:

"I told HR to change your LOA to compassionate leave. Open-ended. Call me when you're ready to talk. About anything. Thinking of you."

Josh. In all the chaos, I'd completely forgotten about him. Simone must've let him know what had happened. I will call him. But not today.

When Hicks and the contractors arrive, I watched dispassionately from the shaded coolness of Diane's porch, like it's someone else's house. Someone else's mess to clean up. Sometimes I wonder if I'll ever be able to go back inside again.

The days are blurring into one another, following a similar pattern. I get up, shower and dress, make tea, sit on the front porch. Diane tries to tempt me with my mother's favorite recipes. I politely refuse. How can I eat when I can't get the image of Anthony's bloodied body out of my head? *I had done that to him.*

I try to shut out memories of the time we'd spent together in that house, but they force their way in. My parents, Marco, Leonora, and Frankie. *Marco.* What can he possibly be going through right now? Small mercies that Leonora isn't here. But she would have been a huge comfort to her husband, if she were still alive.

Dear God.

I drink my tea, focus on the rhythm of the swing like it's a metronome or a mantra, and try to forget what I did. But I can only forget by blocking out everything. And everyone. It's the only way my shattered brain can cope.

ON DAY FOUR, Simone shows up. Although we've been texting since the day after it happened, she hadn't mentioned anything about coming over today.

"You look like hell," she says by way of greeting. "Glad to know it's not just me." She looks at me expectantly, waiting for my usual sarcastic reply.

I silently shake my head.

"That bad, huh?" She pulls me into a hug, then we sit down together.

"Simone, I'm so sorry."

"Sorry? Don't be an ass. You saved my life."

"That's not true. I don't get credit for saving your life, not when I'm the idiot who put you at risk in the first place. We should never have been at my house that day."

"If you hadn't done what you did, we probably wouldn't be sitting here right now. So quit beating yourself up, would you? And I'm not staying. I just came by with a message from Luke."

"From Luke?"

"Yes. Saturday, two o'clock. At Dublin's." Her nickname for Declan doesn't prompt its usual smile.

"Simone—"

"Don't make me come out here to get you. That will piss me off no end."

I glare at her.

"We all need this, okay? It's not just about you. Although you do need to get back out into the real world."

"You've been talking to Hicks."

"Of course I have. Now get off your butt and get with the program."

As she walks toward her car, I call after her. "If this is how you invite people to parties, I suggest you refer to your Emily Post for a refresher."

"Refresh this." She raises her middle finger and keeps on walking.

For the first time in four days, I laugh.

ON DAY FIVE, I'm in my usual spot on the swing when a Sprinter delivery van parks in front of my house. A uniformed driver opens the rear door and pulls out the most enormous floral arrangement I've ever seen. I do a double-take, wondering if he's got the wrong address. It's not exactly a funeral spray, but that's what immediately comes to mind: I swear it's that big. No lilies, though, so maybe it's not actually a misdirected sympathy bouquet. Good thing, because ever since my parents' double funeral, the smell of lilies makes me sick.

"May I help you?" I ask, intercepting the driver midway across my yard.

"Catherine Barrow?" he asks.

Ah. There's only one person who calls me Catherine, so I know who the flowers are from before I even look at the card. I thank the driver, who dashes off without a word, his mind already on his next delivery. There are two cards, actually. One with a note from Thomas ending with a smiley-face. Who knew the repp-tie wearing, slightly-intimidating receptionist had a soft side? The other is from Pen, handwritten in bold slashes across heavy card stock. Sending his best, with a promise to call whenever I let him know I'm ready to talk. No smiley face from Pen, though.

I smile myself when I read the post-scripts: "P.S. Don't expect an invoice. P.P.S. Don't let Simone convince you she paid your retainer. You know how she can be."

I lug the massive vase over to Diane's, wrestle the door open, and set the arrangement on the dining table. Since Vince died, Diane doesn't often use the dining room, so I know the flowers won't be in her way here. They are gorgeous, though, and I take a minute to admire them.

"Who died?" Diane asks from behind me, the sound of her voice making me jump.

"That was my first thought, too." Although we know very well that someone died recently, we both struggle to keep a straight face. "Slightly over the top?"

"Just a bit. Nice selection, though," she concedes. "Can I tempt you into joining me for some *bouillabaisse*? I'll be eating it all week otherwise."

"You know, that sounds amazing."

I follow her into the kitchen, where Luna leaps up from her bed to greet me. I let her bury her cold nose in my hand and stroke her sleek black coat. Her entire body wiggles with delight, along with her tail. I can't help but laugh in the face of such unrestrained joy. I feel a pang of guilt for not having paid much attention to her the past few days, wrapped up as I've been in my own head.

"Hey, girl. It's good to be back. I've missed you."

ON DAY SIX, I open the email I've been avoiding for weeks. As usual, it's short and to the point. I can almost hear the sender's voice as I read the message; it makes me smile. I begin to type a reply but as my fingers hover over the keypad, I have a change of heart. A glance at my watch tells me it's not too late to call, even taking into account the time difference.

With a knot in my stomach, I select a name from my contacts list, make the call. After a couple of rings, a woman answers.

"Hello, Fiona? It's Kate. Kate Barrow."

There is a long pause. My first thought is I've reached someone else, that the phone number is no longer hers. My second thought is I have reached Fiona but she's ticked off at me for not getting in touch sooner.

"Well, what bloody time do you call this, Yank?" she finally demands, laughing. Her Irish accent is as strong as ever and so familiar. Very much like Declan's, rich and warm with a trace of a lilt. I inhale deeply, a mixture of relief and regret. Why has it taken me so long?

Then we're chatting and laughing and picking up like no time at all has passed. Because that's how it is with some friends. What's more, we have so very much to talk about.

TWENTY-EIGHT

IT'S SATURDAY, eight days after Anthony Colletti's death.

My heart is pounding as I get out of the car, juggling my shoulder bag, a bottle of wine, and a covered platter. Diane had gone overboard – thrilled, I'm sure, that I'm finally getting out of the house – and had insisted on making an assortment of mini desserts that would rival any pricey bakery's. Not a talent I'd ordinarily expect from, well – a spook. I guess we all have our own ways of coping with the stress of our jobs, whatever they might be.

The sound of my closing car door sets off a volley of barking from inside the house. The front door opens as I approach the covered entryway, my footsteps crunching on the gravel.

"Hey, Kate." The sight of Luke with his tousled blond hair and welcoming, broad smile relaxes me instantly. "Let me give you a hand with that." He takes the platter in one hand and hugs me with the other arm, easily lifting me off my feet. "Thank you," he whispers fiercely into my ear as he puts me down and meets my gaze.

"Don't be nice, okay?" I whisper back in the same tone. "I'll fall to pieces right here if you are."

"Right, then," he says in a normal voice. "I'll be an asshole, shall I?"

"Yes, please."

He winks and holds out an arm as Simone approaches. "Oh, hang on. Here comes the welcoming committee."

Jasper and Finn barrel into the room from outside, and I have just enough warning to hand off the bottle of wine to Simone before the dogs ambush me. I don't even try to tell them to stay or sit. I end up sitting cross-legged in the middle of the floor and let them do their happy doggy dance thing while I try to shield my face from their wagging tails and cold, curious noses.

"You big goofballs." My tone is affectionate as I scratch under their chins and rub their heads. They sit on either side of me, and I wrap my arms around them, inhaling their clean canine scent. God, I need this. No drama, no heartbreak. Just unconditional, unwavering love.

Simone, casually chic in a floral maxi dress with her white-blonde hair twisted into a loose knot, helps me up off the floor and gives me a hug. "I'm glad you made it," she says.

"Me, too."

Declan enters the room, and his welcome is not quite as enthusiastic as Finn and Jasper's had been. Not by a long shot.

"How are you, Kate?"

"Good, thanks, Declan. You?"

For Pete's sake. It's like our early days back at Trident, and I want to throw something. Simone rescues me by pulling me away.

"Am I early?" I ask her. "I thought you said two o'clock."

"I did. Everyone else is coming around two-thirty. I just wanted a few minutes with you before everyone else shows up."

Declan distracts the dogs by putting jumbo-sized dog biscuits into two large Kongs and throwing them out onto the lawn. The dogs rocket after the red rubber toys, having learned long ago that treats will always be much more interesting than any human visitor. Unless said humans happen to have treats, of course.

"I put a couple of bottles of wine in the fridge, and we've left a charcuterie tray out on the island if you want to start with that," Simone says.

"There's some Foster and Guinness in the fridge, too," Luke adds with a glance in Declan's direction. "It's already cold."

Simone and I stay in the kitchen while Declan and Luke get things set up in the outdoor kitchen.

"What's with the bromance?" I ask with a look toward the patio. "I didn't realize Luke and Declan were such pals."

She pours us each a glass of wine while I take the plastic fitted lid off the charcuterie tray. "Yeah, well. I guess with everything that's happened recently, they've kind of connected. They've been talking quite a bit this past week. Hicks has been keeping in touch, too. Everyone's making sure we're all doing okay. Those of us who're answering calls and texts, that is," she adds pointedly.

I look outside where the two men are laughing and talking animatedly as they prep the grill. What do an Aussie chef and an Irish software developer have in common, anyway – besides football or rugby, maybe?

"What's with you and Dublin? It was so cold between you two, you could've scraped frost off the windows."

"A difference of opinion, that's all." I see the expression on my friend's face, one I know all too well. "Not today, Simone, please. As you reminded me, this isn't all about me. How're you really doing?" She looks like she's lost weight, which takes some doing when your husband's a phenomenal chef. It's also weight she really couldn't afford to lose, thin as she was to begin with.

"For fuck's sake. I'm the one who should be asking you that question." This sounds more like the Simone I know and love, and I can't resist a smile.

"I'll survive. Thanks to a certain friend with abysmal social skills who invited me to this little gathering."

She raises her wineglass in a toast, prompting me to do the same. We clink our glasses. "To Upchuck. I'll never say another word against him as long as I live."

"To Upchuck," I repeat.

"Who's upchucking?" Luke asks as he steps into the kitchen and heads for the fridge.

Simone and I look at each other and burst out laughing.

"What'd I say?" His expression is so genuinely innocent and oblivious, it makes us laugh even harder. "You two seriously worry me sometimes." He's smiling, though, not in the least offended by our laughter. He takes two bottles of Guinness from the fridge. "Need a hand with anything?"

"No, thanks, we've got this," Simone tells her husband. She turns back to me. "Are you sure you're ready? Tomorrow seems kind of soon."

"I can't avoid it forever. Diane's been great, but I need to face it eventually."

"She'd understand if you need more time."

"You're the one who told me I needed to get back in the real world, remember? Tomorrow's as good a time as any. Shall we?"

Simone carries a stack of plates topped with silverware and her glass; while I take the tray and some napkins along with my glass before following her outside.

It's a perfect afternoon, not too hot or humid, which is a rarity in August. The deep covered porch runs the length of the house and has an outdoor kitchen area with a gas grill and prep station in one corner, and a seating area with comfy outdoor chairs and a couch that flank a fire pit on the opposite end. A rectangular dining table in the middle comfortably seats eight people, maybe ten in a pinch. We opt for the couch and chairs and settle in for a chat.

"So, what now, Simone? How much longer are you on vacation?"

Simone glances over at Luke before answering. "Well, I'd originally planned to be off for two weeks, but then Pen offered to let us use his summer place on the Vineyard. We're heading up there on Monday for a while."

"Good for you. I can't remember the last time you had a real vacation."

"Neither can I. How about you?"

"Officially, I'm still on a leave of absence. When that ends, I plan on turning in my notice. I need to talk to Josh before I do anything, though. Did you tell him about what happened last week? He sent a text, said he was thinking of me."

"No, I haven't spoken to him in a while, either. Can you believe that Laura and Anne Marie were involved?" Simone's voice is incredulous. "The things people will do for money." I give her what I hope is an appropriately ironic look. She sees and ignores it. "I feel bad for Anne Marie's husband. First he loses his wife, then he finds out – oh, by the way – she was a criminal, paid by a scum like Colletti to keep him in business with the government. Unbelievable."

"I know. The fallout's going to take a long time to settle. At least I won't have to deal with any audits or investigations."

"Right. You pulled the pin, lobbed the grenade, and took cover just in time."

"I had no idea what I'd stumbled into. It's Josh I feel sorry for. He thinks he's responsible for what Anne Marie did, and he's not. Life's going to be hell for him and for Laura's boss until all this is sorted out."

"Josh is a big boy; he'll figure it out. Don't forget, he used to work for the government. He knows better than anyone how this will play out."

"Yeah, I guess. You've spoken to Pen, I assume?"

"Yes. He's seen a lot in his time, but I think even he was shocked when I told him."

Join the club, Pen.

"I haven't spoken to him, but Thomas sent a floral arrangement. I mean, a *massive* arrangement. I was tempted to check the obituaries to make sure I hadn't died." We both freeze, stare at each other. "Oh, my God. Did I just say that? Tell me I didn't say that."

Simone nearly snorts wine through her nose. The headmaster of her former Swiss finishing school would be very impressed, I'm sure. When we've both recovered, I say, "Pen's a good man."

"That, he is." There's something else in her expression that I can't read, but I let it go for now.

The doorbell chimes. Declan calls, "I've got it," from somewhere in the back yard and crosses through the house to answer the door.

More voices, and we hear a high-pitched girl's voice squealing, "Uncle Declan!" Simone and I exchange a startled glance. I can tell we're both thinking, 'Uncle' Declan?

I look into the kitchen to see Declan, Poppy, Raj, and Hicks all gathered around the granite-topped island. And recognizing her from the picture in Hicks' office, I see his daughter, Emma, talking animatedly to Declan. Simone and I go inside to greet everyone.

Before I have a chance to say anything, Poppy flings her arms around my waist, saying, "Kate! Oh my God! How are you? I've been so *worried*."

"I'm fine, Poppy, really." I return her hug, laughing. Raj and I exchange a smile, and he gives my arm a squeeze.

Hicks, bless him, keeps his distance, knowing that two people hugging me would likely trigger a flood of tears, something nobody wants to deal with today. "Elizabeth couldn't make it but sends her best." He turns to the young girl by his side. With a proud paternal hand on his daughter's shoulder, he makes the introductions. Emma, at twelve, is tall like her father and has long straight brown hair and a bit of coltish awkwardness about her. She smiles shyly to reveal blue-tinted braces on her teeth.

Declan shepherds the newcomers out onto the patio after asking what everyone wants to drink, and I hear him introducing Poppy and Emma to Luke. A minute later, he's back inside, pulling bottles and cans from the refrigerator. He pauses when he sees me leaning against the counter where I'm taking refuge for a quiet minute before joining the crowd out back. Any other time, he'd have asked if I was okay, if I needed anything. Now he's simply looking at me, waiting for—I don't know what.

I take this moment to say my piece since this is probably the only time today I'll catch him alone. "Declan, just so you know, I wasn't avoiding your calls and texts. Not for the reasons you might think, anyway. I wasn't replying to anyone – not just you. It's taken me a while to … get my head on straight."

"You've managed to reply to Hicks and Simone without any problem, so I hear." His expression is closed off, with no hint of the familiar amusement in his blue eyes.

"Well, they're different."

He crosses his arms across his chest, the same way he had on Friday night. "Why are they different?"

Maybe because I didn't have a blazing argument with either of them the night I killed a man in self-defense? Maybe because they didn't accuse me of being some sort of nut job for owning a weapon? I could give him a list, if it really comes down to it, but I'm tired down to my bones all of a sudden. Coming here was a bad idea. I rub my temples, something that's become a habit lately.

"Come on, Declan. Simone was there that night. She knows how I'm feeling right now. And Hicks is," I hesitate for a second, "Hicks." I shrug. "He's like Switzerland," I say, grasping for an analogy.

"Switzerland," he says, his tone dry.

"You know – neutral territory. He doesn't take sides. He's just there, quietly getting things done in the background." I think he might be trying to suppress a smile at my description of his longtime friend, but I'm not sure. "Let's not make it awkward for them, okay? That's not fair." I glance at our friends on the patio. "After tomorrow, it doesn't matter anyway." I lower my voice, almost as though I'm talking to myself. "There have been so many bad days lately. I want just one good day. Is that too much to ask?"

He gives me a long look, his expression softening a fraction. "No, it's not too much to ask. Let's have one really good day."

Okay, so it's not exactly the Treaty of Versailles, but it's something, at least.

THE DOORBELL RINGS a few minutes after Declan and I join everyone on the patio. Since it doesn't look as though anyone else has heard or is making a move to answer it, I go myself.

"Hey, Kate." Josh is standing on the front porch. He looks happy to see me, which cheers me up more than it should. "How are you?"

"Hey, Josh, I wasn't expecting you. Come on in."

I lead him into the living room, where noise from the back yard is drifting in through the open French doors. "Declan and Luke invited a few folks over. You're welcome to join us."

"Thanks, but I can't stay long."

"Can I at least get you something to drink?"

"No, I'm good." He looks around the house, at the soaring ceilings, high windows, and the patio beyond the kitchen. "Quite a place."

"Isn't it? Not what you'd expect from the outside."

"Not at all. You look well. I was worried, but Declan's called a few times to let me know how you were doing."

"I think you mean Hicks."

"No, Declan. Irish accent, right? He had my number from when I'd called you here. He called to tell me what had happened. Called me a few times since, invited me over today, actually."

Before I can reply, Declan comes through the patio doors into the house.

"Josh, is it?" he asks, extending a hand in greeting. "Declan O'Rourke. Good to finally meet you."

"Josh Hudson." The two men shake hands, size each other up the way men sometimes do. "Thanks for your calls. I didn't want to bother Kate."

Declan studiously avoids the curious look I'm giving him. "You're welcome. Glad you could join us. We have enough food for a regiment out there."

"Sorry, but I can't stay. I wanted to talk to Kate about work for a minute, and then I have to get going."

"All right, then. Have a good weekend."

Josh waits until Declan's outside before continuing our conversation. "So – you and Declan are—?"

"Friends." Well, we were. Are we now? It's looking less and less likely, today's fragile truce notwithstanding.

"Uh-huh. And Noah?"

"Ancient history."

"Okay. None of my business, but Declan seems like a good guy."

"He is. So are you. Thanks for sticking with me through all of this. I know it hasn't been easy. You said you wanted to talk about work?"

"Yes. We're wrapping up our internal investigation into Ares and our contracts with Michelangelo. Laura was in it up to her neck, and so was Anne Marie. It's probably a terrible thing to say, but Anne Marie might have gotten off easy; at least she's not facing prison time."

"Apparently Atkinson is testifying in exchange for a plea deal. He claims Colletti was blackmailing him into awarding contracts. No details as to how or why or what Colletti might've had on him. Colletti was paying Anne Marie and Laura to keep their mouths shut. Laura might've been happy with her end of the deal, but Anne Marie either got greedy or threatened to expose Colletti. Either way, that car accident is looking less like an accident."

"My God, Josh. What a nightmare."

Daniel Atkinson's last words to me had been: "Let it go, Kate. Please." At the time I'd wondered at his uncharacteristic use of my first name, at what sounded less like a warning and more like a plea. Had he honestly been trying to warn me off, to protect me from Anthony? It was a possibility, if he was being blackmailed. It's doubtful I'll ever know for sure.

"It's not over by a long shot – there's still a government audit and investigation to get through. No one's looking forward to that." From Josh's weary expression, it looks like Simone and I aren't the only ones struggling with sleepless nights.

"I bet."

"David and I have been talking, and we've come up with a proposal for you."

I look at my boss expectantly. "What kind of proposal?"

He's smiling now. "We won Dragonfly."

"Are you kidding? Even after what Atkinson told us? That's fantastic news."

"It's yours if you want it." He holds up a hand before I can respond. "We want you back. I'm not stupid, Kate. I know contracts isn't your dream job. But how would you feel about a job share? Twenty hours a week, with full benefits?"

"HR agreed to that?" I ask skeptically. I have no love for our HR department, obviously.

"Yep. A contracts admin from the Air Force account is due to return from maternity leave but there's no longer a position for her there. She wants to come back part time, and she doesn't need health insurance. So, you'd each work twenty hours, give or take, and you'd get full benefits. You vacation days would be reduced, though. But I thought it might not matter, if you're working half-time. I can give you Alex's contact info if you want to talk to her about it before making a decision. You'd be working closely together, so it would have to be a good fit. What do you say? Will you think about it?"

"How long do I have to decide?"

"A week, maybe. We need to get back to Alex one way or another, so she can make other plans if she has to."

"Okay, I'll let you know within a week. Thank you. And thank David for me. What's going to happen to Ares?" I'm curious, despite myself.

"They're replacing Michelangelo with another sub for that share of the work. Even better, the new contracting officer has accepted our proposed tweaks to the revised delivery schedule."

"It sounds like it's not a total disaster, after all."

"Not totally." I know my boss well enough by now to know there's something he's not telling me. Something I can't put my finger on.

"Who's replacing Daniel Atkinson on Ares?" I ask as we walk toward the front door.

"Beckett."

I groan in exasperation. "I knew there was something else. Damn it, Josh. I love Beckett. That's playing dirty."

"I know."

Spencer Beckett is the best contracting officer I've ever worked with. All the contractors love him because he's fair, reasonable, and has a wicked sense of humor. He's a lot like Josh, actually, but on the other side of the fence.

"And Dragonfly?"

"Beckett again."

"You were saving that for last, weren't you?"

"Yep."

We're standing in the open doorway, and Josh turns to me. "You're a damn good contracts admin, and I don't want to lose you. You can do this and still have time for what really makes you happy." He gives me a quick hug and waves as he walks to his car. "Talk to you in a week."

I watch Josh leave and stand in the doorway long after his car is gone from view, thinking about everything he'd told me. In less than fifteen minutes, I'd gone from knowing exactly what I was going to do next to having absolutely no idea.

Simone comes in with an empty wineglass and walks toward the refrigerator for a refill. "Did I just hear Josh's voice?"

"Yes. He came by to see how I was doing and to ask how I felt about returning to work. I know you two have had your moments, but he's been a good friend."

"I know. I'm going to miss him."

That takes a minute to sink in. "You're going to miss Josh? Simone, what aren't you telling me?" My stomach tightens. I don't know if I can take any more surprises today.

Simone recorks the wine bottle and returns it to the refrigerator before facing me: a delaying tactic. She breaks into a huge smile, which softens some of the traces of the recent strain and sleepless nights from her face.

"Pen offered me a job. I'm rejoining the firm when Luke and I get back from the Vineyard."

"Seriously? Oh, Simone. I'm so happy for you. I've always known you were too good for corporate law. You *belong* in a courtroom."

I grab her in a hug, and we have a little impromptu dance party in the kitchen.

"What about you? What did Josh say about your job?"

I pour myself a glass of sparkling water and tell my best friend everything. Well, almost everything.

THE NOISE LEVEL on the back porch has increased considerably, and someone has linked their phone to the outdoor Bluetooth speakers. I strain to hear the music playing in the background. It must have been Raj or Poppy, because I don't recognize the songs at all.

Standing at the open French doors, I watch happily as Simone plays with Jasper and Finn, tossing tennis balls and playing tug-of-war. She doesn't seem to care in the least if her beautiful, flowing summer dress ends up covered with dog hair or grass stains. Luke is loading up the grill with enough food to feed a battalion, completely in his element. Declan is drinking a Guinness and laughing at something Raj has said. Hicks has his hand on Raj's shoulder and is making a point with a beer bottle. Maybe they're critiquing Luke's grilling skills, because I see him give them all a one-fingered salute without skipping a beat. Two peas in a pod, he and Simone. Everyone doubles over with laughter.

Poppy has pulled out her enormous Harry Potter bag and is in the process of painting Emma's nails a shade that, from where I'm standing, looks pretty similar to the blue of Emma's braces and the streaks in Poppy's hair. I also notice that the tin of British biscuits has somehow made its way from the kitchen cupboard and is open on the outdoor dining table next to Emma.

As Emma peers into the tin, she says accusingly, "Uncle Declan! You've been eating *my* cookies!"

"Not me," he says. His eyes are bright with laughter as they meet mine. Then he totally throws me under the bus, pointing his Guinness bottle in my direction. "There's your biscuit thief."

"Yep, guilty as charged," I admit, throwing up my hands. I hadn't seen Declan touch the tin since he'd offered it to me the night I'd been attacked, and I'd wondered more than once why he even had it in the pantry. Mystery solved.

Raj approaches me as I stand in the doorway, watching all the goings-on. "You all right, Raj?" I ask. "You need another drink or anything?"

"No, thanks," he says, raising a can of cider. "I'm good. How're you doing?"

"I'm getting there. Good days and bad days, you know. But more good than bad, now. This is helping." I wave a hand, taking in the clusters of conversation, the romping dogs, even the unrecognizable music.

"That's great."

"So, I wanted to tell you something without getting all dramatic, okay?"

Raj looks uncertain, waiting for whatever I'm about to say next. "What is it?"

"You've seen the video, right?" He doesn't have to ask which video I'm referring to; I think everyone in the DC metro area has likely seen it by now. "There's a point in the very beginning where I completely froze, the way I always did when we practiced the chokeholds, remember? But after maybe thirty seconds, I finally got my act together and did what I've been training for all this time." I pause. "You know why that was?"

He shakes his head, but I think he knows what I'm about to say. "Why?"

"That was you. Clear as day I heard you telling me to not to panic and to breathe. And then I heard Declan's voice telling me the same thing, to remember to breathe."

Raj's eyes are on me. "And you did it. Not me or Declan. You."

"I have absolutely no doubt that you saved me that night. You, Declan, Hicks – everyone at the gym who's taught me how to protect myself. I'd considered a few other places before finding Trident. It feels right, being there with all of you. It could have gone very badly for me that night, but it didn't. I have you to thank for that. You're not half-bad, for a former cop and all," I say teasingly.

Raj takes a sip of cider, buys some time before he speaks. "I appreciate your saying all that, Kate, I really do. But don't sell yourself short – you saved yourself. We gave you the tools and the means. You did the rest."

I notice that he's called me by my name for the first time. "You can think whatever you like, Choirboy." I can't resist a grin. "But I was there, and I know."

"Have it your way, Wheels." He's smiling as he says it. I watch him trot over to help Emma who, having eaten several of her biscuits, is now being dragged halfway across the lawn by Finn, who refuses to surrender the tug rope toy.

I hear Poppy's voice from behind me. "You okay, Kate?"

"Yeah, Poppy. How're you doing? You must be relieved that this is all over, too. I'm sorry I haven't checked in like I should have."

She doesn't look in the least traumatized by recent events, though. She looks happy and excited. "Everything's amazing. I don't have to wear that hideous security guard uniform anymore, I'm making decent money for once, and I get to work with Declan."

I smile at the face she makes when mentioning the insipid grey outfit she'd had to wear. The poor kid had been practically invisible, but maybe that had been the point of the uniform. She's anything but invisible today. She's wearing a bright red skater-style dress with a swingy skirt, and her usual Doc Martens have been replaced by gold gladiator sandals. The transformation is remarkable.

I lower my voice. "Speaking of money, if you need any help with tuition, I'd be more than happy to help. It's the least I can do. If you hadn't taken that video and brought it to Hicks, I don't know how things might have gone for me."

"Thanks, but I'm good. The bursar's office called a few days ago. A new scholarship for software engineering students was just announced, and I made the list! It covers my tuition plus a monthly stipend. I don't even have to work now, if I don't want to. But who in their right mind would turn down a chance to work with Declan?"

"How is it, working with him?"

"Well, I don't know because we haven't really started yet." At my puzzled expression, she asks, "Didn't he tell you? He says since I've been working my arse off," she grins, trying to mimic his Irish accent, "I deserved some time off. Two whole weeks, with pay! He sent me links to a bunch of articles and said he wanted my opinion on them. Declan O'Rourke wants my opinion! How crazy is that? I mean, he's just brilliant, you know?"

"Yes, Poppy, he is, isn't he?"

HICKS AND I are quietly content in the early twilight. He's joined me in a short stroll around the perimeter of the yard. He has his hands clasped loosely behind his back but his posture is as upright as ever. As we reach the far end of the lawn, we pause and look back toward the house. The porch is aglow with strings of outdoor lights, and music is still playing faintly in the background as everyone mills around with Diane's desserts, coffee and tea. Luke and Declan had outdone themselves with the meal, and I don't know how any of us can move after all we've eaten.

Declan and Emma have roused themselves and are out in the middle of the lawn, both of them barefoot in the grass, throwing frisbees and tennis balls to the dogs. There's a lot of laughter, teasing, and an occasional playful hug – such easy affection between them. Poppy and Raj join in, then Simone tugs Luke to his feet to add to the chaos.

"He'd have made a great father," I say, thinking aloud.

I'm startled when Hicks replies, not realizing he's also been watching his daughter and his good friend. "Yes, but he's a great honorary uncle, too."

"It looks that way. I'm glad he's going home. I don't know the whole story, but it seems like it's time."

"What about you?" he asks. "Are you going back to work soon?"

"Not just yet. I'm taking some time away. I'll be back in couple of weeks."

I'm conscious of a pang of longing when I look at Simone and Luke. What they have. Then I push the feeling down. They deserve to be happy. And so do I. Time to do something about that.

We walk a little more, this time back in the direction of the house. "This is all down to you, Hicks," I tell the older man as I take it all in: these wonderful friends, old and new; and Finn and Jasper, panting madly but unwilling to end their play time with so many willing buddies. And there's Declan, smiling and laughing, in the midst of it all. He glances up, sees me and Hicks. He watches us for moment, his expression relaxed and open. Like a man who's content with the world and his place in it. Ready to go home after too long away.

"Me? No, I can't take any credit for this. This is just life, isn't it? People who care about each other, spending time together. Helping each other through the hard times, celebrating the happy times. I'm glad you're part of our little family."

I squeeze his arm gratefully. "So am I. I'm very lucky to have found you all."

"Luck had nothing to do with it."

"What do you mean?"

"I think we all end up exactly where we're meant to be."

"You really think so?" And what of Declan, then, on his way to Galway? Is that where he's meant to be? Is that what Hicks, in his understated, gentle way, is trying to tell me?

As we meander slowly back to the house, we hear the muted sound of popping champagne corks. I look up in surprise to see Luke and Declan each holding a bottle of champagne.

"Any idea what we're celebrating?" Hicks asks.

"No idea at all. Maybe just life?"

"Glad to see you've been paying attention, Kate."

We're almost at the porch when he pauses and pulls something from his trouser pocket. "The contractors finished the repairs and clean-up this morning. You'll want these back." He holds out my keyring, thoughtfully regarding the silver pectoral cross that hangs among the keys. "I'm curious, though. Why do you have a medal of my namesake on your keyring?"

"Your namesake? It's not your namesake. It's Saint ..." My eyes widen in astonishment.

Hicks is smiling broadly, knowingly. "Exactly."

At first I can't believe it. But then I can. Of all the names beginning with *C*, how could it have been anything else? I look at him, searching his gaze, as if he somehow knows. But no, of course not. He's merely keeping the promise he'd made to tell me his name one day. Nothing more. I accept the keys without a word.

We step onto the porch where Declan is handing around glasses, and everyone's looking expectant, wondering what the occasion is. Simone's looking a bit flushed; at first, I think it's just the quantity of wine she's had to drink. We did start pretty early in the day, after all.

Then Luke lifts his glass and says, "Everyone, please join me in celebrating some very exciting news. My new restaurant, The Twelve Apostles, will be opening early next year in Arlington. I expect to see you all at the grand opening!"

Amidst claps and cheers, I dash over to Simone and throw my arms around her. "Why didn't you *tell* me?" I practically shriek. "I am so, so happy for you."

I realize Simone is looking stunned; this isn't the announcement she'd expected Luke to make.

"What is it?" I ask.

"I had absolutely no idea."

We turn in search of Luke, who is beaming at his wife as we approach. "You found an investor?" she asks incredulously. "Oh my God, Luke, you found an investor!" Simone practically jumps into her husband's arms, and he swings her around before setting her back on her feet and kissing her.

They're talking excitedly, and she is hugging him, kissing him again, long and hard. She looks the happiest I've ever seen her. Luke is gesturing animatedly and laughing, shaking his head as if in disbelief at his good fortune. I blink away tears as I watch them, two dear friends taking another step toward a dream.

Declan makes his way over to me. He has a champagne glass in one hand and a half-full bottle in the other. "Top up?" he asks.

"Thanks, but I can't. I'm driving." Not long ago, that statement might've prompted the offer to stay the night in the guestroom that I'd started to think of as my own. Stupid, the little things that trip you up.

He hesitates. "Ah, right. I've probably had enough myself." He sets the bottle on a nearby table. "It was a good day, yes?"

"A very good day," I agree, taking a sip of the last of my champagne. "It was kind of you and Luke to do this."

"It was nothing. We all needed it."

"Did Luke tell you Simone's going back to work for Pen?"

"Yes, he did." A pause. "Pen and Simone. You think the legal world's ready for them?"

"Not in a million years. I'd give anything for a ringside seat at their first courtroom appearance."

I catch Simone watching me and Declan, see her small smile. I smile in return and raise my glass in a silent toast. There was a time when she'd be spinning some story in her head about me and 'Dublin,' seeing us like this. She knows better now, though. I do a double-take and see Luke glancing in our direction, too. But he's not looking at us, I realize. Both he and Simone are looking at Declan.

I turn and look carefully at him, too, as if expecting to see something in his face, some telltale sign that will confirm the thoughts that are forming at the edge of my consciousness. Luke and Declan's recent friendliness. Their animated conversations while they were setting up today. The realization comes to me slowly, as it had with Hicks' revelation about his name.

"It's you, isn't it? You're Luke's angel investor."

Declan laughs as he strolls away from me toward the house, his champagne glass dangling from one hand, the half-full bottle swinging carelessly in the other.

"There you go again, Kate, with your wild conspiracy theories."

Wild conspiracy theories, my ass.

IT'S NEARLY NINE o'clock by the time everyone leaves; the party's lasted much longer than I'd expected. Everyone seems reluctant to go, as if knowing that things are changing. That this is a special time we might not have again.

Since Declan and Luke had organized and cooked, Raj and Hicks see it as only fair that they take on clean-up duty. And bless them, they knock it out with a military efficiency that's a little scary to watch. All the leftovers are wrapped in neat packages for everyone to take home, and the place is left immaculate.

There are hugs and farewells near the front door, and I watch with amusement as Emma snags a packet of Jaffa Cakes on her way out. Somehow I'm the last to leave, which has me feeling vaguely uncomfortable. I crouch down to give Jasper and Finn a final hug, and I fight back foolish tears as I stand up. I reach blindly for my bag. You will not cry, damn it.

"Who's—"

"The lads will be in good hands. No need to worry."

I can only bring myself to nod in reply.

Declan's by the door, holding Hicks' carefully-wrapped leftovers and Diane's empty platter.

"Thanks." My vision clears enough to where I'm able to look him in the eye now and take the platter and food. "Safe home, Declan."

"Thanks. Goodnight."

I walk past him and out the door to my car.

"Kate, wait up, would you?"

He stands in front of me, looking uncertain. Then he puts his arms around me, doesn't speak for a moment. "I'm glad you're okay." He lets me go and turns back to the house. "Try to stay out of trouble, would you?" I look at his retreating back, resist the impulse to have the last word.

Time to go.

When I'd parked in front of Declan's garage earlier this afternoon, the doors had been closed. They're open now, and his pickup truck is parked in the bay directly in front of me. The doors are both coming down; Declan must've hit the remote from inside the house. Curious as to what his other vehicle is, I glance into the second bay as I back out onto the gravel driveway. I drive slowly past, staring at the vehicle that's parked there before it's hidden behind the closing door: a white, late-model BMW SUV.

TWENTY-NINE

THERE'S NO SUCH thing as ghosts. There aren't, right?

With an unsteady hand, I put my key in the lock and open the door.

It's the same house. It has the same good bones, as Declan had once said. Same as it always was, except for my renovations of a few years ago. And the new windows and front door.

I set my keys, bag, and the accumulated mail on the kitchen table; open the Roman blinds to let in some bright August sunshine. I go through each room, opening the shutters, banishing the dark. Dust motes float lazily in a shaft of sunlight in the living room, a reminder of the time I've been away. I go back to the kitchen, sort the mail into piles for reading, shredding and recycling. Something to do. Mindless. Postponing the inevitable.

Eventually, I make my way to the stairs, my hand on the railing. A polished-oak lifeline. I ascend slowly, each step more leaden than the last. Then I'm at the top. I deliberately turn right, toward the two smaller bedrooms. Everything is just as I'd left it. But something here is different.

The smell. I'd noticed it when I'd walked in the front door. Not offensive, just different. Hicks had arranged for cleaners to come, the ones you call afterward. After events like a week ago. Whatever they'd used to clean had left behind the faintest of odors. I decide I can live with it for now, no need to pull out my own cleaning supplies just yet.

I force myself to walk down the hall, toward my bedroom. Where it happened. Where the memories and the ghosts are. The wide planks of the hall are clean and polished; the same floorboard creaks as it always has. I cross the threshold and enter my room. I walk to the windows and open the shutters here, too. Then I walk around the room, trail my hand over the bed, plump a pillow. Go into the bathroom, see that everything here is the same, too. Back to the bedroom. I go to the closet, that place of brief refuge from the horror that had awaited just inside the threshold. No physical traces of the tragedy remain. That doesn't mean they're not here.

From downstairs, the doorbell chimes, jolting me out of my reverie. I descend the stairs quickly, grateful for an excuse to escape both the room and my thoughts.

My relief is short-lived: Marco Colletti is standing on my front porch.

I know the shock shows on my face because the old man hesitates before speaking, misinterpreting my expression. He's leaning on a cane and looking more frail than I have ever seen him.

"Is this a bad time, *cara*?"

I shake my head, swallowing the lump that's formed in my throat. Of all the times for him to appear. It's not just the timing that's unsettled me – it's the man himself. This wonderful, kind man, who was such a generous and thoughtful friend to me and my parents, appears gaunt and joyless. For once, he looks like the elderly man that he is. Aware of how much I've contributed to his sudden decline, I am truly at a loss as to what to say.

I look past him out the open front door and see a minivan parked in the driveway. Marco's daughter, Frankie, is behind the wheel. When she sees that I'm at home and have answered the door, she gets out of the vehicle and joins us, carrying a shopping bag.

"Please, won't you both come in?" I ask, thinking that this house, where a son and brother was killed, must be the absolute last place they would want to be.

"Are you sure? Only for a minute, then, Papa?" She takes her father's arm and leads him into the house.

"I'm so sorry, I've been away, and I wasn't expecting ..." My voice trails off. I start to close the door behind them, pause when I look into the street and see a white SUV slowly drive past. I close and lock the door, then turn back to my unexpected visitors. "Please, sit down. May I get you something to drink?"

"Thank you, but we're not staying." Marco braces himself on the silver-topped cane, while Frankie walks into the living room. We are all as uncomfortable as three people in our situation can possibly be. Our families' longstanding friendship, which had always been a source of good memories and goodwill, has now been overshadowed by the recent violent and tragic events.

Frankie, bless her, tries to fill the silence with polite small talk. "Kate, this place looks like a different house from the one I remember. How long ago did you renovate? I think the last time I was here was for one of your parents' Christmas parties," she says wistfully. A lifetime ago, then.

"Around five years ago."

She stands in the kitchen and continues to look around, taking in all the changes.

"Are you sure you won't sit down?" I ask Marco again.

"No, *cara*, thank you. We won't keep you long. I've come to apologize," he says somberly.

"Apologize?" I ask, aghast. "What could you possibly have to apologize for?"

"Anthony. I came to apologize for Anthony. And for being a foolish old man who couldn't see what was in front of his eyes."

"You have no reason apologize to me. The only person responsible for Anthony was Anthony." Clumsily, knowing no matter what I say, it'll be the wrong thing – but knowing I have to say *something* – I continue, "I do owe you an apology, Signor Colletti," reverting to my childhood form of address. I cover the elderly man's hand with my own where it rests on the head of the cane. "I'm sorry." I'm barely able to get the words out. "If there had been any other way. . ." I lower my head. "I'm so very sorry."

"He was a good boy, once. He got a little lost along the way, I think." He looks at me thoughtfully for a moment and then he, too, looks around the house, at all the things that have stayed the same and all the things that have changed. "We had a lot of happy times here, didn't we?" he asks, a glimmer of the man I remember in his eyes.

"Yes, we did." And there are so many good memories here. I think of them now, think of my parents, the Collettis, the time they'd spent here when Leonora was still alive, when Anthony, Frankie, and I were kids.

Frankie is watching us, trying to hide the fact that she's crying. I reach out a hand to her, and to my eternal relief, she takes it. We stand in the living room, remembering all the good times we'd shared in this house and trying to forget the bad. We remember, and we mourn. In memoriam. Maybe no formal wake or *shiva* was held here for Anthony, in this place where he died, but this solemn little gathering is a remembrance all the same.

Marco turns to his daughter. "Frankie, do you have it?" She moves to his side and hands him the bag. He removes the contents, and I cover my mouth to stifle a small gasp. I had completely forgotten, in all the chaos and insanity of the past several weeks – had it been only weeks? – about my shoulder bag.

Marco hands me the bag and I take it, almost reverently, turning it over and over in my hands. Just as he'd done when I was a child, he had magically transformed something in need of a little tender loving care into a thing of beauty again.

"*Grazie mille, Signore*," I whisper, hugging him gently. "*È perfetto.*" I look down at the bag again. It's flawless, no sign of the tear, and the soft leather has been polished to a beautiful, high gloss.

"Your parents would be so proud of you, Caterina."

"*Grazie di cuore.*" Thank you with all my heart.

We all hug each other one last time, and Frankie leads her father carefully down the front steps and into the van. They wave and are gone.

So are the ghosts.

BY THE TIME Poppy arrives twenty minutes later, I've taken a couple of vases down from the high cabinet above the refrigerator and have washed and dried them, ready for the flowers I'd promised her yesterday from my cutting garden.

"Are you looking forward to getting back to campus?" I ask as I show her into the kitchen. "Fall semester starts pretty soon, doesn't it?"

"I was looking forward to it. But one of my roommates wants his girlfriend to move in with us when they all come back next week. I'm really not happy about it. It's hard enough getting ready in the morning as it is, even with two bathrooms. Adding another person to the mix is going to be a total pain."

"I'm sorry about that, Poppy. Hopefully you can all find a way to work it out." I pick up two curved wicker flower baskets and a pair of clippers from the storage bench in the mudroom. "Let's go out back. You can take a look around and decide which flowers you want to take home with you."

She walks along the gardens, exclaiming over all the colors and varieties of flowers. "This is amazing. It's like pictures I've seen of English country gardens. It's all so beautiful."

"Thanks. My mother started the gardens back when she and my father first moved into the house. And this is nothing compared to Diane's gardens." I point next door. "I'll have to take you over there sometime to show you. She would love it."

We walk around the yard, and I absent-mindedly deadhead a rose here, pull a weed there as Poppy wanders among the flowerbeds. A thought suddenly occurs to me. "Poppy, how would you like to live here?"

"Here? With you?"

I laugh. "Yes, here, with me. I've got two extra bedrooms that are just sitting empty. A bathroom, too. I mean, I understand if you'd rather not live here because of what happened. But if you're at all interested, I'd love the company. Maybe you'd rather live with someone your own age, though."

"Are you kidding? I'd love to. Are you sure?"

"Yes, I am." Even though the idea had only just come to me, it could be perfect for both of us. "We can work out the details later. I'm going away for a couple of weeks starting

Wednesday. If it'll bother you being here on your own, we could wait until I come back. What do you say?"

"I say you have yourself a roommate. This is going to be so awesome! And I have no problem being here while you're away, if you don't."

"Terrific. When we're done here, I'll show you your new room."

From next door, I can hear the sounds of Diane filling Luna's wading pool and the dog's excited barking.

"Hey, Diane," I call over to my neighbor. "Do you have a minute? There's someone I'd like you to meet."

Diane opens the gate, and Luna rockets through the opening, a black, wet streak of lightning. Poppy shrieks with laughter and darts out of the way just in time. The dog makes an excited circuit of my yard, stopping suddenly when she sees Poppy, then dashes back through the gate and returns a minute later with a plush dog toy in her mouth.

Drops it at Poppy's feet.

There's no doubt about it: It's love at first sight. For both dog and human.

"I'LL BE RIGHT BACK," I tell the two women. "While you cut flowers, I want to do some weeding. I just need to grab my gloves." I hand off the baskets and the clippers and watch as Diane and Poppy meander through Diane's yard, my neighbor pointing and naming flowers as they go.

The doorbell rings – again – right as I get the gloves and am ready to go back outside. I've been home for all of an hour after being away for more than a week, and this will be the third visitor I've had this morning. At least Poppy had been expected. And nothing could be worse than the sad visit from Marco and Frankie.

Nothing except – Noah. Who is now standing in front of me and smiling as though he expects a returning hero's welcome.

The white SUV in the street. I hadn't imagined it. I think about the vehicle I'd seen last night in Declan's garage. What were the odds? If Simone were here, I know exactly what she'd say. I don't say it, but I do think it: *For fuck's sake.*

"Hello, Kate."

"Noah." I'm in the doorway, one hand still on the door.

"How are you?"

"What are you doing here?" I step onto the porch, partially closing the door behind me. This man is not coming into my home.

"I came to apologize for the way I behaved the last time we saw each other. I've missed you. It was a mistake, our splitting up."

"You've got to be kidding." My voice is dripping with sarcasm.

"Of course I'm not kidding. Kate, we were good together. You know that." He glances around, looking uncomfortable. "Do we really have to have this conversation out here?"

"I'm not having a conversation with you. I can't believe you have the nerve to show up here after what you did. You vandalize my house—"

"*What*? I didn't vandalize your house. What're you talking about?"

He puts on a very convincing act; I'll give him that. If I didn't know him better, I just might buy it. But I do know him, all too well. I slide my phone from my back pocket and find the pictures I'd taken for the police report. Just looking at the images makes me furious all over again.

"You're saying you didn't do this?" I show him the phone.

"No, I swear. That wasn't me."

I notice he won't meet my eyes, and that's all the answer I need. He may be a psychopath, but he's a very bad liar when he's put on the spot.

"It doesn't matter. You need to leave."

I hear the sound of the sun porch door squeaking closed at the back of the house. Poppy appears, looking for all the world like some kind of mythical garden sprite, with a pink Gerbera daisy tucked behind an ear and a basket of flowers draped over her arm. She slows when she sees me, the half-open door, and the man standing outside, barely two yards away. She has no idea who Noah is, no clue as to our history. Yet she comes and stands beside me, wraps one arm around my waist. Doesn't say a word.

I hear quiet footsteps as Diane positions herself on my other side. She's holding her own basket of flowers. She casually loops her free arm around my shoulders.

The three of us stand together, facing Noah.

"Everything all right here, Kate?" Diane asks in her honeyed Southern drawl.

"Yes, everything's perfect. Noah was just leaving."

"You're making a mistake," he says to me. "I'm the best thing that ever happened to you."

"Noah Blackstone, you're not the best thing to ever happen to *anyone*. You need to leave, right now."

I think it's the first time I've ever seen him speechless. And my God, is it priceless.

ONCE I'VE CLOSED the door on Noah, I turn to look at Poppy and Diane.

"I never liked that man," Diane says, walking into the kitchen and setting down her basket.

Poppy follows, curious now. "Your ex?"

"Uh-huh," I say.

She looks thoughtful but doesn't say anything else.

We busy ourselves for a few minutes, taking the flowers from the baskets and sorting them by color and height on the counter. I look down at Diane's basket and see something I don't expect to see – at all – among the colorful blooms.

"Adding concealed carry to your flower-cutting routine, Diane?" I ask. Poppy looks confused for a minute, then her gaze follows mine to what lays at the bottom of Diane's basket. Her eyes widen almost comically.

"I saw him driving by earlier today, so I kept an eye out, that's all," she says, her tone casual. "Never hurts to be prepared."

"No, it never does."

"Arrogant jackass," she mutters. "Now, your quiet Irishman. He's a completely different story."

"Totally," Poppy chimes in wholeheartedly. "Kate's quiet Irishman is amazing." I look at her in surprise. "Well, I'm not blind," she says. "Anyone who looks at you can tell you're – you know – together."

"Is that so?" is all I can manage to say. Obviously she hadn't picked up on the tension between Declan and me yesterday. I guess we see what we want to see at times, whatever fits the narrative we've written in our heads.

I watch with interest as Diane expertly arranges flowers in one of the vases, then shows Poppy how to do the same. Diane and my mother had both been way out of my league, with a natural flair for creating beautiful displays. I've never had the knack, but I try. Poppy now has a flower tucked behind each ear and is completely engrossed in the task at hand. Diane and I exchange a glance when Poppy carefully adds the last bloom. The end result would have given my mother a run for her money. "It's absolutely beautiful, Poppy," I tell her.

"Gorgeous," Diane agrees. "Who's ready for chocolate lava cake?"

I think I hear Luna bark from next door.

LATER, POPPY and I take a walk through the house and decide which spare bedroom will be hers. We agree that she'll move in on Tuesday, to give her time to settle in before classes start and before I leave. I see her to the door, where she throws her arms around me.

"This is going to be amazing!"

"I think so, too." I laugh and wave her off from the porch, watching as she carefully backs out of the driveway.

Once she's left, I go upstairs to my room and sit down on the bed. Picking up the black leather shoulder bag and holding it to my face, I inhale the familiar scents of leather and polish. It's unquestionably a beautiful bag, the craftsmanship is exquisite, and I'd missed having it. I can almost picture my mother selecting it from a Florentine vendor's stall during my parents' last trip to Italy and smile at the thought. I can imagine her wrangling over the price, enjoying the friendly banter in Italian, and my father's patient good humor while he waited. Her emerging, triumphant and happy. A fair price and the perfect gift for her graduating daughter.

But it is only a bag, after all.

A knock on the back door makes me look up. I leave the bag and go downstairs. I can't suppress a laugh as I open the door. Diane's a tall woman, but even she's dwarfed by the enormous floral bouquet from Pen, which she holds out to me.

"I thought you'd want these here, now that you're home."

"Thanks, Diane. And thanks for everything." We exchange a look, and I know I don't have to say any more than that.

"I'm always here for you, Kate. You know that."

THIRTY

"HEY, RAJ. I wasn't expecting you and Poppy for another hour or so. Come on in."

"I know; I hope you don't mind. Poppy's on her way, but I wanted to talk to you before she got here."

"Everything okay?"

He looks uncomfortable, much as he had the first time he'd visited a few weeks ago. "Maybe it's better if we sit."

I give him a curious look and lead him into the sunroom. "What's going on? Are you all right?" I ask as we sit down.

"No, not really. I guess I should start at the beginning. Remember I told you I was an MP in the Army? That much is true. But I didn't enlist because I wanted to – I enlisted because I had to. The summer after college graduation, a bunch of us thought it'd be cool to try to hack into a government agency's network. Just a prank. We were so stupid. We actually hacked the CIA, if you can believe it. Of course, we eventually got caught. That's when we were told we had a choice: prison time or the military. I later found out my assignment was just a front for one of the Army's clandestine units. So, I trained as an MP and was attached to a garrison but I didn't actively work as a military policeman."

At my shocked expression, he says, "Yeah, I know, right? And I bet you were thinking I was judging you because you don't like the police. Like I'm in any position to judge anyone."

"Raj, this is none of my business; you don't have to tell me any of this."

"No, I want to. And I need to, because of what I found out. It involves you."

"Me? How?"

He stands up, starts pacing, finally stops to look out at the gardens. "I never worked as an MP, but I was trained in police procedures. Even though your parents' accident was years ago, it really bothered me. Thinking that the police screwed things up so badly that someone could just walk away after killing two people, it just didn't sit right. I wanted to see what I could find out, maybe set your mind at ease somehow."

"What did you do?" I stare at him, my mouth suddenly dry.

"You probably think it's none of my business, that I had no right. I couldn't stop thinking about what you told me. I wondered about the other things that were happening at the time, with you. Mostly, the tracker on your car. Even though you said you had an idea who it might be, it still bothered me. If someone could track your car, what else might they do? Would they try to tap your phone or bug your house?"

I stand up, hold up my hands. "Wait, Raj, stop right there, please. I really appreciate your taking an interest, but this is all sounding a little crazy."

"I know, Kate, but please, hear me out. A few days ago, Hicks asked me to come by and let the contractors in because he couldn't make it. While they were working, I had a look around. And I did a sweep." He looks directly at me now, no longer uncertain. "I found three listening devices in the house. I have no idea how long they'd been there. But I do know that they're not cheap toys you can buy online. These are serious, state-of-the-art devices."

I lower myself slowly back into the chair. "I can't believe this." I start to rub my temples, put my hands in my lap when I catch myself doing it – again. "This is insane." I close my eyes, consider the implications. Someone had put listening devices in my home. In my *home*. "Where did you find them? Where, exactly, were they?"

"There was one behind the mirror in the front entry; one in your office behind some archaeology reference books; and one in the pendant light above the kitchen table."

"None upstairs? None in the bedrooms?" I swallow, my heart racing.

"None. I checked twice."

Small mercies. "Where are they now?"

"Not here – that's all I'll say. I started to do some digging and eventually came across files that weren't meant to be found; they were buried pretty deep. Then I found the connection I was looking for. To your parents." He looks suddenly much older than he should. "What does the name Sam Miller mean to you?"

That name. After all these years. The bastard. "If you've been digging, Raj, you know who he is. He was the drunk driver who killed my parents."

He shakes his head regretfully. "No, he's not. Sam Miller wasn't the driver of the car that killed your parents. No such person exists; I checked everywhere. His identity and the story about the mishandled evidence was completely fabricated, to hide the real driver's identity. A drunk driver did kill your parents, but not one you'd been led to believe all these years."

"No, you're wrong. That's not possible."

"I'm afraid it is." He takes a deep breath. "The person responsible was someone who was very well-connected, someone who could pull strings and make promises as well as threats. Someone who couldn't risk being charged with a DUI and vehicular manslaughter because it would cost them their entire career." He pauses briefly. "Her entire career."

"You know who this person is? Raj, *tell* me. Who killed my parents?"

The sound of quiet clapping makes us both jump in surprise.

Diane is standing in the sunroom door, an amused expression on her face. "Well done, Mr. Singh. Very well done. You haven't lost your touch, I see."

"Diane?" I ask, incredulous. She doesn't reply. "Raj?" I look to him for confirmation. He looks as astonished and horrified as I am at Diane's arrival. It takes him a minute to compose himself. Then he nods resignedly.

I stare in disbelief at my long-time friend and neighbor. "No, no, no. Tell him he's wrong, Diane. Tell him," I plead. When she doesn't respond, I stammer, "You—you told me that a drunk driver named Sam Miller was responsible for killing my parents. That's what you told me."

She just looks at me without saying a word. It feels as though the bottom has dropped out of my world – again.

"All along, it was *you*? *You* killed my parents?" The words nearly choke me.

"Oh, sweetheart. It was an accident. Just an accident."

"*Just* an *accident*?"

"It wasn't deliberate. I loved your parents, you know that. Your mother and I were like sisters."

At that, I leap to my feet. "Sisters?" I practically spit the word. "Are you insane? You killed her and my father and then made up some story to cover your tracks?" My heart feels about ready to burst out of my chest. "You helped me with the funeral arrangements, helped me pack up their things. For years, you lied to me. Every time you opened your mouth. All this time, you should have been locked up for what you did to them."

"But I couldn't go to prison; don't you see? What would have happened to you? You'd just lost your parents. You needed me. You were the daughter I never had."

I stare at her, open-mouthed in astonishment. "Don't you dare call me that. I'm not your daughter."

"My going to prison wouldn't have brought your parents back, Kate. They were dead. That's a fact, regardless of who killed them." Her tone is mildly condescending, as if she's explaining something to a small child.

My mouth is dry, my stomach is churning. As if all this weren't bad enough—I remember the listening devices. "Why … the … hell did you bug my house? And how long have you been spying on me?" I demand.

"Oh, not long. I'm not a voyeur, Kate," she says, sounding insulted at the idea. "A few weeks, maybe?"

"Why would you do that? I tell you everything!"

"No, you don't," she says in a singsong little voice. "You used to. You used to tell me everything – about work, your friends, Noah. And then—you didn't." She gives me a wounded look. "I had to find out you'd been attacked from a video on social media."

"There was a lot going on at the time. I never had the—" I stop myself, realizing that I'm attempting to justify myself to this woman – the person responsible for my parents' death. Standing now in front of me, in my home.

"It was the same day I met your Mr. O'Rourke," she adds with a small smile, then she adopts an aggrieved expression again. "I had absolutely no idea who he was; you'd never even mentioned him."

"My personal life is none of your business!" I'm almost shouting now.

Raj quietly gets to his feet and stands beside me, almost close enough to touch. Does he think I'm going to throw myself at Diane? I'm tempted, believe me.

"Of course it is. But you never said a word to me. About him, the Admiral, and young Raj here. Now why was that? I started to wonder. And since you weren't being as chatty as you usually were, I had to resort to other ways of finding out about your new friends." She leans casually against the doorframe, as if she's settling in for a bit of neighborhood gossip. "Let's start with your Irishman. Too bad about that wife of his, wasn't it? Although she wasn't the innocent everyone seemed to think she was. You play with the big boys; you're bound to get burned." She shrugs philosophically, then gives me a cloying smile. "I hate to say it, sweetheart, but he's way out of your league, anyway. Then there's the Admiral." Her eyes widen playfully. "A bit of a wild card, that one. I'll have to keep my eye on him."

I can only stare wordlessly at her. This woman is completely unhinged. And ever since my parents died, I'd thought she'd been a friend, a trusted confidante. We'd grieved together, buried my parents together, shared meals and drinks and so much more —for *years*. Every single minute had been a lie, a manipulation. Betrayal on a scale I can't even find words for.

"And young Mr. Singh here. You were the biggest threat of all," she says, turning to Raj, her eyes and voice deadly serious now, no longer playful. "I'd read your file, knew what you and your merry little band of social misfits were capable of. I couldn't take any chances you'd find out the truth."

"Get out of my house!" I shout.

"I'm not going anywhere." Diane's voice is ice-cold. No longer casually leaning against the doorframe, she moves further into the sunroom toward us.

Only then do I notice she's pulled out her Glock, not pointing it at us, but holding it down by her side. Every ounce of blood drains from my face.

Again, I'm aware of Raj next to me. He's shifted slightly; I can feel his arm, warm against mine, can feel his slow, steady breathing, while I'm practically hyperventilating, struggling to stay in control. How can he possibly be so calm?

"I don't understand," I say. "Why are you here now? How did you know that Raj came here to tell me all this?"

"Well, Mr. Singh isn't quite as sharp as he thinks he is. He removed all the devices he found last week." She raises her eyebrows expressively. "A lot can happen in a few days."

My skin prickles. There are *more*? The house I'd thought so safe and secure, so private – isn't. Isn't any of those things. Has it ever been?

"How did you get in to plant another device?" I ask, horrified.

"Don't be silly, Kate. I didn't have to lift a finger. You did it for me." That playful expression again, almost taunting, daring me to figure it out.

"I *what*?" I look dazedly around the house, trying to understand what she's saying. The realization finally hits me. My stunned gaze falls on the flower arrangement from Pen. "Oh, my God. The flowers."

Raj looks questioningly at me.

"There." I point to Pen's flowers, which I'd set in a corner of the sunroom. She must've put a device in the vase of flowers before she'd brought them over. Still in a state of shock, I turn back to Diane.

Her focus sharpens. "Now, what to do with you two? Hmm, murder-suicide? A rejected older woman and a handsome young man? Oh, and you are lovely, aren't you, Raj?" She looks at me sympathetically. "I'm sorry, Kate, but you're not exactly cougar material. No one would buy that story." She sighs melodramatically, shakes her head. "How disappointed your parents would be if they could see you now. All that promise – wasted."

My entire body goes rigid. I can no longer hear her words over the sudden buzzing in my ears; can see only through a haze of fury. Blistering rage courses through me like I've never experienced before; worse, even, than the night I'd been attacked.

I stare at her, my mind racing. And from out of nowhere, the words that saved me once before come back to me: *Remember to breathe.*

I take a long, steadying breath, slow my breathing, clear my head. I shift so that my arm brushes Raj's. I speak quietly, say those same three words so only he can hear: "Remember to breathe." I'm acutely aware of him next to me, aware that he's tensed now, ready to move. I'd know it even with my eyes shut.

Then we're in motion, launching ourselves at Diane, catching her completely off guard. We fall in a tangle of bodies, knocking over potted plants and hurricane lanterns, leaving shattered pottery and glass in our wake. Raj wrenches the weapon from Diane, who is no match for the younger, larger man, long-trained in the art of self-defense. Between the two of us, we subdue her, and Raj ties her hands from the of supply gardener's twine I keep on my potter's bench. Not exactly what I'd had in mind when I'd bought it for staking tomatoes and peppers, but – stranger things, I suppose.

Then – miracle of miracles – I, Kate Barrow, call the police.

"HELLO, KATE," a familiar voice says from the front entryway. Hicks is standing there, and for the first time since I've known him, he actually looks rattled, his usual calm composure noticeably absent.

"Hicks?" I watch dazedly as he walks over to Raj, speaks quietly to him, puts a reassuring hand on his upper arm. They nod to one another, then turn their attention to me.

"You all right there? You guys scared the living daylights out of me."

"Scared the daylights out of *you*?" I ask weakly as Raj and Hicks take seats on either side of me in the kitchen. "What are *you* doing here?"

From the yard next door, we hear Luna barking at all the commotion. Forgetting my current situation for the moment, I give Hicks a worried glance. "Luna – Diane's dog. Someone has to get her. She can't be left alone if they're taking Diane into custody."

"Oh, please," Diane says dismissively from the living room, where two burly Arlington County police officers are keeping an eye on her. "No one's taking me into custody. I'll be back home tonight."

Hicks walks over to the floral arrangement, lifts up the large vase and removes a small black device from the recess in the bottom. "This it?"

Raj smiles. "Yep, that'll be it."

"This should do nicely," Hicks replies, looking satisfied. He turns to Diane. "You were saying?"

She shoots us all a petulant look. "Luna can go to the county shelter for all I care. She always did love Vince more than me, anyway."

"No surprise there, you fucking nutcase," I can't help myself from saying. "Luna's not going to some shelter. Poppy and I are taking her. And you? You can go straight to hell. For all *I* care."

"DON'T LET HER get in your head, Kate. What she said back there. You know it's not true."

Raj and I are sitting on the sun porch with tall glasses of iced tea. Poppy is upstairs, unpacking the last of her things. I can hear her moving around, putting things away, going back and forth between her bedroom and bathroom as she gets settled in.

She'd arrived a few hours ago, astonished to see Diane being led away in handcuffs – my cake-baking, flower-arranging kindly neighbor. Or so she thought. Raj had filled her in on the morning's events while I'd cleaned up the aftermath of our little tussle with Diane. Damn. I'd really liked those hurricane lamps, and there are a few plants that might not make it, but such is life.

I rub absent-mindedly at the condensation ring my drink has left on the tempered-glass tabletop. "I'm not. Not really. The thing is, Raj, most of what she said is true. But not for long, not anymore." We're both quiet for a while, thinking about the events of the morning. "I'm such a terrible person," I finally confess.

Raj looks over at me in surprise. "What're you talking about?"

"I've spent more than a decade hating someone named Sam Miller and despising the police. I've let that hate and bitterness cloud my judgement and affect my entire life. That makes me as much of a monster as Diane."

"That's not true and you know it. You believed what Diane wanted you to believe, what she told you. It's what anyone in your position would've done, would've felt. Diane's the one who has to answer for all of that – not you."

"It's still unforgiveable to wish another person dead."

"Yeah, well, I'm not so sure I agree with you." He smiles then, unexpectedly. "It never crossed my mind that you'd want to go for Diane's weapon. Never in a million years. I mean, I know you can handle yourself, but that? That was intense."

"Yeah. I might have a nightmare or two, once I have time to think about it."

We share an edgy, stressed-out laugh.

After Diane had been taken away, Raj had explained it all to me as Hicks listened attentively. Raj had gone to Hicks with what he'd found out about Diane, and he'd told Hicks he was going to tell me everything. I'm still not sure what role the retired admiral has played in all of this, and honestly, I'm not sure I want to know, anyway. As far as the listening device goes? Technically, I don't think it's admissible as evidence, but that's something for all the high-paid lawyers to sort out. Pen would have a field day, I'm sure.

I hear the thud of the large Labrador as she clambers down the stairs; she and Poppy appear a minute later in the sunroom doorway. Luna's been glued to Poppy's side ever since she'd walked in the door. I don't know who's happier about that – Luna or Poppy.

Hicks had helped me carry Luna's bed, basket of toys, and her food and bowls through the back gate before the agents had locked up the house and taken Diane away. The dog seems to be settling in as easily as her new human companion. She and Poppy will be good company for each other while I'm away and once I'm back. And for me. No more coming home to a quiet, empty house.

Poppy's brimming with her usual nervous energy, even after all the trips she and Raj had made out to their cars and after racing up and down the stairs all afternoon as she unpacked. She flashes me and Raj a wide smile. "I don't know about you guys, but I'm famished. Who wants Vinnie's pizza? My treat!"

Luna barks her agreement. Pizza, it is.

AS RAJ IS LEAVING, he takes a wrapped package from beneath his keys on the entryway table and hands it to me.

"Thank you, Raj," I say, touched at the gesture.

"It's not from me. It's from Declan."

"Oh. All right. Thanks." Just one more thing I didn't see coming. "Raj, about Declan." I'm trying to find my way, to find the words. "He can never know. Those things Diane said about Cara. They might not even be true. But if they are—"

"I know, Kate. Hicks will take care of it."

"Make sure, okay?

"Of course."

"Thanks for everything. You took a huge chance, doing what you did for me."

"Same goes," Raj replies. "We make a good team, you know?"

"Yeah, we do. See you at Trident when I get back, Choirboy?"

A wide smile crosses his face. "Count on it. Oh, and Wheels?"

"Yes?"

He leans his head down, speaks quietly against my ear. "You are *so* a cougar."

I stare at him in astonishment. Then I throw back my head and laugh. "Get out of here," I tell him. We hug goodbye, and Poppy and Luna follow him out the door to say good night.

They're friends, Poppy tells me, and I'm happy about that. There's time enough for anything more if that's what they decide; they have their whole lives ahead of them. And we can all use good friends, can't we? Although I can't help but wonder if Hicks had the long game in mind, back when he'd asked Raj to keep an eye on Poppy until the threat from Anthony Colletti had passed.

I take Declan's package into my office and sit down at the desk. A book, from the shape and size of it. There's an envelope taped to the outside, and I peel it carefully away, careful not to tear the paper. Yes, I'm one of those people, the ones who carefully unwrap gifts and neatly fold the paper afterwards. For no particular reason, because the paper just ends up in the recycling. But anyway. I'm stalling, and I know it. I slice open the envelope and remove the thick dove-grey executive card. It has a bold navy border around all four sides. At the top, breaking the border line, is a small, simple, navy graphic of angel's wings.

In black, precise handwriting, like a draftsman's, Declan has written:

Kate, I watched the story of your family play out in the books you loved and the inscriptions you wrote to one another. Thank you for sharing them with me. Perhaps it's time to finally write your own story.

With gratitude, D.

I peel away the gift wrap to reveal a large leather-bound journal with the letter "C" on the cover, depicted in the colorful style of an illuminated initial. I smile, slip the card into the journal, and put them aside for later.

Then I pick up my phone.

"Josh? It's Kate. Tell Alex I'll see you both in McLean in two weeks."

THIRTY-ONE

IT'S BEEN like coming home.

The changes in the town and the university since I'd been a student here have been tremendous; but the familiar sight of the cathedral in the distance as the train approached the station made my heart leap as it always had. Here at last.

I'd had a teary and laughter-filled reunion with Fiona Gallagher, who'd once been a classmate and close friend of mine, all those years ago. She'd joined the university faculty as a lecturer after receiving her PhD and has been here for most of her career. We'd stayed in touch on and off since our student days, although our contact had dropped off in the past few years. Fiona, with her head of jet-black, cascading corkscrew curls, pale skin, and piercing green eyes, looks like a pre-Raphaelite painting. Until she lets loose with a stream of profanity that would make the long-suffering nuns at her former parochial school pull out their rosaries, that is. I'll bet she strikes absolute terror in the hearts of her undergrads. At least until they've made it to their second year and figure out she's really a pushover, once you get to know her.

It was Fiona's recent emails that had planted a seed of possibility, of hope, precisely when I needed it most. My phone call to her had set things in motion that I'd been dreaming of for so long. To be able to do this work and have a life back in Virginia is more than I'd thought possible.

Even better, Viktoriya is here, too, has been since long before the war. She'd accepted a faculty position six years ago and even managed to bring some of her family over when her country was first invaded. Viktoriya's calm and capable demeanor is the perfect counterbalance to Fiona's drama; nothing fazes her. She's the one you call when disaster strikes, or just when you need something done right now and right the first time – no BS, no excuses. She's a beautiful, Ukrainian blue-eyed blonde who's worked hard to get past any misconceptions people have regarding her looks. She's also one of the few people brave enough to go toe-to-toe with Fiona without backing down.

The more I see the two of them together, the more I'm reminded of Simone and Josh. I'd known Fiona and Viktoriya years before I'd met either of my two American friends, and I seem to have duplicated them back home, just with different accents and personalities. It's both strangely comforting and slightly alarming.

Despite the years that have passed, the evenings we've spent together in the pub since I arrived are wonderfully familiar. Catching up, telling stories, taking stock – these two women know me as well as anyone ever had, even after all this time. Some things are truly universal; we gripe about work, relationships, politics, and the state of the world in general. Nothing new under the sun. Except just about everything.

I don't have the focus and discipline of Trident routines and workouts here in Durham, but I do have archaeology. For a time, it was enough, and it is again. Fiona's latest project is the ongoing excavation of a medieval abbey. The reason she'd contacted me was the discovery of an illuminated manuscript, which had once been my area of expertise. The work will keep me busy for years, if I play my cards right. I won't start my own work until after the summer dig season, which is fine with me. I need to get up to speed on the latest technology, like digital reconstructions and drone-guided imaging, and I have a lot of research to catch up on before I can actually contribute anything. Fiona has put her faith in me, and I'm not about to let her down.

Being back in the field takes all my energy and focus, which helps me forget Diane's betrayal, my role in Anthony's death – and Declan's absence, if I'm honest. Mourning for my parents ended years ago; but Diane's duplicity will haunt me for a very long time. It was calculated and manipulative on a scale I can't wrap my head around. I'd once thought of Noah as a psychopath; his behavior was child's play compared with Diane's. One day I'll forgive myself for being such a mug, as my British friends would say. I have a long way to go, though.

I start my days with an early walk and work all day at the site – sifting, sorting, cataloguing, and sketching finds. Tasks that fill the hours and fill my head. I know it's not what he'd intended it for, but the pages of Declan's notebook are filling up with rough images of artifacts, even though my version won't be part of the team's records. Sketching is meditative and calming, and some of them aren't half-bad, even if I am a little rusty. I spend my evenings in the pub and drop into bed each night, more exhausted than I can ever remember being. If I dream, at least there are no nightmares. For now, that's enough.

"SEE YOU DOWN the pub?" Fiona's voice calls from the far end of the trench where I'm working.

"Sure, as soon as I've cleaned up." I'm crouched down, gathering my tools, when a shadow falls across the damp soil of the trench. I don't glance up, expecting that it's one of the students or a volunteer, also getting ready to call it a day.

"You just can't stay out of trouble, can you?" That voice, that accent, with its hint of humor. I'd know it anywhere. And it's here – *he's* here – in Durham. I swear my heart stops, for just a second.

I shield my eyes from the glare of the lowering sun with my cupped hands and look up.

Declan, as handsome as ever, is standing just outside the boundary of the trench. He's wearing a T-shirt the same blue as his eyes, grey cargo trousers, and battered hiking boots.

"I've never been on an archaeological site before," he says conversationally, looking out across the trenches. As if he'd just happened to be in the neighborhood and dropped by.

"Declan. What are you doing here?" I manage to ask.

"Hello, Kate," he says finally. "I went to see you and found Poppy. And Luna. Not exactly what I was expecting. Poppy told me what happened with Diane. Some of it, anyway. Hicks and Raj filled in the rest."

Oh, Poppy. I'd given her my contact information here so she could reach me in case of an emergency. She wouldn't have thought twice about passing it along to her new boss if he'd asked for it.

"I can't talk about that here."

"Can we go somewhere else and talk, please, if you're done for the day?" he asks.

"We are. We're all meeting up at the pub later, though."

"Afterwards, then?"

I've risen to my feet and look across at Fiona now, who's watching us with undisguised interest. I exit the trench using the planks we've put in place for that purpose, careful not to disturb any ongoing work, and stand beside Declan on the grass.

He follows my gaze, and he and Fiona engage in a brief stare-down. Declan's the first one to look away. Fiona can be rather intimidating on the best of days. "Friend of yours, is she? Or your bodyguard?" he asks wryly. He looks back at me. "I'm here to apologize, Kate. I was a bloody idiot, and I'm sorry."

"You still haven't quite grasped the concept of mobile phones, have you?" I ask, which prompts a smile. "Wouldn't it have been easier to call or text?"

"I wanted to see you, to tell you in person. Look, can we start over? Pretend like the past few weeks never happened?"

I don't want to forget it all, though. "There were some good days."

"There were. But there were a few moments I'd rather forget."

"Agreed." We go quiet, each of us thinking, I'm sure, of everything that's happened since the summer began.

"Fresh start?"

I hesitate at first, then hold out my hand.

Declan catches on, takes my hand and shakes it. "Declan O'Rourke. Software geek. Pleasure to meet you." I feel the beginnings of a smile at the memory. That had been a good day, as I recall, sharing a simple lunch on a Sunday afternoon. And there had been others.

"Nice to meet you, Declan. Kate Barrow. Archaeologist."

"Well past time, too." He looks as though he's deep in thought for a minute. "So, Poppy *and* Luna?"

"Uh-huh. I didn't realize it was going to be a package deal. But it's kind of perfect, if you think about it."

"It is." We exchange a genuine smile for the first time in what feels like ages. In contrast, Fiona's openly glaring at us now; I should go have a word.

"There's a little café on Palace Green, right by the Cathedral. Meet me there at six o'clock?"

"All right. See you then."

I watch as Declan walks to his hire car in the team's makeshift parking lot.

"Is that the gobshite from Galway?" Fiona's hostile glare has diminished to only a frown as she comes to stand next to me. Viktoriya has joined us and is watching, too. I haven't shared all the details of what happened with Declan, but my friends have picked up on what I haven't said as much as what I have. They're concerned and protective, and I love them for it.

"He's not a gobshite, Fiona," I say, playfully mimicking her Irish accent. "I'm no saint, as you well know. Besides, he came to apologize."

"Well, I can see why you've been in bits, anyway." She gives a low whistle. "Hey," she protests when Viktoriya elbows her lightly in the side. "Just stating the obvious, for feck's sake."

"He wants to meet later to talk. Take a raincheck on the pub tonight?"

"Of course. We'll see you in the morning. And we'll want details."

"How old are you, anyway, Fi – twelve?" Viktoriya asks. "See you in the morning, Kate."

***

HOW I LOVE this place.

I arrive a few minutes before I'm due to meet Declan, giving myself just enough time for a quick visit. I'm on the

Palace Green, facing the Cathedral, with the library on my right and the Castle looming behind me.

The university's music students are rehearsing in a building across the green, and choral music drifts out the open windows. It feels like a scene from a movie, the music having been timed so perfectly with my visit, the young voices rising and falling in harmony in this spectacular setting.

Behind the Norman cathedral's silhouette, the sinking sun is casting its last rays of light, gently illuminating the iconic building. I stand outside the entrance with its bronze lion-shaped sanctuary knocker, listening to the music, my face tilted toward the final rays of the sun, enjoying the fading warmth as the wind picks up slightly.

A perfect moment in time.

I enter the cool dimness of the majestic building, enjoying that initial moment of hushed stillness. Now, as I always have, I can almost feel the weight of its history, the presence of all who have come before, down through the centuries. It gives me a sense of peace; knowing it was here long before I existed and will be here well after I'm gone. There are only a handful of visitors aside from me, and except for the fading voices from outside, the silence is almost absolute. I resist the impulse to genuflect before slipping into a pew, this not being a Catholic church, and kneel down for a quick prayer.

If I hurry, I'll have just enough time to make it. I could come back another time, and I will again, before I go home. But somehow, it seems important that I do this today. Now. As I approach the shrine, I stop and take in the hallowed space.

I wait for a small crowd who arrived before me to take their turn, pay their respects, light a candle.

Once I'm alone, I crouch down to lightly trace the lettering engraved on the cool stone floor with my fingers. CVTHBERTVS: The name of the patron saint of Northumberland and Durham, whose medal I've carried with me since my first visit here as a student. I reach into my pocket now, feel the silver cross, worn smooth in places from wear and time. Fretted over and fingered like rosary or worry beads, an almost-constant companion.

I notice that someone else has made their way to the shrine, too, and I move over slightly so that I'm not blocking their view.

"Cuthbert," says a quiet voice. "Did you know?" I turn in surprise to see Declan crouched next to me, smiling.

"Not until the party. He didn't come right out and say it, but he as good as told me, anyway." I pull the cross from my pocket and show him.

"Well, I'll be damned." He covers his mouth, fighting laughter, when I quietly exclaim at his choice of words. I glance nervously around to make sure he hadn't been overheard, mindful of where we are.

"We'd better leave before we get thrown out," I whisper. We're both trying hard not to laugh, like a couple of naughty schoolchildren, as we make our way back the way we'd come, through the hushed, cool dimness and out to where the sweet voices are fading along with the day.

"THAT'S THE BEST meal I've had since I've been in Durham."

We're sitting on the patio of a riverside restaurant, enjoying the last of a leisurely dinner. Declan's too polite to mention the weight I've lost since we've last seen each other, but he'd let me know in his own way it hadn't gone unnoticed. He'd ordered tiramisu for dessert, which had surprised me, until he'd slid the plate across the table next to my own chocolate mousse with an admonition to, "Eat, will you?"

"Why are you really here?" I ask as I set my spoon down on my empty plate.

"I told you; I wanted to apologize. That's not something you can do over the phone or in a text, not properly. The night you shot Anthony, I made it all about me, and it wasn't. You were devastated by what had happened, and I walked away. That was unforgiveable."

"Don't be so hard on yourself. I sent you away, if you recall. I didn't exactly handle it well myself. It's over. Fresh start, remember?"

He twirls the stem of his empty wineglass on the white tablecloth, weighing his words. "While I was in Galway, I visited Cara's family. It wasn't easy, but it was long overdue. Let's just say I learned some things no one shared with me when she died. Things that might have helped, if I'd known. The world isn't as black-and-white as I thought it was, I guess."

I recall what Diane said to me and Raj about Cara, the promise he and I had made to never tell Declan. I look down at my plate, unable to meet his eyes.

I hear him exhale, look up to see him gazing past me at the river flowing behind us. I give him a minute, then admit, "I thought you'd decide to stay in Galway for good."

Declan looks at me in surprise. "Why would you think that?"

"The party. I thought it was because you were leaving."

"No. Ireland will always be where I'm from, where my family is. But my life is in Virginia. That hasn't changed. I just needed to put a few ghosts to rest."

"Yes. I know all about ghosts."

"Raj told me what happened with Diane. I know you said you don't want to talk about it, about her. But what you two did? That took more presence of mind than most people will ever have. Especially given the circumstances."

"I'm no hero, Declan. Raj is the one who really put his life on the line. He could've gone to prison for trying to help me. And speaking of Raj, he did give me your gift. The journal is perfect, thank you. Illuminated manuscripts are kind of my thing. Or they used to be," I say with a smile.

"I know. I read your dissertation."

"You what?"

"I read your dissertation. I had some time on my hands," he says casually. "So I tracked it down and read it."

This man, honestly. "You must've been desperate. No one reads doctoral dissertations unless they're forced to." I'm about to add "at gunpoint," but stop myself just in time. Declan and I have only just reached a fragile peace. I don't want to screw it up already. And personally, I don't care if I ever see another weapon for a very long time. "I spoke with Pen the other day."

"How is Wainwright?"

"Interesting, as always. He filled me in on a few things about the case. The police finally identified the man who attacked me. Turns out he was just a contractor for Anthony, someone he'd hired to do his dirty work. The police found burner phones at his apartment, which answered a lot of their questions. One of the phones was tied to the serial number of the AirTag we found on my car, and there were texts connecting him to Anthony. He was responsible for running Anne Marie off the road, on Anthony's orders. And I don't know if I mentioned it to you earlier, but Anne Marie's laptop had been missing. They found it at Anthony's house."

"So Blackstone hadn't been following you, at least."

"He might not have been responsible for the AirTag, but he'd still been keeping tabs on me in his own way, and I know he was behind the graffiti. The creep."

Declan gives me a half-smile. "What about the cameras in the garage?" he asks. "It's too much of a coincidence that they just happened to go down the night you were attacked."

"Remember Poppy said that Anthony was a regular at Sam's? He'd gotten friendly with one of the security guards and paid him to take the cameras offline, then go home early. That's why Poppy was working alone that night."

"Unbelievable," he says quietly. We sit in silence for a minute, taking it all in.

I notice him looking at the scar on my arm as I reach for my water glass. "I know, I know," I say in a resigned voice. "I should've gotten it stitched."

"I wasn't looking at the scar."

"What then?"

"Don't take this the wrong way, but you don't strike me as the tattoo type." At my amused look, he continues, "I mean, they're commonplace now. But they weren't when you got them, were they?"

"No, not really." I meet his smile with one of my own. "I'll tell you about my tattoos when you tell me why you and Hicks have boxes of burner phones laying around."

His only answer is the lift of one eyebrow.

"Uh-huh. I thought as much. For the love, Declan."

He laughs.

I look at my watch. "If you're feeling brave, there's still time for a drink at the pub."

"Is that a challenge?" His blue eyes are bright with mischief.

"There's someone you really have to meet." And I leave it at that.

"YOU COULD HAVE warned me, you know."

It's two hours later; Declan is walking me back to my hotel.

"It was like being interrogated by Simone the first time we met, all over again. Only with a Dublin accent and a worse mouth. She's actually in charge of the project you'll be working on?"

He's wearing the same shell-shocked expression he'd worn the first time he'd met Simone.

"Yep. Isn't she something?"

"You do like living dangerously, Kate."

The expression I give him needs no verbal translation.

"When're you leaving?" he asks.

"The day after tomorrow. I have an early flight out of Newcastle."

"We could fly home together."

"We could. What would you do with yourself tomorrow while I'm working?"

"I'm sure I can find ways to amuse myself."

"Reading ancient dissertations?" I ask with amusement. "I'll text you my flight details so you can try to get on the same flight."

"Ah, let me rephrase my earlier statement. You could fly home *with* me."

"But I already have a flight." He's watching me, waiting patiently for me to catch up.

When I do, I gasp. "You do *not*."

"No, I don't," he admits with a laugh. "I have more important things to do with my money. But one of my former business partners does, and he's pretty generous if he's not using it himself. Not bad for a couple of software geeks, wouldn't you say?"

"Seriously? Wow. I've never flown on a private jet before."

THERE ARE HUGS all around but no tears this time. This time, I know I'll be returning.

"We've got a Zoom call early next week. You'll have the details in your email by the time you land."

"Thanks, Fi. Talk to you then. I'll come out before next summer, I promise. I have no idea yet what my new work schedule will be, but we'll figure it out."

"I'll see you before the summer – in April." At my confused expression, she says, "I told you." When I still look at her blankly, she says, "I didn't tell you? Feck, where's my head? We'll be at the annual conference in Washington; Viktoriya's presenting a paper. The department got a massive donation from some fancy endowment. We can afford travel and conferences and all that now. I can actually pay you without having to go begging for funding. And who knows? I might even be able to hire another post-grad and find time to finish that bloody book."

I tilt my head to one side, considering whether to ask. Oh, all right – I can't resist. "You wouldn't happen to remember the name of the fancy endowment, would you?"

"Let me think. It's something daft. 'Angel' something-or-other. What kind of name is that for an endowment, anyway?"

"I have no idea, Fi," I say, laughing despite myself. Another round of hugs, and then I'm off.

OUR DRIVER PULLS up alongside the waiting Gulfstream jet on the tarmac; two airport staff rush over and open the vehicle's doors. Declan's enjoying my reaction to all of this, I can tell – this slightly over-the-top, VIP service. It's pretty cool, actually, and not something I ever thought I'd experience. I step out of the vehicle and watch as our luggage and several large cardboard boxes are unloaded, ready to be put on the plane.

Curious, I read the labels on the boxes as they're loaded on board. I turn to Declan, laughing. "Jammie Dodgers, Hobnobs, and Jaffa Cakes? What on earth?"

"Oh, right. Emma's been looking after the lads. Well, Raj is, more likely. Anyway, in exchange, I promised Emma some of her favorite biscuits."

"You do know you can get these at Wegmans, right?" I can't resist asking.

"But not in bulk," he says, completely serious.

"Hicks is going to have your head when he sees all these. There's like, six months' worth here."

He looks sheepish. "Well, I did promise. And besides, I noticed Emma sharing some with Poppy at the party. And Poppy'll be working with me at my place. So, they'll be good to have on hand." His expression changes to one that's becoming all too familiar.

"What?"

"I also happen to know a certain archaeologist who has a bit of a sweet tooth, if memory serves."

"You just like saying that, don't you?"

"I do. 'Contracts administrator' doesn't have quite the same ring to it."

"I'm still that, too, remember. For my sins." We exchange a smile.

As I climb the jetway stairs, I turn and look back toward the city. I can barely make out the cathedral in the distance, perched high above the river. But I know it's there. I reflect on the medieval city's storied history, with the majestic cathedral, castle, and university as its backdrop. For me, as a student, Durham had been simply magical, with its warrens and winding backstreets, small cafes, shops and friendly shopkeepers, inviting paths and footbridges across the meandering River Wear.

I think of the countless hours I'd spent in lecture halls, in libraries, and out on digs. The summer my parents had joined as volunteers when I'd been one of the dig supervisors, and how proud they'd been of me then. Of growing up, of growing into a young adult over the several years I'd spent here in the North East of England.

I consider Cuthbert, the city's patron saint and a draw for pilgrims throughout the centuries. Then my thoughts turn to another Cuthbert, whose face doesn't grace any of the religious medals or prayer cards that are sold in the cathedral giftshop. I think of me, Declan, Raj, and Poppy. And who knows how many others whose lives have been forever changed by the kind and generous heart of one man.

Little had Declan and I known we'd had no need of our respective religious medals and talismans; instead, we'd had a human patron saint interceding on our behalf. Our very own patron saint of lost souls.

"Hicks is something special, isn't he?" I ask. And so are you, I can't help but think.

"He certainly is. My life would be very different today if he and I hadn't met," Declan says.

"Mine, as well."

There are other people whose lives would be very different if they hadn't met Declan: Hicks and his family, Luke and Simone, Poppy, Fiona and my archaeology colleagues – and me. Regardless of what happens after this jet lands at Dulles.

Declan misinterprets my wistful expression. "You'll be back."

"I know." I face the stairs, continue to climb. Only then do I notice the discreet image on the side of the fuselage: a simple set of angel's wings. "I thought you said this wasn't your plane."

"Ah, it's just a harmless little thing, isn't it? It can't hurt, having the angels on your side. If Liam's noticed, he's not mentioned it to me." His blue eyes are bright with mischief.

So typically Declan. Like when he'd slipped the St. Jude medal into my bag.

He's behind me, waiting patiently for me to board the plane. "Ready to go home?" he asks.

"Yes, I'm ready to go home."

To a house that's no longer too quiet; to the boisterous welcome of Poppy and Luna; to wonderful friends; and to work that will add joy and meaning to my life. Perhaps Hicks was right; perhaps we do end up exactly where we're meant to be.

As we settle into our seats, I glance at this quiet Irishman, who may just be on the side of the angels, after all.

Time will tell – for so many things. And I can't wait to see what happens next.

ACKNOWLEDGEMENTS

Until I wrote this novel, I had no idea just how many people were involved in bringing a story to life on the page. Now that I do know, I have an even greater respect for those who have done so and somehow managed to retain their sanity.

I want to thank my parents, Fred and Pat McGarrahan, for their unwavering support throughout this whole process, from the time I quit my job to write full-time through to the book's publication. To my daughter, Brianna Wolf; and my sisters, Maureen Cashin and Nancy McGarrahan. Thank you all for being my beta readers, my support system, and for your sense of humor and perspective when I had nearly lost mine.

To Harry Bingham, the gifted creator of one of my favorite heroines, Fiona Griffiths, and founder of Jericho Writers. Thank you for establishing an uplifting and talented community of writers. And to all the staff at Jericho Writers who help to educate, motivate, and inspire writers on a daily basis.

To Debbie Young, marvelous mentor and teacher, who provided priceless guidance on self-publishing and so much more. You are the best, and I couldn't have done this without you. To Mary Torjussen, who went miles above and beyond my expectations. For your generous insight, suggestions, and wonderful wit, I thank you.

To Wendy Goldman Rohm, thank you for your inspirational Paris writers workshop and your advice on the opening chapters. And to Lesley McDowell, for your assessment and critical tips on how to handle romance in a series.

To Christian Storm, whose wonderful designs grace the cover and interiors of the book. Thank you for bringing my dream to beautiful, colorful life.

To Karen Aguirre and Kim Fitzgerald, many thanks for your painstaking and detailed feedback to the excerpts I shared in class and again when you finally were able to see the big picture. To Ashley Stokes, thank you for your encouragement and thoughts on the early chapters.

To the incomparable Judith Babb Chandler and my fellow Experienced Writers classmates; and to the Travelers Rest cohort of the South Carolina Writers' Association – thank you for helping me find my tribe when I needed one most.

To my readers, thank you for spending time with the characters and the world I've created. There's more to come, and I hope you'll stay along for the ride.

— Trish McGarrahan
www.trishmcgarrahan.com

AUTHOR'S NOTES

As a former dog owner and eternal dog lover, I realize that human food and canines, for the most part, is not a good combination. And while Luna may make her feelings known at the mention of chocolate lava cake and pizza, she's merely picking up on her human's excitement and tone of voice. Kate and Poppy would never let Luna have chocolate or pizza. Just for the record.

ABOUT THE AUTHOR

Trish McGarrahan has worked for more than two decades in the defense contracting and government consulting industries. She holds an MA in archaeology from Durham University in the UK and lives in Greenville, South Carolina. *Saint of Lost Souls* is her debut novel.